# I'LL WALK ALONE

# MARY HIGGINS CLARK

## I'LL WALK ALONE

SIMON &
SCHUSTER

London · New York · Sydney · Toronto

A CBS COMPANY

First published in the US by Simon & Schuster, Inc., 2011
First published in Great Britain by Simon & Schuster UK Ltd, 2011
A CBS COMPANY

1 3 5 7 9 10 8 6 4 2

Simon & Schuster UK Ltd
1st Floor
222 Gray's Inn Road
London
WC1X 8HB

www.simonandschuster.co.uk

Simon & Schuster Australia
Sydney

A CIP catalogue record for this book is available from the British Library

Hardback ISBN 978-0-85720-242-0
Trade Paperback ISBN 978-0-85720-243-7

Designed by Jill Putorti

Printed in the UK by CPI Mackays, Chatham ME5 8TD

# Acknowledgments

I have often said, seemingly in jest, that my favorite two words are "THE END."

They *are* my favorite two words. They mean that the tale has been told, the journey completed. They mean that the people who at this time last year were not even figments of my imagination have lived the life I chose for them, or to put it better, they chose for themselves.

My editor, Michael Korda, and I have made this same journey for thirty-six years, since that first day in March 1974 when I received the unbelievable call that Simon and Schuster had bought my first book, *Where Are the Children?*, for three thousand dollars. All this time, Michael has been the Captain of my literary ship, and I cannot be more joyful and honored than to have shared our collaboration. Last year at this time he suggested, "I think a book about identity theft would make a good subject for you." Here it is.

Senior Editor Kathy Sagan has been my friend for many years. A decade ago, she was the editor of *The Mary Higgins Clark Mystery Magazine*, and for the first time has worked with me, in conjunction with Michael, on a suspense novel. Love you, Kathy, and thank you.

Thanks always to Associate Director of Copyediting Gypsy da Silva and my readers-in-progress Irene Clark, Agnes Newton, and Nadine Petry and to my retired publicist, Lisl Cade.

Once again Sgt. Steven Marron and Detective Richard Murphy, Ret., of the New York District Attorney's office have been my guides in presenting accurately the step-by-step law enforcement that occurs when a major crime is committed.

Of course, and always, love beyond measure to my spouse extraordinaire, John Conheeney and our combined family of nine children and seventeen grandchildren.

Finally, to you, my readers, thank you for all the years we've shared together. "May the road rise to meet you . . ."

*In memory of Reverend Joseph A. Kelly, S.J.*
*1931–2008*

*Always a twinkle in this Jesuit's eye*
*Always a smile on his handsome face*
*Always faith and compassion overflowing his soul*
*He was the stuff of which saints are made*
*When all heaven protested his absence*
*His Creator called him home*

# 1

Father Aiden O'Brien was hearing confessions in the lower church of St. Francis of Assisi on West Thirty-first Street in Manhattan. The seventy-eight-year-old Franciscan friar approved of the alternate way of administering the sacrament, that of having the penitent sit in the Reconciliation Room with him, rather than kneeling on the hard wood of the confessional with a screen hiding his or her identity.

The one time he felt the new way did not work was when, sitting face-to-face, he sensed that the penitents might not be able to allow themselves to say what might have been confided in darkness.

This was happening now on this chilly, windswept afternoon in March.

In the first hour he had sat in the room, only two women had shown up, regular parishioners, both in their mideighties, whose sins, if any had ever existed, were long behind them. Today one of them had confessed that when she was eight years old she remembered telling a lie to her mother. She had eaten two cupcakes and blamed her brother for the missing one.

As Fr. Aiden was praying his rosary until he was scheduled to leave the room, the door opened and a slender woman who looked to be in her early thirties came in. Her expression tentative, she moved slowly toward the chair facing him and hesitantly sat down on it. Her auburn hair was loose on her shoulders. Her fur-collared suit was clearly expensive, as were her high-heeled leather boots. Her only jewelry was silver earrings.

His expression serene, Fr. Aiden waited. Then when the young woman did not speak, he asked encouragingly, "How can I help you?"

"I don't know how to begin." The woman's voice was low and pleasant, with no hint of a geographical accent.

"There's nothing you can tell me that I haven't already heard," Fr. Aiden said mildly.

"I . . ." The woman paused, then the words came rushing out. "I know about a murder that someone is planning to commit and I can't stop it."

Her expression horrified, she clasped her hand over her mouth and abruptly stood up. "I should never have come here," she whispered. Then, her voice trembling with emotion, she said, "Bless me, Father, for I have sinned. I confess that I am an accessory to a crime that is ongoing and to a murder that is going to happen very soon. You'll probably read about it in the headlines. I don't want to be part of it, but it's too late to stop."

She turned and in five steps had her hand on the door.

"Wait," Fr. Aiden called, trying to struggle to his feet. "Talk to me. I can help you."

But she was gone.

Was the woman psychotic? Fr. Aiden wondered. Could she possibly have meant what she said? And if so, what could he do about it?

If she was telling the truth, I can do nothing about it, he thought, as he sank back into the chair. I don't know who she is or where she lives. I can only pray that she is irrational and that this scenario is some kind of fantasy. But if she is not irrational, she is shrewd enough to know that I am bound by the seal of the confessional. At some point she may have been a practicing Catholic. The words she used, "Bless me, Father, for I have sinned," was the way a penitent used to begin to confess.

For long minutes he sat alone. When the woman exited, the green light over the Reconciliation Room door had automatically gone on, which meant that anyone waiting outside would have been free to enter. He found himself praying fervently that the young woman might return, but she did not.

He was supposed to leave the room at six o'clock. But it was twenty minutes after six when he gave up hope that she might come back. Finally, aware of the weight of his years and the spiritual burden of his role as confessor, Fr. Aiden placed both hands on the arms of his chair and got up slowly, wincing at the sharp thrust of pain in his arthritic knees. Shaking his head, he began to walk to the door but stopped for a moment in front of the chair where the young woman had been sitting.

She wasn't crazy, he thought sadly. I can only pray that if she really has knowledge that the crime of a murder is about to be committed, she does what her conscience is telling her to do. She must prevent it.

He opened the door and saw two people lighting candles in front of the statue of St. Jude in the atrium of the church. A man was kneeling on the prie-dieu in front of the Shrine of St. Anthony, his face buried in his hands. Fr. Aiden hesitated, wondering if he should ask the visitor if he wanted to go to confession. Then he reflected that the posted hours for hearing confessions had been over for nearly half an hour. Maybe this visitor was begging for a favor or giving thanks for receiving one. The Shrine of St. Anthony was a favorite stop for many of their visitors.

Fr. Aiden walked across the atrium to the door that led to the passage to the Friary. He did not feel the intense gaze of the man who was no longer deep in prayer but had turned, pushed up his dark glasses, and was studying him intently, taking note of his rim of white hair and slow gait.

She was only in there less than a minute, the observer thought.

How much did she tell that old priest? he wondered. Can I afford to take the chance that she didn't spill her guts to him? The man could hear the outer doors of the church being opened and the sound of approaching steps. Quickly he replaced his sunglasses and pulled up the collar of his trench coat. He had already copied Fr. Aiden's name from the door.

"What do I do about you, Fr. O'Brien?" he asked himself angrily, as he brushed past the dozen or so visitors entering the church.

For the moment he had no answer.

What he did not realize was that he, the observer, was being observed. Sixty-six-year-old Alvirah Meehan, the cleaning woman turned columnist and celebrity author who had won forty million dollars in the New York Lottery, was also there. She had been shopping in Herald Square and then, before going home to Central Park South, had walked down the few blocks to the church to light a candle in front of St. Anthony's Shrine and drop off an extra donation for the breadline because she had just received an unexpected royalty check for her memoir *From Pots to Plots*.

When she saw the man seemingly deep in prayer in front of the shrine, she had paid a visit to the grotto of Our Lady of Lourdes. A few minutes later, when she saw Fr. Aiden, her old friend, leave the Reconciliation Room, she had been about to run up and say a quick hello to him. Then to her astonishment, the man who had seemed so engrossed in prayer suddenly jumped up, his dark glasses raised. No mistake about it, he was watching Fr. Aiden make his way to the door of the Friary.

Alvirah dismissed any passing thought that that guy might have wanted to ask Fr. Aiden to hear his confession. He wanted to get a good look at Father, she thought, as she watched the man pull his glasses back over his eyes and turn up the collar of his coat. She had taken off her glasses so he was too far away for her to see him clearly, but from the distance she judged him to be about six feet tall. His face was in the shadows but she could see he was on the thin side. Her impression, when she had passed him at the statue, was that he had no gray in his full head of black hair. He had been covering his face with his hands.

Who knows what makes people tick, Alvirah asked herself as she watched the stranger, now moving quickly, exit by the door nearest him. But I'll tell you this much, she thought. As soon as Fr. Aiden left the Reconciliation Room, whatever that guy had to say to St. Anthony, he wound it up fast.

# 2

It is March 22. If he is still alive, my Matthew is five years old today, Zan Moreland thought as she opened her eyes and lay still for long minutes, brushing back the tears that often dampened her face and pillow during the night. She glanced at the clock on the dresser. It was 7:15 A.M. She had slept almost eight hours. The reason, of course, was that when she went to bed, she had taken a sleeping pill, a luxury she almost never permitted herself. But the awareness of his birthday had left her almost sleepless for the last week.

Fragments of her recurring dream of searching for Matthew came back to her. This time she had been in Central Park again, searching and searching for him, calling his name, begging him to answer. His favorite game had been hide-and-seek. In the dream she was telling herself that he wasn't really missing. He was just hiding.

But he *was* missing.

If only I had canceled my appointment that day, Zan thought for the millionth time. Tiffany Shields, the babysitter, had admitted that while Matthew was sleeping she had positioned his stroller so that the sun would not be in his face and had spread a blanket on the grass and fallen asleep herself. She had not realized he wasn't in the stroller until she woke up.

An elderly witness had phoned the police after she read the headlines about the missing toddler. She reported that she and her husband had been walking their dog in the park and noticed the stroller was empty nearly half an hour before the babysitter had told the police she had looked into it. "I didn't think anything of it at the time," the witness said, sounding upset and angry. "I just thought that someone, the mother maybe, had taken the child over to the playground. It never occurred to me that young woman could possibly be watching anyone. She was out like a light."

Tiffany had also finally admitted that because Matthew was asleep when they left the apartment, she did not bother to strap him in.

Did he climb out by himself and then someone noticed he was alone and took his hand? Zan asked herself, the question dull with repetition. There are predators who hang around. *Please, God, don't let it be that.*

Matthew's picture had been in newspapers all over the country and on the Internet. I prayed that some lonely person might have taken him and then was afraid to admit it, but finally would come forward or leave him in a safe place where he'd be found, Zan thought. But after almost two years, there was not a single hint of where he might be. By now he's probably forgotten me.

She sat up slowly and twisted her long auburn hair back on her shoulders. Even though she exercised regularly, her slender body felt stiff and achy. Tension, the doctor had told her. You're living with it, 24/7. She slid her feet to the floor, stretched, and stood up, then walked over to the window and began to close it as she absorbed the early-morning view of the Statue of Liberty and New York Harbor.

It had been that view that had made her decide to sublet this apartment six months after Matthew disappeared. She'd had to get away from the building on East Eighty-sixth Street where his empty room with his little bed and toys were daily arrows piercing her heart.

That was when, realizing she had to try to have some semblance of normalcy in her life, she had thrown her energies into the small interior design business she had started when she and Ted separated. They had been together for such a short time, she didn't even know that she was pregnant when they split.

Before her marriage to Ted Carpenter, she had been the chief assistant to the famed designer Bartley Longe. Even then she'd been recognized as one of the bright new stars in the field.

A critic who knew that Bartley had left an entire project in her hands while he was on a lengthy vacation had written about her stunning ability to mix and combine fabrics and color and furnishings for a home that reflected the taste and lifestyle of the owner.

Zan closed the window and hurried to the closet. She loved a cold room for sleeping, but her long T-shirt was no protection from the drafts. She had deliberately given herself a busy schedule for today. Now she reached for the old wraparound robe that Ted had so hated and which she laughingly had told him was her security blanket. To her it had become a symbol. When she got out of bed and the room was freezing, the minute she put on the robe she was warm as toast. Cold to warm; empty to overflowing; Matthew missing; Matthew found; Matthew in her arms, home with her. Matthew had loved to snuggle inside it with her.

But no more hide-and-seek, she thought, blinking back tears, as she knotted the belt of the robe and wiggled her feet into flip-flops. If Matthew climbed out of the stroller himself, was that what he was trying to play? But an unattended child should have been noticed by other people. How long was it before someone took his hand and disappeared with him?

It had been an unseasonably hot day in June and the park had been filled with children.

Don't get into that, Zan warned herself as she walked down the hallway to the kitchen and headed straight for the coffeemaker. It had been set to go at seven o'clock, and now the pot was full. She poured a cup and reached into the refrigerator for the skim milk and the container of mixed fruit she had bought at the nearby grocery store. Then, on second thought, she ignored the fruit. Just coffee, she thought. That's all I want now. I know I should eat more than I do, but I'm not planning to start today.

As she sipped the coffee, she mentally ran through her schedule. After she stopped at the office, she was meeting the architect of a stunning new condominium high-rise on the Hudson River to discuss decorating three model apartments for him, a significant coup if she got the job. Her principal competition would be her old employer, Bartley, whom she knew bitterly resented her opening her own business instead of coming back to work for him.

You may have taught me a lot, Zan thought, but boy that nasty temper of yours wasn't anything I was going to be around again. Not to say anything about the way you came on to me. Then she closed her mind to that embarrassing day when she had had a breakdown in Bartley's office.

She carried the coffee cup to the bathroom, laid it on the vanity, and turned on the shower. The steaming water took some of the tautness out of her muscles, and after she poured shampoo on her hair, she massaged her scalp with deep pressure from her fingertips. Another trick for reducing stress, she thought sardonically. There's really only one way for me to reduce stress.

Don't go there, she warned herself again.

When she was toweling dry, she picked up the pace, briskly drying her hair, then, back in her robe, she applied the mascara and lip gloss that were her only makeup. Matthew has Ted's eyes, she thought, that gorgeous shade of dark brown. I used to sing him that song, "Beautiful Brown Eyes." His hair was so light but I think it was starting to get some reddish tones in it. I wonder if he'll get the bright red I had as a kid? I hated it. I told Mom that I looked like Anne of Green Gables, stick thin and with that awful carrot hair. But on him, it would look adorable.

Her mother had pointed out that when Anne grew up, her body had filled out and her hair had darkened to a warm, rich auburn shade.

Mom used to joke and call me Green Gables Annie, Zan thought. It was another memory not to be dwelt on today.

Ted had insisted they have dinner tonight, just the two of them. "Melissa will certainly understand," he'd said when he phoned. "I want to remember our little boy with the only other person who knows how I'm feeling on his birthday. Please, Zan."

They were meeting at the Four Seasons at 7:30. The one problem with living in Battery Park City is the traffic jams to and from midtown, Zan thought. I don't want to bother coming back downtown to change, and I don't want to bother dragging a different outfit with me to the office. I'll wear the black suit with the fur collar. It's dressy enough for the evening.

Fifteen minutes later she was on the street, a tall, slender young woman of thirty-two, dressed in a black fur-collared suit and high-heeled boots, wearing dark sunglasses, her designer shoulder bag in hand, her auburn hair blowing across her shoulders as she stepped down from the curb to hail a cab.

# 3

Over dinner, Alvirah had told Willy about the funny way that guy was looking at their friend Fr. Aiden when he was leaving the Reconciliation Room, and at breakfast she brought it up again. "I was dreaming about that guy last night, Willy," she said, "and that's not a good sign. When I dream about a person, it usually means there's going to be trouble."

Still in their bathrobes, they were sitting cozily at the round table in the dining area of their Central Park South apartment. Outside, as she had already pointed out to Willy, it was a typical March day, cold and blustery. The wind was rattling the furniture on their balcony, and they could see that across the street, Central Park was almost deserted.

Willy looked affectionately across the table at his wife of forty-five years. Often referred to as the image of the late legendary Speaker of the House Tip O'Neill, he was a big man with a full head of snow-white hair and, as Alvirah told him, the bluest eyes under the sun.

In his fond eyes, Alvirah was beautiful. He didn't notice that no matter how hard she tried, she'd always be trying to lose ten or fifteen pounds. Neither did he notice that only a week after coloring her hair, the gray roots became visible around her hairline, the hair that, thanks to Dale of London, was now a subdued russet brown. In the old days, before they won the lottery, when she colored it herself over the bathroom sink in their apartment in Queens, it had been a flaming red-orange shade.

"Honey, from what you tell me that guy had probably been getting up the courage to go to confession. And then when he saw Fr. Aiden leaving, he was trying to decide whether or not to catch up with him."

Alvirah shook her head. "There's more to it than that." She reached for the teapot and poured herself a second cup and her expression changed. "You know that today is little Matthew's birthday. He'd be five years old."

"Or *is* five years old," Willy corrected her. "Alvirah, I have intuition, too. I say that little guy is alive somewhere."

"We talk about Matthew as if we know him," Alvirah sighed as she added a sugar substitute to her cup.

"I feel as though we do know him," Willy said, soberly.

They were silent for a minute, both remembering how nearly two years ago, after Alvirah's column about the missing child in the *New York Globe* had been posted on the Internet, Alexandra Moreland had phoned her. "Mrs. Meehan," she had said, "I can't tell you how much Ted and I appreciate what you wrote. If Matthew was taken by someone who desperately wanted a child, you conveyed in that article how desperately we want him back. The suggestions you made about how someone could leave him in a safe place and avoid being recognized on security cameras might just make a difference."

Alvirah had agonized for her. "Willy, that poor girl is an only child, and she lost both her parents when their car crashed on their way to pick her up at the Rome airport. Then she splits with her husband before she realizes she is pregnant, and now her little boy disappears. I just know she must be at the point where she doesn't want to get up in the morning. I told her that if she ever wanted to have someone to talk to, she should just call me, but I know she won't."

But then shortly thereafter Alvirah read on Page Six of the *Post* that the tragedy-haunted Zan Moreland had gone back to work full-time at her interior design firm, Moreland Interiors, on East Fifty-eighth Street. Alvirah immediately informed Willy that their apartment needed to be redone.

"I don't think it looks so bad," Willy had observed.

"It's not bad, Willy, but we did buy it furnished six years ago, and to tell you the truth, having everything white, curtains, rugs, furniture, has made me feel sometimes as though I'm living in a marshmallow. It's a sin to waste money, but I think in this case it's the right thing to do."

The result was not only their transformed apartment, but also a close friendship with Alexandra "Zan" Moreland. Now Zan called them her surrogate family and they saw her frequently.

"Did you ask Zan to have dinner with us tonight?" Willy asked now. "I mean, this has got to be a horrible day for her."

"I did ask," Alvirah replied, "and at first she said yes. Then she phoned back. Her ex-husband wants to be with her, and she didn't think she could refuse. They're meeting at the Four Seasons tonight."

"I could see where the two of them might be some comfort for each other on Matthew's birthday."

"On the other hand, that's a pretty public place, and Zan is too hard on herself about letting her emotions show. When she talks about Matthew, I wish she'd let herself cry once in a while, but she never does, not even with us."

"I'll bet there are many nights when she cries herself to sleep," Willy said, "and I agree it won't do her any good to be with her ex tonight. She told us that she's sure Carpenter has never forgiven her for allowing Matthew to go out with such a young babysitter. I hope he won't bring that up again on Matthew's birthday."

"He is—or was—Matthew's father," Alvirah said, then more to herself than to Willy added, "From everything I've ever read, in a case like this, even if they're not present, one parent takes the blame for the situation, be it a careless babysitter, or being away when he or she had wanted to stay home that day. Willy, there's always blame, more than enough to go around when a child is missing, and I just pray God that Ted Carpenter doesn't have a couple of drinks and start in on Zan tonight."

"Don't borrow trouble, honey," Willy cautioned.

"I know what you mean." Alvirah debated then reached for the other half of her toasted bagel. "But, Willy, you know it's true that when in my bones I feel trouble coming, it always does come. And I know, I just know, that impossible as it seems, Zan is going to be hit real hard with something more."

# 4

Edward "Ted" Carpenter nodded to the receptionist without speaking as he strode through the outer room of his thirtieth-floor suite on West Forty-sixth Street. The walls of the room were filled with pictures of his current and former celebrity clients covering the past fifteen years. All were inscribed to him. Usually he made a left turn into the large room where his ten publicity assistants worked. But this morning he headed directly for his private office.

He had warned his secretary, Rita Moran, not to bring up the subject of his son's birthday to him and not to bring any newspapers to work. But when he approached her desk, Rita was so absorbed in reading a news story on the Internet that she did not even see him when he stood over her at the computer. She had an image of Matthew pulled up on her screen. When she finally heard Ted, she looked up. Her face turned crimson as he leaned over her, grabbed the mouse, and turned off the computer. In quick strides, he went into his office and took off his coat. But before he hung it up, he went to his desk and stared at the framed picture of his son. It had been taken on Matthew's third birthday. Even then he looked like me, Ted thought. With that high forehead and dark brown eyes, there was no mistaking that he was my son. When he grows up, he'll probably look just like me, he thought as he angrily turned the frame face down. Then he went to the closet and hung up his coat.

Because he was meeting Zan at the Four Seasons, he had chosen to wear a dark blue suit instead of his preferred sport jacket and slacks.

At dinner last night, his most important client, the rock star Melissa Knight, had been visibly upset when he told her he could not escort her to some affair this evening. "You're having a date with your ex," she had said, her tone apprehensive and angry.

He could not afford to antagonize Melissa. Her first three albums had all hit over a million sales and, thanks to her, other celebrities were signing up with his public relations firm. Unfortunately, somewhere along the way, Melissa had fallen, or thought she had fallen, in love with him.

"You know my plans, princess," he had said, trying to keep his tone mild. And then added with the bitterness he could not conceal, "and you certainly should understand why I'm meeting the mother of my son on his fifth birthday."

Melissa had been instantly remorseful. "I'm sorry, Ted. I'm truly sorry. Of course I know why you're meeting her. It's just . . ."

The memory of that exchange was grating. Melissa's suspicion that he was still in love with Zan was always there, a constant jealousy that caused her to explode regularly. And it was getting worse.

Zan and I separated because she said our marriage was just an emotional reaction to her parents' sudden death, he thought. She didn't even realize she was pregnant when we broke up. That was well over five years ago. What has Melissa got to be upset about? I can't afford to let her get angry at me. If she were to walk out, it would be the end of this place. She'd take all her friends with her, which would mean the most lucrative ones we have. If only I hadn't bought this damn building. What was I thinking?

A subdued Rita was carrying in the morning mail. "Melissa's accountant is a dream," she said with a tentative smile. "The monthly check and all the expenses came in this morning right on time. Don't we wish all our clients were like that?"

"We sure do," Ted said heartily, knowing that Rita had been upset by his curtness when he arrived.

"And her accountant wrote a note telling you to expect a call from Jaime-boy. He just fired his PR firm and Melissa recommended you. That would be another terrific client for us to have."

Ted felt genuine warmth now as he looked at Rita's troubled face. Rita had been with him every day for the last fifteen years, ever since as a cocky twenty-three-year-old he had opened his PR firm. She had been at Matthew's christening and at his first three birthday parties. In her late forties, childless and married to a quiet schoolteacher, she loved the excitement of their famous clients and had been enraptured when he brought Matthew here to the office.

"Rita," Ted said. "Of course you're remembering that it's Matthew's birthday, and I know you've been praying for him to come home. Now start praying that a year from now we'll be celebrating his next birthday with him."

"Oh, Ted, I will," Rita said fervently, "I will."

When she went back outside, Ted stared for a few minutes at the closed door, then with a sigh reached for the phone. He was sure Melissa's maid would pick it up and take a message. Melissa and he had attended a red carpet movie premiere the night before and Melissa often slept in. But she answered on the first ring.

"Ted."

The fact that his name and phone number had come up on her caller ID still caught him off guard. Not that kind of service when I was growing up in Wisconsin, he thought, but it probably wasn't happening in New York then, either. He forced a cheerful note into his voice as he greeted her, "Good morning, Melissa, the queen of hearts."

"Ted, I thought you'd be too busy planning for your date tonight to even think of calling me today." As usual her tone was petulant.

Ted resisted the temptation to slam down the phone. Instead, in the even tone that he used when his most valuable client was being both impossible and insensitive, he said, "Dinner with my ex won't last more than two hours. That means I'll be leaving the Four Seasons around 9:30. Could you make room in your calendar for me around 9:45?"

Two minutes later, sure that he was back in Melissa's good graces, he hung up and put his head in his hands. Oh, God, he thought, why do I have to put up with her?

# 5

Zan unlocked the door of her small office in the Design Center, the magazines under her arm. She had promised herself that she would avoid any references to Matthew that might be in the media. But as she passed the newsstand she had not been able to keep from buying two weekly celebrity magazines, the two most likely outlets for any follow-up stories. Last year on Matthew's birthday both of them had extensive write-ups about his kidnapping.

Only last week someone had snapped her picture when she was walking to a restaurant near her home in Battery Park City. She was bitterly aware that it would probably be used in some sensational article rehashing Matthew's abduction.

In a reflex gesture, Zan turned on the lights and took in the familiar trappings of her office, with several bolts of cloth stacked against the stark white walls, carpet samples scattered on the floor, and shelves filled with heavy books containing swatches of fabrics.

When she and Ted separated, she had started her venture as an interior designer on her own in this small office and, as satisfied clients sent her referrals, had elected to keep it that way. The antique desk with the three Edwardian chairs surrounding it was wide enough for her to sketch suggested designs for homes and rooms and lay out possible color combinations for a client's approval.

It was here in this room that she could sometimes not think about

Matthew for hours and thus force the heavy unsettled pain of losing him to retreat into her subconscious. She knew that wouldn't be the case today.

The rest of the suite consisted of a back office barely large enough to hold a computer desk, files, a table for her inevitable coffeepot, and a small refrigerator. The clothes closet was opposite the lavatory. Josh Green, her assistant, had observed with ironic accuracy that the dimensions of closet and lavatory were exactly the same.

She had resisted Josh's suggestions that they lease the suite next door when it became available. She wanted to keep her overhead to a minimum. That way she would be able to hire yet another private detective agency that specialized in finding lost children to look for Matthew. She had gone through what was left of the money that she had received from her parents' modest life insurance in the first year that Matthew had been missing, spending it wildly on private investigators and psychic quacks, none of whom had turned up a shred of evidence that might lead to finding him.

She hung up her coat. The fur trimming on the collar was one more reminder that she was going to meet Ted tonight for dinner. Why does he bother? she asked herself impatiently. He blames me for letting Tiffany Shields take Matthew out to the park. But he loved Matthew passionately and no amount of blame that he could throw at her could possibly match the blame and guilt she carried herself.

To get it out of the way, she opened the celebrity magazines and scanned them quickly. As she had suspected, one of them was carrying the picture of Matthew that had been released to the media when he vanished. The caption read, "Is Matthew Carpenter still alive and celebrating his fifth birthday?"

The article ended with the quote Ted had made the day Matthew disappeared, a caution to parents about leaving their children with a young babysitter. Zan ripped out the page, crumpled it, and threw both magazines in the wastebasket. Then wondering why she had subjected herself to looking for this kind of article, she hurried to the big desk and settled in a chair.

For the hundredth time in the past few weeks she unrolled the drawings she was going to submit to Kevin Wilson, architect and part owner of the thirty-four-story apartment building that overlooked the new walkway bordering the Hudson River on the lower west side. If she did get the job of furnishing three model apartments, it would not only be a major breakthrough for her, it would be her first successful toe-to-toe with Bartley Longe.

It still was incomprehensible to her that the employer who had so valued her while she was his assistant had so utterly turned on her. When she first began to work for him nine years ago, right after she graduated from FIT, the Fashion Institute of Technology, she had eagerly embraced the demanding schedule and put up with his volatile temper because she knew she was learning a lot from him. Divorced, then in his early forties, Bartley was very much a man about town. He had always been extremely difficult, but it was when he turned his attention to her and she made it clear that she was not interested in an involvement that he had begun to make her life miserable with his biting sarcasm and endless criticism.

I kept putting off going to see Mom and Dad who were living in Rome, Zan thought. Bartley would get furious if I said I needed a couple of weeks off. I delayed that trip for six months. Then when I finally told him I was going, whether he liked it or not, it was too late.

She had been in the airport in Rome when the car her father was driving to meet her had crashed into a tree, killing him and her mother instantly. An autopsy showed that her father had suffered a heart attack at the wheel.

Don't think about them today, she warned herself. Concentrate on the model rooms. Bartley will be submitting his plans. I know the way he thinks. I'll beat him at his own game.

Bartley would have undoubtedly created designs for both a traditional and an ultramodern décor and one that combined elements of both. She made herself concentrate to see if there were any better way she could find to improve the sketches and color samples she would be offering.

As though it mattered. As though anything mattered except Matthew.

She heard a key turn in the door. Josh was there. Her assistant was also a graduate of FIT. Twenty-five years old, smart, looking more like a college kid than a gifted interior designer, Josh had become something of a younger brother to her. It almost helped that he had not been with her when Matthew disappeared. Somehow she and Josh just clicked.

But today the expression on his face made Zan realize that the concern she was seeing was different. Josh began without a greeting, "Zan, I stayed here last night catching up on the monthly statements. I didn't want to call you because you said you were going to take a sleeping pill. But, Zan, why did you buy a one-way ticket to Buenos Aires for next Wednesday?"

# 6

The little boy heard the sound of a car coming down the driveway even before Glory heard it. In an instant, he slid off the chair at the breakfast table and ran down the hall into the big closet where he knew he must stay "like a little mouse" until Glory came back for him.

He didn't mind. Glory had told him it was a game to keep him safe. There was a light on the floor of the closet, and a rubber raft just big enough for him to lie down and go to sleep on if he was tired. It had pillows and a blanket. When he was there, Glory told him, he could pretend he was a pirate and sailing on the ocean. Or, he could read one of his books. There were lots of books in the closet. The one thing he must *never do*, however, was to make a single sound. He always knew when Glory was going to go out and leave him alone because she would make him go to the bathroom even if he didn't have to go, then she would leave a bottle in the closet for him to pee in. And she would leave a sandwich and cookies and water, and a Pepsi.

It had been that way in the other houses, too. Glory always made a place for him to hide, then put some of his toys and trucks and puzzles and books and crayons and pencils in it. Glory told him that even though he never played with other children he was going to be smarter than all of them. "You read better than most seven-year-olds, Matty," she told him. "You're really smart. And it's because of me that you're so smart. You're really *lucky*."

In the beginning, the boy didn't feel lucky at all. He would dream of being wrapped up in a warm, fuzzy robe with Mommy. After a while he couldn't exactly remember her face, but he still remembered how he felt when she hugged him. Then he would start to cry. But after a while the dream stopped coming. Then Glory bought soap and he washed his hands just before he went to bed, and the dream came back because the way the soap made his hands smell was the way Mommy smelled. He remembered her name again and even the feeling of being wrapped with her inside her robe. In the morning he took the soap back to his room and put it under his pillow. When Glory kept asking him why he did it, he told her, and she said it was okay.

Once he wanted to play a game and hide from Glory, but he didn't do that anymore. Glory raced up and down the stairs calling his name. She was *really* mad when she finally looked behind the couch and found him. She shook her fist in his face and said not to ever, ever, ever do that again. Her expression was so angry that he was really scared.

The only time he saw other people was when they were driving in the car, and that was always at night. They didn't stay long in any place and wherever they stayed, there weren't other houses around them. Sometimes Glory would take him out in the back of the house and play a game with him and take his picture. But then they would move to another house, and Glory would make a new secret room for him again.

Sometimes he would wake up after Glory had locked him in his room at night and hear her talking to someone. He wondered who it was. He could never hear the other voice. He knew it couldn't be Mommy because if she was in the house, she would definitely come upstairs to see him. Whenever he was sure someone was in the house, he would hold the soap in his hand and pretend it was Mommy.

This time the door of the closet opened almost right away. Glory was laughing. "The owner of this place sent over the guy from the security system to make sure it works. Isn't that a riot, Matty?"

# 7

After Josh told Zan about the airline charge to her credit card, he suggested they check all the other cards in her purse.

Bergdorf Goodman had new purchases of expensive clothing charged to her account, clothing that was in her size, but that she knew nothing about.

"On this day of all days," Josh muttered as he notified the store to cancel the card. Then he'd added, "Zan, do you think you can handle this appointment alone? Maybe I should go with you?"

Zan promised she would be okay, and promptly at eleven o'clock she was standing at the door of the office of Kevin Wilson, the architect of the stunning new apartment building overlooking the Hudson River. The door was partially open. She could see that the office was a makeshift space on the main floor of the new building, the kind an architect would keep for convenience to observe the progress of an ongoing project.

Wilson's back was to her, his head bent over the papers on the table behind the desk. Were they Bartley Longe's drawings? Zan wondered. She knew his appointment had been earlier than hers. She knocked on the door and Wilson, without turning around, called out for her to come in.

Before she reached his desk, Wilson swiveled around in the chair, stood, and pushed his glasses up on his head. Zan realized that he was younger than she expected, certainly not more than midthirties. With his tall, lanky frame, he looked more like a basketball player than an award-winning architect. His firm jaw and keen blue eyes were the most prominent features in his ruggedly handsome face.

He extended his hand. "Alexandra Moreland, glad to meet you and thank you for accepting our invitation to submit design plans for our model apartments."

Zan tried to smile as she took his hand. In the almost two years since Matthew disappeared, she had usually managed to compartmentalize herself, to force Matthew from her mind when she was in a business situation. But today the combination of Matthew's birthday and the shock of knowing that someone was piling up bills on her credit card and charge accounts was suddenly breaking down the wall of reserve she had built so carefully.

She knew her hand was ice cold and was glad that Kevin Wilson didn't seem to notice it, but she could not trust herself to speak. First she had to let the lump that was crowding her throat begin to dissolve, otherwise she knew that silent tears would begin to run down her face. She could only hope that Wilson would mistake her silence for shyness.

Apparently he did. "Why don't we take a look and see what you've come up with?" he suggested, gently.

Zan swallowed hard, then managed to speak in an even tone. "If you don't mind, let's go up to the apartments and I can explain to you how I've chosen to put things together."

"Sure," he said. In a long stride, Wilson was around the desk and had taken the heavy leather folder from her. They walked down the corridor to the second bank of elevators. The lobby was in the final stages of construction, with overhead wires dangling and narrow strips of carpet scattered on the dusty floors.

Wilson kept up a running conversation, surely, Zan felt, to help her get over what he must have thought was her nervousness. "This is going to be one of the most energy-efficient buildings in New York," he said. "We've got solar energy and we've maximized the window sizes throughout to give all the apartments the constant feeling of sun and light. I grew up in an apartment house where my bedroom faced the brick wall of the building next door. Day and night it was so dark I could hardly see my hand in front of my face. In fact I put a sign on the door when I was ten years old, 'The Cave.' My mother made me take it down before my father came home. She said it would make him feel bad that we didn't have a better place to live."

And I grew up living all over the world, Zan thought. So many people think that's wonderful. Mother and Dad loved the diplomatic life, but I wanted permanence. I wanted neighbors who would still be there in twenty years. I wanted to live in a house that was ours. I didn't want to have to go to boarding school when I was thirteen. I wanted to be with them, and even sometimes resented them for being on the move so much.

They were stepping into the elevator. Wilson pushed a button on the panel and the elevator door closed. Zan searched for something to say. "I guess you may have heard that since your secretary phoned and invited me to submit design plans for the model apartments, I've been in and out of here any number of times."

"I heard that."

"I wanted to see the rooms at different times of day, so that I could get a feel for them, and of how it would be for different kinds of people to walk in and say, 'I'm home.'"

They started in the one-bedroom, one-and-a-half-bath apartment. "My guess is that the people looking at this one fall into two categories," Zan began. "The apartments are expensive enough so that you're not getting any kids just out of college, unless Daddy is paying the bills. I think you'll probably have a lot of young professionals looking at this model. And unless it's a romance situation, most of them won't want roommates."

Wilson smiled. "And the other category?"

"Older people who want a pied-à-terre, and even if they could afford it don't want a guest room because they don't want overnight guests."

It was getting easier for her. She was on safe territory. "This is what I've come up with." There was a long counter separating the kitchen from the dining area. "Why don't I lay out my sketches and swatches here?" she suggested as she took the portfolio from him.

She was with Kevin Wilson for nearly two hours as she explained her alternate approaches for each of the three model apartments. When they were back in his office, he laid her plans on the table behind his desk and said, "You've put an awful lot of work into this, Zan."

After the first time he had called her Alexandra, she had said, "Let's keep it simple. Everybody calls me Zan, I guess because when I was starting to talk, Alexandra was too big a mouthful for me."

"I want to get the job," she said. "I'm excited about the layouts I showed you and it was worth the time and effort to give them my best shot. I know you invited Bartley Longe to submit his plans, and of course he's a superb designer. It's that simple. The competition is stiff and you may not like anything that either of us has planned."

"You're a lot more charitable about him than he is about you," Wilson observed dryly.

Zan was sorry to hear the note of bitterness in her throat when she answered, "I'm afraid there's no love lost between Bartley and me, but on the other hand I'm sure you're not treating this assignment as a popularity contest." And I know I'll come in at least a third cheaper than Bartley, she thought, as she left Wilson at the imposing entrance to the skyscraper. That will be my ace in the hole. I won't make much money if I get this job, but the recognition will be worth it.

In the cab going back to the office, she realized that the tears she had been able to hold back were streaming down her cheeks now. She grabbed her sunglasses out of her shoulder bag and put them on. When the cab stopped on East Fifty-eighth Street, as usual she gave a generous tip because she believed that anyone who had to make a living driving every day in New York traffic deserved one.

The cabbie, an elderly black man with a Jamaican accent, thanked her warmly, then added, "Miss, I couldn't help notice you were crying. You're feeling real bad today. But maybe tomorrow everything will look a lot brighter. You'll see."

If only that were true, Zan thought, as she whispered, "Thank you," gave a final dab to her eyes, and stepped out of the cab. But everything *won't* look brighter tomorrow.

And maybe it never will.

# 8

Fr. Aiden O'Brien had spent a sleepless night worrying about the young woman who, under the seal of the confessional, had told him that she was taking part in an ongoing crime and would be unable to prevent a murder. He could only hope that the very fact that her conscience had driven her to begin to unburden herself to him would also force her to prevent the grave sin of allowing another human being's life to be taken.

He prayed for the woman at morning Mass, then with a heavy heart went about his duties. He especially enjoyed helping with the meals or the clothing distribution that the church had been carrying on for the needy for eighty years. Lately the number of people they fed and clothed had been rising. Fr. Aiden assisted at the breakfast shift, watching with satisfaction as hungry people's faces brightened when they began to eat cereal and scrambled eggs and sip steaming hot coffee.

Then, in the midafternoon, Fr. Aiden's own spirits were cheered considerably when he received a call from his old friend Alvirah Meehan, inviting him to dinner that evening. "I've got the five o'clock Mass in the upper church," he told Alvirah, "but I'll be there about 6:30."

It was something to look forward to, even though he knew that nothing could remove the burden the young woman had laid on his shoulders.

At 6:25 he got out of the uptown bus and crossed Central Park South to the building where Alvirah and Willy Meehan had lived ever since the forty-million-dollar lottery windfall. The doorman got on the speaker to announce him, and when the elevator stopped at the sixteenth floor, Alvirah was waiting to greet him. The delicious aroma of roasting chicken floated into the hall and Fr. Aiden grate-fully followed Alvirah to its source. Willy was waiting to take his coat and prepare his favorite drink, bourbon on the rocks.

They had not been sitting too long before Fr. Aiden realized that Alvirah was not her usual cheery self. There was a concerned look in her expression and he got the feeling she was trying to bring some-thing up. Finally he decided to put it on the table. "Alvirah, you're worried about something. Anything I can do to help?"

Alvirah sighed. "Oh, Aiden, you can read a person like a book. Well, you know I've told you about Zan Moreland, whose little boy disappeared in Central Park."

"Yes. I was in Rome at that time," he said. "No trace of the child ever?"

"Nothing. Absolutely nothing. Zan's parents died in a car acci-dent and she spent every cent of their insurance money hiring pri-vate detectives, but there simply hasn't been a trace of the little guy. He'd be five today. I'd asked Zan to come to dinner, but she's meet-ing her ex-husband, and that's a mistake, too. He blames her for al-lowing a young babysitter to take Matthew out."

"I'd like to meet her," Fr. Aiden said. "I sometimes wonder which is worse, to bury a child or to have a child disappear."

"Alvirah, ask Fr. Aiden about that guy you saw in church last eve-ning," Willy urged.

"That was something else, Aiden. I stopped in at St. Francis yesterday—"

"Probably to slip a donation into St. Anthony's box," Aiden interrupted with a smile.

"Actually, yes. But there was a guy there and his face was in his hands, and you know sometimes you get the feeling you don't want to crowd next to someone?"

Fr. Aiden nodded. "I understand, and that was very thoughtful of you."

"Maybe it wasn't such a good idea," Willy disagreed. "Tell Aiden what you saw, honey."

"Well, anyhow, I walked across the back to the last pew, where I could watch for this fellow when he left. Unfortunately, I didn't get a good look at him, but then you came out of the Reconciliation Room and started across the atrium to the Friary. I was going to see if I could catch up with you, but then Mr. Devout, whoever he is, jumped up, lifted his dark glasses, and Aiden, let me tell you, he didn't take his eyes off you for one minute until you were out of sight."

"Perhaps he wanted to go to confession and couldn't work up his courage," Fr. Aiden suggested. "Unfortunately, that happens, too. People want to unburden themselves, but then can't bring themselves to admit to what they've been doing."

"No. It's more than that. It just has me worried," Alvirah said firmly. "I mean it does happen sometimes that some crazy person decides he's mad at a priest. If there's anyone you know who's mad at you, keep an eye out for him."

The wrinkles on Fr. Aiden's forehead deepened as a thought occurred to him. "Alvirah, you say that this person was kneeling at the Shrine of St. Anthony for a few minutes before I left the Reconciliation Room?"

"Yes." Alvirah put down the glass of wine in her hand and leaned forward. "You suspect someone, don't you, Aiden?"

"No," Fr. Aiden protested unconvincingly. That young woman,

he thought. She said she was powerless to prevent someone from being murdered. Was she followed into church or did someone accompany her? She had rushed into the Reconciliation Room. Maybe she came in on an impulse and then obviously regretted it?

"Aiden, do you have security cameras at the church?" Alvirah asked.

"Yes, at all the doors that lead into the church."

"Well, couldn't you check them and see who might have come in between 5:30 and 6:30? I mean there weren't many people there."

"Yes, I could do that," Fr. Aiden agreed.

"Would you mind if I took a look at them tomorrow morning?" Alvirah asked. "I mean I couldn't see that guy's face, but I did get an impression of him. On the tall side, an all-weather coat, like a Burberry. He did have a lot of black hair."

A tape will also show that young woman coming into church, Fr. Aiden thought. Not that I have any hope of learning who she is, but it would be interesting to get a sense of whether she was being followed. The burden of concern that he had been carrying all day deepened.

"Of course, Alvirah, I'll meet you in the church at nine A.M." If someone followed the young woman and was afraid of what she might have told him, would that young woman's own life be in danger now?

It did not occur to the gentle friar to ask himself if his own life might be at risk because somebody feared the information that the troubled young woman had confided to him.

# 9

Promptly at 7:30 P.M., Zan was at the desk of the Four Seasons Restaurant. She had only to scan the Grill Room to see that Ted was already there, as she had expected he would be. Seven years ago, when they began to date, he had told her that always being early for an appointment was good business. "If it's a client situation, I'm sending a message that I value their time. If it's someone looking for something from me, that person is already nervous and it puts them at a disadvantage. Even if they're on time, they feel as if they're late."

"What would someone want from you?" she had asked him.

"Oh, the manager of a would-be actor or singer who wants me to handle his client. That kind of thing."

"Ms. Moreland, nice to see you again. Mr. Carpenter is waiting." The maître d' led her across the room to the table for two that Ted always booked.

Ted was on his feet when she reached the table. He leaned over to kiss her cheek. "Zan." His voice was husky. When they sat down, his shoulder brushed against hers. "How bad a day have you been having?" he asked.

She had decided not to say a word about the charges on her credit cards. She knew that if Ted learned about them he would want to help, and she did not want to initiate anything that would keep them in contact, except of course if it involved Matthew. "Pretty bad," she said quietly.

Ted's hand closed over hers. "I will not give up hope that some-day the phone will ring and it will be good news."

"I make myself believe that, but then I think that by now Mat-thew has probably forgotten me. He was only three years and three months old when he disappeared. I've lost nearly two years of his life." She stopped. "I mean we've lost nearly two years," she added carefully.

She saw the flash of anger in Ted's eyes and was sure she knew what he was thinking. The babysitter. He would never forgive her for the careless babysitter she had hired because she had an appoint-ment with a client. When would it come up? After he had had a couple of drinks?

There was a bottle of her favorite red wine by the table. At Ted's nod, the waiter began to pour it. When Ted picked up his glass, he said, "To our little boy."

"Don't," Zan whispered. "Ted, I can't talk about him. I simply can't. We both know what we are feeling today."

Ted took a long sip from his glass without answering. As Zan studied him, she thought for the second time that day that Matthew would grow up to look like him, with those wide-spaced brown eyes and even features. By any standards, Ted was a handsome man. Then she forced herself to realize that just as badly as she did not want to talk about Matthew, Ted needed to share some memories of him. But why here? she asked herself bitterly. I'd have cooked din-ner for him at my apartment.

No, I wouldn't, she corrected herself. But we could have gone to some small, out-of-the-way place, where you don't get the feel-ing that the other diners may be people-watching. How many of them in this room might have seen the articles in those magazines today?

She knew she had to allow Ted to talk about Matthew. "This morning I was thinking how when he grows up, he's going to look just like you," she said tentatively.

"I agree. I remember one day, only a few months before he disappeared, I picked him up from you and took him for lunch. He wanted to walk and I had his hand going down Fifth Avenue. He was so darn cute that people were looking at him and smiling. I ran into one of my old clients and he joked, 'You'll never be able to deny that child.' "

"I don't think you'd ever have denied him." Zan tried to smile.

As if he realized what an effort she was making, Ted changed the subject. "How's the design business going? I read somewhere that you were bidding to decorate those model apartments in the Kevin Wilson building."

It was safe ground. "I honestly think it went well." Because she thought Ted was genuinely interested and because she absolutely had to steer the conversation away from Matthew, Zan described the designs she had suggested and said she felt she had a good shot at getting the job. "Of course, Bartley Longe is in there pitching, and from a chance remark Kevin Wilson made, I guess he's been bad-mouthing me again."

"Zan, that man is dangerous. I've always felt that about him. He was jealous of *me* when we started going out together. It isn't just that he's a business rival now. He didn't want to let you out of his sight then, and I would bet anything he's still crazy about you."

"Ted, he's twenty years older than I am. He's been divorced and has had numerous affairs. He's got a nasty temper. If he has any feelings about me, it has to do with the fact that I didn't feel flattered by his attention when he decided to try to hit on me. The great regret of my life is that I kept allowing him to bully me when something in my very soul was telling me to fly to Rome and visit Mom and Dad."

She remembered it all: Arriving at Da Vinci Airport. Looking for their faces when she came through security. The letdown. Then the worry. Then collecting her bags and waiting uncertainly in the terminal. Then the call on her international cell phone. The Italian authorities telling her about the accident that had killed them.

The hustle and bustle of Rome at the airport in the early morning. Zan could see herself, standing with the phone frozen at her ear, her mouth shaped into a silent scream. "And then I called you," she told Ted.

"I'm glad you did. When I got to Rome you were absolutely out of it."

I was out of it for months, Zan thought. Ted took me in like some kind of stray. That's how good he is. There were plenty of women who would have loved to marry him. "And you married me to take care of me, and I rewarded you by allowing an inexperienced baby-sitter to lose your son." Zan could not believe she had said those words.

"Zan, I know I said that the day Matthew disappeared. Can't you ever understand that I was distraught?"

Around and around we go and where we stop nobody knows, she thought. "Ted, no matter what you say I still blame myself. Maybe none of those private detective agencies I hired did us any good . . ."

"They were a waste of money, Zan. The FBI has the case open and so does the NYPD. You fell for every charlatan who claimed they could find Matthew. Even that weird psychic who had us riding down Alligator Alley in Florida."

"I don't think anything that might help us find Matthew is ever a waste of money. I don't care if I have to consult every private agency in the phone book. Maybe I'll eventually find the one person who can follow Matthew's trail. You asked me about this model apartment job. If I get it, it will open a lot of doors. I'll be making more money, and every cent I make over my living expenses will be spent trying to find Matthew. Somebody must have seen something. I still believe that."

She knew she was trembling. The maître d' was standing near them. She realized her voice had been raised and he was discreetly trying to pretend that he had not overheard her.

"Ready for the specials?" he asked now.

"Yes, we are," Ted said heartily. Then he whispered, "For God's sake, Zan, try to keep it down. Why do you keep torturing yourself?" A surprised look came over his face and she turned.

Josh was hurrying across the room. His face ashen, he stopped at their table. "Zan, I was just leaving the office when some reporters with cameras from *Tell-All Weekly* came in looking for you. I said I didn't know where you were. Then they told me some guy from England who was in the park the day Matthew disappeared just had some photos he took that day enlarged for his parents' wedding anniversary. The reporter told me this guy realized that in the background of a couple of those enlarged photos you can see a woman lifting a child out of a stroller that was parked beside a woman asleep on a blanket . . ."

"Oh, dear God," Ted cried. "How much can they tell from them?"

"When they blew them up even more, other background details were clear. The boy's face isn't visible, but he's wearing a matching blue plaid shirt and shorts."

Zan and Ted stared at Josh. Through lips almost too dry to form words, Zan said, "That's what Matthew was wearing. Did that man bring the photos to the police?"

"No. He sold them to that rag *Tell-All*. Zan, this is crazy, but they swear that you're the woman who's picking up the child. They say there's no mistaking that it's you."

As the sophisticated diners in the Four Seasons Grill Room turned their heads to find the source of the sudden outburst, Ted grabbed Zan by the shoulders and pulled her to her feet. "Damn you! Damn you, you self-pitying lunatic," he shouted. "Where is my son? What did you *do* to him?"

# 10

Penny Smith Hammel, like many heavyset women, moved with natural grace. When she had been young, despite her weight she had been one of the most popular girls in high school, with her pleasant features, infectious humor, and ability to make even the most awkward partner on the dance floor feel as if he were Fred Astaire.

A week after high school graduation she had married Bernie Hammel, who immediately started work as a long-distance truck driver. Content with where they grew up, Bernie and Penny had raised their three children in rural Middletown, New York, a little more than an hour drive from Manhattan and eons away in lifestyle.

Now fifty-nine years old, the children and grandchildren scattered from Chicago to California and with Bernie on the road so much, Penny had kept happily busy by being available as a baby-sitter. She loved all her charges, giving them the affection that she would have showered on her grandchildren if they had lived nearby.

The only real excitement in her life had occurred four years ago, when she and Bernie, together with Bernie's ten fellow drivers, had won five million dollars in the lottery. They were one of the larger groups ever to win, and after taxes it netted them each about three hundred thousand dollars, which Bernie and Penny immediately put into a college fund for their grandchildren.

Part of the excitement was that they accepted an invitation to go into Manhattan and meet Alvirah and Willy Meehan and attend a meeting of their Lottery Winners' Support Group. The Meehans had started the group to help people learn not to squander their winnings on crazy investments or by playing Santa Claus to newly discovered relatives.

Penny and Alvirah had immediately realized they were kindred souls and kept in touch regularly.

Penny's best friend since childhood, Rebecca Schwartz, was a real estate agent who kept Penny informed about houses being bought or sold in her local neighborhood. On March 22, she and Penny had lunch in their favorite diner and Rebecca filled Penny in on the fact that the farmhouse on the dead-end road near her had finally been rented. The new tenant had moved in on March 1.

"Her name is Gloria Evans," Rebecca confided. "About thirty. Really attractive. Natural blonde. You know I can always tell when it's being helped along. Great shape, not like you and me. She just wanted a three-month rental, but I told her that Sy Owens wouldn't dream of renting it for less than a year. She didn't bat an eye, just said she was willing to pay for the year in advance because she's finishing a book and needs to be by herself without interruptions."

"Not a bad deal for Sy Owens," Penny commented. "Then I guess he rented it furnished?"

Rebecca laughed. "Oh sure. What else would he do with all that tacky stuff? He wants to sell that place as is, lock, stock, and barrel. You'd think it was Buckingham Palace!"

As was her custom with any new neighbors, the next day Penny drove over to welcome Gloria Evans with a plate of her homemade blueberry muffins. When she knocked on the door, even though there was a car in the breezeway, it was a few minutes before the door was cautiously opened.

Penny had one foot poised to step inside, but Gloria Evans kept the door partially closed and Penny could tell right away that this woman wasn't the least bit happy at the interruption. Penny was immediately apologetic. "Oh, Miss Evans, I *know* you're writing a book, and I'd have called if I had your cell phone number. I just want to welcome you to town with some of my famous blueberry muffins, but please don't think I'm one of those people who will be pestering you with phone calls or drop-in visits—"

"That's nice of you. I did come here to be completely isolated," Evans snapped, as with obvious reluctance she took the plate of muffins from Penny's extended hand.

Refusing to be affronted, Penny continued. "Don't worry about the plate. It's a throwaway. I wrote my phone number for you on a Post-it I stuck on the bottom, just in case you should ever have an emergency."

"That's very kind, but unnecessary," Evans replied stiffly. She had been forced to open the door wider to accept the plate, and looking past her Penny spotted a toy truck on the floor.

"Oh, I didn't know you had a child," Penny exclaimed. "I'm a good babysitter if you ever need one. I have references from half the people in town."

"I don't have a child!" Evans snapped. Then following Penny's glance she turned and saw the toy truck. "My sister helped me get settled. That belongs to her son."

"Well, if she ever visits and you two want to go off for lunch, you have my phone number," Penny said amiably. The last three words were addressed to the door that had closed in her face. For the moment she stood uncertainly, then wishing she had the courage to ring the bell again and grab her blueberry muffins out of the woman's hand, she turned and hurried back to her car.

"I hope Gloria Evans isn't writing a book on manners," she sniffed as, thoroughly humiliated, she backed up her car, turned it around, and sped away.

# 11

Alvirah and Willy heard the breaking news that Zan Moreland might have been responsible for the disappearance of her son on the eleven o'clock news that night. They had been preparing for bed after their dinner with Fr. Aiden. Shocked, Alvirah called Zan and left a message when she did not answer her cell phone.

In the morning, Alvirah met Fr. Aiden in the Friary adjoining St. Francis of Assisi Church. Together with Neil the handyman, they went to the office to view the playback of the tapes from the security cameras starting at 5:30 P.M. on Monday evening. For the first twenty minutes there was nothing unusual in the frames of people entering or leaving the chapel. As she waited, Alvirah, her voice filled with concern, told Fr. Aiden that the media was reporting that Zan might be involved in Matthew's disappearance.

"Aiden," Alvirah said, insistently, "they might just as well be saying that Willy and I stole Matthew from his stroller. It's so absolutely ridiculous that you wonder how anyone would swallow it. If they have some kind of pictures, I can only say that that guy in England doctored them to make money from that magazine." Then she leaned forward and gasped. "Neil, can you stop the video? That's Zan. She must have paid a visit here on Monday evening. I know how upset she had to have been because Matthew was turning five yesterday."

Fr. Aiden O'Brien had also recognized the expensively dressed young woman in the dark glasses with the long hair. It was the woman who had come into the Reconciliation Room and told him that she was involved in an ongoing crime and that there was a murder about to be committed. He tried to keep his voice calm as he asked Alvirah, "Are you sure that is your friend Zan?"

"Aiden, of course I'm sure. Look at that suit. Zan bought it last year after it was reduced. She's so careful about money. She went through every cent her mother and father had left her, spending it on private detectives to help find Matthew. Now she's saving so that she can get someone new to start hunting for him."

Before Aiden could reply, Alvirah urged Neil to start running the tape again. "I'm dying to see if I can pick up the guy who was eyeing you, Aiden."

Aiden phrased his words carefully. "Do you think he might have been accompanying or following your friend, Alvirah?"

Alvirah seemed not to have heard the question. "Oh, look," she exclaimed, "there he is coming in, the guy I'm looking for." Then she shook her head. "Oh, you can't see his face, and his collar is up. He's got those dark glasses on. All you can see is that mop of hair."

For the next half hour, she reviewed the rest of the tapes. They could easily distinguish the agitated figure of the woman Alvirah identified as Zan leaving the church. She was still wearing her dark glasses, but her head was bent and her shoulders shaking. Holding a handkerchief to her mouth as if she were trying to stifle sobs, she had rushed out of the church and out of the sight of the camera.

"She didn't stay five minutes," Alvirah said sadly. "She's so darn afraid of breaking down. She told me that after her parents were killed in that accident, she simply couldn't stop crying. She was afraid to go out in public. She said that if that happened again because of Matthew, she wouldn't be able to work and she needed to work to keep herself from going insane."

"Insane." Fr. Aiden whispered the word so softly that neither Alvirah nor Neil could possibly have heard it. "I am an accessory to a crime that is ongoing and to a murder that is going to happen very soon. I don't want to be part of it, but it's too late to stop." In the last two days that frantic statement was embedded in his mind.

"There's that guy again, leaving. But you can't tell anything about him." Alvirah signaled to Neil to turn off the tape. "You see how upset Zan appears Monday night? Can you imagine how she feels right now with the news story about her kidnapping Matthew?"

That was the other thing the young woman told him, Fr. Aiden thought: *You'll read about it in the headlines.* Had the murder she claimed she could not prevent already *been* committed? Had she already killed her own child, or probably even worse, was the poor thing still alive and about to die?

# 12

After Ted's explosive accusation, Josh grabbed Zan's hand and pulled her through the tables of shocked diners at the Four Seasons, rushed her down the stairs, through the lobby, and onto the street. "God, they must have followed me," he muttered as paparazzi lunged forward and cameras began flashing.

A cab had stopped in the street in front of the entrance. Josh, his arm now around Zan, sprinted to it and the instant the previous occupant had both feet on the ground, pushed her into it. "Just move," he snapped to the driver.

The driver nodded and started the cab, catching the light at Fifty-second Street and Third Avenue. "Make a right on Second Avenue," Josh told him.

"Is she a movie star or a rock singer?" the cabbie asked, then shrugged when he did not get an answer.

Josh still had his arm around Zan. Now he removed it. "You okay?" he asked her.

"I don't know," Zan whispered. "Josh, what does it mean? Are they crazy? How could they possibly have a photo of me taking Matthew out of his stroller? For God's sake, I have proof that I was at the Aldrich town house. Nina Aldrich had invited me over there to discuss doing the interior for her."

"Zan, take it easy," Josh said, trying to sound calm even as he visualized what it was going to look like when Ted's outburst hit the news. "You can prove where you were that day. Now what do you want to do? I'm afraid if you go home, the paparazzi may be waiting for you there."

"I have to go home," she said, her voice becoming stronger. "You can drop me off, but if there are any photographers, have the cab wait and walk with me until I can get inside. Josh, what's going on? I feel as if I'm living in a nightmare and I can't find my way out of it."

You *are* living in a nightmare, Josh thought.

They were silent the rest of the way to Battery Park City. When the cab pulled up to Zan's apartment building, as Josh had antici-pated the cameras were waiting for them. Ducking their heads, they ignored the cries to "Look this way, Zan," or "Over here, Zan," until they were safely inside the lobby.

"Josh, the cab is waiting. You go ahead home," Zan told him as they stood at the elevator.

"Are you sure?"

"I'm sure."

"Zan . . ." Josh bit off what he was about to say. He was going to warn her that the police would undoubtedly want to question her again and that before she spoke to them, she had better get a lawyer.

Instead, he squeezed her hand and waited until she was safely inside the elevator before he left. Outside, the paparazzi, seeing him alone and sensing that there would be no more photo opportunities, were beginning to disperse. They'll be back, Josh thought, as he got back in the cab. If there's anything at all we can be sure of, it's that they'll be back, damn them.

# 13

After his outburst in the Four Seasons, Ted Carpenter had gone down to the men's room. When he had jumped up and grabbed Zan, the glass of red wine he'd been holding had spilled all over his shirt and tie. Grabbing a towel, he'd futilely dabbed at the spots then looked in the mirror.

I look as if I'm bleeding to death, he thought, momentarily distracted from the stunning revelation that a tourist's camera had caught Zan taking Matthew from Central Park.

He felt the vibration of his cell phone in his jacket pocket. He knew it would be Melissa.

It was.

He waited until he was sure she had finished leaving a message, then listened to his voice mail. "I know you can't talk now, but meet me at Lola's by 9:30." There had been nothing of Melissa's normally sexy voice in her message. Ted knew it was clearly an order. "It'll be just the two of us. Then we'll go down to the Club around 11:30," Melissa continued. Then her voice turned petulant: "Don't kiss your ex good night."

I can't be seen out partying when it's just been reported that my ex-wife has kidnapped and probably hidden my child, he thought, aghast. When I call Melissa back and tell her what has happened, she'll surely understand that.

The photos.

She probably hasn't heard about them yet.

Why am I worried about Melissa? he asked himself. The question I should be screaming is: Are those photos fakes?

I know how photos can be manipulated. How many times have we eliminated unimportant people from our publicity shots? If you can take them out, you can put them in, too. It's common practice to put a star's face on a better-shaped body. Is this claim that Zan took Matthew just trick photo editing? How much did that tourist get for selling them to that *Tell-All* rag?

A man entering the restroom looked at Ted sympathetically. Ted exited quickly, not wanting to engage in conversation. If those photos turn out to be phonies, I'll look despicable for attacking Zan the way I did, he thought in near despair. I'm supposed to be a master of public relations when it comes to crisis management.

He had to talk to Melissa. He would meet her. He had time to go home, change his shirt, and meet her at Lola's. If the media was waiting outside, he would tell them that, on reflection, he abjectly begged Matthew's mother's pardon that he had been so quick to believe she had abducted their son.

Bracing himself, he walked out the lobby door where, as he had expected, camera crews were waiting for him. A microphone was stuck in his face. "Please," he said, "I want to make a statement but can't if you won't give me room."

As the shouted questions diminished, he took the microphone from the hand of one reporter. His voice firm, he said, "First, I must apologize to Matthew's mother, my former wife, Alexandra Moreland, for my unspeakable behavior this evening. Both of us are desperate to find our little boy. When I heard that there were photographs in existence showing that Matthew's mother had taken him, I quite literally lost it. A moment of reflection would have made me realize that those photos have got to be fake, or doctored, whatever name you want to give it."

Ted paused, then added, "I am so sure that the photos are a hoax that I am going now to meet my client, the talented and beautiful Melissa Knight, for dinner at Lola's Café. As you can see, in my unfortunate response to hearing about those pictures, I spilled wine on my shirt. I am going home to change, then to Lola's."

Ted could not conceal a tremor in his voice. "My son, Matthew, is five years old today. Neither his mother nor I believe that he is dead. Someone, perhaps a lonely woman who desperately wanted a child and seized the opportunity to steal him, is with him at this moment. If that person is watching us, please tell Matthew how much Mommy and Daddy love him and long to see him again."

The reporters kept a respectful silence as Ted walked to the curb where Larry Post, his high school friend and long-time driver, was holding the car door of the backseat open for him.

# 14

After Josh left her, Zan went upstairs, double-locked the door of the apartment, and stripped off her clothes, wrapping herself in her warm old bathrobe as she had done when she woke up in the morning. The message light was blinking on the telephone. She walked over and turned off the ringer. For the rest of the night, she sat in the bedroom chair with one single light shining on Matthew's picture. Her eyes searched each feature of his face longingly.

The spike of hair that by now had probably developed into a cowlick. The hint of red in that mop of sandy hair. Was he now an out-and-out redhead?

He had always been a friendly child, sunny and welcoming to strangers, not like some children who are naturally shy at age three. Dad was an extrovert, Zan thought. So was Mother. What happened to me?

So many of those months after they died are a blur. Now they are saying that *I* took Matthew out of his stroller that day.

"Did I?" she whispered aloud.

The shock of the question, the enormity that she could actually voice it, stunned her. She forced herself to ask the logical next question. "But if I took him, what did I do with him?"

She had no answer.

I would never have hurt him, she told herself. I never laid a finger on him. Even when I had given him a "time out" if he was be-having badly, my heart would melt for him, sitting in his little chair, looking so miserable.

Is Ted right? Do I wallow in self-pity and want other people to pity me? Does he mean that I'm one of those crazy mothers who harm their children because they need to be pitied and comforted?

She had thought she was beyond it, that sense of numbness, the feeling that she was withdrawing into herself from the pain. In the airport in Rome that day, when she had called Ted only minutes after she learned of her parents' death, she had felt her legs crumble under her. But even though she could not reach out to the people who had gathered around her, who had lifted her onto a stretcher, who had rushed her to the hospital in an ambulance, she had been aware of every word they said. It was just that she couldn't open her eyes, or make her lips form words, or lift her hand. It was as if she had been in a sealed room and could not find her way back to tell them that she was still with them.

Zan knew that was happening to her again. She leaned back in the soft armchair and closed her eyes.

A merciful emptiness engulfed her as she whispered his name: "Matthew . . . Matthew . . . Matthew . . ."

# 15

How much had Gloria told that old priest? It was the question that haunted him day and night. She was beginning to crack, and now at this crucial time, when it all was coming to a head, when everything he had planned during these two years was about to happen, she had rushed into that room.

He had been born a Catholic, and knew that if what Gloria said was under the seal of the confessional, the priest would have to keep his mouth shut. But he wasn't sure if Gloria was a Catholic, and if she wasn't, and just had gone in for a little heart-to-heart chat, maybe the old priest would consider it okay to say that Zan had a lookalike, someone who was impersonating her.

If that happened the cops would keep digging, and it would soon be all over. . . .

The old priest. That neighborhood around West Thirty-first Street wasn't any great shakes, he thought. And stray bullets were hitting people all over the city these days. Why not one more?

He would have to take care of it himself. He couldn't take the chance of having one more person alive who could tie him to the disappearance of Matthew Carpenter. The best thing would be to go back into the church, and try to get a line on when that priest was hearing confessions. There must be a schedule.

But that might take time. Maybe if I call, he thought, and ask when Fr. O'Brien is scheduled to hear confession next, whoever answers won't think it unusual. I'm sure some people want to talk to the same guy about their problems every time they go. Besides I can't sit around like this and wait for him to go to the cops.

The decision made, he placed the call and was told that Fr. O'Brien was scheduled for the next two weeks, Monday through Friday from four to six P.M.

*It's about time for me to go to confession,* he thought.

Before he paid Gloria to mind the child, he'd known that she was a consummate makeup artist. She told him that she sometimes made up herself and her friends to look like celebrities, and that they'd fooled everyone. She said they all had a good laugh when according to Page Six of the *Post* the celebrities they were mimicking were sighted having a quiet dinner at an out-of-the-way spot and graciously signing autographs.

"You wouldn't believe how often we don't get a check," she had giggled.

I always wear the wig she gave me when we meet in town, he thought. With that wig and the raincoat and dark glasses, even my best friends wouldn't know me.

He laughed aloud. As a kid, he'd always enjoyed being in plays. His favorite was when he had played Thomas à Becket in *Murder in the Cathedral.*

# 16

After speaking to the reporters outside the Four Seasons, Ted Carpenter turned on his iPhone on his way downtown and found the photos of the person who seemed unmistakably to be Zan taking Matthew from the stroller. Shocked, he stopped at his duplex condo in the newly gentrified Meatpacking District of lower Manhattan. There he had agonized briefly about whether or not to meet Melissa at Lola's Café. *What will it look like for me to be there when these photos are showing my ex-wife stealing my child?*

He phoned the Central Park Precinct and was put through to a detective who told him that it would be at least twenty-four hours before they could verify that the pictures were not doctored. *At least if I'm questioned by the paparazzi, I can tell them that,* he thought, as he changed his shirt and rushed back to the car.

The paparazzi on the sidewalk outside the popular café were kept back behind velvet ropes. One of the bouncers had held the door of his car open and he had ducked out toward the entrance. But then he stopped, unable to ignore the shouted question, "Have you seen those photos yet, Ted?"

"Yes, I have and I have been in touch with the police. I believe they are a cruel hoax," he snapped.

Inside the café he braced himself, knowing he was a half hour late meeting Melissa. He fully expected to find her in a filthy mood, but she was sitting at a large table with five old friends from the band she had once been in as the lead singer. She was clearly enjoying their adulation. Ted knew all of them and was grateful for their presence. If Melissa had been waiting alone, there would have been hell to pay.

Her greeting to him, "Hey, you're getting more coverage than I am," was met with hoots of laughter from her tablemates.

Ted leaned over Melissa and kissed her on her lips.

"What'll you have, Mr. Carpenter?" The waiter was at the table. There were already two bottles of their most expensive Champagne chilling in a bucket beside him. I don't want that damn Champagne, Ted thought as he sat down next to her. I always get a headache from it. "A gin martini," he said. Only one, he promised himself. But I need it. What in the hell does it look like for me to be here when there may be a break in the search for my son?

He was careful to drape his arm lovingly around Melissa and keep his eyes fixed on her for the benefit of the stringers who were paid to contribute items to the columnists. He knew that tomorrow Melissa would want to read something like "Top recording artist Melissa Knight has bounced back from her well-publicized breakup with rock singer Leif Ericson and is now madly in love with public relations dynamo Ted Carpenter. They were canoodling at Lola's last night."

I remember hearing about the time Eddie Fisher, then married to Elizabeth Taylor, sent a telegram from Italy signed "The Princess and her love slave," Ted thought. That's the kind of rot I'm supposed to provide for Melissa. She's kidding herself into thinking that she's in love with me.

But I need her. I need her nice fat check every month. If only I hadn't bought the building when our lease was up. It's been draining me dry. Melissa will move on from me fast enough, he thought, as he gulped rather than sipped the gin martini. The trick is to make sure that when she decides to drop me, she doesn't go to another PR firm and take her buddies with her.

"The same, Mr. Carpenter?" the waiter asked when he came by.

"Why not?" Ted snapped.

At midnight Melissa decided to leave for the Club. Another four a.m. morning once they get settled there. Ted knew he had to escape. There was only one way he could do it.

"Melissa, I feel lousy," he said, speaking under the din of the noisy café. "I think I may be getting a bug or flu or something. I can't expose you to it any longer. You've got a full schedule and you can't afford to get sick."

Keeping his fingers crossed, he saw the appraising look she gave him. Odd how her genuinely exquisite features could suddenly become distorted and lose all semblance of beauty when she was upset or angry. Her depth-of-the-ocean dark blue eyes narrowed and she twisted her long blond hair into a single curl that she pulled forward over her shoulder.

She's twenty-six years old and as totally self-centered as any personality I've ever dealt with in this business, Ted thought. I wish I could tell her to go to hell.

"You're not hooking up with your ex, are you?" she demanded.

"My ex-wife is the last woman I want to see right now. You ought to know by now that I'm crazy about you." Taking a chance, Ted deliberately let a note of irritation creep into his expression and tone of voice. He could afford to do that only occasionally but he knew, when he did, it sent the message to her that it would be insane to imagine he could look at another woman.

Melissa shrugged and turned to the others at the table. "Teddy's chickening out," she laughed. "Everyone who's going with me to the Club, let's split."

They all got up.

"You have your car?" Ted asked.

"No. I walked. For God sake, of course I have my car." She tapped him on the cheek, a playful slap for the benefit of the onlookers.

Ted signaled to the waiter to put the bill on his house account as usual and the group left the café together. Melissa held his hand and stopped to smile for the paparazzi. Ted walked her to her limo, wrapped her in his arms, and kissed her a long, deep kiss. A little more fodder for the gossip mills, he thought. That should keep her happy.

Her former bandmates piled into the limo with her. As his own car was brought up to the curb, a reporter stepped forward, holding something in his hand. "Mr. Carpenter, have you seen the photos the English tourist took that day your son was kidnapped?"

"Yes, I have."

The reporter held up an enlarged version of them. "Would you care to comment?"

Ted stared at them, then taking them, he moved closer to the brightly lit window as if to get a better look. Then he said, "As I said before, I believe these pictures will turn out to be a cruel hoax."

"Isn't that your ex-wife, Zan Moreland, picking up your child from the stroller?" the reporter demanded.

Ted was aware of the cameras surrounding him now. He shook his head. Larry Post was holding open the door of his car. He rushed to get into it.

When he got home, too shocked to feel anything, he undressed and took a sleeping pill. His night filled with tortured dreams, he awoke aching and nauseous, feeling as though the fictitious flu bug had become a reality. Or was it those damn gin martinis? he asked himself.


At nine o'clock the next morning, Ted called his office and spoke to Rita. Cutting off her shocked reaction to the photos, he told her to call Detective Collins, who had been in charge of the investigation the day Matthew disappeared, and make an appointment for him to see Collins tomorrow. "I'm going to stay home at least until midafternoon," he told Rita. "I may have a fever, but I've got to get in by then. I need to look at the proofs of that photo shoot that Melissa did for *Celeb Magazine* before I can okay them. Tell anyone in the media who calls that I will have no statement until the police have investigated the authenticity of those pictures."

At three o'clock, ghastly pale, he finally arrived at the office. Without asking, Rita made a cup of tea for him. "You should have stayed home, Ted," she said matter-of-factly. "I promise I'm not going to say another word about it, but there is one fact that you should keep in mind. Zan adored Matthew. She would never hurt him."

"Notice you use the word 'adored,'" Ted snapped. "That's past tense in my book. Now where are the *Celeb* proofs of Melissa?"

"They're gorgeous," Rita said reassuringly, as she took them from an envelope she had laid on his desk.

Ted stared at them. "To you they're gorgeous. To me they're gorgeous. But I can tell you right now that Melissa is going to hate them. There are shadows under her eyes, and her mouth looks too thin. And don't forget I was the one who told her she ought to accept posing for that cover story. Good God, can it get any worse?"

Rita looked at her boss of fifteen years with compassion. Ted Carpenter was thirty-eight years old but he looked years younger than his actual age. With his thick hair, brown eyes, firm mouth, and lean frame, she always believed that he was better looking and had a lot more charisma than many of the clients he represented. But right now he looks as if someone attacked him with a machete.

And to think of all the pity I've wasted on Zan these two years, Rita thought. If she'd done something to that darling little boy, I honestly think I could shoot her myself!

# 17

Zan blinked, opened her eyes, and closed them again. What happened, she asked herself. She wondered why she was sitting in the chair, why even though she was wearing the bathrobe, she felt so chilled, why her whole body ached.

Her hands were numb. She rubbed them together, trying to get feeling back into her fingers. Her feet were asleep. She moved them in a circular motion, almost unaware of what she was doing.

She opened her eyes again. Matthew's picture was directly in her vision. She could tell that the bulb in the lamp next to it was still on, even though dim, cloud-filled light was filtering through the partially drawn shade.

Why didn't I go to bed last night? she asked herself as she tried to get past the dull throbbing in her head.

Then she remembered.

They think I took Matthew from the stroller. But that's impossible. That's crazy. Why would I do that? What would I have done with him?

"What would I have done with you?" she moaned, as she stared at Matthew's picture. "Can anyone seriously believe I could harm you, my own child?"

Zan sprang to her feet, then in quick strides crossed the room to grab Matthew's picture and hug it against her body. "Why do they think that?" The question was now a whisper. "How could those pictures be of me? I was with Nina Aldrich. I spent that afternoon in the new town house she bought. I can prove it. Of course I can prove it.

"I know I didn't take Matthew out of his stroller," she said aloud, trying to control the quavering tone of her voice. "I can prove it. But I can't let what happened to me last night happen again. I can't have those blanks in my memory, the way I did after Mom and Dad died. If there is a photo of a woman picking up Matthew from the stroller, it would be the first real break in trying to trace him. I've got to think like that. I can't let myself retreat again. Please, God, don't let me be overwhelmed again. Let me hang on to the hope that there may be something in those photos that will give some clue, some lead, to finding Matthew . . .

It was only six o'clock. Instead of showering, Zan turned on the taps in the Jacuzzi, knowing that the swirling hot water would help relieve the aching of her body. What should I do? she asked herself again. I'm sure that Detective Collins must have those photos by now. After all, he was the lead investigator on the case.

She thought of the way the media had been outside the Four Seasons waiting for her last night, how they had been here outside the apartment when Josh took her home. Would they try to follow her around today? Or would they be at the office waiting for her?

She turned off the taps of the Jacuzzi, tested the water, then realized it was too hot. The phone, she thought. She remembered that she had turned off the ringer when she got into the apartment last night. She walked into the bedroom and over to the night table. The message light was blinking. There had been nine phone calls.

The first eight were from reporters asking to interview her. Determined not to allow them to upset her, Zan carefully deleted the calls one by one. The final one was from Alvirah Meehan. Gratefully, Zan listened to it, savoring Alvirah's reassurance that that guy who claimed he had a picture of Zan picking up Matthew in the park must be some con artist. "It's a shame you have to go through non-sense like this, Zan," Alvirah's outraged voice boomed. "Of course it will be exposed as a sham, but it's still terrible on you emotionally. Willy and I know that. Please call us and come over and have dinner tomorrow. We love you."

Zan listened to the message twice. Then, when the computer-ized voice instructed, "Push three to save, push one to delete," she pushed the SAVE button. It's too early to call Alvirah, she thought, but I'll get back to her when I'm in the office. It would be good to be with her and Willy tonight. Maybe by then, if Detective Collins can see me this afternoon, all this will be cleared up. And maybe, oh, please, God, if that man from England was snapping photos when someone was taking Matthew from the stroller, Detective Collins will have something to go on.

Somewhat comforted at the thought, Zan reset the coffeepot from the seven-o'clock setting so that it would begin to brew at once. She got into the Jacuzzi and felt the healing warmth of the water begin to deflate the tension in her body. Coffee cup in hand, she dressed in slacks, a turtleneck sweater, and low-heeled boots.

When she was dressed, it was still only a few minutes before seven, but she realized it might be early enough to leave the apart-ment without running into reporters. That possibility made her twist her hair into a bun and drape a scarf securely around it. Then she dug into a dresser drawer and found an old pair of sunglasses with a wide, round frame that was a totally different shape from the kind she usually wore.

Finally she grabbed a faux-fur vest from the closet, picked up her shoulder bag, and took the elevator down to the basement. From there she made her way through the rows of parked cars in the ga-rage and exited onto the street at the back of the building. With swift steps she hurried toward the West Side Highway, encountering only the early-morning dog walkers and joggers. When she was sure she was not being followed she hailed a cab and started to give the office address on East Fifty-eighth Street, then changed her mind. Instead she directed the cabbie to drop her on East Fifty-seventh Street. If there's any sign of the media I can go in through the delivery entrance, she thought.

It was only when she was able to sit back, knowing that at least for the length of the trip uptown she could be sure that no one would shout questions at her or aim a camera in her direction, that she was able to focus on the other problem, the fact that someone was charging clothes and an airline ticket to her name. Will that affect my credit rating? she worried. Of course it will. If I get the job with Kevin Wilson, I'll be ordering very expensive fabrics and furniture.

Why is all this happening to me?

Zan found herself pushing back against the almost physical feeling of being caught in a riptide, of a fierce current dragging her underwater. She gasped for air, as the sense of not being able to breathe overwhelmed her.

Panic attacks.

Don't let them come back, she pleaded to herself. She shut her eyes and forced herself to inhale deep, measured breaths. By the time the cab pulled to the corner at Fifty-seventh Street and Third Avenue, she had managed to regain some measure of calm. Even so, her fingers were trembling as she handed the cabbie the folded bills.

It had begun to drizzle. Cold, wet drops brushed her cheeks. The vest was a mistake, she thought, I should have worn a raincoat.

Ahead of her a woman was hurrying a little boy who looked to be about four years old toward a waiting car. Zan rushed to pass them so that she could look into the child's face. But of course it wasn't Matthew.

When she turned the corner there didn't seem to be any sign of the media waiting for her. She pushed the revolving door and went into the lobby. The newsstand was to the left. "The *Post* and the *News* please, Sam," she told the elderly clerk.

There was nothing of his usual friendly smile in Sam's demeanor when he handed the folded copies to her.

She did not permit herself to look at them until she was safely in her office. Then she laid them on her desk and unfolded them. The front page of the *Post* was a picture of her bending over the stroller. The front page of the *News* was a picture of her carrying Matthew away.

Disbelieving, her eyes darted from one to the other. But it *isn't* me, she protested. It *can't* be me. Someone who *looks* like me took Matthew. . . . It made no sense.

Josh wasn't due in until later. Zan tried to focus, but by noon she gave up. Zan grabbed the phone. I've got to call Alvirah back. I know she has the *Post* and the *Times* delivered every morning.

Alvirah answered on the second ring. When she heard Zan's voice, she said, "Zan, I saw the papers. You could have knocked me over with a feather. Why would someone who looks like you take Matthew?"

What does Alvirah mean by that question? Zan asked herself. Was she asking what reason someone would have for making herself look like me and taking Matthew, or does she mean that she thinks I took him?

"Alvirah," she said, choosing her words carefully, "someone is doing this to me. I don't know who, but I have my suspicions. But even if Bartley Longe would go to this length to harm me, there is one thing I'm sure of: He would never hurt Matthew. Alvirah, thank *God* for those pictures. Thank God for them. I'm going to get Matthew back. Those pictures are going to be my proof that someone is impersonating me, that someone hates me enough to steal my child and now is stealing my identity . . ."

For a moment there was silence, then Alvirah said, "Zan, I know a good private detective firm. If you don't have the money to pay for it, I do. If these pictures have been doctored, we'll find out who paid to have it done. Wait a minute. Let me correct myself. If you say these pictures are phonies, I absolutely believe you, but I think that whoever has done this has overplayed his hand. I guess you lit a candle to St. Anthony the other night when you stopped into St. Francis of Assisi."

"When I stopped in . . . where?" Zan was afraid to ask the question.

"Late Monday afternoon at 5:30, quarter of six. I had dropped in to the church to make a donation I promised to St. Anthony and I noticed that some guy was eyeing my friend Fr. Aiden, and I didn't like it. That's why I checked the security camera tapes this morning to see if he was anyone Fr. Aiden might know. With all the crazies in New York, forewarned is forearmed. I didn't see you then, but you are on the tape. You came into the church and left just a few minutes later. I figured you were saying a prayer for Matthew."

Monday afternoon at 5:30 or quarter of six. I decided to walk home, Zan thought. I went straight home. I did go west on Thirty-first or Thirty-second Street, but by then I knew I was tired and took a cab the rest of the way.

But I didn't stop in the St. Francis chapel. I *know* I didn't.

*Or did I?*

She realized that Alvirah was still speaking and was asking about dinner.

"I'll be there," Zan promised, "at 6:30." She replaced the phone on the cradle and put her head in her hands. Am I having blackouts again? she asked herself. Am I going crazy? Did I kidnap my own son? And if I took him, what did I do with him?

If I can forget what happened less than forty-eight hours ago, what else have I blacked out? she asked herself in despair.

# 18

In the days when he had worked as an undercover cop it had been easy for Detective Billy Collins to pass as a down-and-out drifter. Thin to the point of boniness, with a sharp-angled face, sparse graying hair, and mournful eyes, he was easily accepted by drug dealers as a likely customer to purchase a fix.

Now that he was assigned to the Central Park Precinct, and arriving for work in a business suit, shirt, and tie, together with his mild, self-effacing manner, people tended to dismiss him on first acquaintance as an ordinary, run-of-the-mill guy, who probably wasn't too bright.

That judgment was shared by many suspected felons who were deceived by Billy's routine questions and seeming acceptance of their version about a criminal event. For most of them, that turned out to be a serious mistake. Billy's forty-two-year-old steel-trap mind retained information that had seemed trivial and unimportant at the time it was given, but when circumstances changed, he could retrieve that data from his memory bank in a heartbeat.

Billy's private life was simple. Despite his funereal appearance, he had a keen sense of humor, was a good storyteller, and was devoted to his wife, Eileen, whom he'd started dating when they were in high school. He said she was the only person alive who considered him handsome, and that was the reason he had fallen permanently in love with her. His two sons, who fortunately for them resembled their very attractive mother, were both students at Fordham University.

Billy had been the first detective to arrive on the scene when the 911 call came that a three-year-old was missing in Central Park nearly two years ago. He had rushed there with a sinking heart. For him the worst part of his job was to respond to a crime involving a dead or missing child.

That hot summer day in June it had been Tiffany Shields, the babysitter, who sobbed hysterically that she had fallen asleep next to the stroller and when she woke up Matthew was gone. While every inch of the park was being searched and nearby visitors questioned, the divorced parents had arrived separately. Ted Carpenter, the father, had been on the verge of attacking Shields, who admitted that she had fallen asleep; Zan Moreland, the mother, had been eerily calm, a reaction that Billy had attributed to shock. Even as the hours had passed without a trace of Matthew, and not one single witness who might have observed him being taken had come forward, the mother had remained impassive in demeanor.

In the nearly two years since that day, Billy Collins had kept Matthew's file on the top of his desk. He had scrupulously followed up on both parents' explanation of where they had been when their child disappeared, and both their statements were backed up by other witnesses. He asked them about any enemies who might have hated them enough to kidnap their child. Zan Moreland had hesitantly confided that there was one person she did consider an enemy. He was Bartley Longe, a prominent interior designer, who scoffed at the idea that in any way he would kidnap the child of a former employee.

"That statement from Zan Moreland validates everything I have ever said about her," Longe had told Billy, his tone furious and disgusted. "First she practically accused me of causing her parents' deaths, because if they hadn't been on their way to pick her up at the airport, her father might have had his heart attack at home and wouldn't have been in the accident. Then she told me that it was because she was working for me that she didn't see her parents more often. Now she's telling you that I kidnapped her child! Detective, do yourself a favor. Don't waste your time looking anywhere else. Whatever happened to that poor child was because his deranged mother made it happen."

Billy Collins had listened, but then trusted his own instincts. From what he had learned, Bartley Longe's anger at Zan Moreland was triggered by the fact that she had become his business competitor. But Billy had quickly decided that neither Longe nor Moreland had anything to do with the little boy's disappearance. In his heart and soul he firmly believed that Zan was a victim, a deeply wounded victim who would have moved heaven and earth to get her child back.

That was why when he received a call on Tuesday evening about a breaking development in the Matthew Carpenter case, Billy had been tempted to jump in his car and drive from his home in Forest Hills, Queens, to the precinct.

His boss told him to stay put. "For all we know those photos that were sold to that gossip magazine may have been doctored. If they're on the level, you need to have a clear mind to start reworking the case."

On Wednesday morning, Billy woke at seven A.M. Twenty minutes later, showered, shaved, and dressed, he was on his way into the city. By the time he arrived there, the photos that were published in *Tell-All Weekly* and online were on his desk.

There were six in all; the original three the English tourist had taken, plus the three he had blown up for the family album. They were the ones whose background seemed to indicate that Zan Moreland had kidnapped her own son.

Billy whistled softly, his only physical response to the fact that he was both shocked and chagrined. I really did believe that sob-sister, he thought, as he studied the three photos that showed Zan bending over the stroller, then picking up the sleeping child, and finally walking down the path away from the camera. There's no mistake, Billy thought as he went from one photo to the next. The long, straight auburn hair, the slender frame, the fashionable sunglasses . . .

He opened the file that was always on the corner of his desk. From it he extracted pictures that had been quietly taken of Zan by the police photographer when she rushed to the crime scene. The short flowered dress and the high-heeled sandals she was wearing when she arrived in the park that day were identical to the clothing worn by the kidnapper.

Billy normally patted himself on the back that he was an excellent judge of human nature. His sharp sense of disappointment in his own bad judgment was immediately vanquished by his overriding concern about what Zan Moreland might have done with her own son.

Zan's alibi about her whereabouts that day had seemed straightforward. Clearly he had missed something. I'm starting with the babysitter, Billy thought grimly. I'll pick apart Zan Moreland's account of every minute of that day and find out how she's gotten away with lying. Then by God, I'm going to make her tell me what she did with that little kid.

# 19

Tiffany Shields was still living at home, completing her second year at Hunter College. The day that Matthew Carpenter disappeared had been a turning point in her life. It wasn't only that she had been in charge of Matthew and had fallen asleep, it was that whenever the case came up in the media, she was branded as the careless babysitter who had not only not bothered to strap him into the stroller, but who had stretched out on a blanket and, as one reporter wrote, "passed out."

Almost every article referred to the hysterical call she had made to 911. The tape of it was played on some of the TV coverage. In the past two years when a child was missing anywhere, Tiffany had been forced to read or hear that it was or wasn't a Tiffany Shields–sleeping-babysitter kind of situation. Whenever she read or heard those media reports, Tiffany's anger at the unfairness of it grew into a block of solid fury.

The day was still vivid in her mind. She woke with what felt like the beginnings of a cold. She canceled plans to meet some of her girlfriends to celebrate their impending graduation from Cathedral High School. Her mother had gone to work at Bloomingdale's where she was a sales clerk. Her father was the superintendent of the apartment building where they lived on East Eighty-sixth Street. At noon, the phone rang in their apartment. If only I hadn't answered it, Tiffany thought over and over again in the next twenty-one months. I almost didn't. I figured it was some tenant calling to complain about some damn leaking faucet.

But she did answer it.

It was Zan Moreland. "Tiffany, can you possibly help me?" she had pleaded. "Matthew's new nanny was supposed to start this morning and just phoned that she can't be here until tomorrow. I've got a terribly important appointment. It's with a potential client, and she's not the kind of person who would care about my babysitting problems. Would you be an angel and take Matthew out to the park for a couple of hours? I just fed him and it's his naptime. I promise you he'll probably sleep the whole time."

I used to mind Matthew once in a while when the nanny had an evening off and I loved that little guy, Tiffany thought. But that day I told Zan that I thought I was getting sick, but she was so insistent that I finally gave in. And ruined my life in the process.

But on Wednesday morning, as she glanced at the morning paper over a glass of orange juice, Tiffany had two reactions. Explosive anger that Zan Moreland had manipulated her, and unbelievable relief that she would no longer be the victim of Matthew's disappearance. I told the cops that I had taken some antihistamines and felt kind of groggy and that I didn't really want to babysit, she thought. But if they come back to talk to me again, I'm going to rub it into them that Zan Moreland *knew* I was feeling tired. When I picked up Matthew, she offered me a Pepsi. She said it would make me feel better, that the sugar in it was beneficial when a cold was coming on.

Looking back, Tiffany thought, I wonder if Zan may have put something in that soda to make me really sleepy? And Matthew never even stirred while he was in the stroller. That's why I didn't bother him to put the strap on . . . He was out like a light.

Tiffany reread every word of the story and studied the photos carefully. That's the dress Zan was wearing, she thought, but the shoes aren't the same. By mistake, Zan had bought two pairs that were alike and had another pair that was almost the same. All of them were high-heeled beige step-in sandals. The only difference between the two styles was that one crossover strap was narrower than the other. She gave me one of the identical pairs with the narrower strap. We were both wearing them that morning. I still have them.

I'm not going to tell that to anyone. If the cops knew they may want my sandals and by God I *earned* them!

Three hours later, when she checked the messages on her cell phone after her history class, Tiffany saw that one of them was from that Detective Collins who had questioned her over and over again when Matthew disappeared. He wanted to talk with her again.

Tiffany's narrow mouth hardened into a slit. Her normally pert features suddenly lost their attractive, youthful expression. She pressed the button to return Billy Collins's call.

I want to talk to you, too, Detective Collins, she thought.

And this time I'll be the one to make *you* squirm!

# 20

Glory was putting that gooey stuff on his hair again. Matthew hated it. It made his scalp feel burned and some of it almost got in his eye. Glory rubbed hard to catch it, but the washcloth went in his eye and it hurt. But he knew that if he said he didn't want her to put the stuff in his hair, she would only say, "I'm sorry, Matty. I don't want to do it, but I have to."

Today he didn't say one single word. He knew Glory was really mad at him. This morning, when the doorbell rang, he had run into the closet and closed the door. He didn't mind this closet at all because it was bigger than some of the other ones, and it had a light big enough that he could see everything. But then he remembered he had left his favorite truck in the hall. It was his favorite because it was bright red and had three speeds, so when he played with it in the hall he could make it go very fast or really slow.

He had opened the closet door and ran to get it. Just then, he saw that Glory was closing the door and saying good-bye to some lady. After Glory locked the door she turned around and saw him. She looked so mad he was scared that she would hit him. "Next time I'll stick you in the closet and never let you out," she had said in a mean, low voice. He'd been so scared that he ran back into the closet and started to cry so hard that he couldn't get his breath.

Even after a while, when Glory said it was all right to come out, that it wasn't really his fault, that he was just a little kid, and that she was sorry she had yelled at him, he still couldn't stop crying. He was saying, "Mommy, Mommy," over and over, and he wanted to stop but he couldn't.

Then, later, when he was watching one of his DVDs, he heard Glory talking to someone. He tiptoed to the door of his room, opened it, and listened. Glory was on the phone. He couldn't hear what she was saying but her voice sounded really mad. Then he heard her shout, "I'm sorry, I'm sorry," and he could tell she was really scared.

Now he sat with the towel around his shoulders and the stuff dripping on his forehead and waited until Glory told him to get over to the sink, that it was time to rinse out his hair.

Finally she said, "Okay, I guess you're about ready." When he leaned over the sink, she said, "It's really too bad. If you ever get the chance, you'll be a cute redhead."

# 21

With intense satisfaction, Bartley Longe sauntered down the corridor to his office at 400 Park Avenue with the morning newspapers
under his arm. Fifty-two years old, with silver threads in his light
brown hair, ice blue eyes, and an imperious manner, he was the
kind of man who could intimidate a headwaiter or a subordinate
with a single chilling glance. On the flip side of his personality, he
was a charming and welcome guest among his many clients, both
the current celebrities and the quietly wealthy.

His staff always nervously anticipated his 9:30 A.M. arrival. What
kind of mood would Bartley be in? A furtive peek at him answered
that question. If his expression was pleasant and he graced them with
a hearty "Good morning," they relaxed at least for the present. If he
was frowning and tight-lipped, they knew something had displeased
him and that somebody was in for a nasty dressing-down.

By now, every one of the eight full-time employees had read or
heard the stunning news that Zan Moreland, who had once worked
for Bartley, was a person of interest in the disappearance of her own
son. They all remembered the day she had burst into the office after
her parents died in that accident and screamed at Bartley: "I hadn't
seen my mother and father in nearly two years and now I'll never see
them again. You made it impossible for me to leave because you said
I was too valuable on this project or that project. You're a nasty, self-

centered bully. You're more than that. You're a stinking devil. And if you don't believe it, ask any of these people who work for you. I'm going to open my own firm and you know what, Bartley? I'm going to rub your nose in my success."

She had broken into racking sobs and Elaine Ryan, Bartley's longtime secretary, had put an arm around her and taken her home.

Now Bartley opened the door of his office, the smirk on his face a clear signal to both Elaine and the receptionist, Phyllis Garrigan, that all was well for his employees, at least for the present. "I guess unless you're deaf, dumb, and blind, you know about Zan Moreland?" Bartley asked the women.

"I don't believe a word of it," Elaine Ryan said flatly. Sixty-two years old, her dark brown hair stylishly shaped, her hazel eyes the best feature in her narrow face, she was the single employee in the office with enough courage to occasionally challenge Bartley. As she often told her husband, the only thing that kept her working for Bartley was the good pay and the fact that at any time she could afford to walk out if he got too nasty. Her husband, a retired state trooper, was now head of security at a discount department store. Anytime Elaine came home fuming at something Bartley had said or done, he silenced her with one word, "Quit."

"It doesn't matter what you believe, Elaine. The proof is in the photos. You don't think that magazine would have bought them if there was any doubt about what they show, do you?" The smirk was leaving Bartley's face. "It is clear now that Zan picked up her own little boy and walked out of the park with him. It's up to the police to find out what she did with him after that. But if you want my theory, I'll give it to you."

Bartley Longe pointed his finger at Elaine for emphasis. "When she worked here, how often did you hear Zan whine that she wished she had grown up in one home in the suburbs instead of moving from place to place because of her father's job?" he demanded. "My theory is that all the sympathy she got after her parents' death was over and she needed a new tragedy in her life."

"That's absolutely crazy," Elaine said, heatedly. "Zan may have mentioned that she would have preferred not to have moved around all the time, but she said it in a general way when we were talking about our backgrounds. It certainly doesn't mean she said it all the time to gain sympathy. And she was crazy about Matthew. What you're insinuating is disgusting, Mr. Longe."

Elaine realized that Bartley Longe's cheeks were becoming flushed. Thou shall not contradict the boss, she thought. But how could he possibly suggest that Zan might have kidnapped Matthew to get sympathy?

"I forget how partial you were to my former assistant," Bartley Longe snapped. "But I will bet you that, as we speak, Zan Moreland is hunting for a lawyer, and I can assure you that she's going to need a good one."

# 22

Kevin Wilson admitted to himself that it was almost impossible to concentrate on the drawings on his desk. He was looking at the landscaper's sketches for the plantings in the lobby of 701 Carlton Place, as the new apartment complex would be called.

The name had been agreed upon only after a heated discussion with the directors of Jarrell International, the multibillion-dollar company that was financing the building. Several members of the board of directors had suggestions of names they thought would be more appropriate. Most of them were in the romantic or would-be historical vein, Windsor Arms, Camelot Towers, Le Versailles, Stonehenge, even New Amsterdam Court.

Kevin had listened with increasing impatience. Finally it had been his turn. "What is considered to be the most exclusive address in New York?" he had asked.

Seven of the eight board members named the same address on Park Avenue.

"Exactly," Kevin had told them. "My point is that we've got a very expensive building to fill. As we speak, there are many very expensive residential buildings in Manhattan under construction. I don't have to remind you that this is a tough economy, or that it's our job to make our pitch to potential buyers a very special one. Our location is spectacular. Our views of the Hudson River and of the city are spectacular. But I want us to be able to tell our prospective buyers that when the name 701 Carlton Place is mentioned, everyone hearing that address will know that the person giving it is lucky enough to be living in a privileged location."

I guess I carried the day, he thought as he turned his chair from the table to the desk, shaking his head. Dear God, if Pop were around what would he think if he heard that spiel? His grandfather had been the superintendent of the building next door to where he and his parents had lived. The name, Lancelot Towers, had been carved in stone over the six-story walk-up with its dreary railroad flats, creaking dumbwaiters, and ancient plumbing, on Webster Avenue in the Bronx.

Pop would have thought I was crazy, Kevin acknowledged, and so would Dad, if he were still alive. Mom is used to my salesmanship pitch by now. After Dad died, when I finally got her to move to East Fifty-seventh Street, she said I could sell a dead horse to a mounted policeman. Now she loves Manhattan. I swear she falls asleep at night humming "New York, New York."

All these random thoughts are going nowhere, he acknowledged silently, as he leaned back in his chair. From down the hall he could hear the relentless sound of hammering and the shrill, ear-piercing whine of machines beginning to polish the marble floors.

To Kevin, the din of construction was more beautiful than hearing a symphony in Lincoln Center. From the time I was a kid, I told Dad I'd rather go to a construction site than to the zoo, he thought. Even then, I knew I wanted to design buildings.

The landscaper's sketches weren't right, he decided. He'll have to start all over, or I'll get someone else. I don't want the entrance to look like a conservatory, Kevin thought. This guy just doesn't get it.

The model apartments. Last night he had studied both Longe's and Moreland's submissions for hours. They were both mighty impressive. He could understand why Bartley Longe was considered one of the foremost interior designers in the country. If he got the job, the apartments would be spectacular.

But Zan Moreland's sketches were marvelously attractive, too. He could see how she had studied under Longe, but then broken off from his ideas to pursue her own. There was more warmth, more of a sense of this-is-my-home in the deft way she put small touches in her layouts. And she was 30 percent cheaper in her prices.

He admitted to himself that he had not been able to get her out of his mind. She was a beautiful woman, there was no doubt about that. Slender, even a shade too thin, those enormous hazel eyes dominating her face . . . Odd that she was so shy, almost to the point of diffidence, until she got into explaining her vision for the model apartments. Then it was as if a light turned on and her face and voice became animated.

When she left yesterday, I watched her walk out to the curb and hail a cab, Kevin thought. It had gotten so windy that I wondered if that suit she was wearing was warm enough for her, even though it had a fur collar. I had the feeling that a strong gust of wind would have knocked her to the ground.

There was a tap on the door of his office. Before he could respond, his secretary, Louise Kirk, was in the office and walking to his desk. "Let me guess. It's exactly nine o'clock," he said.

Louise, a forty-five-year-old pear-shaped dynamo, with a head of fluffy blond hair, was the wife of one of the construction chiefs. "Of course it is," she replied briskly.

Kevin was sorry he had given Louise that opening. Now he hoped she wouldn't repeat her oft-told comparison of herself to Eleanor Roosevelt. As Louise, a history buff, explained it, Eleanor was always exactly on time, "Even to the moment when she descended the stairs in the White House to arrive precisely when the ceremony at FDR's casket in the East Room was about to begin."

But today Louise clearly had other things on her mind. "Did you have a chance to read the papers?" she asked.

"No. The breakfast meeting started at seven o'clock," Kevin reminded her.

"Well, then take a look at this." Gleeful at being able to be the bearer of startling news, Louise laid the morning papers, the *New York Post* and the *Daily News*, on his desk. Both of them had a picture of Zan Moreland on the front page. Their headlines were similar, and sensational. Both alleged that Zan Moreland had kidnapped her own child.

Kevin stared at the photos in disbelief of what he was seeing. "Did you know her child was missing?" he asked Louise.

"No, I didn't connect her name with it," Louise said. "Don't forget, I was in the main office yesterday. Of course, I knew the child's name, Matthew Carpenter. The papers were full of the story when he disappeared, but as I remember they always referred to the mother as Alexandra. I didn't put two and two together. What are you going to do about it, Kevin? She's bound to be arrested. Should I return her sketches to her office?"

"I would say that we have no choice," Kevin said quietly, then added, "The funny thing is I'd just about decided to give her the job."

# 23

On Wednesday morning, after celebrating the seven-o'clock Mass, Fr. Aiden watched CNN news as he sipped a cup of coffee in the kitchen of the Friary. Deeply disturbed, he shook his head as the breaking news unfolded that Alexandra Moreland had kidnapped her own child. He watched as the camera showed the same young woman who had come into the Reconciliation Room Monday leave the Four Seasons Restaurant last night. She tried to hide her face when she was rushing into a cab past the reporters and photographers, but there was no mistaking her.

Then he saw the photos that seemed to be the unmistakable proof that she had abducted little Matthew.

"I am involved in an ongoing crime and I am unable to prevent a murder that is about to be committed," she had said.

Was the ongoing crime the fact that Alexandra Moreland had taken her own son and lied to the authorities about his disappearance?

Fr. Aiden watched as the news anchorman spoke to June Langren, a nearby diner in the Four Seasons, about the shocking outburst by Ted Carpenter. "I honestly thought he was going to attack her," Langren said, breathlessly. "My boyfriend jumped up to restrain him if necessary."

In the fifty years he had been hearing confessions, Fr. Aiden thought he had heard virtually the full range of iniquities that the human spirit is capable of committing. Many years ago he had listened to the wrenching sobs of a young woman, little more than a girl herself, who had given birth to a child, and in fear of her parents had left it to die in a garbage bag in the Dumpster.

The saving mercy was that the child had not died, that a passerby had heard the cries of the wailing infant and saved it, he reflected.

This was different.

"A murder is about to be committed."

She did not say, "I am going to commit a murder," Fr. Aiden thought. She spoke of herself as an accomplice. Maybe now that those pictures have proven that she stole the child, whoever she is involved with will be frightened off. I can only pray that that will be the case.

Later that morning after he had reviewed the security tapes with Alvirah and she had gone home, Fr. Aiden opened his calendar. He had several dinner appointments in the next week with generous sponsors of the friars' ongoing food and clothing charity who had become close personal friends. He wanted to verify the time he was meeting the Andersons this evening.

His memory was accurate: 6:30, at the New York Athletic Club on Central Park South. Right down the street from Alvirah and Willy, he thought. That's perfect. I just realized I left my scarf in their apartment last night. I guess Alvirah didn't notice it or she would have mentioned it when she was here. After dinner, I'll give them a call and if they're home, I'll run over and get it. His sister, Veronica, had knitted that scarf for him, and if she noticed that he wasn't wearing it on a cold day, he'd be in big trouble.

As he was leaving the Friary after lunch, Neil was coming out of the chapel, a dustcloth and can of furniture polish in his hands. "Father, did you see that the woman, I mean the one your friend recognized on our security tape, is the one who stole her own kid?"

"Yes, I did," Fr. Aiden said abruptly, making it very clear to Neil that he did not wish to hear anything more about it.

Neil had been about to make the comment that when he had seen the tape it had jostled something in his mind. He'd been walking home to his apartment on Eighth Avenue Monday night around the time that Moreland woman had been caught on the security tape, but just as he got to the corner, a young woman who was walking ahead of him had darted out in traffic and hailed a cab. She damn near got hit by a car, he thought. I got a good look at her.

That was why he had gone back and run the security tape again, stopping it where Alvirah Meehan had recognized her friend. You'd swear the woman getting in the cab was the one who's on the tape, he thought. But unless she can change clothes in the middle of the street, it can't be the same person.

Neil shrugged. That was what he'd been about to tell Fr. Aiden, but it was clear Fr. Aiden didn't want to hear it. None of my business anyhow, Neil decided. In his forty-one years, thanks to his drinking problem, Neil had run the gamut of jobs. The one he'd liked best was being a cop, but that had only lasted a few years. No matter how much you pleaded that you'd go on the wagon, getting drunk three times when you were on duty meant getting tossed out on your ear.

I had the makings of a good cop, Neil thought reflectively, as he headed for the utility closet. All the guys joked about me that I could see a mug shot once and pick the guy out of Times Square a year later. Wish I'd lasted in the department. Maybe by now I'd be the police commissioner!

But he hadn't gone to AA then. Instead, after drifting from job to job, he'd ended up on the streets, begging for handouts and sleeping in shelters. Three years ago when he'd come here for food, one of the friars had sent him to the Inn at Graymoor where they had a rehab program for men like him, and there he'd finally kicked the booze.

Now, he liked working here. He liked staying sober. He liked the friends he'd made at the AA meetings. The friars called him their majordomo, a fancy way of saying handyman, but still, it had a certain dignity.

If Fr. Aiden did not want to talk about the Moreland woman, that's the way it is, Neil decided. Mum's the word. He probably wouldn't care anyhow that I saw someone who looked just like her.

Why should he?

# 24

The elderly man who timidly entered the offices of Bartley Longe was clearly not a potential customer. His thinning white hair was straggly on his skull, his worn Dallas Cowboys jacket in need of replacing, his jeans hanging loose on his body, his feet clad in old sneakers. He made his way slowly to the reception desk. At the first sight of him, Phyllis, the receptionist, took him to be a messenger. Then she dismissed that possibility. The frailness of the man's body and the sallow complexion of his wrinkled face suggested that he was, or had been, seriously ill.

She was glad that the boss was huddled in a meeting with Elaine, his secretary, and two fabric designers, and that his door was closed. Bartley Longe would have thought that whatever this man wanted, he didn't belong in the rarefied atmosphere of these surroundings. Even after six years, kindhearted Phyllis cringed at the way Bartley treated any person with a shabby appearance. Like her pal Elaine, Phyllis stayed at the job for the pretty decent salary, and the fact that Bartley was out of the office often enough to give them all a break.

She smiled at the obviously nervous visitor. "How can I help you?"

"My name is Toby Grissom. I'm sorry to bother you. It's just that I haven't heard from my daughter in six months and I can't sleep at night because I'm so worried that maybe she's in some kind of trouble. She used to work here about two years ago. I thought someone in your office, maybe, might have heard from her."

"She worked *here*?" Phyllis asked, as she mentally reviewed the list of employees who might have quit or been fired around two years ago. "What is her name?"

"Brittany La Monte. At least that's her stage name. She came to New York twelve years ago. Like all kids she wanted to be an actress, and she did get a little part off-Broadway now and then."

"I'm sorry, Mr. Grissom, but I've been here six years, and I can absolutely tell you that no one named Brittany La Monte was working in this office two years ago."

As though afraid of being dismissed out of hand, Grissom explained, "Well, not exactly worked for you *here*. What I mean is that she made her living as a makeup artist. Sometimes when there were cocktail parties to show off those model apartments Mr. Longe decorated, he asked Brittany to do the makeup for the models. Then he invited her to be one of the models. She's a real pretty girl."

"Oh, that could be why I never met her," Phyllis said. "What I can do is ask Mr. Longe's secretary about her. She's at all those model-apartment parties, and she has a phenomenal memory. But she's tied up in a meeting now and I know she won't be free for a couple of hours. Can you come back later?"

Make it after three, Phyllis reminded herself. King Tut said he was going to his place in Litchfield tonight, and he's leaving after lunch. "Mr. Grissom, anytime after three would work," she said sweetly.

"Thank you, ma'am. You're very kind. You see, my daughter always wrote to me regularly. She did say she was going on a trip two years ago, and sent me twenty-five thousand dollars to make sure I had something in the bank. Her mother passed away a long time ago and my little girl and I have been real pals. She said she wouldn't be in touch too often. Every once in a while I would get a letter from her. The postmark would be New York, so I know she's been back here. But like I say, it's been six months and no letter, and I've just got to see her. The last time she was in Dallas was almost four years ago now."

"Mr. Grissom, if we have an address for her, I promise we'll have it for you this afternoon," Phyllis said. Even as she spoke she knew that there probably wasn't any financial record of payment to Brittany La Monte. Bartley always paid people like her off the books so that he could get away cheaper than paying union wages.

"You see, I just got a pretty bad report from my doctor," Grissom explained, as he turned to go. "That's why I'm here. I don't have long and I don't want to die before I see Glory again and be sure she's okay."

"Glory? I thought you said her name was Brittany."

Toby Grissom smiled reminiscently. "Her real name is Margaret Grissom, after her mother. Like I said, her stage name is Brittany La Monte. But when she was born, I took one look at her and said, 'Little girl, you're so gorgeous your mama may call you Margaret, but my name for you is Glory.' "

# 25

At 12:15, a few minutes after they had spoken, Alvirah called Zan back. "Zan, I've been thinking," she said. "There's no question but that the police are going to want to talk to you. But before they do, you need to have a lawyer."

"A lawyer! Alvirah, why?"

"Zan, because the woman in those pictures looks just like you. The police are going to be knocking at your door. I don't want you answering questions without a lawyer beside you."

Zan felt the numbness that had pervaded her mind and body begin to change into a deadly calm. "Alvirah, you really aren't sure whether I'm the woman in those pictures, are you?" Then she added, "You don't have to answer that. I understand what you are saying. Do you know a lawyer you would recommend?"

"Yes, I do. Charley Shore is a top-drawer criminal defense attorney. I did a column on him for my newspaper, and we became good friends."

Criminal defense lawyer, Zan thought, bitterly. Of course. If I *did* take Matthew, I committed a crime.

*Did* I take Matthew?

Where would I have taken him? Who would I have given him to?

Nobody. It can't have happened that way. I don't care if I forgot that I stopped in at St. Francis's the other night. I was so desperately unhappy with Matthew's birthday coming up that maybe I did go in and light a candle for him. I've done that before. But I know that I never could have taken him out of that stroller and put him out of my life.

"Zan, are you still there?"

"Yes, Alvirah. Can you give me that lawyer's number?"

"Sure. But don't call him for ten minutes. I'll get in touch with him first. After I speak to him, he'll want to help you. I'll see you tonight."

Slowly Zan put the phone back on the cradle. A lawyer will cost money, she thought, money I could use to hire someone new to search for Matthew.

Kevin Wilson.

The thought of the architect's name made her sit bolt upright. Of course he would see those photos and think that she had kidnapped Matthew. Of course he would expect her to be arrested. He'll give the job to Bartley, Zan thought. I've spent so much time on it. I can't lose it. I'll need the money more than ever. I've *got* to talk to him!

She wrote a note for Josh and hurried out of the office, going down in the service elevator, and leaving the building by the service entrance. I don't even know if Wilson will be there, she thought, as she hailed a cab. But if I have to sit outside his office all afternoon, I'll do it.

I've got to ask him to give me a chance to clear myself.

It took nearly forty minutes in even heavier than usual traffic for Zan to reach the newly named 701 Carlton Place. The cab fare with tip was twenty-two dollars. It's a good thing I have a credit card, she thought, as she looked in her wallet and realized she had only fifteen dollars in the billfold section.

It had been her cardinal rule to use the credit card as sparingly as possible. Whenever she could, she walked to her appointments. Funny how you concentrate on something like cab fare, she thought, as she entered the apartment building. It's like when Dad and Mother died. At the funeral Mass I kept thinking that there was a spot on the jacket I was wearing. I kept asking myself why I hadn't noticed it. I had another black jacket that I could have worn.

Is it that I'm taking refuge in trivia again? she asked herself, as she pushed the revolving door and walked into the deafening sound of the machines polishing marble in the lobby.

Kevin Wilson obviously only wants working space, she thought, as she walked down the equipment-laden corridor to the room he was using as an office. She knew that when everything was in place that area would serve as a delivery drop for tenants' packages.

The door of his temporary office was partially open. She knocked, and without waiting for a response went in. There was a woman with blond hair standing at the table behind Wilson's desk. From the astonished expression on her face when she turned around and saw her, Zan knew she had read the morning papers.

Even so, she introduced herself. "I'm Alexandra Moreland. I met with Mr. Wilson yesterday. Is he here?"

"I'm his secretary, Louise Kirk. He's in the building, but . . ."

Trying not to cringe as she saw the agitation that was exuding from the other woman, Zan interrupted her. "It's a beautiful building, and from what I saw of it yesterday the people who move in here will be very, very happy. I certainly hope to be part of it."

I don't know how I can sound so calm, she thought. And then immediately she had the answer. Because I must get this job. Zan waited silently, her eyes fixed on the other woman's face.

"Ms. Moreland," Kirk began, hesitantly. "There really isn't any point in your waiting to see Kevin—I mean Mr. Wilson. Earlier this morning, he asked me to pack your proposal and return it to you. In fact, it's right there if you want to take it now, or else I'll have it delivered to you, of course."

Zan did not look at the package on the table. "Where is Mr. Wilson?"

"Ms. Moreland, he really doesn't . . ."

He's in one of the model apartments, Zan thought. I know he is. She turned, walked around the desk and picked up the package of her fabrics and sketches. "Thank you," she said.

In the lobby she headed straight for the elevators.

Wilson was not in the first apartment or in the second. She found him in the third, the largest unit. Sketches and fabric samples were laid out on the kitchen counter. Zan knew they had to be Bartley Longe's designs for this apartment.

She walked over to stand next to Wilson and set her package down. Without greeting him, she began, "I'm going to tell you right now," she said, "if you go with Bartley, the effect will be ravishing and damn hard to live with." She picked up a sketch. "Beautiful," she said. "But take a look at that love seat. It's too low. People will avoid it like the plague. Look at those wall hangings. Simply gorgeous, and so-oo-oo formal. But this is a very large apartment. Maybe somebody who has kids will be interested in it, but this design isn't going to inspire them. And no matter how much money you have, when you come home you want a home, not a museum. I offered you three different apartments that will make people feel comfortable."

She realized that for emphasis she had grabbed his arm. "I'm sorry for barging in," she said, "but I had to talk to you."

"You have, so are you finished?" Kevin Wilson asked quietly.

"Yes, I am. You've probably heard that photographs have surfaced that appear to show me kidnapping the child I've been hungering to find for almost two years. We'll know soon enough if I can prove that no matter how much the woman in those photos looks like me, it's not me. Just answer one question. If the photos that I'm talking about didn't exist, would you have given the job to Bartley Longe or me?"

Kevin Wilson studied Zan for a long minute before answering. "I was inclined to give it to you."

"Well, then, I ask you, I beg you, don't make a decision yet. I am going to be able to prove that whoever the woman in those photos is, it isn't me. I'm going to see the client who is the reason I hired the babysitter to take Matthew to the park that day, and ask her to come with me to the police and prove that I could not have been in the park at that time. Kevin, if you go with Bartley simply because you prefer his designs, that's one thing. But if you would have given me the job because you like my designs better, I implore you to let me clear my name. I implore you to wait before announcing a decision."

She looked up into Wilson's face. "I need this job. That doesn't mean I'd expect you to give it to me out of pity, because that would be ridiculous. But every cent I can save is being squirreled away so that I can hire another agency to try to find my Matthew. And something else that you should think of. I bet I'm thirty percent cheaper than Bartley. That ought to count for something."

Suddenly all the energy and fire was gone from her. She pointed to the package with her samples and sketches on the counter. "Would you consider looking at them again?" she asked.

"Yes."

"Thank you," Zan said, and without looking at Kevin Wilson again left the apartment. As she passed the floor-to-ceiling window at the elevator bank, she could see that the earlier drizzle had turned into a hard, driving rainstorm. She stopped for a moment to look out. A helicopter was hovering over the West Side Heliport preparing to land. She watched as the wind tossed it from one side to another. Finally, it settled down safely on the tarmac. It made it, she thought.

Dear God, please let me make it through this storm, too.

# 26

Billy Collins's partner was Detective Jennifer Dean, a handsome African-American woman his own age whom he had met at the Police Academy, where they had become fast friends. After a stint in the Narcotics Division, Jennifer had been promoted to detective and transferred to the Central Park Precinct. There, to their mutual satisfaction, she had been assigned to be his partner.

Together, they met with Tiffany Shields at Hunter College during her lunch break. By that time Tiffany had convinced herself that Zan Moreland had deliberately drugged both her and Matthew. "Zan insisted I have that Pepsi that day," she told them, her mouth tightened into a narrow line. "I felt lousy. I didn't want to babysit. She gave me a pill. I thought it was Tylenol for colds, but I think now it was the kind that makes you sleepy. And let me tell you something else. Matthew was out like a light. I bet anything she drugged him, too, so that when she grabbed him out of the stroller, he wouldn't wake up."

"Tiffany, you didn't tell me that you thought Zan Moreland drugged you the day Matthew disappeared. You never hinted that you thought that," Billy said quietly. His tone did not reflect the fact that to him what the girl was saying made sense. If Moreland had been looking for a way to kidnap her own child, Tiffany may have given her a priceless opportunity. That day was unseasonably warm, the kind that made anyone sleepy, never mind someone who was drowsy from having a cold and then possibly drugged.

"There's something more I've been thinking about," Tiffany went on, her voice sullen. "Zan put an extra blanket at the foot of the stroller just in case I wanted to sit on the grass. She said that it was so warm that every bench in the park would probably be filled. I thought she was being nice, but now I think she was just hoping that I'd fall asleep right away."

The detectives looked at each other. Was Moreland possibly that manipulative? they both wondered. "Tiffany, you never suggested the day Matthew disappeared—or any time after that when we spoke to you—that you had been drugged," Jennifer Dean reminded her calmly.

"I was hysterical. I was so scared. All those people and cameras around and then Zan and Mr. Carpenter coming, and I knew they were blaming me."

Because of the heat, the park had been unusually crowded that day, Billy thought. If Moreland had waited her chance, then casually walked past the stroller and picked up Matthew, no one would have thought it unusual. Even if Matthew had awakened, he wouldn't have cried. We attributed Moreland's calm to shock. When Ted Carpenter arrived on the scene, he did what most fathers in his position would have done. He tore into the babysitter for falling asleep.

"I've got a class," Tiffany said, as she stood up. "I can't be late for it."

"We don't want you to be late for it, Tiffany," Billy agreed, as he and Jennifer rose from the hallway bench where they had been sitting.

"Detective Collins, those photos prove that Zan Moreland took Matthew and set me up to be the fall guy. You don't have a clue how miserable these two years have been for me. Try listening to my 911 call to you. You can still find it on the Internet."

"Tiffany, we can understand how you feel." Jennifer Dean's tone was soothing.

"No, you can't. No one can. But do you think Matthew might still be alive?"

"We have no reason to think that he is not alive," Billy hedged.

"Well, if he's not, I just hope that that lying, lousy mother of his spends the rest of her rotten life in a jail cell. Just promise me that I get a front seat at her trial. I've earned it."

Tiffany spat out the words.

# 27

He had put the plan in motion. Step by step he was now bringing it to a head. He knew it was time. Gloria was getting too restless. Also, he had made a terrible mistake when he told her that it would be necessary to kill Zan and make it look like a suicide. Gloria had only gotten into it for the money he promised her. She didn't understand that it would not be enough simply to make Alexandra Moreland dangle in the wind to public ridicule.

He would not be happy until Zan was dead.

Last night when he called Gloria, he told her that he was planning to have her come back to the church with him soon, but he didn't tell her why. She started to object, and he shouted her down. He didn't tell her that he planned to get rid of the old priest and that she had to be caught looking like Zan on the security cameras.

Zan's suicide would be believable.

The plan was that on the same day, Gloria would abandon Matthew in a public place where he would be noticed. He could see the headlines already: MISSING CHILD FOUND HOURS AFTER MOTHER'S SUICIDE.

He could savor the story that would follow. "Alexandra 'Zan' Moreland was found dead in her apartment in Battery Park City, an apparent suicide. The troubled interior designer, suspected of kidnapping her own child . . ."

Those photos that the tourist has taken. Why had they come to light now? The timing couldn't be worse. On the other hand, they could be a magnificent, unexpected gift.

He had pored over them himself, studied them, enlarged them on his computer. Gloria looked just like Zan. If the cops believed they were authentic, Zan's denials about making all the purchases to her credit cards would only be one more proof that she was crazy, that she had staged the kidnapping herself.

By now they were undoubtedly wondering if she might have done away with her own child.

But if the cops, or anyone else, could find one single discrepancy in those photos, they wouldn't believe that any of the rest was true. The whole thing would fall apart.

Would they interview the babysitter again?

Of course they would.

Would they interview Nina Aldrich, the potential client Zan claimed to have been with when her son disappeared?

Of course they would.

But Nina Aldrich had had a good reason to be vague about that time frame two years ago and that reason still existed. She wouldn't want to be pinned down now, he thought.

The greatest threats to him were Gloria herself, and the photos that tourist had taken.

He never phoned Gloria during the day. There was always the chance that the boy might be within earshot and no matter how much he warned her, Gloria had a bad habit of calling him by name when they talked.

He looked at the clock. It was almost five. He couldn't wait any longer. He had to talk to Gloria. He had bought two prepaid cell phones, one for her and one for himself. He locked the door of his office and tapped in her number.

She answered on the first ring. From the angry tone of her voice he could tell that the call was going to be trouble.

"I've been seeing the story plastered all over the Internet," she said. "They keep showing those pictures."

"Was the boy nearby when you were on the computer?"

"Of course he was. When he saw his picture, he loved it," Gloria snapped.

"Don't try your lamebrained sarcasm on me. Where is he?"

"He's in bed already. He didn't feel well. He threw up twice."

"Is he getting sick? I can't have him going to a doctor."

"Not that kind of sick. I put that coloring stuff in his hair again this afternoon and he hates it. This crazy life is getting to him. It's getting to me, too. You said one year tops, and it's been nearly two years."

"It's going to be over very soon. I can promise you that. Those pictures of you in the park will bring it to a head. But you've got to rack your brain. Look at them on the Internet again. See if there's *anything* that the cops might notice that would make them suspect that the woman there isn't Zan."

"You paid me to follow her around, to study her photos, to learn how to walk and talk like her. I'm a damn good actress and that's what I want to be doing, not babysitting that little kid and keeping him from his mother. God Almighty, he keeps a bar of soap under his pillow because it's the kind she used and the scent reminds him of her."

He had not missed the moment of hesitation in Gloria's voice and then her answer, first defensive, then trying to steer the conversation to the subject of the child.

"Gloria, concentrate," he warned firmly. "Is there *anything* about the way you dressed, or jewelry that you wore, that would make the police take seriously Zan's claim that she was not the woman in that picture?"

Enraged when she did not answer, he asked, "And something else, exactly *what* did you tell that priest?"

"If you keep bugging me about that, I'll go crazy. So here's the way it was. I told him that I am a participant in an ongoing crime, that a murder is going to be committed, and that I can't stop it."

"You told him that?" The caller's voice was deadly calm.

"I told him that, damn you. But I told him under the seal of the confessional. If you don't know what that seal means, look it up. And I'm giving you fair warning. One week more and I'm out of here. And you better have two hundred thousand dollars in cash for me. Because if you don't, I'll go to the cops and tell them you forced me to keep the kid because otherwise you would have had him killed. I'll trade everything I know about you for immunity from prosecution. You want to know something? I'll be a hero! I'll get a book contract for a million dollars. I've got it all figured out."

Before he had time to answer, the woman, known to Matthew and her father as Glory, had pressed the END button on her cell phone.

Despite his frequent and frantic efforts to reach her again, she did not answer his calls.

# 28

After she left Kevin Wilson, Zan went directly back to the office, once again using the delivery entrance to get into her building.

Josh was waiting for her. She had left the note saying that she was going to try to meet with Wilson. When she saw the expression of deep concern on the face of her young assistant, she attributed it to his fear they might have lost the job of decorating the model apartments, and said reassuringly, "Josh, I think we might get a break with Wilson. He'll hold off making a decision until I can clear myself."

Josh's expression did not change. "Zan, exactly how can you clear yourself?" he asked, his voice trembling with emotion. He pointed to the front page of the two newspapers that were lying on the desk.

"Josh, I'm not in those pictures," Zan said. "That woman looks like me, but she isn't me." The protest came from lips that were suddenly dry. Josh has been my dear friend as well as my assistant, she thought. Last night he came rushing to get me out of the Four Seasons and past all those reporters. *But he hadn't seen the pictures yet.*

"Zan, a lawyer named Charles Shore called you," Josh told her. "He said that Alvirah had recommended him. I'll dial him back for you. You need to be protected right away."

"Protected from whom?" Zan demanded. "The police? Ted?"

"You need to be protected from yourself," Josh shot back, as tears glistened in his eyes. "Zan, when I first came to work for you after

Matthew disappeared, you told me about those blackouts you had after your parents died." He came around the desk and put his hands protectively on her shoulders. "Zan, I love you. You're a brilliant interior designer. You're the big sister I never had. But you need help. You've got to prepare a defense before the cops start questioning you."

Zan pushed his hands away and stepped back. "Josh, you mean well, but you've got to understand. I can prove I was with Nina Aldrich when Matthew was taken from the stroller. I'm going to see her right now. Tiffany took Matthew to the park at about 12:30. By two when she woke up, he was gone. I can prove I was meeting with Nina Aldrich during that time. I tell you, I can prove it! Something crazy is going on, but I am *not* the woman in those photos."

Josh did not look convinced. "Zan, I'm calling that lawyer for you right now. My uncle is a cop. I talked to him this morning. He said it's obvious you're a suspect now in Matthew's disappearance, and he'd be surprised if you're not brought in for questioning before the end of the day."

Nina Aldrich is my only hope, Zan thought. "Call that lawyer," she said. "Tell me his name again."

"Charles Shore." Josh reached for the phone.

As Josh was dialing, Zan steadied herself by putting both palms on the desk. The panic was building up. She felt herself wanting to retreat to escape it. Not now, she prayed. Please God, not now. Give me the strength to hang on. Then from a distance, she heard Josh shout her name, but she no longer had the strength to answer him.

It all became a blur. She thought she felt people pressing around her, people shouting at her, the wail of an ambulance. She heard herself sobbing, calling for Matthew. Then she felt a prick in her arm. It was real.

When she finally woke, she was in the emergency room of a hospital. Josh and a man with iron gray hair and steel-rimmed glasses were sitting beside her in the curtained-off cubicle. "I'm Charley Shore," the older man said. "I'm Alvirah's friend, and your lawyer if you'll have me."

Zan struggled to focus on him. "Josh called you," she said slowly.

"Yes. Don't try to talk now. We'll have plenty of time tomorrow. As a precaution, the doctor would like you to stay here overnight."

"No. No. I have to go home. I have to talk to Nina Aldrich." Zan tried to pull herself up.

"Zan, it's nearly six o'clock." Shore's voice was soothing. "We'll talk to Mrs. Aldrich tomorrow. It would be better if you stayed here, I promise you."

"It would be so much better if you stayed, Zan," Josh told her soothingly.

"No. No. I'll be all right." Zan felt her head clearing. She had to get out of here. "I'm going home," she said. "But first, I promised Alvirah I would have dinner with her and Willy tonight. I want to go there now." Alvirah will help me, she thought. She'll help me prove that I am not the woman in those photos.

Things were coming back to her. "I fainted, didn't I?" she asked. "And then I was in an ambulance?"

"That's right." Josh covered her hand with his.

"Wait a minute. Am I wrong, or were people crowding around me? Were reporters there when they took me out to the ambulance?"

"Yes, Zan," Josh admitted.

"I had another blackout." Zan pulled herself up, then realized a hospital gown was hanging loosely from her shoulders. She folded her arms, hugging herself. "I'll be okay. If you two will just wait outside, I'll get dressed."

"Of course." Charles Shore and Josh rose quickly but were stopped by her sudden, anxious question.

"What is Ted saying about all this? Obviously, he's seen the photos himself by now."

"Zan, get dressed," Shore told her. "We'll talk on the way to Alvirah and Willy's place."

As they left the emergency room, Zan realized, in a moment of absolute clarity, that neither Josh nor Charley Shore had responded to her insistence that Nina Aldrich would verify the fact that she had been with her when Matthew disappeared.

# 29

On Wednesday afternoon, Penny Hammel phoned her friend Rebecca Schwartz and invited her to come over for dinner. "I cooked a nice pot roast for Bernie because the poor guy's been on the road for two weeks and it's his favorite meal," she explained. "He was supposed to be home by four o'clock but wouldn't you know it, his darn truck started having problems in Pennsylvania. He's got to stay in King of Prussia overnight while they figure out what's wrong. Anyhow, I pulled out all the stops for the dinner and I'm not going to eat it alone."

"I'll be there with bells on," Rebecca assured her. "I don't have anything in the house for dinner, as it happens. I was going to get takeout from Sun Yuan, but honest to God, I do that so often I feel as if I'll turn into a fortune cookie."

At 6:15 the two friends were sipping Manhattans in Penny's combined kitchen–family room. The mouthwatering aromas emanating from the stove combined with the warmth of the fireplace filled both women with the sense of well-being.

"Oh, have I got a story to tell you about the new tenant in Sy's farmhouse," Penny began.

Rebecca's expression changed. "Penny, that woman made it clear that she was holing up there to finish her book. You didn't go over, did you?"

Even as she asked the question, Rebecca knew the answer. She should have guessed that Penny would want to get a look at the new tenant.

"I had no intention of paying a visit," Penny said defensively. "I brought over six of my blueberry muffins just to be neighborly, but that woman was downright rude. I mean I started by saying that I didn't want to interrupt her but thought she might enjoy the muffins, and I'd put my phone number on a Post-it on the bottom of the plate. If I were the one moving into a strange neighborhood, I'd like to know that there was someone to call if an emergency came up."

"That was real nice of you," Rebecca conceded. "You're the kind of friend everyone should have. But I wouldn't go there again. She's a loner, that one."

Penny laughed. "For two cents I would have asked her for my muffins back. And anyhow, when you think about it, she has a sister she can call if she needs help."

Rebecca drained the last of her Manhattan. "A sister? How do you know she has a sister?"

"Oh, I saw a toy truck on the floor in the hall behind her and I told her that I'm a good babysitter. She told me that the truck belonged to her sister's kid. Her sister helped her move in and had left it."

"That's funny," Rebecca said slowly. "When I gave her the key, she said she had a meeting with her editor and would be arriving late at night. I drove by early the next morning and saw her car in the breezeway. There wasn't another car there. So I guess her sister and her kid came later."

"Maybe there *is* no sister and she likes to play with toy trucks herself," Penny laughed. "I can tell you, with a nasty attitude like hers, I bet she doesn't have many friends."

She got up, reached for the cocktail shaker, and split the last of the Manhattans between them. "Dinner's about ready to be put on the table. Why don't we sit down and get started? But I do want to catch the 6:30 news. I'd love to know if they arrested that crazy woman who kidnapped her own child. I can't believe that she's still running around loose."

"Neither can I," Rebecca agreed.

As they had expected, the photos taken in Central Park allegedly showing Alexandra Moreland lifting her son Matthew out of the stroller were the lead story on the evening news. "I wonder what she did with him, poor kid?" Penny sighed as she swallowed a succulent bite of pot roast.

"Moreland wouldn't be the first mother to kill her own child," Rebecca said soberly. "Do you think she was nuts enough to do that?"

Penny did not answer. Something about those photos was bothering her. What *is* it? she asked herself. But then the segment about the missing child ended and she clicked the television off with a shrug. "Who needs three minutes of sales pitches about sex pills and nose sprays?" she asked Rebecca. "Then you hear all the problems that stuff can give you, like heart attacks and ulcers and strokes, and you wonder who would be dopey enough to buy them."

For the rest of the meal the two good friends gossiped about their mutual friends in town, and whatever it was about the photographs that had disturbed Penny retreated into her subconscious.

# 30

The meeting Bartley Longe had been conducting in his office when Toby Grissom stopped in to inquire about his missing daughter lasted all morning. Then, contrary to his usual pattern, instead of going out, Bartley ordered a lunch delivered from a nearby restaurant.

As was their habit, his secretary, Elaine, and the receptionist, Phyllis, shared their diet-conscious salads in the kitchenette down the hall from the reception room. A weary-looking Elaine confided that Bartley was in as terrible a mood as she'd ever seen him and that was saying a lot. He had bitten off poor Scott's head when Scott suggested not putting valances in the smaller bedrooms of the Rushmore job, and he tore Bonnie apart over the fabric designs she chose for him to approve. Both of them were almost in tears. "He's treating them the way he treated Zan," she said.

"Scott and Bonnie are not going to last any longer than all the other assistants he's had since Zan," Phyllis said vehemently. "But I've been looking at those photos in the newspapers. He's right about one thing. There's no question but that Zan stole her own child. I only hope she left him with someone she can trust."

"I blame Bartley for causing her to have a breakdown," Elaine said sadly. "And you know what's crazy? In the midst of all that was going on with Scott and Bonnie, he kept the television on the whole morning. It was on mute, so there was no sound, but he kept an eye on it and the minute those photos of Zan taking Matthew were shown, he was all attention."

"Is that what has him all fired up today?" Phyllis asked. "I thought he would be thrilled to see that Zan was lying about Matthew."

"You wouldn't believe how much he hates Zan, and how he loves to see her twisting in the wind. And actually it was when Scott suggested that those photos might have been staged that Bartley lost it. Don't forget Zan just bid against him for that job with Kevin Wilson. If Zan could somehow prove those photos are phonies and she gets that job, it will be a horrible blow for Bartley. There's no question about that. There are at least four younger designers besides Zan who have been cutting into his business."

Phyllis glanced at her watch. "I'd better get back to the desk. I swear he begrudges me breaking for lunch, even though if anyone rings the doorbell, I can buzz it open in about ten seconds. But first, do you remember someone named Brittany La Monte?"

Elaine sipped the last of her diet soda. "Brittany La Monte? Oh sure I do. She started out doing makeup for the models or would-be actresses that Bartley hired to serve cocktails and hors d'oeuvres when he was showing off those model apartments a couple of years ago. Just between us, I think Bartley took a big shine to Brittany. He told her he thought she was prettier than the girls she was making up and gave her a job passing out Champagne. I always thought he was seeing her on the side. We haven't done one of those apartments in at least a year, and he's never brought her to any of his other events. I guess he dumped her the way he dumps all of them."

"Brittany's father, Toby Grissom, was in this morning looking for her," Phyllis explained. "The poor old guy's worried. The last postcard he got from her was six months ago, from Manhattan. He's sure she's in trouble. I told him I'd talk to you because you would remember her if she worked on any of those jobs. He's coming back after three. I figured Bartley would be on his way to Litchfield by then. What can I tell Grissom?"

"Only that she did some freelance work for us a few years ago and that we have no idea where she might be working or living now," Elaine said. "That's the truth."

"But if you think Bartley might have had a thing going with Brittany, could you ask him if he's been in touch with her? The father said that he's had some bad news about his health, and I can tell he's desperate to see her."

"I'll ask Bartley," Elaine agreed nervously. "But if there was any romance going on between them, he won't like to have her name brought up. He's still steaming about that model who sued him for sexual harassment. He settled big on that one and might be afraid that this will develop into that kind of problem. Was there a postmark on the card Brittany sent her father?"

"Yes, New York. That's why he's here. But Mr. Grissom did say that just about two years ago, Brittany told him that she had some kind of job and wouldn't be in touch with him often."

"Oh, brother," Elaine sighed. "I wonder if Bartley got her pregnant? What time did you say Brittany's father is coming in?"

"Anytime after three o'clock."

"Then let's just hope that Bartley takes off for Litchfield, and I can talk to the father quietly."

But at three o'clock when Toby Grissom timidly rang the bell and Phyllis released the lock, Bartley Longe was still incommunicado in his office. Grissom's sneakers were squishing and Phyllis looked with horror as they deposited muddy soil on the Aubusson carpet.

"Oh, Mr. Grissom," she said, "I wonder if you'd mind wiping your feet on that mat." She tried to soften the request by adding, "The weather certainly is miserable today, isn't it?"

Like an obedient child, Grissom walked back to the mat and rubbed the soles of his sneakers on it. Seemingly oblivious to the stain on the carpet, he said, "I've spent the day chasing down the girls my daughter lived with while she was in New York. I want to see Bartley Longe now."

"Mr. Longe is tied up in a meeting," Phyllis said, "but his secretary, Elaine Ryan, will be happy to speak to you."

"I didn't ask to speak to Longe's secretary. I'll sit in this fancy waiting room no matter how long it takes until I see that Bartley Longe fellow," Grissom said, his manner unquestionably determined.

Phyllis could see the weariness in his eyes. His jacket and jeans looked soaked through to the skin. I don't know what else is wrong with him, but he's lucky if he doesn't catch pneumonia, she thought. She picked up the phone. "Mr. Grissom is here," she told Elaine. "I explained Mr. Longe is in a meeting, but Mr. Grissom plans to wait until he's free."

Elaine caught the cautionary note in the receptionist's voice. Brittany La Monte's father was going to wait Bartley out. "I'll see what I can do," she told Phyllis. She replaced the phone in the cradle, and deliberated. I have to tell our fearless leader about this guy, she thought. I've got to warn him. The light on the phone panel showed that Bartley had made an outside call himself. When the light went out, she got up and knocked on Bartley's door. Without waiting for a response she went into his private office.

The television was still on, muted. Bartley's lunch tray was pushed to one side of his massive desk. The norm would have been for Bartley to call for someone to take out the tray when he had finished eating. Now he looked at Elaine, his expression both surprised and angry. "I wasn't aware I sent for you."

It had been a long day. "Nobody sends for me, including you, Mr. Longe," Elaine said, crisply. Fire me if you don't like that, she thought. I'm sick of the sight of you. She did not wait for Longe to react before continuing. "There is a man out here who insists on seeing you. I gather he'll wait in the reception room until the cows come home, so unless you want to sneak out the back door, you'd better meet with him. His name is Toby Grissom and he's Brittany La Monte's father. I'm sure you'll remember her name. She freelanced for you about two years ago when we were showing the Waverly apartments."

Bartley Longe leaned back in his chair, a puzzled expression on his face, as if trying to remember Brittany La Monte. He knows perfectly well who I'm talking about, Elaine thought, as she noticed the way he clasped his hands tightly together.

"Of course I remember that young woman," he said. "She was trying to be an actress and I even introduced her to some people who might have helped her. But as I recall, the last time we had one of those situations where we used the models, she wasn't available."

Neither Elaine nor Bartley Longe had heard Toby Grissom come through Elaine's office and stand at the partially opened door. "Don't give me that stuff, Mr. Longe," Grissom said, his voice rising in fury. "You gave Brittany a line about making her a star. You had her up to your fancy place in Litchfield plenty of weekends. Where is she now? What did you do to my little girl? I want the truth and unless I get it, I'm going straight to the cops."

# 31

It was 7:30 P.M. by the time Zan, against all medical advice, was in a cab on her way to Alvirah and Willy's apartment with Charley Shore. She had insisted Josh go home after flatly refusing his offer to sleep on the couch of her apartment. If there's anything I need now, she thought, it's to be alone later on and gather my wits about me.

"Shouldn't you be on your way home, too?" she asked Shore as the cab inched its way along York Avenue.

Charley Shore decided not to tell Zan that he and his wife had theatre tickets for a play they both wanted to see and that he had phoned his wife to tell her to leave his ticket at the box office, that he'd be there when he could make it. Once again he thanked heaven for the fact that Lynn was always understanding when a situation like this came up. "I don't think I'll be terribly late," he had told her. "Zan Moreland is in no condition to have a long discussion with me tonight."

That opinion was more than reinforced by the deadly paleness of Zan's complexion and the way she was shivering inside the fake-fur vest she was wearing. I'm glad she's going to be with Alvirah and Willy, Charley thought. She trusts them. Maybe she'll even tell them where her son is.

When Alvirah had called him earlier this afternoon about Alexandra Moreland, she had been direct with him. "Charley, this is someone you've got to help. I thought a tree had fallen on me when I saw those photographs. I don't see how they can be fake. But there's nothing fake about the way she's been suffering and trying to find Matthew. If she took him, she doesn't remember it. Don't people go into zombielike states when they've had breakdowns?"

"Yes, it's not frequent, but sometimes they do," he told her.

Now in the cab, Charley wondered if Alvirah had not diagnosed Moreland's condition with deadly accuracy. When he got to the hospital earlier, she had still been out of it, but was mumbling her son's name over and over again. "I want Matthew . . . I want Matthew . . ."

The words had torn his heart. When he was ten years old, his two-year-old sister had died and he could still vividly remember that terrible day at the grave, and his mother's plaintive wail. "I want my baby. I want my baby."

He looked at Zan. The cab was dark, but from the headlights of other cars and the brightly lit signs on stores along the way, he could clearly see her face. I am going to help you, he vowed. I've been in the business forty years and I'm going to give you the best defense that I possibly can. You're not faking this memory loss. I'll bet my life on it.

He had expected to go up with her to the Meehans' apartment and stay for a while, but as the cab approached Central Park South, he changed his mind. Alexandra Moreland obviously trusted Alvirah and Willy. She'd be better off alone with them this evening. Certainly it was no time to start to question her about details.

The cab stopped in the semicircular driveway, and he told the cabbie to wait for him. Despite Zan's insistence that he didn't need to get out, he escorted her up in the elevator. The doorman had announced them and Alvirah was waiting in the hall when they got off on the sixteenth floor. Without a word, she wrapped her arms around Zan and looked at Charley. "You go ahead, Charley," she directed. "What Zan needs is to relax now."

"I couldn't agree more and I know you'll take good care of her," Charley said with a smile, as he stepped back into the elevator and pushed the button for the lobby. The cab got him to the theatre in time for the curtain, but even though the show was lighthearted and amusing, and he had been looking forward to it, he still could not settle down and enjoy it.

How do I defend a woman who may not be capable of contributing to her own defense? he asked himself. And how long will it be before they decide to slap handcuffs on her?

He had an ominous feeling that when that happened, it would push her over the edge.

A blanket wrapped around her, a pillow behind her head, sipping hot tea with honey and cloves, all had the effect of making Zan feel as though she was coming out of a kind of dark alley. At least those were the best words she could use to explain to Alvirah and Willy about why she had collapsed. "When I saw those photos, I thought I was dreaming. I mean, I can prove I was with Nina Aldrich when Matthew was in the park. But why would anyone go to the trouble of looking exactly like me? I mean, isn't that crazy?"

Not waiting for a response, she said, "You know what I was running through my head . . . that song from A *Little Night Music* . . . 'Send in the Clowns.' I love that song and it seemed so appropriate. This is a farce. It's a circus. It has to be. But I know it will be all right when I talk to Nina Aldrich. I was going to do that today and then I fainted."

"Zan, it's no wonder you fainted with all this going on. You may remember that Josh was on the phone with Charley Shore and Charley dropped everything to be with you. That's the kind of lawyer and friend he is. Josh told me about last night at the Four Seasons with

Ted. The way I figure it, you never did get to have dinner last night, and how much did you eat today?" Alvirah asked.

"Well, not much. Just coffee this morning, and I hadn't had lunch by the time I got back to the office. And then I fainted." Zan sipped the last of the tea. "Alvirah, Willy, you both believe that those photos show me taking Matthew. I heard it in your voice this afternoon, Alvirah. Then when Josh told me right away that I needed a lawyer, I could see that he believes they're real, too."

Willy looked at Alvirah. Of course she thinks they're the real McCoy, he thought. I do, too. But that doesn't mean this poor gal isn't positive they're not her. What's Alvirah going to say now?

Alvirah's response was hearty but evasive. "Zan, if you say those pictures are not of you, then I would guess Charley's first job will be to get a copy of the negatives or whatever they do with those cell phone cameras if that's what the man used, and get an expert to prove that they're phony. Then my bet is that the time frame when you saw that woman about decorating her new town house would vindicate you. Didn't you say Nina Aldrich was her name?"

"Yes."

"Charley's the kind of lawyer who will make sure that every second you spent with Nina Aldrich is accounted for."

"Then why didn't Josh or Charley respond when I told them that my meeting with Aldrich would prove I couldn't have been in the park?" Zan asked.

Alvirah stood up. "Zan, from what I gather, you didn't have any real conversation with Josh before you fainted. Buh-lieve me, we're not going to leave a stone unturned until we get at the truth and find Matthew," she promised. "But the first thing you've got to remember is that you are going to be bombarded from all sides and you can't go through all this unless you're strong. And I mean physically strong. Dinner's simple. When you promised to come I put on my thinking cap and remembered that you love chili. So that's what it is, chili, a salad, and hot Italian bread."

Zan tried to smile. "Sounds good to me."

And it *was* good, she decided, as the warmth of the comfort food and a glass of red wine made her feel that she was getting her balance back.

She had told Alvirah and Willy about the possibility of decorating the model apartments for the architect Kevin Wilson at his ultra chic building, 701 Carlton Place. "It's between me and Bartley Longe," she explained. "I realized that when Wilson read the morning papers, he'd probably believe that I had staged that kidnapping. I went straight to his office and asked him to give me a chance to prove that I couldn't have taken Matthew that day."

Alvirah knew she had only a small sense of how much Zan had worked on her designs for those apartments. "Did he give you that chance?"

Zan shrugged. "We'll see. He let me leave my sketches and fabrics, so I guess I'm still in the running."

They all passed on dessert, deciding to have just cappuccino. Knowing that Zan would be getting ready to leave, Willy got up from the table, went into the bedroom, and quietly picked up the phone and ordered a car to take her to Battery Park City then bring him back. *Just in case they're hanging around her building, there's no way I'm letting that girl face a battery of reporters and photographers alone,* he decided. *I'm going to escort her home and get her upstairs.*

"Fifteen minutes, Mr. Meehan," the car dispatcher assured him.

Willy had just gotten back to the table when the phone rang. It was Fr. Aiden. "I'm crossing the street from the club," he announced. "If it's still all right, I'd like to pick up my scarf."

"Oh, that's perfect," Alvirah assured him. "There is someone here I've been hoping you'd arrive in time to meet."

Zan was finishing the last of her coffee. As Alvirah replaced the phone, Zan said, "Alvirah, I honestly don't want to meet anyone. Please, let me get away before whoever that is arrives."

"Zan, this isn't just anyone," Alvirah pleaded. "I didn't say anything but I was really hoping that you'd still be here when Fr. Aiden dropped by. He's an old friend and he left his scarf here last night, and because he had dinner practically across the street, he's stopping by to pick it up. I don't want to interfere with your plans, but I'd love it if you got to know him. He's a wonderful priest at St. Francis, and I think he could be a real comfort to you."

"Alvirah, I'm not feeling very religious these days," Zan said, "so I'd like to just slip away fast."

"Zan, I called a car. I'm riding home with you. That's that," Willy said.

The phone rang. It was the doorman to announce Fr. O'Brien. Alvirah rushed to open the door and a moment later the elevator stopped at their floor.

A smiling Fr. O'Brien was hugged by Alvirah, shook hands with Willy, and then turned to be introduced to the young woman who was their guest.

The smile vanished from his face.

Holy Mother of God, he thought, she's the woman who's involved in a crime.

She's the one who claims she can't prevent a murder.

# 32

On the short drive over from Hunter College to the Aldrich town house on East Sixty-ninth Street, Detectives Billy Collins and Jennifer Dean admitted to each other that never for one minute had either of them suspected that Zan Moreland had abducted her own child.

They reconstructed the day Matthew Carpenter disappeared. "All I was thinking was that we were looking for a predator who sized up the situation and acted on it," Billy said somberly. "The park was crowded, the babysitter asleep on the grass, the little boy asleep in the stroller. I saw it as a perfect set-up for a pervert on the lookout for a child."

"Tiffany was absolutely hysterical," Jennifer said, reflectively. "She was screaming, 'How can I face Zan, how can I face her?' But why didn't we dig further? The thought that Tiffany may have been drugged never crossed my mind, either."

"It should have crossed our minds. It was a hot day, but not many teenagers, even with the onset of a cold, would pass out midday in a deep sleep on the grass," Billy said. "Oh, here we are." He pulled to a stop in front of the handsome residence, double-parked, and slapped his ID on the windshield. "Let's keep reconstructing our first impressions for a couple of minutes," he suggested.

"Alexandra Moreland had a hard-luck story that would make a sphinx take pity on her," Jennifer Dean said. "Parents killed on the way to the airport for a long-delayed reunion, marriage when she was an emotional wreck, a single mother struggling to start a business, and then her little guy gets abducted." Her voice was becoming more disgusted with every word.

Billy tapped his fingers on the steering wheel as he tried to recall every detail of the events that had taken place nearly two years ago. "We spoke to the Aldrich woman that night. She backed up Moreland's story right away. They had an appointment. Moreland was with her going over sketches and fabrics in the new town house Aldrich just bought when I called Moreland to tell her her son was missing." Billy stopped, then added angrily, "And we didn't ask any more questions."

"Let's face it," Jennifer said as she fished in her pocket for her handkerchief. "We had it all figured out. Working mother. Irresponsible babysitter. Predator snatching the opportunity to grab a child."

"When I got home, Eileen had been watching television," Billy recalled. "She told me she cried when she saw the expression on Moreland's face. She said that she thought it was going to be like Etan Patz, that little boy who disappeared all those years ago and was never found."

Looking out at the blustery wind and the persistent rain, Jennifer raised the collar of her coat. "All of us were willing to believe the sob story. But if those photos are legit, they prove that Moreland couldn't have been with Nina Aldrich that whole time," she said. "And if Aldrich can swear they were together, then the photos are probably fakes."

"They're not going to be fakes," Billy said grimly, "so Aldrich wasn't on the level when I spoke with her. But why would she have lied?" Without waiting for an answer, he said, "Okay, let's go in."

With that they dashed from the car to the door of the town house and rang the bell. "I imagine Aldrich paid a minimum of fifteen million bucks for this little nest," Billy muttered.

They could hear the chimes inside, but before they had stopped ringing, the door was opened by a Latina woman in a black uniform. She appeared to be in her early sixties. Her dark hair, streaked with gray, was drawn back into a neat bun. Her face was lined and there was a weary expression in her heavily lidded eyes.

Billy gave her their cards.

"I am Maria Garcia, Mrs. Aldrich's housekeeper. She is expecting you, Detective Collins and Detective Dean. May I take your coats?"

Garcia hung the coats in the closet and invited them to follow her. As they walked down the hall, Billy glanced into the formal living room and slowed his pace to get a longer look at the painting over the mantel. He was a frequent visitor to museums and said to himself, I bet that's a genuine Matisse.

The housekeeper led them into a large room that seemed to serve a double purpose. Butter-soft dark brown leather sofas were grouped around a recessed flat-screen television. Floor-to-ceiling mahogany bookcases covered three walls. All the books on the shelves were aligned in perfect symmetry. No casual reading in here, Billy thought. The walls were dark beige and the carpet a geometric brown and tan pattern.

Not my taste at all, Billy decided. Probably cost a fortune, but a little dab of color would go a long way in here.

Nina Aldrich kept them waiting close to half an hour. They knew she was sixty-three years old. When she swept into the room with her impeccable carriage, flowing silver hair, flawless complexion, patrician features, black caftan, silver jewelry, and frosty expression, she gave the impression of a monarch greeting an intrusive visitor.

Billy Collins was not impressed. As he stood up, for a split second he remembered what his uncle, a chauffeur for a family in Locust Valley, Long Island, had told him. "There are a lot of smart people in this town, Billy, who have plenty of money they made on their own. I know, because that's the kind of people I work for. But they're not the same as the really rich, who have been that way for generations. Those people live in a world of their own. They don't think like the rest of us."

It was clear to Billy, as it had been the first time he met her, that Nina Aldrich fit into that category. And she wants to put us on the defensive, he thought. Okay, lady, let's talk. He opened the conversation. "Good afternoon, Mrs. Aldrich. It's very accommodating of you to see us on short notice, because it's obvious you're having a very busy afternoon."

From the narrowing of her lips, he could see that she had gotten his point. Without being invited, he and Jennifer Dean both sat down again. After a moment's hesitation, Nina Aldrich took a seat behind the narrow antique desk opposite them.

"I've seen the morning papers and the Internet," she began, her voice cold and contemptuous. "I can't believe the way that young woman could have been so flagrant as to kidnap her own child. When I think of the sympathy I felt for her and the caring note I wrote to her, I am simply outraged."

Jennifer Dean opened the questioning. "Mrs. Aldrich, when we spoke to you hours after Matthew Carpenter disappeared, you verified that you had an appointment with Alexandra Moreland, and that she was with you when I first phoned her to tell her that her child was missing."

"Yes, that was about three o'clock in the afternoon."

"What was her reaction to our call?"

"Looking back, after having seen those photos, I can tell you that she's quite a marvelous actress. As I told you at our previous meeting, after speaking to you, Ms. Moreland went white as a sheet and jumped up. I wanted to call a cab, but she ran out of the house and raced to the park on foot. She left all her books with her fabric and paint samples and pictures of antique furniture and lamps and carpets and so forth scattered here."

"I see. The babysitter took Matthew to the park between 12:30 and 12:40. From my notes I see that your appointment with Ms. Moreland was at one P.M.," Jennifer continued.

"That's right. She called me on her cell phone to say that she'd be just a few minutes late because of the babysitter problem."

"You were here."

"No. I was in my former apartment on Beekman Place."

Billy Collins was careful to keep his expression from showing his excitement. "Mrs. Aldrich, I don't think you told me that the first time we spoke. You said that you met Ms. Moreland here."

"That's the way it turned out. I told her I didn't mind her being a little late, but then when an hour passed, I called her back. By then she was sitting in this house."

"Mrs. Aldrich, you are now telling me that when Alexandra Moreland spoke to you after two o'clock that you still hadn't seen her?" Billy persisted.

"That's exactly what I'm saying. Let me explain. Zan Moreland had a key to this house. She had been letting herself in while she was preparing to submit her suggestions for the décor. She just assumed we were meeting here. So actually it was closer to an hour and a half before we got together. When we finally did talk, she apologized for the confusion and offered to come to Beekman Place, but I was meeting friends at the Carlyle for cocktails at five so I told her I would come meet her up here. Frankly, by then I was getting pretty irritated with her."

"Mrs. Aldrich, do you keep a written record of your appointments?" Dean asked.

"Of course I do. I keep them in one of those daily planners."

"Would you happen to have kept yours from two years ago, and is it on hand?"

"Yes. It would be upstairs." With an impatient sigh, Nina Aldrich got up, walked to the door of the room, and called the housekeeper. Glancing at her watch, a gesture Billy Collins was sure was intended for them, she directed Garcia to go to her desk, open the top drawer, and get the appointment book for the year before last.

While Nina Aldrich and the detectives waited, she said, "I do hope we're not going to be involved in this situation beyond this meeting. My husband despises this sort of sensationalism, and he was not happy when the papers made so much of the fact that Moreland's meeting was with me that day."

Billy did not deem it wise to tell her that if this came to trial, she would end up being a star witness. Instead he said quietly, "I'm sorry about the inconvenience."

Maria Garcia returned, a small red leather book in her hand. She had already opened it to June 10.

"Thank you, Maria. Wait right here." Nina Aldrich glanced at the page and handed the book to Billy. Next to the one P.M. slot was Alexandra Moreland's name. "This doesn't say where you were planning to meet her," Billy observed. "If you were discussing decorating this house, why would you meet her at the other residence?"

"Ms. Moreland had taken extensive pictures of all the rooms here. We had no furniture other than a card table and a couple of chairs in the entire house. Why would I not make my choices in comfort? But since, as I said, I was planning to meet friends at the Carlyle for cocktails at five, I told Ms. Moreland to wait for me instead of coming down to Beekman Place."

"I see. Then you weren't here long before we called her?" Jennifer asked.

"Little more than a half hour."

"When you arrived here, how would you describe Ms. More-land's demeanor?"

"Flurried. Apologetic. Anxious."

"I see. And how big is this house, Mrs. Aldrich?"

"It's five stories high and forty feet wide, which as you can see makes it one of the larger town houses in the area. The top floor is now an enclosed garden. We have eleven rooms." There was no mis-taking the pleasure Nina Aldrich displayed in disclosing the dimen-sions of her town house.

"What about the basement?" Billy asked.

"It has a second kitchen, a wine cellar, and a very large finished room, which my husband's grandchildren enjoy when they are visit-ing. Also a storage area."

"You say there were only a few chairs and a card table here the day Matthew disappeared and you met Ms. Moreland here?"

"Yes. The architectural renovation had been done by the previous owners. Because of sudden financial problems, the house went on the market and we bought it. For the most part we were very satisfied with the architect's work and wanted no part of long delays by starting any further renovations. The interior decorating had not begun and that was when Alexandra Moreland was recommended to me."

"I see." Billy looked at Jennifer and they both got up to go. "You say Ms. Moreland had a key to the house. Did she ever come back after Matthew disappeared?"

"I never saw her. I know that she did come back at some point for her briefcase, samples, and so forth. Frankly, I don't remember if she ever did return the key, but of course we had all the locks changed when we moved in."

"You did not have Ms. Moreland do the interior design work for you?"

"I thought it was quite obvious that she would be in no emotional condition to take on such a project, and I wouldn't have expected it of her. And obviously I couldn't take a chance that she wouldn't have some kind of breakdown and leave me in a mess."

"May I ask who decorated this house?"

"Bartley Longe. Perhaps you've heard of him. He's quite brilliant."

"I guess what I'm asking is, when did he come on the job?" Billy's mind was racing. This house had been empty the day Matthew disappeared. Zan Moreland had access to it. Was it possible that she brought her child here and perhaps had hidden him in one of the rooms or in the basement? No one would have dreamt of looking for him here. She could have come back in the middle of the night and, alive or dead, taken him somewhere else.

"Oh, Bartley took over quite soon," Nina Aldrich said. "Don't forget, I hadn't given the job to Moreland at that point. I was only considering hiring her. And now, Detective Collins, if you don't mind—"

Billy interrupted her. "We're on our way, Mrs. Aldrich."

"Maria will see you out."

The housekeeper escorted them down the hall and retrieved their coats from the closet. Although her face remained impassive, inwardly she was churning with anger. You bet Bartley Longe took right over from that nice young woman, she thought. Mrs. High-and-Mighty began having a fling with him after she let that nice young Moreland woman do all those design plans. She won't admit it now, but she was going to turn down Moreland's designs even before the child disappeared.

Jennifer began to button her coat. "Thank you, Ms. Garcia," she said.

"Detective Collins," Maria began, then stopped. She had been about to say that she was in the room when Mrs. Aldrich absolutely told Alexandra Moreland to meet her here, not at Beekman Place. But who would take my word against hers? Maria Garcia asked herself. Besides, what difference does it make? I saw those photos in the paper. There's no question. Whatever her reason, Ms. Moreland stole her own child.

"Did you want to tell me anything, Ms. Garcia?" Billy asked.

"Oh, no, no. I just wanted to wish you both a nice day."

# 33

He had tried Gloria again and again that evening, but the phone just rang. Was she playing a game with him? He finally reached her at midnight and was quick to notice that at some point her defiant bravado had collapsed. Her voice sounded tired and listless when she answered. "What do you want?"

He was careful to keep his tone moderated and warm. "Gloria, I know how tough this has been for you." He was about to add that it had been tough for him, too, but clamped his teeth over that sentence. It would have given her an opening and, worse than that, a golden opportunity to rekindle her sense of being entrapped.

"Gloria," he continued, "I've been thinking. I'm not going to give you two hundred thousand as we agreed. I'm going to triple it. I'm going to give you six hundred thousand dollars in cash by the end of next week."

He was delighted to hear her astonished gasp. Was she stupid enough to really fall for it? "You only have one more thing to do," he continued, "and that is to show up in the Franciscan church one more time about quarter of five. I'll let you know what evening."

"Aren't you afraid I'll go to confession again?"

If she were in this room, I'd kill her right now, he thought. Instead he laughed. "I looked it up. You're right about the seal of the confessional."

"Aren't you torturing Matthew's mother enough? Why do you have to kill her?"

Not for the same reason I'm going to kill you, he thought. You know too much. I'd never be sure that so-called conscience of yours wouldn't start bubbling to the surface. As for Zan, I won't be happy until they are planning her funeral.

"Gloria, I'm not going to kill her," he said. "That was just angry talk."

"I don't believe you. I know how much you hate her." The edge of anger and even panic was creeping back into Gloria's voice.

"Gloria, how did we start this conversation? Let me remind you. I'm going to give you six hundred thousand dollars in cash, in genuine U.S. dollars, that you'll be able to put in a safe-deposit box and live on while you give yourself a chance to do the only thing you really want to do and that is to walk across the stage in a Broadway play or on a movie set. You're a beautiful woman. Unlike most of the look-alike Barbie dolls in Hollywood, you're also a chameleon. You can look and walk and talk like someone else. You remind me of Helen Mirren in *The Queen*. You've got that level of talent. I'm asking you for a week. At the most ten days. I'll want you to go to that church, and I'll let you know what to wear. The minute you leave, it's all over. We'll meet someplace nearby and I'll give you five thousand dollars right away. That's as much cash as you should carry in case your bags are opened in an airport."

"Then what?"

"You go back to Middletown. You wait until about nine or ten o'clock that night, then drop Matthew off in a department store or mall. After that, you're on a plane to California, or Texas, or wherever you like, to start your new life. I know you're worried about your father. You can tell him you were on a mission for the CIA."

"Not more than ten days." Now her voice was tentative, almost convinced. Then she added, "But how will I get the rest of the cash?"

You'll never have that problem, he thought. "I'll have the money packaged and mailed to you anywhere you want."

"But how can I trust that the package will arrive or that, if it does, that it won't be stuffed with old newspapers?"

You can't trust me, he thought. Reaching for the straight-up double scotch that he had promised himself he wouldn't touch until after he spoke to her, he said, "Gloria, if that ever happened, and it won't, you can go back to plan B. Get a lawyer, tell him your story, get him to arrange a book deal, and then go to the cops. In the meantime, Matthew has been found, nice and healthy, and the only thing he knows is that Glory took care of him."

"I read him a lot of books. He's smarter than a lot of kids his age."

I'm sure you were a real Mother Teresa, he thought. "Gloria, this will be over soon and you'll be rich."

"All right. I'm sorry I got so upset before. It's just that this woman who lives near here showed up with some stupid muffins this morning. I know she was just sniffing around to see what kind of person I am."

"You didn't tell me about her earlier," he said quietly. "Did she see Matthew?"

"No, but she saw his toy truck and told me she was such a great babysitter if I ever needed one. I told her my sister had helped me move in and that it was her little boy's truck."

"That sounds all right to me."

"The real estate agent is this woman's big friend. I had told the real estate agent that I was coming in by myself at night. She's another nosy one. I know she drove by early the morning after I got here."

He felt himself begin to perspire. *For want of a horse the rider is lost . . .* Incongruous that he should remember that old saying right now. His mind explored the possible scenarios. The nosy blueberry muffin lady checking with her real estate friend. He didn't want to think about that.

Time was running out.

It was hard to keep the reassuring note in his voice. "Gloria, you're borrowing trouble. Just start counting down the days."

"You bet I will. And not just for my sake. This little kid doesn't want to stay hidden anymore. He wants to go look for his mother."

# 34

Kevin Wilson arrived at his mother's apartment at seven P.M., just as the evening news on Channel 2 was ending. He had rung the bell twice, then let himself in with his own key. It was an arrangement that was long in place. "That way if I'm on the phone or still dressing, I don't have to run to the door," was the way his mother put it.

But when he walked in, diminutive, white-haired, seventy-one-year-old Catherine "Cate" Kelly Wilson was neither in her bedroom nor on the phone. She was glued to the television set and did not even look up as he entered the living room.

The three-room apartment he had bought for her was on Fifty-seventh Street, near First Avenue, a location which offered a crosstown bus stop on the corner, a movie theatre within walking distance, and, most important to her, St. John the Evangelist Church only one block away.

The unwillingness with which his mother had vacated the old neighborhood three years ago when it had become financially possible for him to buy her this new apartment still amused Kevin. Now, she loved it.

He went over to her chair and kissed her forehead.

"Hello, dear. Sit down a minute," she said, switching the channels without looking up at him. "*Headline News* is coming on now and there's something I want to see."

Kevin was hungry and had been looking forward to going immediately to Neary's Pub. It was not only a favorite dining spot, but also had the advantage of being directly across the street.

He settled down on the couch and looked around. The couch and the matching chair where his mother was sitting had been part of her original furniture, and no amount of persuasion had induced her to part with them when she moved. Instead Kevin had both pieces reupholstered for her as well as having her bridal bedroom set refinished. As she pointed out, "That's ribbon mahogany, Kevin, and I'm not giving it up." He'd also repaired her dining room furniture, which was "too good to throw out." She did allow him to replace the threadbare, machine-made Oriental carpet with one in a similar design. He did not tell her how much the new one cost.

The result was a cozy apartment filled with pictures of his father and grandparents, various cousins, and lifelong friends. Whenever he walked into it, no matter how busy his day, it lifted his spirits. It felt like a home. It *was* a home.

That was just what Zan Moreland had pitched to him in her plea to withhold judgment on his decision between her and Bartley Longe until she could prove her innocence in the alleged kidnapping of her own child. People want to feel as though they're living in a home, not a museum, she had told him.

Kevin realized that he had spent a good part of the day wondering why he hadn't simply returned Moreland's sketches and fabric samples to her with a brief note saying he had decided that Bartley Longe was the right person for the project.

What was keeping him from doing it? God knows he'd taken enough flak from his secretary, Louise, about how astonished she was that he would waste his time on a lying kidnapper. "I can tell you, Kevin, it took my breath away when that woman had the nerve to come here, and then ignore what I told her, that she could take her stuff, or I'd mail it to her. What did she do? Go running up to find you, and try to hold on to her chance of getting the job. Mark my words, she'll be on Rikers Island in handcuffs before this is over."

Not bothering to hide his annoyance, he had told Louise dryly, "If she's arrested, I believe she'll be out on bail." Finally he had told Louise flat out to drop the subject altogether, which of course had brought on a wounded, reproachful attitude from her that she made doubly clear by calling him "Mr. Wilson" for the rest of the day.

"Kevin, watch! They're showing those pictures of that Moreland woman picking up her child out of the stroller. The nerve of her, lying to the cops. Can you imagine how the father must be feeling all this time?"

Kevin sprang up and rushed across the room. There was a picture of Alexandra Moreland taking a little boy out of a stroller, and then one of her carrying him down the path. They stayed on the screen as the commentator continued, "She is seen here when she rushed back to Central Park after learning from police that her son was missing."

Kevin studied the image. Zan Moreland looked in shock. The suffering in her eyes was unmistakable. That same look had been there this afternoon, he thought, when she begged him to give her the chance to prove her innocence.

Begged? That was too strong a word. And she had given him an out by saying that if he preferred Bartley Longe's designs, she would understand.

She looks so wounded, he thought. He listened intently as the news announcer said, "Yesterday was Matthew Carpenter's fifth birthday and now the speculation is about whether his mother gave him to someone to keep for her—or if he is no longer alive."

In this past month or two Zan had been going back and forth to the apartments any number of times and putting hours upon hours of work into creating the designs for them, Kevin thought. I realize now that when I met her at Carlton Place yesterday, I could sense her suffering even though she seemed so calm. Why would she be in so much pain if she knew her child was safe? Is it possible she killed him?

No, it was not possible, he thought. I'd stake my soul on that. She's not a killer.

Kevin realized that his mother had stood up. "It's hard not to believe that kind of solid evidence," Catherine Wilson said. "But the look on Zan Moreland's face when she found out her child was missing! Of course, you're too young to remember, but when the Fitzpatrick baby fell out the window of our apartment building and was killed, that's the expression I saw in Joan Fitzpatrick's eyes, so much pain that you bled for her. That Moreland woman must be some actress."

"*If* she's acting." Kevin was surprised to hear himself defending her.

Startled, his mother looked at him. "What do you mean, if? You saw those pictures, didn't you?"

"Yes, I did, and I don't know what I mean. Come on, Mom, let's eat. I'm starved."

It was later, at their usual table in Neary's, that Kevin told his mother over coffee that he had been considering hiring Alexandra Moreland to decorate three model apartments.

"Well, of course this ends that," Catherine Wilson said decisively. "But tell me, what's she like?"

Her face would haunt you, Kevin thought. Those expressive eyes, that sensitive mouth. "She's about five eight, I would say. She's very slender and graceful. She moves like a dancer. Yesterday her hair was loose on her shoulders, the way you see it in the pictures. Today, she had tied it back in a bun or chignon or whatever you call it." He realized he was describing Zan to himself as much as to his mother.

"My God, you sound as though you have a crush on her," his mother exclaimed.

Kevin thought for a long moment. That's crazy, he decided, but there is something about Zan. He remembered the feeling of having her shoulder brush his when she was pointing out some of the aspects in Bartley Longe's sketches that she felt would put off a prospective buyer. By then she had seen those photos from Central Park and she knew what she was up against.

"She asked me to give her time to prove that those photos are fakes," he said. "I don't have to make a decision between her and Bartley Longe yet. And I'm not going to. I'm sticking to my guns and giving her the chance she asked for."

"Kevin, you've always been for the underdog," his mother said. "But this may be carrying it too far. You're thirty-seven years old and I was beginning to worry that I would be stuck with an Irish bachelor on my hands. But, for God's sake, don't get involved with someone in a hopeless situation."

Just then their longtime friend Jimmy Neary stopped at their table to say hello. He'd caught Catherine's last words. "I couldn't agree more with your Mom, Kevin," he said. "And if you're ready to settle down, I've got a list a mile long of young ladies who already have their eye on you. Do yourself a favor. Steer clear of trouble."

# 35

As he had promised, Willy took Zan home in a hired car. He offered to drop Fr. Aiden along the way, but he did not accept the ride. "No, you go along. I'll visit with Alvirah for a little while," he said.

When Fr. Aiden said good-bye to Zan, he looked directly into her eyes and said, "I will pray for you." Then he reached out and took her hands in his.

"Pray that my little boy is safe," Zan answered. "Don't bother to pray for me, Father. God has forgotten that I exist."

Fr. Aiden did not try to reply. Instead he stepped aside to let her pass into the hallway. "I'll just stay five minutes, Alvirah," he promised after the door closed behind Zan and Willy. "I could see that the young woman wanted no part of my company, and I didn't want to wish it on her even for a short ride in the car."

"Oh, Aiden," Alvirah sighed. "I'd give anything if I could believe that Zan didn't take Matthew out of his stroller that day, but she did. There's no question about it."

"Do you think the child is alive?" Fr. Aiden asked.

"I could no more conceive of her hurting Matthew than I could imagine running a knife through Willy."

"I think you told me that you only came to know Ms. Moreland after her son disappeared," Fr. Aiden said. *Be careful*, he warned himself. There is no way you can possibly let Alvirah think that you've met Alexandra Moreland before.

"Yes. We became friendly because I wrote a column about her, and she phoned to thank me for it. Oh, Aiden, I believe that Zan must have been in some sort of catatonic state, or maybe even has a split personality. The point is, I don't know anyone she has ever mentioned who might be raising Matthew for her."

"There are no other family members?"

"She was an only child. So was her mother, and her father had one brother who died when he was still a teenager."

"How about a close friend?"

"I'm sure she has friends, but I don't care how good a friend you are, who would be party to a kidnapping? But, Father, suppose she just abandoned Matthew somewhere and doesn't know where? The one thing I would swear is that in her mind, her child is missing."

*In her mind, her child is missing.* Fr. Aiden was still pondering that thought when, a few minutes later, the doorman hailed a cab for him downstairs.

*I am an accessory to an ongoing crime and to a murder that is about to be committed.*

Does that young woman indeed have a split mind — or what is the new term for it, a dissociative identity disorder? And if so, was it Alvirah's friend, the real personality, trying to break through when she rushed into the Reconciliation Room?

The cab the doorman hailed was waiting. Grunting from the pain in his arthritic knees as he climbed into the backseat, Fr. Aiden thought, I am bound by the seal of the confessional. There is no way I can hint as to what I know. She asked me to pray for her child. But oh, dear Lord, if a murder is in the offing, I beg you to intercede and stop it.

What the elderly friar could not even begin to imagine was that there were now three murders being planned. And that *he* was first on the list.

# 36

Josh was already in the office when Zan arrived at eight A.M. Thursday morning. From the expression on his face, she knew immediately that something else had happened. By now too numb to feel anything except cold acceptance, she merely asked, "What is it?"

"Zan, you told me that Kevin Wilson agreed to hold off on deciding between you and Bartley over those model apartments."

"Yes. But I know with those pictures in this morning's papers of me being carried out to the ambulance yesterday, it's all over for that job. I'll be surprised if everything I left with him isn't back here before noon."

"Zan," Josh said passionately, "that's probably true, but it's not what I'm talking about. Zan, how could you have ordered all the fabrics and furniture and wall hangings for those apartments before you got the okay on the job?"

"You've got to be joking," Zan said flatly.

"Zan, I wish I were. You put the order in for the fabrics and the wall hangings and the custom furniture and the fixtures. My God, you've ordered *everything*. We've got delivery notices on the fabrics. Forget the money! Where are we going to *put* all that stuff?"

"They never would have begun delivering without being paid," she said. This, at least, I can prove is a mistake, Zan thought frantically.

"Zan, I called Wallington Fabrics. They have a letter from you requesting deferment of the usual ten percent down because time is of the essence, and saying you'll be able to pay in full as soon as the contract with Kevin Wilson comes in. You claim he's already signed it, and the check will be arriving very soon."

Josh grabbed a paper from his desk. "I asked them to fax me a copy of the letter. Here it is. On our stationery and that's your signature."

"I didn't sign that letter," Zan said. "I swear on my life that I didn't sign that letter, and I didn't order anything for those model apartments. Absolutely all I ever took from any of our suppliers were the upholstery fabric, drapery and wall hanging samples, and pictures of the furniture and Persian carpets and window treatments that I would use if we got the job."

"Zan," Josh began, then shook his head. "Look, I love you like you're my own sister. We've got to call Charley Shore right now. When I phoned Wallington Fabrics, I thought someone had made a mistake. Now they're going to start worrying about getting paid. And you *did* send minimal deposits to hold the carpets and some of the antiques. You must have written the checks from your personal account."

"I didn't sign that letter," Zan said, her voice now quiet. "I didn't write any checks from my personal account. And I am not crazy." She saw the look of combined disbelief and concern on the face of her associate. "Josh, I accept your resignation. If this is going to turn out to be a scandal with our suppliers suing us, I don't want you caught in it. They might accuse you of being in some kind of rip-off scheme along with me. So why don't you get your stuff together and take off?"

As he stared at her, she added, sarcastically, "Admit it. You think I kidnapped my own son and that I've lost my mind. Who knows, maybe I'm dangerous? Maybe I'll clobber you over the head when your back is turned."

"Zan," Josh snapped. "I'm not leaving you, and I'm going to find a way to help you."

The phone rang, a sharp, ominous sound. Josh picked up the receiver, listened, then said, "She's not here yet. I'll give her the message."

Zan watched as Josh scribbled a phone number. When he hung up, he said, "Zan, that was Detective Billy Collins. He wants you to come to the Central Park Precinct with your lawyer today, as soon as possible. I'm going to call Charley Shore right now. It's early but he told me he always gets to his office by 7:30."

Yesterday I fainted, Zan thought. I can't, I won't, do that again.

During the night, after Willy dropped her off, she lay in bed in quiet, absolute despair, a single light shining on Matthew's picture again. For some reason, the look of compassion in the eyes of the priest who was Alvirah's friend kept coming back to her. I was rude to him, she thought, but I could feel that he wanted to help me. He said he'd pray for me, but I told him to pray for Matthew instead. When he took my hands, it felt as though he were blessing me. Maybe what he was doing was helping me to face the truth?

All night long, except for brief periods when she dozed off, Zan had kept her vigil, looking at Matthew's picture. As dawn was breaking she said quietly, "Little guy, I don't believe that you're still alive. I've always sworn that I would know if you were dead, but I've been fooling myself. You are dead, and it's over for me, too. I don't know what's happening, but I can't fight anymore. I guess in my soul, all these many months, I've really believed that you were grabbed by a predator who abused and then killed you. I wouldn't have thought I would come to this, but there is a bottle of sleeping pills in this drawer that will bring us back together. It's time to take them."

A sense of relief and exhaustion had come over her, and she finally closed her eyes. With Fr. Aiden's face before her, she had prayed for forgiveness and understanding before she reached for the pills.

It was then that she heard Matthew's voice calling out to her. "Mommy, Mommy." She had leapt up from the bed screaming, "Matthew! Matthew!" In that moment, against all rational belief, she knew with absolute certainty that her little boy was still alive.

Matthew is alive, she thought fiercely, as she heard Josh talking to Charley Shore. When he replaced the receiver, Josh said, "Detective Collins wants to question you this morning. Mr. Shore will pick you up at 10:30."

Zan nodded. "You said that I must have paid any deposits on the furnishings for the model apartments out of my savings account. Pull my bank account up for me on the computer."

"I don't have the password for your account."

"You'll have it now. It's 'Matthew.' I have a little over twenty-seven thousand dollars in it."

Josh sat down in front of the computer and began to send his fingers flying across the keyboard.

Zan saw the expression on his face, troubled, but not surprised. "What is my balance?" she asked.

"Two hundred thirty-three dollars and eleven cents."

"Then there is a computer hacker at work," she said flatly.

Josh ignored that. "Zan, what are we going to do about all the orders you placed?" he asked.

"You mean, what are we going to do about all the orders I *didn't* place," Zan said. "Look, Josh, I'm not afraid to go to the police station and talk with Detective Collins. I believe there is an answer to all this. Somebody hates me enough to try and destroy me, and his name is Bartley Longe. I told Detective Collins and his partner about him when Matthew disappeared. They didn't take me seriously. I know they didn't. But if Bartley hates me enough to try to destroy my reputation and my business, I think he may hate me enough to kidnap my son and maybe turn him over to a friend who wanted a child."

"Zan, don't repeat that to the cops. They'll turn that kind of talk against you in a heartbeat," Josh implored.

The intercom phone rang. Josh picked up the receiver. It was the service manager of the building. "Shipment arriving for you. It's a large load and pretty heavy."

Ten minutes later twenty long rolls of fabric were delivered to the office. Zan and Josh had to push the desk to one side and pile the chairs in the back room in order to make room for it. When the delivery men left, Josh opened the statement that was attached to one of the rolls and read it aloud. "One hundred yards of discontinued fabric at one hundred and twenty-five dollars a yard. Special arrangement nonrefundable purchase agreement. Full payment due within ten days. Total including tax, thirteen thousand eight hundred and seventy-four dollars."

He looked at Zan. "We have forty thousand dollars in the bank and sixteen thousand in accounts receivable. You've been concentrating so much on the model apartments, you haven't done anything on at least four of the smaller jobs we have lined up. The rent is due next week and so is the payment on the start-up loan you got to open this place, to say nothing of the usual overhead and our salaries."

The phone rang again. This time Josh made no effort to answer, and Zan hurried to pick it up. It was Ted. His voice bitter and angry, he snarled, "Zan, I'm on my way to meet Detective Collins. I have rights as Matthew's father, rights that you have willfully taken from me. I am going to insist that they arrest you immediately, and I'll move heaven and earth to make you tell me what you have done with my son."

# 37

Toby Grissom pushed open the door of the 13th Precinct in Manhattan and, ignoring the comings and goings in the busy reception area, approached the sergeant behind the desk.

"I'm Toby Grissom," he began timidly, but there was nothing timid in his voice when he added, "My daughter is missing and I think some big shot interior decorator may be the reason for it."

The sergeant looked at him. "How old is your daughter?"

"Thirty last month."

The sergeant did not show the relief he felt. He'd been afraid that it might be another case of a young teenage runaway who sometimes gets picked up by a pimp and ends up a hooker or disappearing for good. "Mr. Grissom, if you'll just take a seat, I'll ask one of our detectives to take down the information."

There were a couple of benches in the area near the desk. Toby, his wool cap in hand, a manila envelope under his arm, sat on one of them and watched with detached curiosity as uniformed cops went in and out of the building, sometimes accompanying people in handcuffs.

Fifteen minutes later, a large-framed man in his midthirties with thinning blond hair and a quiet manner approached Toby. "Mr. Grissom, I'm Detective Wally Johnson. Sorry to keep you waiting. If you'll follow me to my desk, we can talk."

Obediently Toby stood up. "I'm used to waiting," he said. "Seems to me I've been waiting for one thing or another most of my life."

"I think we all have times when we feel like that," Wally Johnson agreed. "It's this way."

The detective's desk was one of many in a large, cluttered room. Most of the desks were empty, but the files strewn on them suggested that each of the missing occupants was actively working cases.

"We got lucky," Johnson said as, arriving at his desk, he pulled up a chair beside it. "I not only got promoted to being next to the window with the view, such as it is, but it's one of the quieter spots in the whole precinct."

Toby did not know where he got his courage to speak up. "Detective Johnson, I don't really care if you like where you sit. I'm here because my daughter is missing, and I think either something has happened to her, or she's mixed up in some kind of trouble that she has to get out of."

"Can you explain what you mean by that, Mr. Grissom?"

By now, after visiting Bartley Longe's office and speaking with the two young women Glory had been living with when she disappeared, Toby felt as though he could not go through the full story again. But that's crazy, he told himself. If I don't come across to this detective as a guy to believe, he'll just blow me off.

"My daughter's legal name is Margaret Grissom," he began. "I always called her Glory because she was such a glorious, beautiful baby, if you know what I mean. She left Texas when she was eighteen to come to New York. She wanted to be an actress. She won best actress in the senior play at her high school."

Oh God, Johnson thought, how many of those kids who were best actress in the school play come running to New York? Talk about the "field of dreams." It was an effort to keep his mind on what Grissom was telling him, about his daughter taking the name of Brittany La Monte, and what a good person she was. She was so pretty she was offered jobs in porno films but wouldn't touch them, how she got started doing makeup because that way she could make enough money to support herself and even send nice little gifts to him on his birthday and Christmas. And—

It was time for Johnson to interrupt. "You say she came to New York twelve years ago. How many times have you seen her since then?"

"Five times. Like clockwork. Glory always spent Christmas with me every other year. Except almost two years ago this coming June, she phoned and said she wouldn't be coming next Christmas. She said she was working on a new job that was real hush-hush, but that she'd be getting paid a lot of money for it. When I asked if she was talking about some guy keeping her, she said, 'No, Daddy, no, I promise you.' "

And he believes that, Wally Johnson thought sympathetically.

"She said that she had an advance payment for the job and was giving almost all of it to me. *Twenty-five thousand dollars.* Can you imagine? It was to be sure I wouldn't need anything, because she had to be out of touch. I thought maybe she was working for the CIA or something."

Or more likely, Margaret-Glory-Brittany found herself a billionaire, Detective Johnson thought.

"The last I heard from her was a postcard from New York six months ago saying that the job was taking longer than she expected and that she was worried about me and missed me," Grissom continued. "That's why I finally came to New York. I got some real bad news from my doctor, and besides that I have a feeling now that maybe somebody is holding Glory somewhere. I went to see the girls she shared an apartment with and they told me that this big shot designer was snowing her about how he'd introduce her to theatre people and make her a star. He made her go up to his house in Connecticut on weekends so she could meet important people."

"Who was this designer, Mr. Grissom?"

"Bartley Longe. He has fancy offices on Park Avenue."

"Did you speak to him?"

"He gave me the same line he gave Glory. He told me that he hired her as a kind of model when he was showing off places he'd decorated and he'd introduced her to a lot of theatre big shots. But they all told him that Glory didn't have what it takes, and finally he couldn't pester people about her anymore. And according to him, that was that."

And it probably was, Wally Johnson thought. The usual thing. The guy promises her the moon, has a little fling, gets tired of her, and tells her not to bother showing up at his place next weekend.

"Mr. Grissom, I'm going to follow up on this, but I warn you that I'm afraid that we're not going to get very far. I'm more interested in the job your daughter was so mysterious about. Is there anything more specific you know about it?"

"Not a thing," Toby Grissom said.

As he asked the question, Wally Johnson felt like a phony. I'd be better off telling this poor old guy that his daughter is a hooker who got involved with some guy, and it's worth her while to stay under the radar, he thought.

Nevertheless, he asked the usual perfunctory questions. Height. Weight. Color of eyes. Color of hair.

"All this is on Glory's publicity shots," Toby Grissom said. "Maybe you'd like one." He reached into the envelope he was carrying and brought out a half dozen eight-by-ten photographs. "You know, they want the girls to look kind of sweet and innocent in one picture, and kind of sexy in another, and if they have short hair like Glory, they try them with different wigs or extensions or whatever you call that stuff."

Wally Johnson rifled through the photos. "She *is* very pretty," he said sincerely.

"Yeah, I know. I mean, I always liked her better with long hair, but she said that it's easier to have good wigs 'cause you can be anybody you want."

"Mr. Grissom, why don't you leave me the photograph with the montage showing her in her different poses. That will be more useful to us."

"Of course." Toby Grissom stood up. "I'm going back to Texas. I need my chemo treatments. They won't save my life, I guess, but maybe they will keep me alive long enough to see my Glory." He started to walk away, then came back to Johnson's desk. "You will talk to that Bartley Longe?"

"Yes, I will. And if anything develops we'll be in touch with you, I promise."

Wally Johnson tucked Margaret-Glory-Brittany's glossy photo montage under the clock on the corner of his desk. His gut instinct was that the young woman was alive and well and probably involved in something dirty, if not illegal.

I'll give that Longe guy a call, Johnson thought, then I'll put Glory's picture where it belongs, in the dead letter file.

# 38

At nine A.M. Thursday, Ted Carpenter arrived at the Central Park Precinct. Haggard and worn from the events and the emotional seesaw of the past day and a half, his tone was brusque when he said he had an appointment with Detective Billy Collins. "And I believe he said something about his partner would be with him," Ted added before the desk sergeant could respond.

"Detectives Collins and Dean are expecting you," the sergeant said, ignoring the hostility in Carpenter's voice. "I'll let them know that you're here."

Less than five minutes later, Ted was sitting at a conference table in a small office, facing Billy Collins and Jennifer Dean.

Billy thanked him for coming in. "I hope you're feeling better, Mr. Carpenter. I know that when your secretary phoned yesterday to make an appointment, she said you were ill."

"I was and I am," Ted replied. "And it's not just physical. Knowing what I've gone through for almost two years, to see those photos and realize that my ex, Matthew's mother, has been guilty of abducting my son, just about drove me over the edge."

An unmistakable note of anger crept into his voice. "I have wasted my time blaming that babysitter who fell asleep when she was supposed to be minding my son. Now I have begun to wonder if she wasn't in collusion with my ex-wife. I know Zan regularly gave Tiffany clothes she no longer wore."

Billy Collins and Jennifer Dean were trained not to show surprise at anything that was said to them, but each knew the other's thoughts. Was this an angle they had not considered? And if there was any truth to it, what made Tiffany Shields turn on Zan to the point of suggesting that both she and Matthew had been deliberately drugged that day?

Billy chose not to follow up on Ted Carpenter's reasoning that Shields was involved. "Mr. Carpenter, you and Ms. Moreland were married for how long?"

"Six months. What has that got to do with it?"

"Her mental health is what we're getting at. At the time of Matthew's disappearance, she told us that after her parents' death, you flew to Rome and saw her through the funeral, the packing of their personal items, the usual details following a demise. She made it clear that she was very grateful to you."

"Grateful! That's one way of putting it. She didn't want me out of the room. She had hysterical crying fits and fainting spells. She blamed herself for not having visited her parents sooner. She blamed Bartley Longe for not letting her take a vacation. She blamed the traffic in Rome for causing her father's heart attack."

"But with that kind of emotional baggage, you still chose to marry her?" Jennifer Dean asked quietly.

"Zan and I had been dating, somewhat casually, but we were definitely becoming interested in each other. I guess I was half in love with her then. She is a beautiful woman, as I'm sure you've observed, and very intelligent. She is a gifted interior designer, thanks, I might add, to the fact that Bartley Longe took her on after she graduated from FIT and gave her the chance to be his right-hand apprentice."

"Then you don't feel that Ms. Moreland was fair when she

blamed Bartley Longe for making it impossible to visit her parents earlier?"

"No, I don't. She knew perfectly well that much as he might rant and rave if she took a few weeks off, he never would have fired her. She was far too valuable to him."

"You say you were dating and half in love with Ms. Moreland during that time. Did you express your feelings about her job with Longe at that time?"

"Of course I did. The fact is, Longe had given her the chance of a lifetime for a young designer. He had taken on a high-profile job to decorate the TriBeCa penthouse of Toki Swan, the rock star, but because he was up to his elbows doing a Palm Beach mansion, he virtually turned the job over to Zan. She was thrilled. You couldn't have dragged her onto a plane at that point."

"Did Ms. Moreland show any signs of overwork, or of approaching a breakdown, before she flew to Rome?"

"From what I understand, after she finished that job Longe wanted her to stay a few weeks longer and help him finish the Palm Beach place. That's when the big quarrel took place and she quit. As I just told you, that so-called firing was a joke."

"After her parents' death, couldn't you have helped her without marrying her?" Jennifer Dean asked.

"That's like asking a bystander watching someone trapped in a burning car, why didn't you dial 911 instead of taking immediate action? Zan needed to feel as if she had a home and a family. I gave that to her."

"But she left you very quickly."

Ted bristled. "I didn't come in here to have a consultation about my brief marriage to the woman who abducted my son. Zan felt that she had taken advantage of me, and decided to move out. It was only after she was gone that she realized she was pregnant."

"What was your reaction?"

"I was pleased. By then I realized there was nothing between us, and I told her I would give her generous support so that she could always live comfortably and raise our child. She told me she intended to open her own interior design business. I understood that, but after my son was born, I did insist on meeting the nanny she planned to hire so I could judge for myself if that person was competent."

"Did you do that?"

"Yes. And the nanny, Gretchen Voorhees, was a blessing. Frankly, I would say that she was more of a mother to Matthew than Zan. Zan was consumed with her need to beat out Bartley Longe for jobs. I can tell you the amount of time she spent working to get that job with Nina Aldrich was unconscionable."

"How do you know that?"

"Gretchen told me that on the last day she worked for Zan. I was picking Matthew up for the afternoon. Gretchen was flying back to Holland because she was getting married."

"Had Ms. Moreland hired a new nanny, and if so, did you meet her?"

"I met her once. Her references were good. She seemed perfectly pleasant. However, she was obviously not reliable. She didn't show up the first day for work, and Zan grabbed Tiffany Shields to take my son to Central Park so she could fall asleep on the grass, if indeed she *did* fall asleep."

Ted Carpenter's face turned a deep crimson red. He swallowed, unable to go on. Then, his hands clenched into fists, his voice raised, he said, "I'll tell you what happened that day. Zan realized that Matthew was going to be in her way. Maybe she had realized it for a long time before that. Gretchen told me of the many times she had to work on her day off because Zan was too busy to stay home with her child. Zan was, and is, all about becoming a famous interior designer. That's it! She's well on her way to it. That baloney about spending every cent she can scrimp to have private detectives search for Matthew is strictly PR. If anyone should know, it's me. I'm in the business. Take a look at that article *People* magazine did on her last year on the first anniversary of Matthew's disappearance. She's showing them her modest three-room apartment, whining about how she walks rather than take cabs so that every cent she makes is saved to try to find Matthew and so on . . . Then notice how she always talks about what a great interior designer she is."

"You are saying that you believe your ex-wife got rid of your child because he had become a liability?"

"That's *exactly* what I'm saying. She's a born martyr. How many people have lost their parents in an accident and even though they're grieving, have gone on with their lives? If she had asked me to take full custody of Matthew, I would have done it in a heartbeat."

"Did you *request* full custody?"

"That would have been like asking the earth to stop revolving around the sun. How would that have looked in the newspapers?"

Ted stood up. "I have nothing more to say to you except this. I assume that by now you have checked out those photos that were taken in Central Park. Unless they are doctored—and you have given me no indication that you think that is the case—then I want to know why Alexandra Moreland has not been arrested. You have proof positive that she stole my son. Clearly she lied to you every step of the way. I'm sure there is a law about withholding a child from the other parent who has visitation rights. But the charge you really should be pursuing now is that Matthew was abducted and murdered by his own mother. What are you waiting for?"

As he pushed back his chair and stood up, Ted Carpenter, tears running down his cheeks, again demanded, "What are you waiting for?"

# 39

It was not just the pain in his arthritic knees, which he ruefully referred to as his nocturnal visitor, that kept Fr. Aiden awake for a good part of Wednesday night. It was the woman who had confessed to being part of an ongoing crime and an impending murder, the woman whose name he now knew: Alexandra Moreland.

The incredible irony of meeting her at Alvirah and Willy's apartment! Between two and four in the morning, Fr. Aiden relived every second of those few moments they had been together. It was apparent to anyone that Zan, as Alvirah had called her, was suffering. The expression in her eyes was like that of a soul in hell, if such a comparison could be imagined. She had said, "God has forgotten that I exist."

She truly believes that, Fr. Aiden thought. But she did ask me to pray for her child. If only I could help her! When she confessed, she was clear about what she was doing, and about what was being planned. No mistake about it, and no mistake that it was her.

Alvirah, who knew Zan well, had recognized her face on the security camera in the church and said that she was absolutely the person in those Central Park pictures. If I could only broach the subject that if Zan has a split personality, they might try to have a doctor give her some medication to release what is hidden in her mind, Fr. Aiden thought. But I cannot reveal anything, even if it would help her. . . .

He would pray that in another way, some way, somehow, the truth would come out to save her child, if it was not already too late. After a while his eyes began to close. Just before dawn, he woke again. Zan's face filled his mind. But there was something else. Something he had dreamed. And it troubled him. There was a seed of doubt in him, and he didn't know where it was coming from.

Once again he whispered a prayer for her and her little boy, then mercifully fell back asleep until his alarm woke him in time to be ready to celebrate the eight o'clock Mass in the lower church.

At almost half past ten, while Fr. Aiden was going through the mail on his desk, a call was put through to him. It was Alexandra More-land. "Father," she said, "I'll have to make this quick. My attorney is going to be here in a minute to go with me to the police station. The detectives on Matthew's case want to talk to me. For all I know, I'm going to be arrested. I apologize for being so rude to you last night, and thank you for praying for Matthew. And I want you to know this: I was as close as you can get to swallowing a bottle of sleeping pills early this morning, and something about the kind way you looked at me and then took my hands in yours stopped me. Anyhow, I won't think of that again. I had to say thank you and please keep praying for Matthew, but if you don't mind, say a word for me as well."

Then there was a click in his ear. Stunned, Fr. Aiden sat quietly at his desk. That's what I've been trying to remember, the feel of her hands when I held them, he thought.

But what is it?

What could it possibly be?

# 40

After the cozy dinner she had shared with her friend Rebecca, and the fact that they both had enjoyed several glasses of wine, Penny had slept soundly through the night and even allowed herself the luxury of bringing her morning cup of coffee back to bed. Propped up on pillows, she had watched the news on television. Once again the Central Park photos of Zan Moreland taking her child out of the stroller and the others of her being carried to the ambulance were briefly shown.

"Unless those photos are proven to be doctored, in my opinion, the arrest of Alexandra Moreland is imminent," the network's legal expert explained on the *Today* show.

"Should have happened yesterday!" Penny barked to the television screen. "What are they waiting for, a sign from heaven?" Shaking her head, she got out of bed a second time, put on a warm robe, and carried the coffee cup to the kitchen, where she began to prepare her usual generous breakfast.

Bernie phoned as she was running the last scrap of toast over the plate to catch the remnants of the yolk of her fried egg. His voice sounded disgruntled as he told her that it would be another couple of hours before the truck was fixed, so he wouldn't get home till midafternoon. "Hope you and Rebecca didn't eat all the pot roast," he told her.

"More than plenty for you," Penny assured him before saying good-bye. Men, she thought, shaking her head indulgently. He's upset because he's stuck in a gas station in King of Prussia, and he's trying to find a reason to get mad so he can have a fight with me and get it off his chest. I should have told him that Rebecca and I ate the whole thing and tonight we're having frozen pizza.

As she loaded the dishwasher, Penny saw that the mailman was delivering to their box at the end of the driveway. After his van disappeared, she tightened the belt on her robe and hurried outside. Spring may have just arrived, but boy you'd never know it, she thought, as she opened the box, closed her hand on the small pile of letters, and at an even quicker pace made her way back to the warmth of the house.

The first few envelopes were solicitations from various charities. The next contained a fingernail-sized sample of a new facial cream. The last envelope brought an unconscious smile to Penny's face. It was from Alvirah Meehan. Quickly she ripped it open. It was a notice that the semiannual meeting of the Lottery Winners' Support Group was being held the following week in Alvirah and Willy's apartment.

Alvirah had written a personal note on the notice. "Dear Penny, hope you and Bernie can make it. Always so good to be with you."

We can make it, Penny thought happily, as she mentally reviewed Bernie's schedule. I'd love to get her opinion on that Moreland woman now. I know Alvirah's been friendly with her.

The sense of pleasant anticipation wore off as Penny went upstairs, showered, and dressed. Something was gnawing at her and it had to do with that snippy Gloria Evans, who was renting the Owens farmhouse. It wasn't just the fact that Gloria Evans had been so rude when I gave her the blueberry muffins, and it wasn't just the toy truck on the floor, Penny decided. That woman was supposed to be finishing a book, but even writers who want privacy don't practically slam the door in a person's face, do they?

Penny was by nature thrifty. That was why another thing that Rebecca had told her about Gloria Evans—that Evans didn't bat an eye about paying for a year's lease when she only planned to stay for three months—seemed strange.

There's something going on with that lady, she decided. She wasn't just being rude. She was downright nervous when she answered the door. I wonder if she's doing something illegal, like selling drugs out of there? No one would know if someone came late at night and turned onto that dead-end road. Sy's is the only house on it.

I'd love to keep an eye on the place, she thought. The trouble is, if Gloria Evans happens to be at the window she'll see me driving past, then turning around and coming back. If she is up to anything, I'd be tipping her off.

As Penny, her lips pursed, applied bright red lipstick, her only tribute to glamour, she began to laugh, smearing the lipstick on her cheek. "Oh, for heaven's sake," she said aloud. "I know what's bugging me about that Evans bird. She reminds me of the Moreland woman. Isn't that a riot? Wait till I tell Alvirah that I was trying to hatch a mystery. She'll get a real laugh out of that!"

# 41

Charley Shore could not conceal his look of astonishment when Josh opened the door of Moreland Interiors and he saw the rolls of carpet stacked against the walls and covering the floor of half the office.

"It's a misunderstanding with one of our suppliers," Josh began to explain.

"No, it isn't," Zan corrected him. "Mr. Shore, or Charley, since we've agreed we're on a first-name basis, somebody is ordering materials on a contract that we don't have yet and has hacked into my bank account."

She really is out of it, Shore thought, but was careful not to show any reaction except concern. "When did you find out about this, Josh?"

"The first indication was the other day, when someone bought a first-class one-way ticket to South America in Zan's name for next week and charged it to our business account," Josh said, his tone carefully matter-of-fact. "Then there are bills for expensive clothes charged to Zan's store accounts. Now we're hearing from our suppliers about carpets and fabrics and wall hangings that we didn't order."

"Josh is trying to convey to you that he thinks I'm delusional and doesn't believe that there's a computer hacker at work," Zan said, calmly, "but there is, and that shouldn't be too hard to prove."

"How did the orders to the suppliers get placed?" Charley Shore asked.

"By phone, and—," Josh began.

"Give Charley the letter, Josh," Zan interrupted.

Josh handed it to the attorney, who read it carefully. "This is your stationery," Charley Shore asked.

"Yes," Zan said.

"Is this your signature, Zan?"

"It looks like mine, but I didn't sign that letter. In fact, I'd like to take it to the police station with us. I believe that someone is impersonating me and trying to ruin my life and my business, and I think that person has taken my son."

Charles Robert Shore was an experienced criminal lawyer with an impressive list of verdicts that favored his clients to the point that he was a thorn in the side of many prosecutors. But now for a split second he regretted that his friendship with Alvirah Meehan had put him in the position of defending her clearly psychotic friend.

Choosing his words carefully, he asked, "Zan, have you reported this identity theft crime to the police?"

Josh answered for her. "No, we haven't. Too much has been going on in the past few days. You can understand that."

"I would agree," Charley said, quietly. "Zan, I don't want this problem to come into the conversation with Detectives Collins and Dean today. Can you promise me that you won't bring it up?"

"Why wouldn't I bring it up?" Zan demanded. "Can't you see? This is part of an ongoing scheme, and when we get to the bottom of it, we will know where Matthew is being kept."

"Zan, trust me. We must thoroughly discuss this before we decide if and when we tell the detectives." Charley Shore looked at his watch. "Zan, we'd better get going. I have a car waiting downstairs."

"The delivery entrance is my usual mode of entrance and exit,"

Zan told him. "There's always someone from the media hanging out around the front door."

Charley Shore studied his new client. There was something different about her. When he delivered her to Alvirah last night, she'd been fragile in every way, pale, shivering, and broken in spirit.

Today, there was a resolute firmness in her. She was wearing light makeup that enhanced her beautiful hazel eyes and long lashes. The auburn hair that she had worn in a tight bun yesterday was flowing on her shoulders. Yesterday she had been wearing jeans and a fake-fur jacket. Today, her slender, fine-boned body was fashionably dressed in a dark gray pantsuit with a multicolored scarf draped around her neck.

Charley's wife, Lynn, dressed well. If he ever needed confirmation of that fact, he received it from the American Express bill he got every month. He considered her mild extravagance a small price to pay for the many times he missed a dinner party or was late for an event at Lincoln Center because he was preparing for an important trial. But if he had to choose, he much preferred the image of Zan Moreland as a victim than the one the media would see if they took pictures of her today.

There was absolutely nothing he could do about it. He reached for his cell phone and directed his driver to meet them at the back of the building.

The day was still unseasonably cold, but the sun was shining and the drifting white clouds held no hint of rain. Charley glanced up, hoping that the brightness of the day might be a good omen, but he had serious doubts that would be the case.

When they were in the car, choosing his words carefully, he said, "Zan, this is terribly important. You have got to follow my lead on anything I tell you to do. If Collins or Dean asks you a question and I tell you not to answer, that's the way it has to be. I understand that there will be times when you're burning to try to put them straight, but you must *not* do that."

Digging her nails into her palms, Zan tried not to show how frightened she was. She liked Charley Shore. He had been so kind, so fatherly at her bedside in the hospital yesterday, then in the cab when he escorted her to Alvirah's apartment. She also knew that he didn't doubt for one minute that she was the woman in the Central Park photos. And even though he tried not to show it, it was obvious he believed the letter to Wallington Fabrics with her signature was on the level as well.

One of her favorite books as a child had been *Alice in Wonderland*. Now the words "Off with her head, off with her head," ran through her mind. But Charley does want to help me, and the least I can do is trust his advice. I don't have any choice.

"Mommy . . . Mommy . . ." I heard Matthew's voice this morning, she reminded herself. I must keep holding on to the certainty that he is alive and that I will find him. It's the only way I can possibly keep going.

The cab was pulling up to the Central Park Precinct. There were people with television cameras and microphones at the entrance.

"Oh, hell," Charley Shore muttered. "Somebody tipped them off that you're expected here."

Zan bit her lip. "I'll be all right."

"Zan, remember, do *not* answer their questions. If they shove a mike in your face, ignore it."

The cab stopped and Zan followed Shore out of it. The reporters rushed to intercept them. Zan tried to close her eyes to the shouted questions, "Will you be making a statement, Ms. Moreland?" "Where is Matthew, Ms. Moreland?" "What did you do with him, Zan?" "Do you think he is still alive?"

As Charley Shore, his arm around her back, tried to propel her forward, she broke away from him and turned around to the cameras. "My son is alive," she said, her voice steadily rising. "I believe I know who hates me enough to go to the level of kidnapping him. I tried to tell that to the police two years ago and they didn't listen, but I am going to make them listen now."

She turned and looked straight into Charley Shore's eyes. "Sorry," she said, "but it's about time somebody starts to listen to me and look for the truth."

# 42

Kevin Wilson's present home was a furnished sublet in TriBeCa, the area below Greenwich Village that at one time had been the location of grimy factories and printing presses. It was a roomy loft with an open area that included a kitchen with a well-equipped bar, a living room, and a library. The furniture was starkly modern, but the den beyond it was equipped with a roomy leather sofa and matching chairs with hassocks. His bedroom was comparatively small, but that was because the owner had moved the wall to accommodate a fully equipped gym. An oversized corner room served as his office. The large windows in every room guaranteed sunshine from dawn till dark.

Kevin was happy to sublease the loft and recently had put in a bid to buy it. He already was making plans for the architectural changes he would make, like leaving the exercise room only big enough to hold a few pieces of equipment, enlarging the master bedroom and bath, and turning the corner room into two other bedrooms with a shared larger bath.

As for the furnishings, he already was marking which ones he would keep and which would end up at Goodwill. His mother told him he was getting the nesting instinct. "You're the last one of your good friends to be single," she regularly reminded him. "It's about time you got over the casual dates and found a nice girl and settled down." Lately she had begun to expand on that. "By now all my friends are bragging about their grandchildren," she complained.

After having dinner with his mother, Kevin had gone straight home to bed. He slept soundly and in the morning awoke at his usual six A.M. Cereal, juice, and coffee with a quick glance at the front page of the *Wall Street Journal* and the *Post* was followed by an hour on the gym equipment. He watched the morning news, catching a segment of the *Today* show with some legal expert giving his opinion that the arrest of Alexandra Moreland was imminent.

My God, Kevin thought, is that really possible? He felt again the electrical reaction that he had experienced when their shoulders brushed. If those pictures in Central Park aren't doctored, then there is something wrong with her, he regretfully acknowledged.

As he showered and dressed, he could not get Zan's face out of his mind. Her eyes, so beautiful and expressive, had been so sad. It didn't take a Rhodes scholar to see the pain in them. Louise had made the initial call to Moreland Interiors inviting Zan to bid on the job for decorating the apartments. Oddly enough, in all the times she had come and gone, he had not run into her until the other day when she delivered her sketches and samples. She had brought them in herself. Bartley Longe, on the other hand, had been accompanied by his assistant walking behind him carrying his designs.

That's another reason I don't like that guy, Kevin thought. Longe's attitude was galling. "I look forward to working with you, Kevin," as though it were a done deal.

It was ten minutes of eight, and he was ready to go. Because he was planning to be at 701 Carlton Place all day, he had dressed casually in a sport shirt, sweater, and khakis. He took a quick glance in the mirror. It was about time to get a haircut, and he wanted to be sure that his hair was brushed down sufficiently.

When I was a kid, I had such curly hair that Mom used to say that I should have been a girl. Zan Moreland has long, straight hair, the dark auburn of a Japanese maple. I didn't know I was a *poet*, he thought, as he reached for a jacket and left the apartment.

If Louise Kirk did not come in at the stroke of nine, Kevin had to endure her usual indignant outburst about her belief that one day, all the traffic in New York will just stop dead. Today, though, she arrived fifteen minutes early.

Kevin had told her he surfed the channels during his workout.

"Kevin, did you by any chance catch the *Today* show when they were talking about Zan Moreland?" she asked eagerly.

I guess we're friends again, he thought. I'm back to being on a first-name basis with her.

"Yes, I did," he said.

Louise did not seem to notice his abrupt answer. "Everybody can see that unless those pictures were doctored, which I'd give ten years of my life to say that they're not, the poor girl is deranged."

"Louise, the 'poor girl,' as you describe Alexandra Moreland, is an extremely gifted interior designer and a very attractive human being. Could we withhold judgment and drop the subject?"

Kevin almost never played employer/employee with anyone in his office or on a job, but this time he did not try to hide his genuine anger.

When he was a child, at his mother's insistence, he had taken piano lessons. It had become painfully obvious to all three—his mother, his teacher, and himself—that he had absolutely no talent as a musician, but that had not diminished his pleasure in playing. There was one song that he had learned to play very well, "The Minstrel Boy."

Now a fragment of the words echoed through his head. *"Tho' all the world betrays thee . . . One sword, at least, thy rights shall guard . . . One faithful harp shall praise thee!"* Who did Zan Moreland have to praise or defend her? Kevin wondered.

Louise Kirk got the message. "Of course, Mr. Wilson," she answered, her voice subdued.

"Louise, will you knock off the 'Mr. Wilson' stuff? We're going to take a tour through this whole building. Bring your notebook. I've been seeing some sloppy work, and I have a number of people who are going to hear about it today."

At ten o'clock, as Kevin, trailed by Louise, was pointing out uneven grouting in three of the shower stalls in apartments on the thirtieth floor, his business cell phone rang. Not wanting to be interrupted, he gave the phone to Louise to answer.

She listened, then said, "I'm sorry, Mr. Wilson is not available but I'll give him your message." She disconnected and handed him back the phone. "That was Bartley Longe," she said. "He wants to invite you to have lunch with him today, or if that doesn't work, to have dinner this evening or tomorrow night. What shall I tell him?"

"Tell him to forget it for now." Longe's probably gloating that he has the job, he thought, and then reluctantly concluded that maybe he did. The model apartments needed to be finished. The consortium that owned the building was already grumbling about the cost overruns and the inevitable delays in construction. They wanted the apartments decorated so that the sales department could take over. Certainly if Zan Moreland was arrested, she wouldn't have any time to oversee the day-to-day progress. A decorator had to be on top of the job when any interior work was done.

At quarter of eleven, when he and Louise were finally back in his office, one of the workmen came in to see him. "Which apartment do you want us to stack the fabrics and all that other stuff in, sir?"

"What do you mean, where do I want to put what stuff?" Kevin asked.

The workman, a leathery-faced man in his sixties, seemed bewildered by the question.

"I mean all the stuff that decorator ordered for the model apartments. It's starting to arrive."

Louise answered for Kevin. "Tell whoever is delivering anything for those model apartments to take it right back to where it came from. Not one single order has been authorized by Mr. Wilson."

Kevin did not believe what he heard himself saying. "Put any deliveries in the largest apartment." He looked squarely at Louise. "We'll sort this out," he said, "but if we don't accept whatever is coming, we'll be part of the sensational stories about Zan Moreland. Those suppliers will go screaming to the media. I don't want potential buyers to see this building in that kind of light."

Not daring to show what she was thinking, Louise Kirk nodded. You're attracted to that young lady, Kevin Wilson, she thought.

*Fools rush in . . .*

# 43

Matthew had begun to be really scared of Glory. It had started yesterday when she yelled at him for forgetting his truck and leaving it where that lady saw it. He had run back into the closet and then she locked him in and then after a while she said she was sorry, but he couldn't stop crying. He wanted Mommy.

He kept trying to think about Mommy's face but it was like seeing shadows. But he could remember her wrapping him inside her bathrobe, and he could even remember when her long hair would tickle his nose and he would brush it away. If she was with him now, he wouldn't brush it away. He'd hold it so tight that he'd never let go even if it hurt her.

Later on, after Glory had put that smelly stuff in his hair, she gave him one of the muffins the lady brought. But afterward he felt sick and threw up. It wasn't the muffin. He knew that. It was because some days when Mommy didn't go to work, she used to bake muffins with him. It was like the soap that he kept under his pillow. The muffins made him think of Mommy.

After that Glory had tried to be nice. She read a story to him, but even though she told him he was really smart and read grown-up words better than any kid his age, he hadn't felt any better. Then Glory told him to make up a story. He did make up one—that a little boy had lost his mother and knew he had to go out and find her.

Glory didn't like that. He could tell that she was tired of taking care of him. He was tired, too, and went to sleep early.

After he had been asleep for a long time, he woke up when he heard a phone ring. Even though his door was only opened a little, he could hear some of what Glory was saying. He heard her talking about keeping this kid from his mother. Was he the kid she was talking about? Was it her fault he wasn't with Mommy? She had told him that Mommy wanted him to hide because bad people were going to steal him.

Was she lying to him?

# 44

When he left the police station at ten A.M., Ted Carpenter pushed through the assembled media, his eyes resolutely fixed on his waiting car. But when he reached it, he stopped and spoke into the microphone that had been thrust in front of him. "For nearly two years, despite her emotionally unstable personality, I have tried to believe that my ex-wife, Alexandra Moreland, was in no way responsible for my son's disappearance. Those pictures are absolute proof that I was wrong. I can only hope that she will now be forced to tell the truth and that by the grace of God Matthew is still alive."

As questions began to be thrown at him, he shook his head. "Please, no more." Tears glistening in his eyes, he got into the car and buried his face in his hands.

His driver, Larry Post, pulled away, then when they were clear of the police station, asked, "Will you be going home, Ted?"

"Yes, I will." I can't face going into the office, he thought. I can't face talking to people. I can't face trying to persuade Jaime-boy, that no-talent, egocentric, crude jackass whose so-called reality show is making him millions, that he should sign up with me. What in the hell was I doing even going to dinner with that blood-sucker Melissa and her hangers-on the night of Matthew's birthday? My ex-wife is going to be grilled by the cops, and maybe she'll say or do something that will break this wide open.

Larry glanced in the rearview mirror and took in the haggard, strained expression on Ted's face. "Ted," he said, "I know it's none of my business, but you look as though you're getting sick. Maybe you should see a doctor."

"There's no medicine available to solve my problems," Ted said wearily. He leaned his head back and closed his eyes. His meeting with the detectives replayed itself, moment by moment, in his mind. The expression on both their faces had been inscrutable.

What's the matter with them? he asked himself. Why haven't they arrested Zan? Is there something wrong with those photos? And if so, why wouldn't they tell me? *I'm* the father. I have every right to know. Zan had always insisted that Bartley Longe hated her enough and was jealous enough of her success to do anything to hurt her. But did those cops honestly believe that a high-class interior designer would go to the extent of kidnapping and maybe even killing a child just to get back at a former employee? His head pounded at the notion.

Larry Post knew what was going through Ted Carpenter's mind. Ted was worried sick. It's really a crime that he ever met that Moreland woman who dumped him after he was so good to her and then didn't even want him when she started to get better, he thought, even though she was pregnant with his kid.

Larry's weathered skin and balding hair made him seem older than his thirty-eight years. His tightly muscled body was the result of rigorous daily exercise. That had started when he was twenty and serving a fifteen-year sentence for killing a drug dealer who had been trying to cheat him. When he got out he couldn't find a job anywhere in Milwaukee and phoned Ted, his closest friend in high school, begging for help. Ted had told him to come to New York. Now Ted called him his right-hand man. Larry cooked for him when Ted wanted a night home, chauffeured him everywhere, and did general maintenance in the building Ted had so foolishly bought three years ago.

Ted's cell phone rang. As he had expected, it was Melissa. When he answered, she said, "I didn't like the fact that you claim you were too sick to go to the Club with me the other night. I notice that you were able to be at the police station bright and early today."

Enraged, Ted waited a long moment, then forced a reasonable tone into his voice. "Melissa, sweetheart, I told you that the police needed to talk with me. I put them off yesterday and anyhow I didn't want you to catch any kind of bug I may be carrying. I still feel absolutely lousy and much as I want to meet Jaime-boy, I'm not up to it today. I've got to just get home and sit by the phone. My ex is meeting with the detectives in less than an hour. With any luck they'll arrest her and maybe get her to talk. I'm sure you can understand how I'm feeling right now."

"Forget Jaime-boy. He made up with his publicist. But don't worry. He'll break up with him again before the week is over. Listen, I've figured out a great way to get publicity. Call the media and tell them to be in your office for a three o'clock news release. I'll be with you, and I'll announce that I'm offering a five-million-dollar reward for anyone who finds your kid alive."

"Melissa, are you totally crazy?" Ted's raised voice made Larry Post look quickly into the rearview mirror.

"Don't you *dare* talk to me like that. I'm trying to *help* you." Melissa made no attempt to hide her fury at Ted's response. "Think about it. Suppose that Bartley Longe, that miserable snob who I hate—you know the remarks he made about my last album, when he told the paparazzi why he hadn't invited me to that big party he threw. . . . Anyhow, you told me your ex keeps saying Longe took your kid. Maybe he did."

"Melissa, think this through. You're on record as saying, not once but many times, that you believe that Matthew was molested and killed by a predator the same day he was abducted. Why would anyone believe you would change your mind now? That kind of offer will only look like a cheap publicity stunt and will hurt your career. They'll compare it with O. J. Simpson putting up a reward to find the person who killed his wife and her friend. Added to that, it will open the door to hundreds of people calling in claiming they saw a child who looks like Matthew. I put up a million-dollar reward myself when Matthew disappeared, and the police ended up wasting valuable time tracking down the bunch of lunatics who called."

"Look," Melissa insisted, "they've got those pictures of your ex taking the kid. Suppose she doesn't break down? Suppose the kid is alive somewhere and someone is minding him? Don't you think that person would jump at the chance to get five million bucks?"

"That same person would have a long time to wait in prison before being able to spend that money."

"That's not true. Look at that mob guy who killed a zillion people and didn't even go to jail because he helped the cops convict his buddies. Maybe there's more than one person in on it. Maybe one of them will confess and help the cops find your son. Then that person gets a good deal from the DA and a lot of money from me. Listen, Ted, I *like my* idea. Your kid is going to be in the headlines when your ex is arrested and for a long time after until she goes to trial. My sister's husband, no great shakes of a guy, is a public defender. God help the poor slobs he defends, but he does know law. You know how much money I make. If I had to pay the five million, I can afford it, and just the offer makes me look like a saint. Angelina Jolie and Oprah get all that publicity doing good for kids. Why not me? So be at your office at three o'clock and have a statement for us to give them."

Without any good-bye, Melissa's phone went dead.

Ted leaned his head back against the seat and closed his eyes. *Think*, he told himself. *Think*. Get control of yourself. Consider the consequences if she goes ahead with this. If I could only afford to quit right now. If I could only afford to kiss her good-bye. If only I didn't have to put up with her moods and tantrums and outbursts and have to cover her backside when she makes a fool of herself . . .

He touched the REDIAL button on his cell phone. As he expected, Melissa did not answer. "Leave a message" was the response he heard. At the signal he took a deep breath. "Baby," he began, his tone wheedling, "you know how much I love you and how every minute of my life is dedicated to building you up to be the number one star that you deserve to be. But I also want the public to know the sweet and generous side of you. I can't begin to thank you for this breathtaking offer, but as your lover, your best friend, your publicist, I want you to think about making this offer in a different way."

A beep told him that his allotted time to leave a message was up. Gritting his teeth, Ted pressed REDIAL again. "Sweetheart, I have an idea that will have a long-lasting effect. We'll call a press conference tomorrow or whenever you want to arrange the meeting. At it, you announce that you are donating five million dollars immediately to the Foundation for Missing Children. Every parent of a missing child will love you and that way you won't have to respond to the sleazes who will try to turn your generosity into something it isn't. Think about it, darling. And call me."

Ted Carpenter turned off his cell phone and managed to wait until he reached home before he went into the bathroom and became violently sick to his stomach. Minutes later, chilled and shaking, he went into the bedroom and picked up the phone.

Rita Moran answered, her voice motherly and concerned. "Ted, I saw you on the breaking news on the Internet. You look terrible. How are you doing now?"

"Just as bad as I look. I'm going to bed. No calls at all unless . . ."

Rita finished the sentence for him. "Unless the witch dials from her broom."

"She won't for a while. Some commonsense advice I gave her may be filtering into her brain as we speak."

"How about your appointment with that Jaime-boy nut?"

"It's been canceled, or maybe just postponed." He knew that Rita understood the financial ramifications of losing that potential client.

"Maybe it's just been postponed."

Ted caught the false hardiness in her tone. She was the only one of his employees who knew the degree to which the purchase of the building had been a big drain and a horrible mistake. "Who knows?" he asked. "I'll talk to you later. Zan is being questioned by the detectives right now. If Collins or Dean happens to call, tell them they can reach me here."

Stripping off his clothes to his underwear, he got into bed and pulled the covers around him until only the top of his head was showing.

For the next four hours, he dozed intermittently.

Then at three o'clock, his phone rang again.

It was Detective Collins.

# 45

Zan remembered keenly the kindness with which Detectives Billy Collins and Jennifer Dean had treated her when Matthew disappeared. That day, after Ted's outburst about leaving Matthew with a young babysitter, they had even said to her, "At times like these, some people have to handle tragedy by blaming it on someone. Try to understand that."

She knew they had then interviewed Nina Aldrich, who had verified their appointment that day. When Tiffany Shields had finally calmed down, she had told the detectives that the new nanny had not shown up, and that Zan had called her at the last minute and begged her to watch Matthew because she had an important client she could not risk losing.

Zan had told them that the only person who she felt honestly hated her was Bartley Longe, but even then she had realized that they were dismissing him as a possibility.

They had tried to suggest that Ted's outburst about hiring an inexperienced babysitter might suggest some underlying hostility, a scenario Zan had dismissed. She had told them that Ted had approved both Matthew's first nanny and the new one she had hired just before Matthew disappeared.

The photos. Of course they had to be doctored! With her new-found strength in the sure knowledge that she had heard Matthew's voice early that morning, Zan, with Charley Shore guiding her arm, followed Detectives Collins and Dean into the room where they would be questioning her.

They all took seats, Charley Shore next to her, Billy Collins and Jennifer Dean across from them. In the weeks immediately following Matthew's disappearance, Zan realized she had originally seen the detectives only in a blur. This time she studied them carefully. They were both in their early forties. Billy Collins had the kind of face that blended into the crowd. He had no distinguishing features. His eyes were narrowly set, his ears a little too large for his long, thin face. His eyebrows shaggy. His manner low-key. He looked slightly rumpled, as though he hadn't taken the time to straighten his tie. When they were settled in the seats, Billy solicitously asked if they would like to have coffee or water.

On the other hand, Jennifer Dean, his attractive African-American partner, immediately made Zan feel uncomfortable today. There was a crisp, no-nonsense air about her now. Zan remembered the warmth of her touch when Zan almost fainted shortly after she arrived in Central Park that day. Jennifer had been the one who rushed forward and grabbed her before she fell. Today she was wearing a dark green suit with a white turtleneck sweater. Her only jewelry was a wide gold wedding band and small gold earrings. Streaks of gray were untouched in her midnight black hair. Unsmiling, she looked appraisingly into Zan's face as though she were seeing her for the first time.

Zan had shaken her head at the offer of coffee, but the unexpected change in Dean's attitude startled her. "Maybe I will have that coffee," she said.

"Sure thing," Collins said. "Anything in it?"

"Nothing, thanks," Zan said.

"I'll be back in a minute."

It was a long minute. Detective Dean made no attempt to start a conversation.

In a casual gesture, Charley Shore gently placed his arm over the back of Zan's chair, a reassuring move that signaled to her he was there to protect her.

But protect her from what?

Billy Collins was back with a paper cup filled with coffee that was little more than tepid. "Starbucks it's not," he commented.

Zan nodded her thanks as Collins took his seat and handed her the enlarged photographs of a woman taking the sleeping Matthew from his stroller in Central Park. "Ms. Moreland, is that you in these pictures?"

"No, it isn't," Zan said firmly. "It may look like me, but it isn't me."

"Ms. Moreland, is this your picture?" He held up another one.

Zan glanced at it. "Yes, that must have been taken right after I got to Central Park after you called me and said that Matthew was missing."

"Can you see any difference in the women in these pictures?"

"Yes. The woman taking Matthew out of the stroller is an imposter. The one of me arriving in the park after he was kidnapped is genuine. You certainly must know that by now. I was with a client, Nina Aldrich. I know you checked that out immediately."

"You did not tell us that instead of meeting Mrs. Aldrich at her Beekman Place home where she waited for you for well over an hour, you were in her town house on East Sixty-ninth Street alone for all that time," Jennifer Dean said, her tone accusing.

"I was there because she told me to meet her there. I was not surprised she was late. Nina Aldrich was chronically late for our appointments whether they were in the town house she was decorating or the apartment where she still lived."

"The town house is minutes from the spot in Central Park from which Matthew disappeared, isn't it, Ms. Moreland?" Billy Collins asked.

"I would guess it's about a fifteen-minute walk. When I got the call from you, I ran all the way."

"Ms. Moreland, Mrs. Aldrich is very sure that she told you to meet her on Beekman Place," Detective Dean said.

"That's not true. She told me to meet her at the town house," Zan said heatedly.

"Ms. Moreland, we're not trying to attack you," Collins said, his voice soothing. "You say Mrs. Aldrich was chronically late for appointments."

"Yes, she was."

"Do you know if she has a cell phone?" Collins asked.

"She has a cell phone, of course she does," Zan answered.

"Do you have the number of her cell phone?" As he spoke, Billy Collins took a sip of his own coffee and made a face. "Even worse than usual," he commented amiably.

Zan realized she was still holding the cup in her hand and took another sip of it. What had Collins just asked her? Of course. He asked me if I had Nina Aldrich's cell phone number. "Her number is in my phone," she said.

"How long since you've spoken to Mrs. Aldrich?" Dean asked, her voice steely.

"Almost two years. She wrote me a note about Matthew and said she knew that it would be far too much responsibility for me to take on such a major project as decorating her large home, meaning, of course, she was afraid to take a chance on me concentrating on the job."

"Who got the job of decorating her town house?" Collins asked.

"Bartley Longe."

"Isn't he the person you claim might be responsible for kidnapping Matthew?"

"He is the only person I know who thoroughly hates me and is jealous of me."

"Where are we going with these questions?" Charley Shore asked as he applied slight pressure to Zan's shoulder.

"We're simply asking if Ms. Moreland was frequently in touch with Mrs. Aldrich at the time she was bidding for the job of decorating her town house."

"Of course I was," Zan broke in.

Again she felt the light pressure of Charley's hand on her shoulder.

"Were you friendly with Mrs. Aldrich?" Dean asked.

"In a client-relationship kind of way, I guess you'd call it. She liked my vision for how I saw the town house should be decorated to best show off, or rather emphasize, some of the architectural features that exist in those wonderful late nineteenth-century homes."

"How many rooms are in that town house?" Jennifer Dean asked.

I can't imagine why they're so interested in the layout of that place, Zan thought as she mentally retraced the rooms in the Aldrich home. "It's very large," she said. "Forty feet wide, which I assure you is unusual. There are five stories. The top floor is an enclosed roof garden. There are eleven rooms as well as the wine cellar, and a second kitchen and storage room in the basement."

"I see. So you went there to meet Nina Aldrich. Were you surprised she didn't show up?" Collins asked.

"Surprised? No, not really. She was always late. The one time she wasn't and I was five minutes late, she let me know how important her time was and that she wasn't in the habit of being kept waiting."

"Didn't the fact that the babysitter minding Matthew had a cold and didn't feel well make you anxious enough to pick up your cell phone and call her?" Dean asked.

"No." Zan felt as though she were in a morass where everything she said made her sound as though she were lying. "Nina Aldrich would have resented my reminding her that she was late."

"How often did she keep you waiting as long as an hour or more?" Dean asked.

"That was by far the longest."

"Wouldn't it have been reasonable to phone and ask if you had been mistaken about the time and place of your meeting?"

"I knew the time and place she had told me. You don't remind the Nina Aldriches of this world that they may have made a mistake."

"So you stood or sat there for an hour or more before she finally called you?"

"I was going over my sketches and the pictures of antique furniture and chandeliers and sconces that I was planning to show her. In a few cases, I was choosing between several selections as my top recommendations. The time went quickly."

"I understand there was almost no furniture in the town house," Collins commented.

"A card table and two folding chairs," Zan answered.

"So you sat at the card table for more than an hour going over your sketches?"

"No. I went up to the master bedroom on the third floor. I wanted to check once more and see how the patterns I had chosen worked in the strong sunlight. Remember the day was unusually warm and sunny."

"Would you have heard Mrs. Aldrich if she had come in while you were on the third floor?" Jennifer Dean asked.

"She would have seen my portfolio and sketches as soon as she walked through the door," Zan said.

"You had your own key to the town house, Ms. Moreland?"

"Of course. I was submitting plans to decorate the entire house from top to bottom. I went back and forth regularly for weeks."

"You got to know the house pretty well, then, didn't you?"

"I would think that's obvious," Zan snapped.

"Including the basement with its second kitchen, wine cellar, and storage room. Were you planning to decorate the storage room?"

"That space was large and dark and virtually inaccessible. It was really a kind of subcellar reached by a door at the back of the wine cellar. There were plenty of other storage areas in closets throughout the house. I suggested painting the room, putting in good lighting, and building shelves to accommodate items like skis for Mrs. Aldrich's step-grandchildren."

"It would have made a pretty good hiding place if someone wanted to hide something—or someone—wouldn't it?" Jennifer Dean asked.

"Don't answer that question, Zan," Charley Shore ordered.

Billy Collins did not look disturbed. "Ms. Moreland, when did you give Mrs. Aldrich her key back?"

"It was about two weeks after Matthew disappeared. That was when she wrote the note saying that she thought the stress of Matthew's disappearance would be too much for me to handle the job."

"In those two weeks, did you still think you had the job?"

"Yes, I did."

"Could you have handled it, given the fact that your son was missing?"

"Yes, I could have handled it. In fact, concentrating on it was the only way I thought I could preserve my sanity."

"Then you went back and forth often to that empty house after your son disappeared?"

"Yes."

"Did you go there to visit Matthew?"

Zan jumped up from the chair. "Are you crazy?" she demanded.

"Are you trying to tell me that you think I kidnapped my own child and hid him in that storage room?"

"Zan, sit down," Charley Shore said firmly.

"Ms. Moreland, as you have said several times, that is a large town house. Why would you suggest that we think you hid Matthew in the storage room?"

"Because you *are* suggesting it," Zan cried. "You are insinuating that I stole my own child, brought him back to that house, and hid him there. Why are you wasting your time? Why aren't you finding out who doctored those photos to make them look as though I'm taking Matthew from the stroller? Don't you understand that's the key to finding my son?"

Detective Dean shot back at her, "Ms. Moreland, our tech people have gone over the photographs very carefully. They are not 'doctored,' as you put it. These photos have not been altered."

Try as she would, Zan could not hold back the sobs that racked her shoulders. "Then someone is impersonating me. Why is this happening?" she cried. "Why don't you listen to me? Bartley Longe hates me. From the minute I opened my own firm, I took business from him. And he's a womanizer. He used to come on to me when I worked for him. He's the worst kind of sleaze. He can't stand to be rejected. That was another reason to hate me."

Neither Collins nor Dean showed any emotion. Then when Zan, her tearstained face buried in her hands, managed to stifle her anguished reaction to the relentless questions, Jennifer Dean said, "Ms. Moreland, this is a new twist on your story. You never once referred to Bartley Longe as having come on to you sexually."

"I didn't because I didn't think it was that important at the time. It was only a part of the pattern."

"Zan, how often did you suffer fainting spells and memory lapses after your parents died?" Collins asked. Now his voice was concerned and kindly.

Zan tried to brush away tears, realizing that he, at least, was not openly antagonistic to her. "Everything was a blur for those six months," she said. "Then I started to be able to think clearly and realized I had been so unfair to Ted. He was putting up with my crying spells and my spending days in bed and he was giving up evenings to be with me when he should have been out at clients' events and openings, and endless awards events. When you run a public relations firm, you just can't neglect that."

"Did you tell him you were leaving as soon as you decided?"

"I knew he would be too worried about me and try to talk me out of it. I looked around and found a small apartment. My mother and father had insurance policies, no fortune, fifty thousand dollars in all, but it gave me a safety net to get started. And I took out a small loan."

"What was your husband's reaction when you finally told him you were leaving and wanted a divorce?"

"He had to go to California for the premiere of Marisa Young's new movie. He was planning to get a nurse to stay with me. That was when I told him that I was eternally grateful to him, but I couldn't be a burden to him any longer, that our marriage was a total act of kindness on his part, but now I knew I could go it alone and give him his life back. I told him I had decided to move out. He was kind enough to get me settled."

At least they're not accusing me when they ask me about Ted, she thought.

"At what point did you realize you were pregnant with Matthew?"

"I didn't have a period for several months after my parents died. The doctor told me that wasn't unusual in cases of extreme stress. Then my periods were irregular. So it was a few months after I left Ted before I realized that I was expecting Matthew."

"What was your reaction to finding out you were pregnant?" Dean asked.

"Shocked, then very happy."

"Even though you had taken out a bank loan to start your own business?" Collins asked.

"I knew it would be hard, but that didn't bother me. Of course I told Ted, but I told him that he should not feel any financial responsibility."

"Why not? He was the father, wasn't he?"

"Of course he was," Zan said heatedly.

"And he has a very successful public relations firm," Dean pointed out. "Weren't you as much as telling him that you wanted no part of him having anything to do with your child?"

"*Our* child," Zan said. "Ted insisted that until I got my business going that he would pay for the nanny I would need to hire, and that if I didn't need his financial help, he would put the money he would normally pay for support into a trust fund for Matthew."

"You paint a rosy picture, Ms. Moreland," Jennifer Dean observed sarcastically. "Wasn't it a fact that Matthew's father was concerned over the amount of time you left Matthew with the nanny? In fact, didn't he indicate that he was willing to take over full custody of Matthew when you became more and more involved in your business?"

"That's a lie," Zan shouted. "Matthew was my life. In the beginning I only had a part-time secretary and unless I had a client in the office or was outside on appointments, Gretchen, the nanny, would bring Matthew to the office on her way to and from the park. Look at my appointment books from the time he was born till he disappeared. I was home almost every night with him. I didn't want to be out. I loved him so much."

"You *loved* him so much," Dean snapped. "Then you do think he is dead."

"He is not dead. He called out to me this morning."

The detectives could not conceal their astonishment. "He called out to you this morning?" Billy Collins demanded.

"I mean, early this morning, I heard his voice."

"Zan, we're leaving now," Charley Shore said, himself clearly rattled. "This inquisition is over."

"No. I'm going to explain. Fr. Aiden was so kind when I met him last night. I know that even Alvirah and Willy don't believe that I'm not the one in those photos in Central Park. But Fr. Aiden gave me a sense of peace that stayed with me all night. Then just as I was waking up this morning, I heard Matthew's voice as clearly as though he were in the room and I knew he was still alive."

This time, when Zan stood up, she pushed back the chair so quickly that it toppled over. "He is alive," she shouted. "Why are you torturing me? Why aren't you searching for my little boy? Why won't you believe me that those photos are not of me? You think I'm crazy. You're the ones who are blind and stupid." Her voice now hysterical, she screamed, " 'There are none so blind as those who will not see.' In case you don't know, that's a quote from Jeremiah in the Bible. Two years ago, when the pair of you wouldn't listen to me about Bartley Longe, I looked it up."

Zan turned to Charley Shore. "Am I under arrest?" she demanded. "If not, let's get the hell out of here now."

# 46

Alvirah had called Zan's office and learned from Josh that Charley Shore had taken Zan to the police station for questioning. And then Josh told her about the one-way ticket to Buenos Aires and the orders Zan had placed with their suppliers.

With a heavy heart, Alvirah filled Willy in on that conversation when he returned from his morning walk in Central Park. "Oh, Willy, I feel so helpless," she sighed. "There's no mistake about those pictures. Now Zan has bought herself a one-way ticket to Buenos Aires and is ordering stuff for a job she doesn't even have."

"Maybe she thinks they're closing in on her, and is planning to run away," Willy suggested. "Listen, Alvirah, if she *did* take Matthew out of the stroller, maybe he's in South America with a friend. Didn't Zan tell you that she speaks a couple of languages, including Spanish?"

"Yes. She moved around with her parents a lot when she was growing up. But oh, Willy, that's as much as saying that Zan is a schemer. I don't think that's true. I think the problem is that she has lapses of memory, or is a split personality. I've read a lot about people like that. One personality simply has no idea of what the other one is doing. Remember that book *The Three Faces of Eve*? That woman was three different people and one didn't know about the other. Maybe Zan, in another persona, took Matthew from the stroller. Maybe she did give him to a friend who took him to South America and in that persona is planning to join him."

"This split personality stuff sounds like hocus-pocus to me, honey," Willy said. "I'd do anything for Zan, but I honestly think she's mentally ill. I just hope that when she was irrational, she didn't do anything to that little kid."

While Willy was out on his morning walk, Alvirah had been cleaning the apartment. Even though they had put most of the lottery money they'd won in triple-A bonds and solid stocks so that they had a nice dividend income, she had never been able to bring herself to hire a cleaning woman. Or at least, when she did try one at Willy's urging, she had immediately realized that she was three times as fast and ten times as thorough as the person they hired to come in once a week.

Now their three-room apartment overlooking Central Park South was sparkling, and the sun that had finally broken through was cheerfully reflected in the shiny surface of the glass-topped coffee table and the mirror on the back wall that reflected the park. Vacuuming and dusting and mopping up the kitchen had helped calm Alvirah, and while she was working she had put on her "thinking cap," as she called the imaginary head covering that helped her find solutions to problems.

It was almost eleven. She turned on the television to the news station just in time to see Zan get out of a car and Charley Shore try to rush her past the media. When Zan stopped and began to speak into the microphone, she could see the dismay on Charley's face. "Oh, Willy," Alvirah sighed. "Anyone listening to Zan now would be sure that she knows exactly where Matthew is. She sounds so positive that he's alive."

Willy had settled in his club chair with the morning papers, but looked up at the sound of Zan's voice. "She sounds so positive because she knows where that kid is, honey," he said emphatically.

"I have to say that judging from her performance when Charley brought her here last night, she's one hell of an actress."

"How was she when you took her home in the car?"

Willy ran his fingers through his thick mane of white hair and frowned in concentration. "Just the way she was here, like a wounded doe. She said we've become her best friends and she doesn't know what she'd do without us."

"Then if she's hidden Matthew somewhere, she doesn't know it herself," Alvirah said positively as she pushed the remote to turn off the television. "I'd be interested to know what impression Fr. Aiden had of Zan. When he said he'd pray for her, I heard what she said to him, to pray for Matthew but that God had forgotten she existed. That almost broke my heart. I just wanted to put my arms around her and hug her."

"Alvirah, I think that dollars to donuts, Zan is going to be arrested," Willy said. "You might as well be prepared for that."

"Oh, Willy, that would be awful. Would they let her out on bail?"

"I don't know. They sure won't like the fact that she bought a one-way ticket to South America. That could be reason enough to keep her locked up."

The telephone rang. It was Penny Hammel calling to say that she and Bernie would be thrilled to join the Lottery Winners' Support Group meeting on Tuesday afternoon.

With her worry about Zan, Alvirah had wished that she had waited to call a Support Group meeting, but the sound of Penny's cheerful voice lifted her spirits. She knew that she and Penny were kindred spirits in a lot of ways. They both wore size fourteen. They both had a good sense of humor. They both had preserved their lottery windfall. They both were happily married. Of course, Penny had three children and six grandchildren and Alvirah had never been blessed with a child. However, she considered herself a surrogate mother to Willy's nephew, Brian, and surrogate grandmother to

Brian's kids. Besides that, she had never wasted time wishing her life away for something she could do nothing to change.

"Solved any crimes lately, Alvirah?" Penny asked.

"Not a one," Alvirah admitted.

"Have you been watching television and seeing that Zan Moreland kidnapped her own kid? I've been glued to the set."

Alvirah did not intend to get into a discussion with the loquacious Penny about Zan Moreland, nor admit she knew her well. "It's a pretty sad case," she said, carefully.

"I'd say so," Penny agreed. "But I've got a funny story to tell you when I see you next week. I thought I was on my way to uncovering a drug deal or something sinister like that, and then I realized that I was getting excited about nothing. Oh well, I guess I'll never write a book about solving crimes like you did. Did I ever tell you that I thought the title *From Pots to Plots* was downright inspired?"

Every time I see you, you tell me that, Alvirah thought indulgently, but said, "I'm pretty happy about the title myself. I think it's catchy."

"Anyhow, maybe you'll get a laugh when you hear about the crime that didn't happen. My best friend in town is Rebecca Schwartz. She's a real estate agent."

Alvirah knew it was impossible to cut off Penny without seeming abrupt. Carrying the phone, she walked across the living room to the club chair where Willy was now attempting to solve the daily puzzle and tapped him on the shoulder.

When he looked up, she mouthed the name "Penny Hammel."

Willy nodded, went to the front door of the apartment, and stepped out into the hall.

"Anyhow, Rebecca rented a house near me to a young woman and I'll tell you why I thought there was something strange about her."

Willy rang the bell, keeping his finger on it long enough that Penny would be sure to hear it.

"Oh, Penny, I hate to interrupt but the doorbell is ringing and Willy isn't in the apartment. I can't wait to see you next Tuesday. Bye, dear."

"I hate to lie," Alvirah said to Willy. "But I'm too worried about Zan to listen to one of Penny's long stories, and it wasn't a lie to say you weren't in the apartment. You were outside in the hall."

"Alvirah," Willy smiled, "I've said it once and I'll say it again. You'd have made a great lawyer."

# 47

At eleven A.M. Toby Grissom checked out of the Cheap and Cozy Motel where he had spent the night on the Lower East Side and started to walk to Forty-second Street where he could get a bus to LaGuardia Airport. His plane wasn't until five o'clock, but he had to be out of his room and anyhow he didn't want to stay in it any longer.

The weather was cold, but the day was clear and bright and it was the kind of day on which Toby used to enjoy taking long walks. Of course, it had been different since he started getting the chemo treatments. They really knocked the stuffing out of him and now he wondered if there was any point in taking them any longer if all they could do was to keep him out of pain.

Maybe the doctor could just give me some pills or something so I wouldn't have to be so tired, he thought, as he trudged up Avenue B. He glanced down at his canvas bag to reassure himself that he hadn't forgotten it. He had put the manila file with the pictures of Glory in it. They were the most recent ones she had sent him before she disappeared.

He always carried the postcard Glory had sent him six months ago folded in his wallet. It made him feel near to her, but ever since he came to New York, his sense that she was in trouble had gotten steadily worse.

That Bartley Longe guy was bad news. You could tell that in a minute. Sure, he wore clothes that any dope could tell were expensive, and he was good looking but in that narrow-nose, thin-lip kind of way. When he looked at you, it was like you were dirt under his feet.

Bartley Longe had work done on his face, Toby thought. Even a run-of-the-mill guy like me would know that. His hair is too long. Not like those rock stars with those wild mops that make them look like a bunch of bums, but still too long. Bet it cost him four hundred dollars to get a haircut. Like the kind of money those politicians pay to barbers.

Toby thought about Longe's hands. You'd never guess he ever did an honest day's work in his life.

Toby realized he was gasping for breath. He was walking close to the curb. Slowly, he worked his way through the stream of oncoming pedestrians, until he reached the nearest building and, leaning on it, dropped his bag and took out his inhaler.

After he used it, he took deep breaths to force more air into his lungs. Then he waited for a few minutes until he felt ready to resume walking. While he waited, he observed the passersby. All kinds of people in New York, he decided. More than half of them were talking on cell phones, even the ones who were pushing strollers. Yak. Yak. Yak. What the devil did they have to say to each other? A group of young women, maybe in their twenties, passed him. They were talking and laughing and Toby eyed them sadly. They were dressed nice. They all were wearing boots that went anywhere from their ankles to past their knees. How did they ever wear those crazy high heels? he asked himself. Some of them had short hair, others had hair down past their shoulders. But they all looked as if they'd just stepped out of the shower. They were so clean they glistened.

They all probably had pretty good jobs in stores or offices, he thought.

Toby resumed his walk. I can understand now why Glory wanted to come to New York. I just wish she'd decided to get a job at an office, instead of trying to be an actress. I think that's what got her into trouble.

I know she's in trouble and it's the fault of that Longe guy.

Toby thought about how his sneakers had made a stain on the carpet in Longe's reception area. Hope they can't get it out, he thought as he dodged a homeless woman pushing a cart laden with clothes and old newspapers.

Longe's private office looks phony, too, Toby mused. Real formal. You'd think you were in Buckingham Palace, but not a paper on the desk. Where does he do all that fancy planning of those houses he decorates?

Deep in thought, Toby almost stepped from the curb after the light turned red. He had to jump back to avoid being sideswiped by a sightseeing bus. I better watch where I'm going, he told himself. I didn't come to New York to get splattered by a bus.

His thoughts immediately turned back to Bartley Longe. I wasn't born yesterday. I know why Longe snowed Glory into going up to his country home. That's the way he talked about his house in Connecticut. "His country home." Glory was a sweet, innocent girl when she came to New York. Longe didn't bring Glory up to Connecticut to play tiddlywinks. He took advantage of her.

If only Glory had married Rudy Schell right out of high school. He was crazy about her. Rudy went to work when he was eighteen and has a big plumbing business now. Big home, too. He only got married last year. When I'd run into him, he always asked about Glory. I could tell he still really liked her.

Toby realized he was not that far from the 13th Precinct, where he'd met Detective Johnson yesterday. A thought struck him. That guy never asked to see Glory's postcard. She printed what she wrote on it, and I thought it was because the card was small and her handwriting was kind of big with all those loops. But suppose she never sent the card herself? Suppose someone figured that I'd be getting nervous about her and decided to put me off looking for her? Maybe that person knows that I'm on my way out.

I'm going to see that Detective Johnson again and sit at his desk, that he says is such a privilege to have, Toby decided, and I'm going to ask him to check this postcard for fingerprints. Then I'm going to tell him that I want him to see Mr. Bartley Longe right now if he hasn't already. Does Detective Johnson think he's kidding me? All he's probably planning to do is to call up Longe and apologize for the inconvenience and then tell him that this old bird came in and he has to follow through. Then he'll ask him if he knew Glory, and what was the nature of their relationship. Longe will give him the same kind of bull he gave me about trying to help Glory's career and that he doesn't hear from her anymore. And Detective Johnson, sitting at his window desk, which doesn't have a view, will apologize for bothering Mr. Longe and that will be that.

If I miss the flight, I miss the flight, Toby thought as he turned down the block heading to the 13th Precinct. But I can't go home until that detective checks the fingerprints on that postcard and until he goes face-to-face with that creep Longe and pins him down about when he last saw Glory.

# 48

Ms. Moreland, you are not under arrest, at least not at the present," Billy Collins told Zan as she started for the door. "But I would suggest you wait."

Zan looked at Charley Shore and he nodded. As she sat back down, to give herself time, Zan asked for a glass of water. While she waited for Collins to get it, she tried to steel herself against making another outburst. Charley had immediately put his arm over the back of her chair again and for a brief moment pressed his hand on her shoulder. But this time she did not find the gesture reassuring.

Why wasn't he objecting to their insinuations? she asked herself. No, they're not insinuations. They're accusations. What good is it to have a lawyer if he won't defend me against these people?

She turned her chair a little to the left to avoid having to look directly at Detective Dean, then realized that Dean was looking down into a notebook that she had taken from her pocket.

Billy Collins returned with the glass of water and took his seat across the table from Zan. "Ms. Moreland—"

Zan interrupted him. "I would like to speak with my lawyer privately," she said.

Collins and Dean stood up immediately. "We'll get a cup of coffee," Collins told her. "Why don't we come back in fifteen minutes?"

The second the door closed, Zan yanked her chair to face Charley Shore directly. "Why are you letting them attack me with those accusations?" she demanded. "Why aren't you taking my part? You're just sitting there and patting my shoulder and letting them suggest that I kidnapped my child and brought him back to that town house and locked him in the storage room."

"Zan, I understand how you feel," Charley Shore said. "I have to do it this way. I need to know everything they'll be using to try to build a case against you. If they don't ask those questions, we won't be able to start building a defense."

"Do you think they're going to arrest me?"

"Zan, I'm sorry to tell you that I believe they will get a warrant for your arrest. Maybe not today but definitely within the next few days. My concern is what charges they may bring against you. Obstruction of justice. Perjury. Depriving your ex of his parental rights. I don't know whether they'd go so far as to charge you with kidnapping since you're the mother, but they may. You just told them that Matthew spoke to you today."

"They knew what I meant."

"You *think* that they know what you meant. They may be deciding that you were on the phone with Matthew." Looking at Zan's stunned expression, Charley added, "Zan, we have to anticipate the worst-case scenario. And I need you to trust me."

They passed the next ten minutes in silence. When the detectives returned to the room, Collins asked, "Do you want more time?"

"No, we don't," Charley Shore answered.

"Then let's talk about Tiffany Shields, Ms. Moreland. How often did she babysit for Matthew?"

It was an unexpected question, but easy to answer. "Not that often, just sometimes. Her father is the superintendent of the apartment building where I lived when Matthew was born and until six months after he disappeared. His original nanny, Gretchen, was off on weekends, which was fine with me, because I liked to take care of

Matthew myself. But after he was past the infant stage, if I did go out for the evening after he was in bed, Tiffany stayed with him."

"Did you like Tiffany?" Detective Dean asked.

"Of course I did. I thought she was a very intelligent, sweet girl and it was clear she loved Matthew. Sometimes on a weekend if I was taking him to the park, she'd come along to keep me company."

"Was your friendship so close that you gave her presents?" Collins asked.

"I wouldn't call them presents. Tiffany is pretty much my size, and sometimes when I was going through my closet and realized I had a jacket or scarf or blouse that I hadn't worn in a while and that I thought she'd like to have, I'd offer it to her."

"Did you consider her to be a careful babysitter?"

"I never would have left my child with her if I didn't think so. That is, of course, until that terrible day when she fell asleep in the park."

"You knew Tiffany had a cold, wasn't feeling well, and did not want to babysit that day," Detective Dean snapped. "Wasn't there anyone else you could have called to help you out?"

"No one who lives close enough to drop everything and rush over. Besides that, almost all of my friends are in the same business I'm in. They're working. You have to realize I was frantic. You just don't call someone like Nina Aldrich and break an appointment at the last minute. I had put untold hours into my sketches and designs for the town house and it wouldn't have been unlike her to dismiss me if I had made that call. I only wish to God I *had* made it."

Zan knew that even though she was trying to follow Charley Shore's instructions that he wanted to know where the detectives were going with their questions, it was impossible to conceal the nervous tremor in her voice. Why were they asking her all these questions about Tiffany Shields?

"So Tiffany reluctantly said she would help you out, and came to your apartment?" Detective Dean said, her tone level and without emotion.

"Yes."

"Where was Matthew?"

"He was asleep in the stroller. Because the weather was so warm overnight I had left his window open, and he woke up that morning at five o'clock from the racket the sanitation trucks were making. He usually sleeps until seven, but he didn't go back to sleep that morning and we got up and had breakfast very early. That was why I gave him an early lunch, and because Tiffany was coming to get him, I laid him down in the stroller and he was out like a light."

"What time would you say it was when you put him in the stroller?" Collins asked.

"I would say about noon. Right after I fed him."

"And what time did Tiffany come to your apartment?"

"Around 12:30."

"He was asleep when Tiffany came to get him, and he was still asleep when he was lifted out of the stroller approximately an hour and a half later." Now there was no mistaking the sneer in Jennifer Dean's voice. "But you didn't bother to strap him in, did you?"

"I had planned to fasten the strap when Tiffany came."

"But you didn't do it."

"I had covered Matthew with a light cotton blanket. I asked Tiffany to make sure the strap was fastened before we left the apartment."

"You were in too much of a rush to make sure your only child was secure in the stroller?"

Zan knew she was about to start screaming in frustration at the detective. *She's twisting everything I'm telling her*, she thought. But then she again felt the firm pressure of Charley Shore's hand on her shoulder and knew he was warning her. She looked straight into

Dean's impassive face. "When Tiffany came up, it was obvious she didn't feel well. I told her that I had put an extra blanket at the foot of the stroller so that if she couldn't find a bench in a quiet place where Matthew could nap, she could spread it on the grass and sit on it."

"Didn't you also offer her a Pepsi?" Detective Collins asked.

"Yes, Tiffany said she was thirsty."

"What else was in the Pepsi?" Dean snapped.

"Nothing. What are you getting at?" Zan demanded.

"Did you give Tiffany Shields anything else? She believes you put something in that soda to make her pass out once she sat down on the grass in Central Park. And you gave her a sedative instead of a cold pill."

"You've got to be out of your minds," Zan shouted.

"No, we're not," Detective Dean said scornfully. "You portray yourself as being so kind, Ms. Moreland. Isn't it a fact that this child was getting in the way of your precious career? I've got kids. They're in high school now, but I remember the nightmare it was if they woke up too early and were cranky for the day. Your career was all that mattered to you, wasn't it? This unexpected little treasure from heaven was getting to be a pain in the butt, and you knew you had the ideal situation to take care of it."

Detective Dean stood up and pointed her finger at Zan. "You deliberately went to Nina Aldrich's town house when she was expecting you at her home on Beekman Place. You went to the town house with all your sketches and fabrics and left them there. Then you walked to the park knowing that it wouldn't be long before Tiffany passed out. You saw your chance and you got it. You grabbed your child and took him back to that nice big, empty town house and hid him in that storage space behind the wine cellar. The question is, what did you do to him, Ms. Moreland? What did you do to him?"

"I object!" Charley Shore shouted and pulled Zan up from her chair. "We're out of here now," he said. "Are you two through with us?"

Billy Collins smiled indulgently. "Yes, counselor. But we do want the names and addresses of the two people you mentioned, Alvirah and the priest. And let me offer a suggestion. Maybe if Ms. Moreland hears her son's voice again real soon, she can tell him—and whoever is hiding him—that it's time for him to come home."

# 49

The real estate business in Middletown, as in most of the country, had been miserable for months. Rebecca Schwartz's thoughts were glum as she sat in her office and stared out at the street. The windows were filled with taped pictures of houses for sale. A number of the pictures had the word SOLD slashed across the front, but some of them were of houses that had been sold five years ago.

Rebecca was a master at describing available housing. The smallest, dingiest Cape Cod was depicted in the flyers she tacked up around town, as "cozy, intimate, and utterly charming."

Once she got prospective buyers to take a look at that kind of house, she painted a verbal picture of how special it would be when a talented homemaker brought out its latent beauty.

But even with her spectacular ability to bring out the hidden virtues of a house that needed a lot of work, Rebecca was experiencing tough sledding. Now, as she anticipated another fruitless day, she reminded herself that she was a lot better off than most of the people in this country. Unlike other fifty-nine-year-olds who were having a lean time, she could afford to keep going until the economy improved. An only child, her parents deceased, she had inherited from them the split level that had been her home all her life and the income from the two rental properties they owned on Main Street.

It isn't just about the money, she thought. I like to sell houses.

I like to see people's excitement the day they move in. Even if the house needs a lot of work, it's a new chapter in their lives. I always bring over a present for the new owners on moving day. A bottle of wine, and cheese and crackers, unless I know they're teetotalers. In that case I bring a box of Lipton tea bags and a crumb cake.

Her part-time secretary, Janie, wasn't due in until twelve. The other agent, Millie Wright, who worked with her on a commission-only basis, had had to give up and take a job in the A&P. As soon as the market picked up, she had promised Rebecca that she'd be back.

So lost was Rebecca in her thoughts that she jumped when the phone rang. "Schwartz Real Estate, Rebecca speaking," she said, keeping her fingers crossed that this was a potential buyer, not just someone else wanting to sell their house.

"Rebecca, this is Bill Reese."

Bill Reese, Rebecca thought, and then felt a surge of hope. Bill Reese had come back twice last year to look at the Owens farm, then decided against buying it.

"Bill, it's good to hear from you," she said.

"Did that Owens place ever sell?" Reese asked.

"No, not yet." Rebecca switched immediately into real estate jargon. "We have several people very interested in it, and one of them seems to be ready to make an offer."

Reese laughed. "Come on, Rebecca. You don't have to try to snow me. On your honor as a girl scout, how many potential buyers are ready to be reined in at this minute?"

Rebecca pictured Bill Reese as she laughed with him. He was a smart, pleasant, heavyset guy in his late thirties with a couple of young kids. An accountant, he lived and worked in Manhattan, but he had been raised on a farm and last year had told her that he missed that kind of life. "I like to grow things," he'd said. "And I'd like my kids on weekends to be able to have the fun of being around horses, the way I did."

"There aren't any offers on Sy's farm," she admitted, "but I'm telling you this right now, and this isn't the usual sales pitch: that is a beautiful piece of property, and when you get rid of all those heavy shades and tired furniture and do some painting and update the kitchen, you'll have a lovely, roomy house that you'll be proud to own. This bad market isn't going to last forever, and somebody is going to come along sooner or later and realize that twenty acres of prime property with a basically sound house is a good investment."

"Rebecca, I tend to agree with you. And Theresa and the kids fell in love with it. Do you think Sy will budge on the price?"

"Do you think an alligator will start singing love songs?"

"All right. I get you," Bill Reese laughed. "Look, we'll take a ride up on Sunday and if it's what we all think we remember, we'll go into contract."

"We have a tenant there now," Rebecca said, "it's a year's lease and she paid it all in advance, but that doesn't matter. In the contract, it clearly says that with one day's notice, we can show the place to a potential buyer, and if the place is sold, the tenant has to be out within thirty days. Of course, her money will be refunded on a per diem basis. But it won't be a problem. Even though this woman has a year's lease, she told me she only planned to stay for three months."

"That's fine," Reese said. "If we decide to buy it, I want to take over by the first of May so I can do some planting. How's this Sunday around one o'clock in your office?"

"It's a date," Rebecca said happily. But when she hung up, some of the exhilaration faded. She did not relish the thought of phoning Gloria Evans to tell her she may have to move. On the other hand, Rebecca reassured herself, the contract was clear and Gloria Evans would have thirty days' notice to get out. I can show her some other places, Rebecca thought, and I'm sure I can find one that will rent on a month-to-month basis. She said she only needed three months to finish her book. This way I can point out that she'll be refunded for the whole time she doesn't use Sy's place.

Gloria Evans answered on the first ring. Her voice sounded annoyed when she said, "Hello."

I've got good news and bad news, Rebecca thought, as she drew in her breath and began to explain the new development.

"*This* Sunday? You want people marching through here this Sunday?" Gloria Evans demanded.

Rebecca caught the unmistakable anxiety in her voice. "Ms. Evans, I can show you at least half a dozen very nice houses that are more up-to-date, and you can save a lot of money by going on a month-to-month basis."

"What time are those people coming on Sunday?" Gloria Evans asked.

"Sometime after one o'clock."

"I see. When I was willing to pay a year's lease for only the three months I plan to use this house, you could have pointed out that you might have people trooping in and out of here."

"Ms. Evans, it was clearly there in the lease you signed."

"I asked about that. You told me that I didn't have to worry about anyone coming near it for the three months I planned to be here. You said the market would be dead until at least early June."

"I honestly thought that. But Sy Owens would not have allowed you to rent the house without that provision in the lease." Rebecca realized she was talking to herself. Gloria Evans had clicked off. Too bad about her, she thought as she picked up the phone to give Sy the good news that she might have a sale on the house.

His reaction was exactly what she had expected. "You made it clear that I'm not budging five cents off the price, didn't you, Rebecca?" he asked.

"Of course that's what I told him," she replied, silently adding, you old skinflint.

# 50

Detective Wally Johnson looked at the tattered postcard Toby Grissom had handed him. "Why do you think your daughter didn't write this card?" he asked.

"I don't say she didn't write it. Like I told you, I've started to think that because it was printed, maybe she didn't, maybe somebody did something to her and then tried to make it look like she's still alive. Now, Glory has big, fancy handwriting, with lots of loops, if you know what I mean, and that's why it didn't occur to me till now that maybe she hadn't sent this card at all."

"You said you received this six months ago," Johnson said.

"Yeah. That's right. And you never asked, but I thought maybe you should check it for fingerprints."

"How many people have handled this card, Mr. Grissom?"

"Handled it? I don't know. I showed it to some of my friends in Texas, and I showed it to the girls Glory used to room with here in New York."

"Mr. Grissom, of course we'll check it for fingerprints, but I can tell you right now that whether your daughter sent it or somebody else did, we'll never be able to get prints off it. Think about it. You've shown it around to your friends and to Glory's roommates. Before that a number of postal clerks and your mailman handled it. Too many people have touched that card."

Toby spotted Glory's photo montage on the corner of Johnson's desk. He pointed to it. "Something happened to my girl," he said. "I know it." Then in a voice tinged with sarcasm, he asked, "Have you called that Bartley Longe, that guy who was taking her up to his country house, yet?"

"I had some other pressing assignments last night. Mr. Grissom, I assure you it is my top priority to talk with him."

"Don't assure me anything, Detective Johnson," Toby told him. "I'm going nowhere until you pick up that phone and make an appointment with Bartley Longe. If I have to miss my plane, that's okay with me. Because I intend to sit here until you've seen that guy. If you want to arrest me, that's okay, too. You just got to get it straight. I won't leave this police station until you're on your way to see Longe, and don't go there with your hat in your hand apologizing for the visit, saying her father is a pest. Go there hard-nosed and get some of the names of the other theatre people who that jerk claims he introduced Glory to, and find out from them if they ever met her."

This poor guy, Wally Johnson thought. I don't have the guts to break his heart and tell him that his daughter is probably a high-priced hooker by now who's with some fat-cat boyfriend. Instead, Johnson picked up the phone and asked information for the phone number of Bartley Longe. When the receptionist answered, he introduced himself. "Is Mr. Longe there?" he asked. "It's very important that I speak with him immediately."

"I'm not sure if he's still in his office," the receptionist began.

If she's not sure if he's in his office, that means that he *is* in his office, Johnson thought. He waited and a moment later the receptionist was back on the phone.

"I'm afraid he's already left, but I'll be happy to take a message," she said, soothingly.

"I'm afraid I'm not planning to leave a message," Johnson answered firmly. "You and I both know that Bartley Longe is there. I can be there in twenty minutes. It is absolutely essential that I see him now. Brittany La Monte's father is sitting at my desk and he needs some answers about her disappearance."

"If you'll just hold . . ." After a brief pause the receptionist said, "If you can come right over, Mr. Longe will wait for you."

"That will be fine." Johnson hung up the phone then looked compassionately at Toby Grissom, taking in the exhaustion in the elderly man's eyes and the deep creases in his face. "Mr. Grissom, I could be gone as long as a few hours. Why don't you go out and get something to eat, then come back here? What time did you say your plane was?"

"Five o'clock."

"It's just a little after twelve now. I could get one of our guys to run you out to LaGuardia after I report back to you. I'm going to speak to Longe, and then, as you suggest, get a list of the people he claims met her at his home. But you staying in New York doesn't make sense at all. You told me that you're supposed to be having chemo treatments. You shouldn't skip them. You know you shouldn't."

Toby suddenly felt as though all the starch were going out of him. The long walk in the cold had taken its toll even though he had enjoyed it. And he was hungry. "I guess you're right," he said. "There's got to be a McDonald's near here." With a humorless smile, he added, "Maybe I'll treat myself to a Big Mac."

"That's a good idea," Wally Johnson agreed, as he got up and reached for the photo of Glory that he had kept on his desk.

"You don't need to bring that," Grissom said angrily. "That guy knows just what Glory looks like. Trust me, he does."

Wally Johnson nodded. "You're right. But I'll take it with me when I talk to the people who met Glory at Bartley Longe's home."

# 51

I'm leaving for an hour or so," Kevin Wilson told Louise Kirk, and did not respond to the obvious curiosity in her expression by explaining where he was going. He knew that after his sharp response to her remarks about Zan Moreland she would not have the nerve to question him. He also knew that later, if he gave her a receipt for a luncheon, she would look it over carefully to see if he had marked a client's name on it or if he had charged it on his personal card.

There had been two more deliveries this morning. One contained rolls of wall coverings, the other boxes of table lamps.

Louise did manage to get in one more question. "Do you want any other deliveries from Zan Moreland's order to be put in the largest apartment? I mean, I could see that some of them were meant for the middle one."

"Keep it all together," Kevin said as he reached for his windbreaker.

Louise hesitated, then said, "Kevin, I know I'm overstepping myself, but I'll bet the ranch that you're on your way to Zan Moreland's office. As your friend, I beg you, don't let yourself get caught up in anything to do with that girl. I mean, she's very attractive, anyone with two eyes can see that, but I think she's mentally ill. When she went into the police station this morning, she told the reporters that her son was alive. If she knows that, she knows where he is, and she's been putting on a big act for nearly two years. On the Internet, they have links to some of the video that the media posted that day after the child was reported missing in Central Park. They show her in the park by the empty stroller. You can tell she's the same woman as in the photos that tourist took."

Louise paused for breath.

"Anything else?" Kevin asked evenly.

Louise shrugged. "I know you're mad at me, and I don't blame you. But as your friend as well as your secretary, I hate to see you get hurt. And any kind of involvement with her will hurt you profession-ally as well as personally."

"Louise, I'm not getting involved. I'll tell you where I'm going. It's to Alexandra Moreland's office. I spoke to her assistant, who sounds like a nice guy. I'd like to settle all this with as little fanfare as possible. Quite frankly, I don't like Bartley Longe. You heard him when he called. He's like the cat who ate the canary, just assuming that I wouldn't dream of having anything to do with Zan Moreland now."

Kevin's hand was on the door, but then he turned and added, "I've studied and compared both of their proposals, and I like hers much more. As Zan pointed out, Bartley Longe doesn't provide a homelike quality to his designs. He's too damn grandiose. That doesn't mean I'll hire Moreland, by the way. But it does mean that I might accept her proposal, use her materials, make some sort of financial deal with her for all the work she's done, and get someone else to execute it. Does that make sense to you?"

Louise Kirk could not resist a parting shot. "It makes sense, but is it sensible?"

Josh had braced himself for the meeting with Kevin Wilson. He had his story straight. He and Zan believed that a hacker had gotten into their computer, and they were having it checked. As soon as they could validate that a hacker had made the orders, they could insist that the vendors who had delivered any goods pick them up immediately.

That will only buy us a little time, he thought. There's no hacker. Zan ordered that stuff from her laptop. Who else would know exactly what to order?

She must have written that letter on her laptop, too.

The phone rang. It was the desk saying that Mr. Kevin Wilson was there and was it all right to send him up?

Kevin did not know what to expect, but he was not prepared to find Moreland Interiors to be headquartered in a relatively small office that was packed with rolls of carpet piled almost to the ceiling and covering half the floor space. He noticed that the furniture had obviously been pushed as far as possible toward the opposite wall to make room for all of it. Nor did he expect Josh Green to be so young. Not more than his midtwenties, Kevin thought, as he extended his hand to Josh and introduced himself.

Recognizing the supplier's name stamped on the heavy paper covering the carpet, he asked, "Is all that stuff intended for my model apartments as well?"

"Mr. Wilson," Josh began.

"No need for formalities. It's Kevin."

"All right, Kevin. This is what happened. A hacker must have gotten into our computer and placed those orders. That's the only explanation I can offer."

"Do you know that we've had three deliveries so far this morning to 701 Carlton Place?" Kevin asked. Then, seeing the stunned expression on the young man's face, he said, "I gather you *didn't* know that?"

"No, I didn't."

"Josh, I know Zan went into the police station with her lawyer this morning. Do you expect her back soon?"

"I don't know," Josh said, making no effort to hide the concern in his voice.

"How long have you been working with her?" Kevin asked.

"Almost two years."

"I chose her to submit a plan for my model apartments based on the fact that I was a guest in a home in Darien, Connecticut, and in an apartment on Fifth Avenue, two separate jobs that she had just finished decorating six months ago."

"That would be the Campion home and the Lyons apartment."

"Did you actively work on those jobs?" Kevin asked.

Where is this going? Josh asked himself. "Yes, I did. Of course, Zan is the designer and I'm her assistant. Since we were doing both jobs at the same time, we alternated covering the day-by-day activity of each project."

"I see." I like this guy, Kevin thought. He's a straight shooter. Whatever Zan Moreland's problems, she designed exactly what's right for those apartments. I don't want to deal with Bartley Longe and I don't like his designs as much. And I can't start inviting other designers to submit plans. The board is already screaming about the delays in having the model apartments completed.

The door opened behind him. He turned to see Zan Moreland come into the office, with some older man who he guessed would be her lawyer. Zan was biting her lip trying to hold back the sobs that were racking her shoulders. Her eyes were swollen from crying and tears were streaming down her cheeks.

Kevin knew he had no business there. He looked at Josh. "I'll call Starr Carpeting," he said, "and tell them to pick up all this stuff and deliver it to Carlton Place. If any more deliveries like this come in, don't accept them. Send them to Carlton Place as well as all the invoices. I'll be in touch."

Zan had turned her back to him. He knew she was embarrassed for him to see her weeping. He left without speaking to her, but as he waited for the elevator he knew that, more than anything, he wanted to go back and put his arms around Zan.

Sense and sensible, he thought wryly, as the elevator door opened and he stepped into it. Wait till I tell Louise what I've done.

# 52

Melissa had listened with mounting fury to Ted's message suggesting that instead of putting up a five-million-dollar reward for information leading to Matthew's return, she make it a five-million-dollar donation to the Foundation for Missing Children.

"Can he be serious?" she asked Bettina, her personal assistant.

Bettina, a savvy, sleek forty-year-old with a cap of gleaming black hair, had come to New York from Vermont at age twenty, hoping for a career as a rock singer. It hadn't taken her long to realize that her reasonably good voice would go nowhere in the music world and instead she had become the personal assistant to a gossip columnist. Melissa had noticed Bettina's efficiency and offered her more money to work for her. Bettina promptly dumped the columnist who, as she aged, had come to count on her.

Now Bettina's emotions ranged between sharing Ted's loathing of Melissa and loving the excitement of being part of a major celebrity's life. And when Melissa was in a good mood, she would grab an extra one of the expensive gift bags that were meant only for the stars at a concert or awards show for Bettina, while she was getting one for herself.

The minute Bettina walked into Melissa's apartment at nine o'clock that morning, she had known it would be a long day. Melissa had immediately sprung on her the notion of offering the reward for

Matthew's safe return. "You notice I say 'safe return,' " Melissa said. "Almost everybody believes that little kid is dead, so I'll get some nice publicity and it won't cost me a nickel."

Ted's negative response had infuriated Melissa. Then, when he left the suggestion that she donate the money to a foundation instead, she was livid. "He wants me to give five million dollars to a foundation. Is he crazy?" she asked Bettina.

Bettina liked Ted. She knew how hard he worked promoting Melissa. "I don't think he's crazy," she said, soothingly. "It certainly would make you seem very, very generous, which of course you would be, but you'd need to write the check in front of the cameras."

"Which I don't intend to do," Melissa snapped, pushing back the blond hair that hung almost to her waist.

"Melissa, I'm here to do anything you want. You know that," Bettina said. "But Ted is right. Ever since you and he became an item, you let everyone know that you think his son was abducted and killed by a child molester. To offer a reward for information leading to his safe return now would be begging for nasty comments on the late-night shows and the Internet."

"Bettina, I intend to make that offer. Call a press conference for one o'clock tomorrow. I know exactly how I'll word it. I'll say that while I have always felt that Matthew is not alive, that uncertainty is destroying Matthew's father, my fiancé, Ted Carpenter. This offer may make someone come forward, maybe someone whose relative or friend is raising Matthew as her own child."

"And if someone does come forward, you're prepared to write him or her a check for five million dollars, Melissa?" Bettina asked.

"Don't be silly. First of all, that poor kid is probably dead. Second, if someone really knew where he is and hasn't come forward all this time, that person is considered an accomplice of some kind and therefore cannot profit from the crime. Got it? Everybody thinks I'm some kind of airhead, but we'll get hundreds of tips from all over the world, and every one of them will be mentioning Melissa Knight's promised reward."

They were in the living room of Melissa's penthouse apartment on Central Park West. Before answering Melissa, Bettina walked over to the window and looked down at the park. It all began there, she thought. One sunny afternoon in June nearly two years ago. But Melissa is right. That little boy is probably dead. She'll get her free publicity and it won't cost her a dime.

# 53

Well, we rattled Moreland's cage," Billy Collins observed with satisfaction as he and Jennifer Dean munched on hot pastrami sandwiches and coffee at their favorite delicatessen on Columbus Avenue.

Detective Dean finished the last bite of the first half of her sandwich before she answered. "What scares me is that this case is almost too perfect. Do you believe that Moreland meant she had heard her son's voice in a kind of dream, or do you think she was actually talking to him on the phone?"

"Whether she was on the phone or dreaming, she said that boy is alive and I believe he's alive," Billy Collins said positively. "The question is where is he, and will whoever is holding him panic with all the publicity about the case now? I'm getting another cup of coffee. Want one?"

"No, I've had enough caffeine today. Why don't I try Alvirah Meehan again and see if she's back yet? Her husband said that she should be finished at the hairdresser by now."

Alvirah answered the phone herself. "Come over, if you want, but I don't know how I can help you," she said cautiously. "My husband and I have been good friends of Zan ever since she decorated our apartment about a year and a half ago. That was after her son disappeared. She's a wonderful young woman and we love her."

"Why don't we just come anyhow? You're practically around the corner," Jennifer Dean said, as Billy returned with his second cup of coffee.

Ten minutes later they were parking in the semicircular driveway at 211 Central Park South. It was wide enough so that other vehicles could pass, and when Tony the doorman saw Billy put his police department ID face up inside the windshield, he made no objection to leaving the car there. "Mrs. Meehan said you should go right up when you get here," he told them. "It's apartment 16B."

"You do realize that some of our guys know Alvirah Meehan?" Jennifer asked Billy as they rode up in the elevator. "She's the cleaning woman who won big in the lottery and became an amateur sleuth, and has even written a memoir about it."

"Just what we don't need is an amateur sleuth involved with the case," Billy commented as the elevator stopped at the sixteenth floor. But after two minutes of being in Alvirah and Willy's home, like everyone else who had ever met them, he felt as if they'd been friends forever.

Willy Meehan reminded Billy of the pictures of his grandfather, a big man with snow white hair who had worked all his life as a cop. Alvirah, her hair freshly set, was wearing slacks and a cardigan sweater. Billy knew her clothes had not come out of a bargain basement, but still Alvirah's outfit reminded him of the housekeeper for the people down the block who had some money.

He was surprised when Jennifer accepted the coffee Alvirah offered. It was not something they usually did, but he suspected that it would not be wise to make an enemy of Alvirah, who had already established on the phone that she was Zan Moreland's good friend. And probably her defender, he thought.

I was right about that one, Billy said to himself a few minutes later as Alvirah emphasized the heartbreak she believed that Zan had been suffering since her son disappeared. "I've known all kinds,"

Alvirah said emphatically, "and there are some things you can't fake. The suffering I've seen in that girl's eyes has made me want to cry."

"Did she talk about Matthew very often?" Jennifer Dean asked, softly.

"Let's put it this way, we never brought it up. I'm a contributing columnist for the *New York Globe* and at the time Matthew disappeared, I wrote a column begging whoever took him to understand the agony his parents were going through. I suggested that that person bring Matthew to a mall, and point out a security guard. Then tell the boy to close his eyes, count up to ten, then go up to the guard and tell him his name and the guard would find Mommy for him."

"Matthew was only a little past three when he disappeared," Billy objected. "Not every child that age can count up to ten."

"I had read in the paper that his mother had said that hide-and-seek was the favorite game they played together. In fact, one of the times that Zan did talk about Matthew, she said that when she got the call that he was missing, she was praying that he had woken up and gotten out of the stroller himself and maybe thought he was playing hide-and-seek with Tiffany." Alvirah paused, then added, "She told me that Matthew could count up to fifty. He was obviously a very bright child."

"Did you see the photos of Zan Moreland taking Matthew out of the stroller on television or in the papers today, Mrs. Meehan?" Jennifer Dean asked.

"I saw the photos of a woman who looked like Zan taking the child out of the stroller," Alvirah said carefully.

"Do you think that was Zan Moreland in those pictures, Mrs. Meehan?" Billy Collins asked.

"I wish you'd call me Alvirah. Everyone else does."

She's stalling for time, Collins thought.

"Let me put it this way," Alvirah began. "It certainly looks as though the woman in those pictures is Zan. I don't know nearly enough about technology because it's going so fast these days. Maybe those pictures were altered. I do know that Zan Moreland is torn in two with missing her son. She was here last night and she was a basket case she was so upset. I know she has friends both here and abroad who invited her to visit them over the holidays. She stayed home by herself. She couldn't bear to go out."

"Do you know what other countries her friends live in?" Jennifer Dean asked, quickly.

"Well, they're from the countries where her parents lived," Alvirah said. "I know one of them is Argentina. Another one is in France."

"And remember her parents were living in Italy when they were killed in that accident," Willy chimed in.

Billy Collins knew that there was nothing more they could learn from Alvirah or Willy. They believe those pictures are of Zan Moreland, he thought as he got up to go, but they won't admit it.

"Detective Collins," Alvirah said, "before you leave, you must understand that if those photos really are Zan taking Matthew out of the stroller, she doesn't know that she did it. I would swear to that."

"Are you suggesting that she may be a split personality?" Collins asked.

"I'm not sure what I'm suggesting," Alvirah said. "But I do know that Zan is not acting. In her mind she has lost her child. I know she's spent money on private detectives and on psychics to try to find him. If she was playing a game, she wouldn't have had to go that far, but she isn't playing a game."

"One more question, Mrs. Meehan—uh, Alvirah. Zan Moreland mentioned a priest, Fr. Aiden O'Brien. By any chance do you know him?"

"Oh, yes, he's a dear friend. He's a Franciscan friar at St. Francis of Assisi Church on Thirty-first Street. Zan happened to meet him here last night. She was just about ready to leave when he came in.

He told her that he'd pray for her and I think that gave her some comfort."

"She had never met him before that?"

"I don't think so. Although I *do* know she stopped into St. Francis just before I was there on Monday evening to light a candle. Fr. O'Brien was hearing confessions that evening in the lower church."

"Did Zan Moreland go to confession?" Billy asked.

"Oh, I don't know, and of course I didn't ask. But you might be interested to hear that I had my eye on some guy who I thought was acting funny. I mean he was kneeling in front of the Shrine of St. Anthony with his hands in his face. But the minute Fr. Aiden stepped out of the Reconciliation Room, he jumped up and didn't take his eyes off Aiden until he was out of sight in the Friary."

"Was Ms. Moreland still in church when this happened?"

"No," Alvirah said, positively. "I only know she was there because yesterday morning I went back and asked to have a look at the tape on the security cameras. I wanted to see if I could spot that guy just in case he ever caused any trouble. I couldn't pick him out in the crowd, but on the camera I did see Zan coming in. That would be about fifteen minutes before I got there. The security tapes showed that she only stayed a few minutes. The guy I was trying to get a look at left just before I did, but there was no way to pick him clearly out of the crowd that was coming into the church."

"Did you think that was unusual for Ms. Moreland to pay a visit there?"

"No. The next day was Matthew's birthday. I thought she might have wanted to light a candle to St. Anthony for him. He's the saint people pray to when they're missing something."

"I see. Thank you both very much for your time," Billy Collins said as he and Jennifer Dean got up to leave.

"Well, that didn't get us very far," Dean commented as they went down in the elevator.

"Maybe, maybe not. What we did find out is that Zan Moreland has friends in a number of countries. I want to see if she's made any trips to any one of those countries since her son disappeared. We'll get a subpoena and check her credit cards and bank accounts. And tomorrow we'll go down and pay a visit to Fr. O'Brien at St. Francis of Assisi. Wouldn't it be interesting if Zan Moreland went to confession to that priest? And if she did, I wonder what she had to say to him."

"Billy, you're *Catholic*," Jennifer Dean protested. "I'm not, but I know that no priest will ever discuss what was said in the confessional."

"No, he won't, but when we question Zan Moreland again, maybe if we work her hard enough, she'll break down and share her dirty little secrets with us."

# 54

Matthew had never seen Glory cry, not even once. She had sounded real mad when she was talking on the phone, but after she slammed it down, she started to cry. Just like that. Then she looked at him and said, "Matty, we can't hide like this any longer."

He thought that meant that they'd be moving to a new place to live, and he wasn't sure if he was glad or sorry. The room he slept in was big enough so that he could put all his trucks on the floor and move them one after the other just like he would see big trucks on the road at night when he and Glory moved to a new house.

And there was a bunk bed and a table and chairs in that room that had been there when they moved in. Glory had told him that some other kids must have lived there because the table and chairs were just right for a kid his size to sit down and draw pictures.

Matthew loved to draw. Sometimes he would think about Mommy and draw a lady's face on the paper. He never could get it to look just like her, but he always remembered her long hair and how it felt when it tickled his cheek, so he would always give the lady in his pictures long hair.

Sometimes he would take the bar of soap that smelled like Mommy from under the pillow and have it next to his hand on the table before he opened his box of crayons.

Maybe the next place they moved wouldn't be as nice. He didn't mind being locked in the big closet in this house when Glory left him alone. She always left the light on, and it was big enough for his trucks, and she always saved some new books for him to read until she got back.

Now Glory looked mad again. She said, "I wouldn't put it past that old bag to make some excuse to come barging in here before Sunday. I've gotta remember to keep the bolt on the front door."

Matthew didn't know what to say. Glory wiped her face with the back of her hand. "Well, we just move up the schedule. I'll let him know that tonight." She walked over to the window. She always kept the shades down all the way and if she looked out, she did it by pushing the shade to one side.

She made a funny sound as if she couldn't get her breath, then said, "That damn muffin jerk is driving by again. What's she looking for?" Then she added, "You got her started, Matty. Go upstairs and stay in your room and make sure none of your trucks are ever downstairs again."

Matthew went up to his room, sat down at the table, reached for his crayons, and began to cry.

# 55

Bartley Longe sat behind closed doors in his Park Avenue office, trying to talk himself into indignation at the rudeness of the detective who had, in effect, ordered him to put off any appointments he might have until they met.

But he could not conceal, even from himself, that he was frightened. Brittany's father had kept his threat to go to the police. He couldn't have them digging into his background again. That sexual harassment suit the receptionist had filed against him eight years ago hadn't looked good in the newspapers.

The fact that he had been forced to settle for a lot of money had hurt him, financially and professionally. The receptionist had alleged that he'd become outraged when she rejected his advances and had slammed her against the wall, and that she had been in fear of her life. "His face had darkened with anger," she had said to the cops. "He can't stand rejection. I thought he would kill me."

How was that going to sit with this cop when he does some digging into my background? Longe asked himself. Should I bring it up right away so that I seem straightforward? Brittany's been missing nearly two years. The only way they'll believe that I didn't do something to her is if she turns up in Texas and visits her Daddy very, very soon.

Something else. Why hadn't Kevin Wilson taken his call this morning? Surely he, or someone in his office, had seen Zan going into the station house with her lawyer. Surely Wilson had to be figuring that she'd probably be arrested, and if she was, how much time would she be able to put into his model apartments?

I *need* that job, Bartley Longe admitted. It's a showcase for whoever gets it. Sure, I get enough business from the celebrities, but an awful lot of them drive a hard bargain. They say they'll get a magazine to do a photo layout of their new homes, and that it would be free advertising for me. I don't need that kind of free advertising.

I lost some of my big-money/old-money customers after that lousy publicity. If I'm involved in another scandal, I'll lose more of them.

Why doesn't Wilson call me back? In his letter when he asked me to bid for the job, he said it was of the utmost importance that I submit my plans as soon as possible because they were already behind schedule. But now, not a word from him.

The intercom on his telephone buzzed. "Mr. Longe, are you planning to go out after your meeting with Detective Johnson, or do you want me to send for something after he leaves?" Elaine asked.

"I don't know," Longe snapped. "I'll decide after I see him."

"Of course. Oh, Phyllis is calling. That means he must be here now."

"Send him in."

Nervously, Bartley Longe opened the top drawer in his desk and looked at the mirror he kept there. The small job that had been done on his face last year had been terrific, he comforted himself. It wasn't obvious, but it got rid of the suggestion of a jowl that had begun to form below his chin. Having the touch of silver in his hair was exactly the right way to go as well. He had worked carefully on his distinguished exterior. He tugged at the sleeves of his Paul Stuart shirt so that the monogrammed cuff links were in place.

Then as Elaine Ryan tapped on the door and opened it with Detective Wally Johnson in tow, Bartley Longe stood up and, with a courtly smile, welcomed his unwelcome guest.

# 56

The minute Wally Johnson entered Longe's office, he took an instant dislike to the man. Longe's condescending smile reeked of superiority and disdain. His opening statement was that he was delaying a meeting with a very important client and hoped that whatever questions Detective Johnson had for him would not take more than fifteen minutes to complete.

"I hope not, either," Johnson answered, "so let's get right to the purpose of my visit. Margaret Grissom, whose stage name is Brittany La Monte, is missing. Her father is sure that something has happened to her or that she is in trouble. Her last known job was working for you as a hostess in your model apartments, and it is also known that she was having an intimate relationship with you and spent many weekends at your home in Litchfield."

"She spent some weekends at my home in Litchfield because I was doing her a favor, introducing her to theatre people," Longe contradicted. "As I told her father yesterday, none of them thought Brittany had that certain something, that almost indescribable spark that would make her a star. They all predicted that at best she would be doing low-budget commercials or independent films where she would not need a SAG or Equity card. In her ten or eleven years in New York, she had never managed to achieve either."

"On that basis, you stopped inviting her to Litchfield?" Johnson asked.

"Brittany was beginning to see the big picture. At that point, she tried to turn our casual relationship into wedding bells. I have been married once to an aspiring actress and it cost me plenty. I have no intention of making that same mistake twice."

"You told her that. How did she accept it?" Johnson asked.

"She made some very uncomplimentary remarks to me and stormed out."

"Of your Litchfield home?"

"Yes. I might add that she took my Mercedes convertible with her. I would have filed charges, but I did receive a phone call from her telling me that she had parked it in the garage in my apartment building."

Johnson watched as Bartley Longe's face darkened with anger. "Exactly when was that, Mr. Longe?" he asked.

"Early June, so that would make it nearly two years ago?"

"Can you give me a more definite date?"

"It was the first weekend in June and she left late Sunday morning."

"I see. Where is your apartment, Mr. Longe?"

"It is at 10 Central Park West."

"Were you living there two years ago?"

"It has been my New York residence for eight years."

"I see. And after that Sunday in early June nearly two years ago, have you ever seen or heard from Ms. La Monte again?"

"No, I have not. Nor did I care to either hear from or see her."

Wally Johnson let a long minute pass before he spoke again. This guy is scared to death, he thought. He's lying and he knows that I'm not going to stop looking for Brittany. Johnson also knew that he wouldn't get more from Longe today.

"Mr. Longe, I'd like to have a list of the guests who would also have been at your home on the weekends that Brittany La Monte was there."

"Of course. You must understand that I entertain frequently in

Litchfield. Being a good host to the wealthy and to celebrities opens the door to many of them becoming very good clients. It is quite possible I will miss some names," Longe said.

"I can understand that, but I would suggest you dig deep into your memory and give me a list by tomorrow morning at the latest. You have my card with my e-mail on it," Johnson said as he rose to leave.

Longe stayed behind his desk, not even rising from his chair. Johnson deliberately walked over to the desk and reached out his hand, giving the designer no choice but to accept it.

As the detective suspected, Bartley Longe's finely manicured hand was wringing wet.

On the way back to the precinct, Wally Johnson decided to make a detour and drive to the garage at 10 Central Park West. He got out of the car there and showed his badge to the attendant who was approaching him, a handsome young African-American. "No parking today," he said. "I just want to ask a few questions." He glanced at the nameplate the young man was wearing. "How long have you worked here, Danny?"

"Eight years, sir, since the doors opened," Danny answered proudly.

Johnson was surprised. "I didn't take you for more than your early twenties."

"Thanks. A lot of people say that." With a smile, Danny added, "It's a mixed blessing. I'm thirty-one, sir."

"Then of course you know Mr. Bartley Longe?"

Johnson was not surprised to see the change in Danny's formerly pleasant expression as he confirmed that he knew Mr. Longe.

"Did you ever know a young woman who was a friend of his, Brittany La Monte?" Johnson asked.

"Mr. Longe has many young women who are his friends," Danny answered, hesitantly. "Different ones come in with him all the time."

"Danny, I have a feeling you remember Brittany La Monte."

"Yes, sir. I haven't seen her in a while, but that's not surprising."

"Why is that?" Johnson asked.

"Well, sir, the last time she came here, she was in Mr. Longe's convertible. I could tell she was mad as hell." Danny's lips twitched. "She had Mr. Longe's toupees and wigs with her. She had cut patches of hair out of all six of them. While we stood there, she Scotch-taped them over the wheel and the dashboard and the hood so no one could miss them. There was hair all over the front seat. Then she said, 'See you guys,' and marched off."

"What happened then?"

"The next day, Mr. Longe came in boiling mad. The manager had put his wigs and toupees in a bag for him. Mr. Longe had a baseball cap on and we guessed that Miss La Monte had rounded up his whole collection. Between us, sir, Mr. Longe isn't very well liked in this garage, so we all got a good laugh out of it."

"I'll bet you did," Wally Johnson agreed. "He looks like the kind who stiffs you at Christmas."

"Forget Christmas, sir. He never heard of it. But his tip when he picks up his car is one dollar, if you're lucky." Danny's expression became concerned. "I shouldn't have said that, sir. I hope you won't repeat it to Mr. Longe. I could lose my job."

"Danny, you don't have to worry about that. You've been an immense help to me." Wally Johnson began to get back in his car.

Danny held the door for him. "Is Miss La Monte okay, sir?" he asked anxiously. "She was always really nice to us when she came in with Mr. Longe."

"I hope she is okay, Danny. Thanks a lot."

                    *        *        *

Toby Grissom was sitting at Johnson's desk when he got back to the precinct.

"Did you have that Big Mac, Mr. Grissom?" Johnson asked.

"Yes, I did. What did you find out from that big phony about Glory?"

"I found out that your daughter and Mr. Longe had a blowup and she drove his convertible to his apartment here in the city and left it parked there. He claims that he never saw her again. The young man in the garage confirmed that she never came after that, at least not to the garage."

"What does that tell you?" Grissom asked.

"It tells me that they broke up for good. As I mentioned to you before, I'm going to get a list of as many of the other weekend guests as we can locate and see if any of them has heard from Brittany, or, as you call her, Glory. I'm also going to visit her roommates and find out exactly when she left that apartment. I promise you, Mr. Grissom, that I am going to follow this through to the end. And now, please, let me get you a ride to the airport and promise me that you'll be in your doctor's office tomorrow morning. As soon as you're on your way, I'm going to call your daughter's roommates and make an appointment to see them."

Leaning on the sides of the chair for support, Toby Grissom stood up. "I've got a feeling I'll never see my girl again before I die. I'm going to trust you to keep your promise to me, Detective. I'll see the doctor tomorrow."

They shook hands. With an attempt at a smile, Toby Grissom said, "All right. Let's find my police escort to the airport. If I ask real nice, do you think he'll turn the sirens on for me?"

# 57

On Thursday afternoon, after her breakdown in her office, Zan let Josh take her home. Emotionally exhausted, she went straight to bed, allowing herself a rare sleeping pill. On Friday morning, feeling heavy and drugged, she stayed in bed, arriving at the office at noon.

"I thought I could handle it, Josh," she said, as they sat at the desk and ate the turkey sandwiches he had ordered from the local delicatessen. Josh had brewed coffee in the coffeemaker, making it extra strong, as she had requested. She reached for her cup and sipped from it, savoring the flavor. "It's a lot better than what Detective Collins served at the station house," she said wryly.

Then, seeing how concerned Josh was, she said, "Look, I know I fell apart yesterday, but I'll be all right. I've got to be. Charley warned me not to talk to the media, and now I'm sure they're twisting what I said about Matthew being alive just the way those detectives did when they questioned me. Maybe next time I'll listen to him."

"Zan, I feel so useless. I just wish I could help you," Josh said, trying to keep the emotion out of his voice. But there were still some questions he needed to ask, too. "Zan, do you think we should report the airplane ticket to Buenos Aires that was charged to your credit card? And the clothes at Bergdorf's and all the stuff that was ordered as if we got the job for the Carlton Place apartments?"

"And the fact that my bank account has been virtually cleaned out?" Zan asked. Then she added, "Because you don't believe that I didn't order any of it, or have any part in those transactions, do you? I *know* that. And I know Alvirah and Willy and Charley Shore all believe that I'm mentally ill, and that's putting it kindly."

She did not give Josh a chance to answer. "You see, Josh, I don't blame you a bit. I don't blame Ted for what he's saying about me, I don't even blame Tiffany who, I just learned from the detectives, thinks that I sedated her so that she would fall into a drugged sleep on a blanket in Central Park, and I could take my own child to that damn town house and leave him tied up and gagged in the storeroom—unless, of course, I'd already murdered him."

"Zan, I love you. Alvirah and Willy love you. And Charley Shore wants to protect you," Josh said, feebly.

"The saddest part is that I know all that is true. You, Alvirah, and Willy love me. Charley Shore wants to protect me. But none of you believe that someone who *looks* like me has taken my child, and that person, or whoever hired her, is trying to destroy my business as well.

"To answer your question, I don't think we should give these detectives any more so-called evidence that I'm a mental case to help them when they continue their inquisition."

Josh looked as if he wished he could deny what she had told him, but Zan could see that he was honest enough not to try. Instead she waited until she had finished her coffee, silently handed him the cup to refill, and then waited until he came back before she spoke. "I was obviously in no state to talk to Kevin Wilson when I got back here yesterday, but I heard what he said to you. Do you think he really means it, that he'll take on the obligation of paying our suppliers?"

"Yes, I do," Josh answered, relieved to get onto a safer subject.

"That's more than decent of him," Zan said. "I can't imagine what the media would have made of it, if he'd said in public that he had never okayed any of the designs I had submitted. In all, the orders amount to tens of thousands of dollars. He wanted top-of-the-line and we gave him top-of-the-line."

"Kevin said he liked our—I mean *your*—plans better than Bartley Longe's," Josh told her.

"*Our* plans," Zan emphasized. "Josh, you're gifted. You know that. You're like me nine years ago when I started working for Bartley Longe. You had a lot of input when I was discussing those model apartments with you."

She picked up the second half of her sandwich, then put it down. "Josh, you know what I think is going to happen? I may be arrested for kidnapping Matthew. I believe in my heart he is alive, but if I am wrong I can assure you that the state of New York won't have to prosecute me for his murder to put me in prison. Because if Matthew is dead, my life will be a prison anyway."

# 58

O n Friday morning, the first thing to hit Ted as he walked into the office was bad news. Rita Moran was waiting for him, her expression tight with anger and frustration. "Ted, Melissa is calling in the media to her apartment to announce she is offering five million dollars for Matthew's safe return. Her assistant phoned to tip us off. She didn't want you to be blindsided. Bettina *did* say Melissa is making it clear she believes Matthew is dead, but said that the uncertainty is killing you."

Sarcastically Rita added, "She did it for you, Ted."

"Good God," Ted shouted. "I told her, I begged her, I implored her . . ."

"I know," Rita said. "But, Ted, keep something in mind. You can't afford to lose Melissa Knight as a client. We just got a new estimate for repairing the plumbing in this building, and let me tell you, it's a horror. Melissa and the friends she's already brought in are keeping your head above water and if Jaime-boy does come through, we've got breathing space. I suggest you discount this white elephant of a building until you find a buyer, take the business loss, and concentrate on getting more clients like Melissa. Only be sure you don't get that lady mad at you. You can't afford it."

"I know I can't. Thanks, Rita."

"I'm sorry, Ted, I know how much you have on your shoulders.

But remember, we still have some terrific singers and actors and bands, who, when their big break comes, won't forget how much you've done for their careers. So I suggest you call the witch when she's finished offering her five million dollars and tell her how grateful you are and how much you love her."

# 59

On Friday Penny Hammel drove past the Owens farmhouse slowly enough that she noticed the movement of the shade in the front window. That woman must have been right there and heard my van rattling down this bumpy road, she thought. What's Gloria Evans got to hide in there? Why is every shade pulled down to the sill?

Sure that she was still being watched, Penny deliberately made a U-turn instead of going as far as the dead end. In case the mystery woman has any doubts, let her know that I've got my eye on her, she thought. What's she doing in there anyhow? It's a gorgeous day, wouldn't you think she'd want to be able to see it? And she claims she's writing a book! I bet most writers don't sit at the computer in the dark when the sun could be pouring in the window!

Penny had made the detour impulsively while she was on her way into town. She wanted to pick up a few groceries and she also wanted to get out of Bernie's way. He was in one of his Mr. Fixit moods, puttering around in his workshop in the basement. The only problem was that every time he finished a job like replacing the handle of a pot or gluing together the broken lid of the sugar bowl, he would yell for her to come down and see what a great job he'd done.

I guess being alone in the truck so much of the time, he likes to have someone hear the sound of his voice, Penny mused as she turned onto Middletown Avenue. She hadn't intended to drop in on Rebecca, but when she found a parking spot it was practically in front of Schwartz Real Estate and she could see her sitting at the desk.

Why not? she decided as with quick steps she walked across the sidewalk and turned the handle on the door of the agency. "*Bonjour, Madame Schwartz*," she boomed in her best imitation of a French accent. "I am here to buy that beeg, ugly McMansion on Turtle Avenue that has been on the market for two years. I wish to tear it down because it is an eyesore. I am carrying four million Euros in the trunk of my limousine. Do we have what you Americans call a deal?"

Rebecca laughed. "Very funny, but let me tell you something that is nothing short of a miracle. I have a buyer for Sy's place."

"What about the tenant?" Penny demanded.

"She has to be out within thirty days."

Penny realized that she felt a twinge of disappointment and that she actually had been having fun building up a mystery surrounding Gloria Evans. "Have you told Evans that?" she asked.

"I did, and she is one unhappy lady. She hung up the phone on me. I told her I could show her at least five or six places that would be much more attractive and that she could use on a month-to-month basis so that she isn't stuck with a year's lease."

"And she hung up on you anyway?" Penny dropped into the chair nearest to Rebecca's desk.

"Yes. She was really upset."

"Rebecca, I just drove past Sy's place. Have you been inside since she moved in?"

"No. Remember, I told you that I drove by early the morning after she was supposed to arrive and saw her car in the carport, but I haven't been inside."

"Well, maybe you should make an excuse to go in. Maybe you

can knock on her door and apologize to her about the inconvenience of the sudden sale and tell her you're sorry she's so upset. If she doesn't have the courtesy to invite you to come in, I'd say that it's proof positive something is going on."

Warmed up to the subject, Penny searched her mind for possible reasons to spur Rebecca into taking action. "That would be a perfect place for distributing drugs," she theorized. "Quiet country road. Dead-end street. No neighbors. Think about it. And if the cops ever raided her, who knows what might happen to your sale? Suppose she's already running from the police?"

Knowing that she had absolutely no basis in fact to support what she was suggesting, Penny said, "You know what I think I'll do. I won't wait until Tuesday. I'll call Alvirah Meehan later on today and tell her everything about Ms. Gloria Evans and ask her for her advice. I mean, suppose Evans is running from the police and there's a reward for finding her? Wouldn't that be just too much?"

# 60

Fr. Aiden O'Brien began his Friday at seven A.M. serving the breadline outside the church. Today, as usual, there had been more than three hundred people waiting patiently for breakfast. Some of them, he knew, had been on line for at least an hour. One of the volunteers whispered to him, "Notice that we're seeing a lot of new faces, Father?"

The answer was that yes, he had noticed. Some of those people attended the senior citizen activities that were now his principal assignment. He had heard from many of them that it was getting to be a choice between food and the medicines they absolutely needed.

Those concerns were with him always, but today, as he woke up, he had prayed for Zan Moreland and for her child. Was little Matthew still alive, and if so, where had his mother been keeping him? He had seen the suffering in Zan Moreland's eyes when he took her hands in his. Was it possible, as Alvirah seemed to believe, that Zan was a split personality and didn't know what was happening in her other persona?

If that were true, was it the other persona who had come to confession and admitted to being part of an ongoing crime and unable to prevent a murder?

The problem was that no matter which one came to confession, he was bound by the seal never to reveal what he had been told.

He remembered how chilled Zan Moreland's elegant hands had felt when he closed his own over them.

*Her hands.* What was it that was nagging him about those hands? There was something, and it was important, but try as he might he simply could not remember it.

After lunch in the Friary, Fr. Aiden was barely back in his office when he received a call from Detective Billy Collins, requesting to pay him a visit. "My partner and I would like to ask you a few questions, Father. Would it be possible for us to come down immediately? We could be there in twenty minutes at the most."

"Yes, of course. May I ask what this is about?"

"It concerns Alexandra Moreland. We're on our way, Father."

Exactly twenty minutes later Billy Collins and Jennifer Dean were in his office. After the introductions, sitting at his desk facing them, Fr. Aiden waited for one of them to open the conversation.

It was Billy Collins who spoke first. "Father, Alexandra Moreland paid a visit to this church on Monday evening, did she not?" he asked.

Fr. Aiden chose his words carefully. "Alvirah Meehan identified her on our security tape as having been here on Monday evening."

"Did Ms. Moreland go to confession, Father?"

"Detective Collins, your name suggests that you are Irish, which means there is a good chance that you are Catholic or, at least, were raised as one."

"I was raised as one and I still am one," Billy said. "Not that I make it to Mass every Sunday, but pretty regularly."

"That's good to hear." Fr. Aiden smiled. "But then, as you must know, I cannot discuss anything about the confessional—not only what may have been said within it, but also who was or wasn't there."

"I see. But you did meet Zan Moreland at Alvirah Meehan's home the other evening," Jennifer Dean asked quietly.

"Yes, I did. Very briefly."

"Anything she said to you then wouldn't be under the seal of the confessional, would it, Father?" Dean persisted.

"It wouldn't necessarily be. She asked me to pray for her son."

"She didn't happen to mention that she just had cleaned out her bank account and bought a one-way ticket to Buenos Aires for next Wednesday, did she?" Billy Collins asked.

Fr. Aiden tried not to show how startled he was. "No, she did not. I repeat, we spoke for less than fifteen seconds."

"And it was the first time you were face-to-face with her?" Jennifer Dean shot the question at him.

"Please don't try to trick me, Detective Dean," Fr. Aiden replied sternly.

"We're not trying to trick you, Father," Billy Collins said. "But you might also be interested to know that after several hours of questioning, Ms. Moreland didn't share with us the fact that she's planning to leave the country. We just found it out ourselves. Well, Father, if you don't mind we'll take a look at those security tapes that show Ms. Moreland coming into the church and leaving it."

"Of course. I'll have Neil, our man for all seasons, show them to you." Fr. Aiden reached for the phone. "Oh, I forgot. Neil isn't here today. I'll ask Paul from our bookstore to help you out."

While they waited, Billy Collins asked, "Father, Alvirah Meehan was worried because she thought somebody was observing you too carefully the other night. Are you aware of anyone who might be antagonistic to you?"

"No one, absolutely no one," Fr. Aiden replied emphatically.

After Paul escorted the detectives to show them the tapes, Fr. Aiden put his head in his hands. She must be guilty, he thought. She was planning to escape.

But what is it about Zan Moreland's hands that I can't remember?

Two hours later, Fr. Aiden was at his desk when Zan called him again. Still holding out hope that he might be able to prevent the murder she had told him would happen, he said, "I was hoping to hear from you, Zan. Do you want to come in and talk with me? Maybe there is some way I can really help you?" Fr. Aiden said.

"No, I don't think so, Father. My lawyer just called. I'm going to be arrested. I have to go with him to the police precinct at five o'clock today. So maybe, if you don't mind, pray for me, too."

"Zan, I *have* been praying for you," Fr. Aiden said fervently. "If you . . ." He did not get to finish the sentence. Zan was no longer on the phone.

He was scheduled to be in one of the Reconciliation Rooms at four o'clock. I'll wait till after I'm finished there, then call Alvirah after six, he thought. By then she may know whether or not Zan is going to be released on bail.

At that moment Fr. Aiden O'Brien had no inkling that someone would be coming into the Reconciliation Room, and that his purpose would be not to confess to a crime but to commit one.

# 61

At 4:15 on Friday afternoon, Zan called Kevin Wilson. "I don't know how to begin to thank you for taking responsibility for everything that was ordered for the apartments," she said, her voice calm, "but I can't let that happen. I'm about to be arrested. My lawyer thinks I'll be given bail, but whether or not I am, I won't be of much use to you as an interior designer."

"You're going to be arrested, Zan?" Kevin could not keep the shock out of his voice even though Louise had warned him that she was surprised the arrest had not already happened.

"Yes. I'm to be at the police precinct at five o'clock. The way it was explained to me is that I'll be processed after that."

Kevin could hear the effort Zan was making to keep her voice from breaking. "Zan, this doesn't change the fact that—" he began.

She interrupted him. "Josh will call the suppliers and explain that everything must go back, and that I'll try to work out some sort of settlement with them," she told him.

"Zan, please don't think that my decision to accept the deliveries was some random act of kindness. I like your designs and I don't like Bartley Longe's. That's the beginning and the end of it. Before you came in, Josh told me that you and he worked on two jobs concurrently, and that while you were at one, he was at the other. Isn't that true?"

"Yes. It is. Josh is truly gifted."

"All right, then. On the business level, I am hiring Moreland Interiors to take over the decorating of my model apartments. Whether or not you receive bail, my decision is firm. And, of course, I need a separate bill for your usual fees over and above the actual cost of the furnishings."

"I don't know what to say," Zan protested. "Kevin, you've got to be aware of the kind of publicity my case is generating and it is bound to get worse. Are you sure that you want people to know that a woman accused of kidnapping and maybe murdering her own child works for you?"

"Zan, I know how bad it looks, but I believe in your innocence, and that there is another explanation for everything that has happened to you."

"There is, and please God, it will be found." Zan attempted to laugh. "I want you to know that you have the distinction of being the first person to express any belief at all in my innocence."

"I'm glad if I'm the first, but I'm sure I won't be the last," Kevin said firmly. "Zan, you've been on my mind constantly. How are you able to handle all this? When I saw you, you were so upset that I was heartsick for you."

"How am I now?" Zan asked. "I've been questioning myself about that, and I think I have the answer. Years ago, when my parents were stationed in Greece, we flew to Israel and visited the Holy Land. Have you ever been there, Kevin?"

"No, I haven't. I've always wanted to go. For a long time I didn't have the money. Now I don't have the time."

"What do you know about the Dead Sea?"

"Not much other than that it's in Israel."

"Then to explain how I feel, I swam in it when we were there. It's a salt lake that is twelve hundred and ninety-three feet below sea level. That means it's the lowest point on earth. It's so thick with salt that you're warned not to get the water in your eyes because if you do, they'll be terribly burned."

"Zan, how does that relate to you now?"

Zan's voice broke as she said, "I feel as if I'm at the bottom of the Dead Sea with my eyes wide open. Does that answer your question, Kevin?"

"Yes, it does. Oh, God, Zan, I'm sorry."

"I really believe you are. Kevin, my lawyer just came in. Time to go get fingerprinted and booked. Thanks again."

Kevin replaced the phone on the cradle, then turned away so that Louise Kirk, who was opening the door of his office, would not see the tears in his eyes.

# 62

Friday afternoon he called Glory. When she answered, as he had expected, her voice was sullen and angry. "It's about time I heard from you," she snapped. "Because your one-week-or-ten-day plan just isn't going to pan out. I probably have to get out of here within thirty days, and Sunday afternoon the real estate broker is going to come trooping in here with the guy who's buying the house. And if you think you're going to dump me in another godforsaken hole like this, you're wrong. By Sunday morning, you'd better have the money in my hands or I go to the police and claim that five-million-dollar reward."

"Gloria, we can wind this up by Sunday. But if you think you can make a deal to collect that reward, you're dumber than I thought. Remember Son of Sam? If not, look him up. He killed a couple of people and shot three or four others. He was writing a book about his crime spree and they passed a law saying that no criminal can profit from his crime. Lady, whether you know it or not, you're up to your neck in this one. You kidnapped Matthew Carpenter and you've been holding him captive for two years. You get caught, you go to prison. Got it?"

"Maybe they make exceptions," Gloria said defiantly. "But this little kid is bright. If you think that once they find him, he won't tell them that Mommy didn't take him that day, you are wrong. I'm pretty sure he remembers. When he woke up in the car, I was still wearing the wig. He started shrieking when I took it off. He remembers *that*. And once, when I thought the door was locked, I tried on the wig after I washed it. My back was to him. He opened the door and came in before I could get it off. He asked me, 'Why do you try to look like my Mommy?' Suppose he tells them that Glory took him out of the stroller? Won't that be great for me?"

"You haven't let him see any of the tapes they've been showing on television, have you?" he asked, as the appalling truth washed over him. If Matthew tells the police he knew his mother had not taken him, every plan I have made would collapse.

"You do ask stupid questions, don't you? Of *course* I haven't," she said.

"I think you're crazy, Brittany. That happened almost two years ago. He's too little to remember."

"Just don't count on him being a dumb bunny when they find him. And don't call me Brittany. I thought we agreed on that."

"All right, all right. Look, we're going to change our plan. Forget about making yourself up to look like Zan and going back to that church. I'll take care of that myself. Pack your car with everything you own. We'll meet tomorrow night instead at LaGuardia Airport. I'll have the money for you, and a plane ticket home to Texas."

"What about Matthew?"

"Do what you've always done, only this time it will have to be a little longer. Put him to bed in the closet, leave the light on, and give him enough cereal or sandwiches and soda to last him. You say those people are coming in on Sunday to go through the house?"

"Yes. But suppose they don't come? We can't leave that little boy locked in the closet."

"Of course not. Tell that real estate agent that you're leaving Sunday morning and that you'll notify her where to send your refund. You can be sure that by noon on Sunday she'll be checking out that house, whether or not she has the new buyer with her. And then she'll find Matthew."

"Six hundred thousand dollars, five thousand in cash, the rest wired to my father's bank account in Texas. Get out your pen. I'll give you the account number now."

His hand was perspiring so much that he couldn't keep the pen from slipping, but he managed to jot down the numbers she was snapping at him.

It was the one possibility that he had never considered—that Matthew would remember it was not his mother who had kidnapped him that day.

If that happened, Zan's story would be believed. All his carefully laid plans would be useless. Even if he killed her, as he had planned to do, they would still start looking to see who else might have planned this hoax and kidnapping.

And somehow they would get to the truth. The same vigilance with which they were hounding Zan would be turned from her in other directions.

He was sorry. He was truly sorry, but Matthew could *not* be found in that closet. He had to be gone when the real estate agent arrived on Sunday afternoon.

I never intended to kill him, he thought regretfully. I never thought that it would have to end like this. He shrugged. And now it was time to go to church.

"Bless me, Father, for I have sinned," he thought grimly.

# 63

This time, Zan did not respond to the media when she and Charley Shore arrived at the Central Park Precinct. Instead, ducking her head, she ran from the car to the front door with Charley's arm under her elbow. They were escorted to the now familiar interrogation room, where Detectives Billy Collins and Jennifer Dean were waiting for them.

Without greeting her, Collins said, "I hope you didn't forget to bring your passport, Ms. Moreland."

Charley Shore answered for her. "We have the passport."

"Good, because the judge will want it," Billy said. "Ms. Moreland, why didn't you share with us that you were planning to fly to Buenos Aires next Wednesday?"

"Because I wasn't," Zan said calmly. "And before you ask, neither did I clean out my bank account. I'm sure you've checked that by now."

"What you are saying is that the same imposter who stole your child also bought you a one-way ticket to Argentina and helped herself to your bank account?"

"That is *exactly* what I am saying," Zan said. "And in case you don't know it yet, that same person ordered clothes at the stores where I have an account, and also ordered all the supplies I would have needed for the interior design job I bid on."

The frown on Charley Shore's face reminded her that he had told her to answer questions, but not to volunteer any information. She turned to him. "Charley, I know what you're thinking, but I don't have anything to hide. Maybe if these detectives look into all those activities, they'll discover that even just one of them couldn't have been done by me. And maybe then it is possible they will look at each other and one of them will say, 'Well, maybe she was telling the truth.' "

Zan looked back at the detectives. "Clap if you believe in miracles," she said. "I am here to be arrested. Can we possibly begin the process?"

They stood up. "We do that downtown at the courthouse," Billy Collins told her. "We'll drive you there."

It doesn't take long to be an accused felon, she thought an hour later, after the arrest warrant was issued, a number was assigned to it, and she had been fingerprinted and had her mug shot taken.

From there she was taken into a courtroom to stand in front of a stern-faced judge. "Ms. Moreland, you are being charged here with kidnapping, obstruction of justice, and interference with parental custody," he told her. "If you can make bail, you cannot leave the country without the permission of the court. Do you have your passport with you?"

"Yes, Your Honor," Charley Shore answered for her.

"Surrender it to the court clerk. Bail is set at two hundred fifty thousand dollars." The judge stood up and walked out of the courtroom.

Zan turned to Charley, panic-stricken. "Charley, I can't raise that much money. You know I can't."

"Alvirah and I spoke about this possibility. She's putting up the deed to her apartment for security with a bondsman and will lend you the bondsman's fee. As soon as I call Willy, he'll be on his way here with it. When the bail is straightened out, you'll be free to go."

"Free to go," Zan whispered, looking down at the black smudges she had not been able to scrub from her fingers, "free to go."

"This way, ma'am." A court officer took her arm.

"Zan, you have to wait in a holding cell until Willy puts up the bail. As soon as I talk to him, I'll come back and wait with you," Charley told her. "You've got to understand this is all routine stuff."

Her feet leaden, Zan allowed herself to be walked through a nearby door. It opened onto a narrow passage. At the end of it was an empty cell with an open toilet and a bench. At the slight prodding of the uniformed officer, she stepped inside the cell and heard the key turn in the lock behind her.

*No Exit*, she thought wildly, remembering the Sartre play by that name. I played the role of the adulteress in it in college. *No exit. No exit.* She turned and looked at the bars, then tentatively put her hands on them. My God, how can it have come to this? she thought. *Why? Why?*

She stood there unmoving for nearly half an hour, then Charley Shore returned. "I spoke to the bail bondsman, Zan," he said. "Willy should be here in a few minutes. He has to sign a few papers, turn over the deed, pay the fee, and you'll be out of here. I know how it must feel for you, but this is the moment your lawyer, meaning me, knows what we're up against and starts to fight."

"An insanity defense? Isn't that what you're thinking, Charley? I'll bet it is. In the office before you got there, Josh and I had the television in the back room on. The CNN anchor was interviewing a doctor who specialized in multiple personalities. In his brilliant opinion, I may be a very likely candidate for that kind of defense. Then he cited a case where the defense pleaded that the core person did not know what the personality who committed crimes was doing.

"You know what the judge said to that defense argument, Charley?" Zan shrieked. He said, *"I don't care how many personalities that woman has. They all have to obey the law!"*

Charley Shore looked into Zan's blazing eyes and knew there was no way he could either reassure or comfort her.

He decided not to insult her by attempting to do either.

# 64

Gloria Evans, born Margaret Grissom, called "Glory" by her adoring father, stage name Brittany La Monte, was not sure if she could believe that it really would be over within forty-eight hours. A thousand times in these nearly two years she had whispered, "If only," to herself during sleepless nights when she had begun to realize the enormity of her crime.

Suppose it doesn't work out? she thought. Suppose they do track me down? I'll go to prison for the rest of my life. What's six hundred thousand dollars? It will only last me a couple of years by the time I get set up, buy new clothes, have new pictures made, take some more acting lessons, and try to get a publicist and an agent. He said he could introduce me to people in Hollywood, but what good were all the people he introduced me to in New York? *Zip.*

And Matty. He was such a nice little kid. I knew I'd mess myself up if I got too tight with him, Glory thought, but how can you *not* like the kid?

I love the boy, she thought, as she packed the clothes that were the same as the ones Zan Moreland wore. By God, I'm good, she thought with a tight-lipped grin. I pay attention to detail. Moreland is a little taller than I am. I had an extra lift put on the heels on those sandals just in case anyone got a picture of me when I took the kid.

Warming to her self-congratulatory stream of thought as she packed her suitcases, Glory remembered how she had worked on that wig to get her hair just right, the color and the blunt cut. Glory padded the shoulders of that dress because Moreland was more broad shouldered than she was. I bet right now the cops are doing all that digital stuff and they'll come back saying that no way was the woman in the picture not Moreland. My makeup was perfect, too.

She looked around the bedroom with its bleak white walls, tired oak furniture, and rag of a carpet. "And what the hell did it all get me?" she asked aloud. Two years of jackassing from one hidden house to another. Two years of leaving Matty locked up in the closet while I went to the store or once in a while to a movie. Or to New York, to make it look like Moreland had been some place or other.

That guy could break into Fort Knox, she thought as she remembered how one day he had met her at Penn Station and thrust the fake credit card into her hand. He had cut out ads of clothes on sale. "This is what I want you to buy," he said. "She already has duplicates of them."

Other times he had mailed her a box of clothes that were identical to some that Moreland had bought. "In case I really want to rub it in," he said.

Glory had been wearing one of those suits, the black one with the fur trimming, and all her makeup when she drove into Manhattan on Monday. He'd told her to buy clothes at Bergdorf's and charge them to Moreland's account. She didn't know exactly what else he planned for her to do, but when she met him, she could tell he was upset. "Just get back to Middletown," he had told her.

That was late Monday afternoon. I got mad, Glory thought. I told him to go to hell and that I'd walk to the parking lot. I should have taken off my wig and tied my scarf around my neck so I didn't look like her, but I didn't. Then when I passed the church, it was crazy, but I stopped in. I don't know what made me go to confession, or start to anyhow. My God, was I losing it? And I ought to have known that he'd be following me. How else would he have known I was there?

"Glory, can I come in?"

She looked up. Matthew was standing at the door. Focusing on him, Glory could see that he had lost weight. Well, he hadn't been eating much lately, she thought. "Sure. Come in, Matty."

"Are we going to move again?"

"I have very good news for you. Mommy is coming to get you in a couple of days."

"*She is?*" he said excitedly.

"You bet she is. That's why I won't be minding you at all any-more. And the bad people who were trying to steal you are all gone. Isn't that wonderful?"

"I miss Mommy," Matthew whispered.

"I know you do. And believe it or not, I'm going to miss you, too."

"Maybe you'll come and visit us sometime?"

"Well, we'll see." Looking into Matthew's intelligent, seeking gaze, Glory suddenly thought, In two years if he sees me on television or in a movie, he'll say, "That's Glory, the lady who minded me."

Oh my God, she thought, that's the way *he's* thinking, too. He knows he can't let Matty be found. Could he possibly . . . ?

Yes, he could. She already knew that.

I can't let it happen, Glory thought. I've got to call and try to get that reward. But right now, I'll do what he said. In the morning, I'll call the real estate woman and tell her I'm leaving Sunday morning. Then I'll meet him in New York tomorrow night, like we planned, but before that I'll go to the cops and make a deal with them. They can tape me so that they'll have absolute proof that I'm on the level.

"Glory, can I go downstairs and get a soda?" Matthew asked.

"Sure, honey, but I'll go down with you and get you something to eat."

"I'm not hungry, Glory, and I don't believe you that I'll see Mommy soon. You always tell me that."

Matthew went downstairs for a soda, brought it back up, lay on his bed, and reached for the bar of soap. But then he pushed it away. Glory tells lies, he thought. She's always telling me that I'll be seeing Mommy soon. Mommy doesn't want to come for me.

# 65

Fr. Aiden made his way from the Friary to the lower church at ten minutes of four on Friday. He walked slowly. He had been sitting at his desk for hours and the arthritis in his back and knees always pained him when he'd been in one position for too long.

Today, as always, there were people queuing up at the two Reconciliation Rooms in the entrance area where confessions would be heard. He could see that someone was paying a visit to the Lady of Lourdes grotto and someone else was at the kneeling bench before St. Jude. A few people were sitting on the bench against the outside wall. Resting their feet, he wondered, or waiting to work up courage to go to confession? It shouldn't take courage, he thought. It only requires faith.

As he passed the recessed Shrine of St. Anthony, he noticed a man in a trench coat with a thick head of dark hair kneeling there. The thought crossed his mind that maybe this was the man who Alvirah claimed was taking an odd kind of interest in him the other night. Fr. Aiden dismissed that thought. If it is, maybe the fellow simply was working his way up to unburdening himself, he thought. I hope so.

At five of four, he put his name on the outside of the Reconciliation Room, went in, and settled in his chair. His personal prayer before he began to receive the penitents was always the same, that he would meet the needs of those who came for healing.

At four o'clock, he pressed the button so that the green light would go on, and the first person on the line would know it was permissible to enter.

It was an unusually busy afternoon even for the Lenten season, and nearly two hours later, Fr. Aiden decided that since there were only a few others waiting, he would not leave until he had heard all their confessions.

Then, at five minutes of six, the man with the unruly hair came in.

The collar of his trench coat was up around his neck. He was wearing oversized dark glasses. His thick mop of dark hair covered his ears and forehead. His hands were in his pocket.

Fr. Aiden felt an instant sense of fear. This man was not a penitent, he was sure of that. But then the man sat down and, his voice husky, said, "Bless me, Father, for I have sinned." Then he paused.

Fr. Aiden waited.

"I'm not sure you'll want to forgive me, Father, because the crimes I am going to commit are quite a bit more serious than the crimes I have been committing. You see, I am going to kill two women and a child. You know one of them, Zan Moreland. And beyond that I can't take a chance on *you*, Father. I don't know what you have heard, or what you suspect."

Fr. Aiden tried to rise, but before he could the man drew a gun out of his pocket and held it against the Friar's robe. "I don't think they'll hear this," he said. "Not with a silencer, and anyway they're all too busy praying."

Fr. Aiden felt a fierce, sharp pain in his chest, and then as everything went black, he felt the man's hands guiding him back into his chair.

Hands. Zan Moreland. That was what he had been trying to remember. Zan had long, beautiful hands.

The woman in confession who he had thought was Zan had smaller hands and short fingers . . .

Then the image passed out of his mind, leaving him in silent darkness.

# 66

When they were finally able to leave the courthouse, Willy stepped out through a sea of cameras, ran out into the street, and hailed a cab.

Biting her lip to keep it from trembling, and holding Charley Shore's hand, Zan raced to get in the taxi. But she could not escape the flashing bulbs and the microphones that were thrust in front of her. "Any statement for us now, Zan?" a reporter called.

Stopping in her tracks, she screamed, "I am not the woman in those photos, I am not, I am not."

At the curb Willy was holding the cab door open. Charley helped her into it. "The big guy will take care of you now," Charley said quietly.

For minutes after the cab pulled away, neither Zan nor Willy said anything. Then when they were almost at Central Park, she turned to Willy. "I simply don't know how to thank you," she began. "My apartment is a sublet. My bank account is nonexistent. There's no way I could have made that bail. I'd be in the Tombs tonight in an orange jumpsuit if it weren't for you and Alvirah."

"There was no way you were going to be in the Tombs tonight, Zan," Willy said. "Not on my watch."

When they reached the apartment, Alvirah was waiting with glasses on the coffee table. She said, "Charley called me, Willy. He said Zan needs something stronger than red wine. What will it be, Zan?"

"I guess a scotch." Zan tried to smile as she untied her scarf and slipped off her outer jacket, but it was a forlorn effort. "Or maybe two or three," she added.

As she reached to take the jacket from her, Alvirah wrapped her arms around Zan. "When Charley called to say you were on your way, he asked me to remind you that this is only the first move in a long process and that he is going to fight every step of the way for you."

Zan knew what she had to say, but she was not sure how to put it. Stalling for time, she sat on the couch and looked around the room. "I'm so glad that you went ahead with these matching club chairs, Alvirah. Remember we debated about having one of them be a wing chair?"

"You told me all along that I should get the matching club chairs," Alvirah said. "When Willy and I were married we, and everyone we knew, bought a couch, a wing chair, and a club chair. And the end tables matched the cocktail table. And the lamps matched, too. Let's face it. There weren't too many interior decorators running around Jackson Heights, Queens, at the time."

As she spoke, Alvirah was studying Zan, taking in the deep shadows under her eyes, the alabaster white of her skin, the fact that although she was naturally slender, she now seemed actually frail.

Zan picked up the drink Willy had prepared for her, shook it slightly to rattle the ice cubes against the side of the glass, and began, "This is terribly hard for me to say because it seems so ungrateful."

She looked up at their concerned faces. "I can read your minds," Zan said quietly. "You think I'm going to come clean and tell you that yes, I did kidnap and maybe even kill my child, the flesh of my flesh.

"That's not what I'm going to say. I am going to tell you that I am not bipolar. I am not neurotic. I am not a split personality. I know what it looks like, and I don't blame you for believing any or all of that."

Her voice rising with passion, she said, "Someone else took Matthew. Someone who cares enough to look exactly like me is the woman in those photos in Central Park. I just read about a woman who spent a year in prison because two of her ex-fiancé's friends claimed she had held them up at gunpoint. Finally one of them broke down and admitted he was lying."

Zan stared into Alvirah's eyes, beseeching her understanding. "Alvirah, on Matthew's life, I swear before God, I am innocent. You're a good detective. I've read your book. You've solved some pretty important crimes. Now I am going to ask you to rethink this awful mess. Say to yourself, 'Zan is innocent. Everything she has told me is true. How do I go about proving her innocence instead of just pitying her?' Is that possible?"

Alvirah and Willy looked at each other, knowing they could read each other's minds. Ever since they had seen those pictures of Zan—or the woman who strikingly resembled her—they had passed judgment on her. *Guilty.*

I never even considered that she isn't the woman in the pictures, Alvirah thought. Maybe there *is* another explanation for all this. "Zan," she began slowly, "I am ashamed, and you are right. I am a pretty good detective, and I've been too quick to judge you. You *are* presumed innocent, which is the foundation of justice, something which I, like many people, have forgotten in your case. Where do I look for answers?"

"I swear Bartley Longe is behind this," Zan said promptly. "I rejected his advances—never smart if you worked for him. I quit and opened my own firm. I've taken some of his clients. Today I learned the job of doing the model apartments at Carlton Place is mine."

She saw the surprised expression that came into both their eyes.

"Can you believe that Kevin Wilson, the architect, hired me even though he knew I might be going to jail? Of course, now that I'm out on bail, I can work with Josh, but Kevin hired us knowing that Josh might have had to handle the job himself."

"Zan, I know how much that assignment means to you," Alvirah said. "And you won it over Bartley Longe!"

"Yes, but if he hates me now, can you imagine how much more he'll hate me when he hears this?"

Alvirah had a frightening thought that Zan may have missed something. If she was right and some woman was skillfully impersonating her, and if Bartley Longe had hired a woman to dress up like Zan and kidnap Matthew, what might happen now? And what might Longe do to Matthew given this new insult of Zan getting a prestigious job that he wanted himself? If Longe is guilty and if Matthew is still alive, will Longe be driven even further in his need to harm Zan?

Before Alvirah could speak, Zan said, "I've been trying to sort everything out myself. For some reason Nina Aldrich told those detectives that I was to meet her at her apartment on Beekman Place. That simply isn't true. Maybe the housekeeper was within earshot when Nina told me to meet her at the town house on Sixty-ninth Street that day."

"All right, Zan, that may be a good lead. I'll try to get to the housekeeper. I'm good at making friends with someone like that. Don't forget I was a cleaning woman for years." Alvirah hurried to get the pad and pen on the shelf under the kitchen phone.

When she returned, Zan said, "And, please talk to Tiffany Shields, the babysitter. She asked for a Pepsi and when I went to get it she followed me into the kitchen. She took it out of the refrigerator and opened it herself. I never touched it. She asked me if I had any cold pills. I gave her a Tylenol for colds. I've never had the

Tylenol with a sedative in my home. Now she's decided that's what I gave her."

The phone rang. "It always rings when we're about to have dinner," Willy grunted, as he went to pick it up.

An instant later his expression changed. "Oh my God! What hospital? We'll go right over. Thanks, Father."

Willy replaced the receiver, then turned to Alvirah and Zan who were staring at him.

"Who, Willy?" Alvirah asked, her hand over her heart.

"Fr. Aiden. Some guy with a lot of heavy black hair shot him in the Reconciliation Room. He's in NYU Hospital, Alvirah. He's in intensive care. His condition is critical. He may not last through the night."

# 67

Alvirah, Willy, and Zan had stayed at the hospital outside the intensive care unit until three in the morning. Two other Franciscan friars were there, keeping watch with them. They had all been allowed to stand at Fr. O'Brien's bedside for a moment.

His chest was swathed in bandages. A breathing tube covered most of his face. Intravenous fluid was dripping into his arm. But the doctor now was cautiously optimistic. Miraculously, all three bullets had missed his heart. While his condition was extremely critical, his vital signs were improving. "I'm not sure if he can hear you, but talk to him briefly," the doctor said.

Alvirah whispered, "Fr. Aiden, we love you."

Willy said, "Come on, Padre. You've got to get better."

Zan covered Fr. Aiden's hand with hers. "It's Zan, Father. With all that's going on, I know it is your prayers that have given me hope. Now I'm praying for you."

When they left the hospital, Alvirah and Willy took Zan home in a cab. Alvirah waited in it while Willy saw her to the door of her apartment. When he returned, he grunted, "It's too cold for the vultures. Not a camera in sight."

\*    \*    \*

They slept until nine o'clock the next morning. On awakening Alvirah grabbed the phone and called the hospital. "Fr. Aiden is holding his own," she reported. "Oh, Willy, I knew when I saw that guy in the church Monday night that he was trouble. If only we could have gotten a good look at him on the security camera, we might have been able to identify him."

"Well, the police are sure going over that security camera with a fine-tooth comb now to see if they got a better view of him last night," Willy assured her.

Over breakfast, they looked at the front page of the tabloids. Both the *Post* and the *News* had a picture of Zan, leaving the courthouse with Charley Shore. Her denial, I AM NOT THE WOMAN IN THOSE PHOTOS, was the headline of the *News*. "NOT ME," SCREAMS ZAN, read the *Post* headline. The *Post* photographer had gotten a close-up that revealed the agonized expression that accompanied her words.

Alvirah cut the *Post* front page and folded it. "Willy, it's Saturday, so maybe that babysitter is home. Anyhow, Zan gave me her address and phone number. But instead of calling, I'm just going to go there. Zan said that Tiffany Shields took the Pepsi from the refrigerator herself. That means there's no way Zan could have tampered with it. And as for the cold pill, Zan says she never bought the kind that has a sedative. You heard her. That young woman fell asleep when she was minding Matthew and now is trying to throw the blame for doing that on Zan."

"Why would the girl have made up a story like that?" Willy asked.

"Who knows? Probably to justify herself for falling asleep on the job."

An hour later, Alvirah was ringing the superintendent's bell at Zan's former apartment building. A young woman in a bathrobe answered the door.

"You must be Tiffany Shields," Alvirah guessed, plastering her warmest smile on her face.

"So? What do you want?" was the hostile reply.

Alvirah had her card in her hand. "I'm Alvirah Meehan and I'm a columnist for the *New York Globe*. I'd love to interview you for a story I'm writing about Alexandra Moreland." That's not a lie, Alvirah told herself. I am going to write a column about Zan.

"You want to write about the stupid babysitter who everybody blamed for falling asleep while all this time it was his mother who was the kidnapper," Tiffany snapped.

"No. I want to write about a teenage girl who was sick and only agreed to babysit because the child's mother had to see a client and the new nanny hadn't showed up."

"Tiffany, who's there?"

Looking past Tiffany into the foyer, Alvirah could see a broad-shouldered, balding man approaching them. She was about to introduce herself when Tiffany said, "Dad, this lady wants to interview me for an article she's writing."

"My daughter has taken enough of a pounding from you people," Tiffany's father said. "Just go home, lady."

"I don't intend to pound anyone," Alvirah said. "Tiffany, listen to me. Zan Moreland has told me how much Matthew loved you, and that you and she were real friends. She told me that she knew you were sick and she blamed herself for insisting that you mind Matthew that day. That's the story I want to tell."

Alvirah kept her fingers crossed as the father and daughter looked at each other. Then the father said, "I think you should talk to this lady, Tiffany."

As Tiffany opened the door wide to allow Alvirah to enter, her father escorted Alvirah into the living room and introduced himself. "I'm Marty Shields. I'll leave you two. I've got to get upstairs to check out someone's lock." Then he looked down at the card. "Hey, wait a minute. Aren't you the lady who won the lottery and wrote a book about solving crimes?"

"Yes. I am," Alvirah acknowledged.

"Tiffany, your mother loved that book. She went to a bookstore and you signed it for her, Mrs. Meehan. She said she had a nice talk with you about it. She's at work now. She's a sales woman in Bloomingdale's. I can tell you right now she'll be real sorry she missed you. Okay, I'm on my way."

What a piece of luck that his wife liked my book, Alvirah thought happily, as she took a straight chair near the couch where Tiffany was curling up. Tiffany is just a kid, she decided, and I can understand what kind of stress she's been under all this time. I've heard her phone call played on the news and so have millions of other people.

"Tiffany," she began, "my husband and I have been good friends with Zan almost since the time Matthew disappeared. I have to stress that I never once heard her blame you for what happened that day. I never ask her about Matthew because I know how hard it is for her to talk about him. What was he like?"

"He was adorable," Tiffany said promptly. "And so smart. That isn't surprising. Zan read to him every night, and on weekends she would take him everywhere. He loved to go to the zoo and he could name all the animals. He could count to twenty and never miss a number. Of course, Zan is a real artist. Her sketches of rooms and furniture and window treatments that she does for her job are wonderful. Even at three you could tell that Matthew had a real talent for drawing. He had big brown eyes that could look so solemn when he was thinking. And his hair was starting to turn red."

"And you and Zan were real friends?"

Tiffany's expression became wary. "Yes, I guess so."

"Over a year ago, I remember she told me that you two were good friends, and that you always admired her clothes. Didn't she sometimes give you a scarf or gloves or a pocketbook that she didn't need?"

"She was nice to me."

Alvirah opened her purse and took out the folded front page of the *Post*. "Zan was arrested last night and is charged with kidnapping. Just take a look at her face. Can you see how much she's suffering?"

Tiffany glanced down at the picture, then quickly looked away from it.

"Tiffany, the detectives told Zan that you think she may have drugged you."

"She may have. That's why I was so sleepy. There may have been something in that Pepsi and then that cold pill. I bet it was a sedative."

"Yes, that's what I understand that you told the detectives, but Tiffany, Zan remembers it clearly. You asked for a soda because you were thirsty. You followed her into the kitchen and she opened the refrigerator door for you. You took the can out and you opened it yourself. She never touched it. Isn't that true?"

"I don't remember it that way." Tiffany's tone of voice was now defensive.

"And you asked Zan if she had any cold medicine. She gave you a Tylenol, but she never kept nighttime Tylenol in the house. At your request she gave you the one that is a cold medication. Now, I grant you that those antihistamines can make you a little drowsy, but you asked for medication. Zan didn't offer it."

"I don't remember." Tiffany was sitting up straight now.

She remembers, Alvirah thought, and Zan is right. Tiffany's trying to rewrite history to make herself look good. "Tiffany, I wish you'd look at that picture again. Zan is suffering from these accusations. She swears she is not the woman in that picture taking Matthew. She doesn't know where he is, and the only thing that's keeping her going is the hope that he'll be found alive. She will be put on trial and you'll be a witness. I just hope that you think carefully when you're under oath, and if Zan's account of that morning is accurate that you will tell the truth. Now, I'm on my way. I promise that when I write this story, I will stress that Zan has always blamed herself, not you, for Matthew's disappearance."

Tiffany did not get up with her.

"I left you my card, Tiffany. It has my cell phone on it. If there's anything else that you think of, call me."

At the door she was stopped. "Mrs. Meehan," Tiffany called. "It may not mean anything, but—" She got up. "I have some sandals to show you. Zan gave them to me. When I saw those pictures of Matthew being taken out of the stroller, I noticed one thing. Wait a minute."

She went down the hall and came back a moment later with a shoebox in one hand and a newspaper in the other. She opened the shoebox. "These sandals are exactly the same as a pair Zan has. She gave them to me. When I thanked her, she said that she had bought a second pair the same color by mistake, and not only that, she had another pair exactly the same except that it had wider straps. She said it was practically like having three pairs of the same shoes."

Not knowing what to expect and not daring to hope that it would be significant, Alvirah waited.

Tiffany pointed to the newspaper she was holding and said, "You see the shoes Zan, or the woman who looks like her, is wearing when she's bending over the stroller?"

"Yes. What about them?"

"See how the strap is wider than it is on this pair?" She took a sandal from the shoebox and held it up.

"Yes. It is different, not much, but Tiffany, what about it?"

"I noticed and I can swear that Zan was wearing the ones with the narrow straps the day Matthew disappeared. She and I left this building together. She rushed into a taxi and I pushed the stroller to the park."

Tiffany's face became troubled. "I didn't tell that to the cops. I've been so mad about the way people think of me that I know I was blaming Zan. But last night when I began to think about it, it didn't make sense. I mean, why would Zan have come back home that day and changed into her sandals with the wide strap?"

Her eyes searched into Alvirah's pleadingly.

"Does that make sense to you, Mrs. Meehan?"

# 68

On Saturday morning, Detective Wally Johnson pushed the intercom button under the name ANTON/KOLBER 3B in the foyer of the brownstone shared by Angela Anton and Vita Kolber. They were the young women who had been Brittany La Monte's roommates before she disappeared.

When they did not answer the messages he left them on Thursday evening, he'd been prepared to go directly to their apartment the next morning and take a chance on catching them at home. But then Vita Kolber called him back at eight A.M. on Friday asking if he could meet with them on Saturday morning instead. They both had early-morning rehearsal calls and the rehearsals were expected to last through the day.

It was a reasonable request and Wally spent Friday following up on the other names Bartley Longe's secretary phoned in to him. "These are regular theatre people who would have met Brittany when she was in Mr. Longe's country home," she explained.

Two of the names were film producers who were both out of the country. The third was a casting director who had to search her brain to remember Brittany La Monte. "Bartley always has a bevy of blondes around him," she explained. "It's hard to tell them apart. If I can't place this girl Brittany, it says to me she didn't grab my attention."

Now as soon as he announced himself a musical voice said, "Come right up." At the sound of a buzzer he pushed the inner door open and climbed to the third floor.

The door of 3B was opened by a tall, slender young woman with long blond hair that cascaded down past her shoulders. "I'm Vita," she told him. "Please come in."

The small living room had clearly been furnished from make-dos and family castoffs, but was cheerful and coordinated with bright pillows on the vintage couch, colorful blinds on the long, narrow windows, and playbill posters of Broadway hits on the whitewashed walls.

When, at Vita's invitation, he sat in one of the armless upholstered chairs, Angela Anton came in from the kitchen carrying two cups of cappuccino. "One for you, one for me," she announced as she laid them on the round metal coffee table. "Vita's a tea drinker but doesn't want a cup now."

Angela Anton was not more than five feet tall, with medium brown hair cut into bangs, and hazel eyes that Wally immediately noticed were more green than brown. There was something in the graceful way she moved that made him suspect she was a dancer, an observation that was absolutely on target.

Both young women settled on the couch and looked at him expectantly. Wally took a sip of the coffee and complimented Anton on it. "I usually have my second cup at my desk," he said, "but, this is much better. As I said in my message, I need to talk to you both about Brittany La Monte."

"Is Brittany in trouble?" Vita asked, anxiously, then didn't give him a chance to answer. "What I mean is that she's been gone almost two years and when she left she was so mysterious about it. She took Angela and me out to dinner and said it was on her. She was all excited. She said that she had gotten an offer of a job that would pay really well, but would take a while, and after that, she was going to California because hanging around New York trying to get in a Broadway show hadn't worked for her."

"Brittany's father is concerned about her, as you know," Johnson said. "He told me he came here to see you."

Angela was the one who answered. "Vita only spoke to him for a couple of minutes. She had a casting call. I had time so I listened to Mr. Grissom's life story, then I had to tell him that we just haven't heard from her."

"He told me that he showed you the postcard Brittany sent him six months ago. It was from New York. Do you think it was genuine?" Johnson asked.

The two young women looked at each other. "I don't know," Angela said slowly. "Brittany's handwriting had curlicues and loops. I can see why she would have printed on a small card. But I just don't know why she wouldn't have called one of us if she was back in Manhattan. We were pretty tight with each other."

"How long did you actually share an apartment together?" Wally asked as he put the coffee cup back on the table.

"It was four years for me," Angela said.

"Three years," Vita responded.

"What do you know about Bartley Longe?"

Wally Johnson was surprised to hear both young women laugh. "Oh, my God," Vita said. "Did you know what Brittany did with that guy's wigs and toupees?"

"I heard about it," Johnson said. "What was that situation? Was Brittany involved with him, or was she in love with him?"

Angela took a sip of her coffee, and Wally wasn't sure if she was considering the question or finding a way to be loyal to Brittany. Finally she said, "I think Brittany underestimated that guy. She was having a fling with him, but she did it for one reason only and that was to meet people at his Litchfield house who might do her some good as an actress. I can't tell you how much she wanted to be famous. It drove her. She made fun of Bartley Longe. She put us in stitches imitating him."

Wally Johnson thought of what Longe had told him, that Brittany wanted to turn their affair into marriage. "Did she want to marry him?" he asked.

Both young women began to laugh. "Oh, good God," Vita said. "Brittany would no more have married him than . . ." She paused. "I swear, I can't come up with a comparison."

"Then what happened that caused her to destroy his hairpieces?" Johnson asked.

"She saw that most of the people he had up to that house in Litchfield were potential clients, not theatre people. She decided he was wasting her time. Or maybe by then this mysterious other job had come up. Bartley Longe had given Brittany some jewelry. I guess he could tell that she was sick of going up there, and he swiped it from her jewelry box. That's what really ticked her off. They had a big fight. He wouldn't give it back. So when he was in the shower, she collected all his wigs and toupees and drove his convertible back to New York. She told us she cut up all the 'rugs,' as she called them, and scattered them all over the convertible so that no one in the garage could miss seeing them."

"Did she ever hear from Longe after that?"

"He left her a message," Vita said, the smile gone from her face. She played it for us. "He wasn't ranting the way he would be if she was late getting to Litchfield. He said. 'You will regret this, Brittany. *If* you live to regret it.'"

"He threatened her that directly?" Wally Johnson asked, his interest aroused.

"Yes. Angela and I were frightened for her. Brittany just laughed. She said he was a big bag of wind. But I made a copy of the voice mail. As I said, I was frightened for her. It was only a few days later that she packed her stuff and left."

Wally Johnson considered what he had heard. "Do you still have that copy of Longe's voice mail?"

"Oh, sure," Vita said. "I was worried that Brittany just laughed it off, but when she left town I figured Bartley Longe would eventually cool down."

"I'd like to have that tape if it's handy," Johnson told her. When Vita went to get it he spoke to Angela. "You're in show business, too, I guess."

"Oh, yes. I'm a dancer. Right now I'm rehearsing for a show that's going to open in two months." Before he asked, she said, "And just so you know, Vita is a really good singer. There's a revival of *Show Boat* opening off-Broadway and she's in the chorus."

Wally Johnson took in the Broadway playbill posters on the walls. "Was Brittany a singer or dancer?" he asked.

"She could get by in both areas, but basically she was a dramatic actress."

Johnson could tell by the hesitancy in Angela Anton's voice that she was not going to be lyrical about the theatrical talents of Brittany La Monte. "Angela," he began, "Toby Grissom is a dying man and is agonized by his worry that his daughter may be in some kind of trouble. How good an actress was Brittany?"

Angela Anton looked reflectively at the framed playbill over the chair where Johnson was sitting. "Brittany was okay," she said. "Would she have made it to become a star? I don't think so. I remember one night about four years ago, when I got home, she was sitting here crying because once again an agent had turned her down. You see, Detective Johnson, she was a fabulous makeup artist. I mean *fabulous*! She could change the way someone looked in a heartbeat. Sometimes, when the three of us didn't have jobs, she'd make us all up to look like celebrities. She had a collection of wigs that would knock you over. We'd get dressed up and go somewhere and everyone would think we were the celebrities we were imitating. I told Brittany that she could be the leading makeup artist to celebrities and that would be her path to success. She didn't want to hear it."

Vita Kolber had come back into the living room. "Sorry," she said. "It wasn't in the drawer where I thought I had put it. Would you like me to play it for you, Detective Johnson?"

"Please."

Vita pushed the button of her tape machine. The voice of Bartley Longe, powerful in its fury, threatening and frightening in its message, reverberated through the room. *"You will regret this, Brittany. If you live to regret it."*

Wally Johnson asked to have it played again. It sent chills down his spine. "I'll have to take that tape with me now," he said.

# 69

Penny Hammel knew she should not take the chance of driving past the Owens farmhouse and being spotted by Gloria Evans. But as she told Bernie, she also knew that something was going on in that house and it was probably a drug deal. "And maybe there's a reward," she said. "You know you can be an anonymous caller, I mean they won't blab all over the news that you're the one who blew the whistle."

There were times when Bernie didn't mind being on the road so much, and one of those times was when Penny got it into her head that something mysterious was going on around her. "Honey, remember the time you thought that stray poodle you found was the missing champion that ran away in the airport? When you checked it out, he was a foot higher and twelve pounds heavier than the other one."

"I know. But he was a nice dog, and then I advertised and his owner came for him."

"Your thank-you was a bottle of the cheapest wine that guy could find in the liquor store," Bernie reminded her.

"So what? The dog was so happy to be found." Philosophically, Penny had shrugged off the incident. It was Saturday morning. Over breakfast they had seen the news clip of Alexandra Moreland leaving the station house last night still screaming denials that she had kidnapped her child. Penny had thoroughly reasserted her opinion of what should be done to that heartless mother.

Bernie was about to leave for an overnighter that would bring him back on Monday evening. Penny had reminded him several times that he absolutely could not miss the Lottery Winners' reunion in Alvirah and Willy's apartment on Tuesday evening.

He zipped up his jacket and pulled on his wool cap. It was then that he noticed that Penny was wearing her tracksuit and thick boots. "Are you going for a walk?" he asked. "It's pretty cold out."

"Oh, I don't know," Penny said dismissively. "I'm considering going into town and stopping by to say hello to Rebecca."

"You're not going to walk into town, are you?"

"No, but I may do a little shopping or something."

"Uh-huh. Well, just don't overdo it." Bernie planted a kiss on Penny's cheek. "I'll call you tomorrow, honey."

"Drive carefully. If you get sleepy, be sure to pull over. Remember I love you and I don't want to be a merry widow."

It was their traditional parting when Bernie went on the road.

Penny gave him plenty of time to get out of town, then around ten o'clock went into the closet to get her heavy jacket, snow hat, and gloves. She had already put the binoculars on the sideboard behind a lamp where Bernie wouldn't see them. I'll park the car on the street that borders the end of Sy's property, she thought, then I'll sneak up and hang out in the woods for a while. It might be silly, but who knows? That Evans woman is up to something. I can feel it in my bones.

Twenty minutes later she was standing behind an evergreen tree with heavy branches. From there she had a good view of the house. She waited for nearly an hour and then, her hands and feet cold, decided to leave. It was at that moment that the side door of the farmhouse opened and she saw Gloria Evans come out carrying two suitcases.

She's leaving now, Penny thought. What's her big hurry? Rebecca said that she has thirty days to get out if the house sells. On the other hand, Rebecca told her that she was bringing the buyers in tomorrow for a look around the house. That's probably what Missy Evans is worried about. Dollars to donuts, I'm right. What's she got to hide in there?

Gloria Evans had put the suitcases in the trunk of her car and returned to the house. When she came out again, she was dragging an oversized trash bag that seemed to be heavy. That, too, she started to put in the trunk. As Penny watched, a paper fell out of the top of the bag and blew back into the yard. Evans looked after it, but did not chase it. Then she went back into the house and for the next half hour did not come out.

Too cold to wait any longer, Penny went back to her car. It was nearly noon and she drove straight into town. Rebecca had left a note on the door: "Back soon."

Disappointed, Penny started to drive home but then, on an impulse, returned to her observation spot behind Sy's farmhouse. This time to her chagrin, the Evans car was gone. Oh, boy, that means nobody's in there, she thought and, holding her breath, walked up to the back of the house. The shades were drawn to the sill except for one of them that was raised about six inches. She peered in and could see into the kitchen with its heavy old furniture and linoleum floor. Can't tell much from here, she thought. I wonder if she's gone for good?

Making her way to the wooded area again, she saw that the sheet of paper that had blown away was caught on a shrub. Pleased, she ran to get it.

It was coloring paper and a childish hand had obviously sketched it. It had the outline of a woman's face with long hair, a face that in some way resembled Evans. Under the sketch was a single word, "Mommy."

So she *has* a kid, Penny thought, and she doesn't want anyone to know it. I bet she's hiding it from the father. That would be just her style. I wonder if she cut her hair recently. No surprise that she didn't want me to see the toy truck. I know what I'll do. I'll call Alvirah and tell her—maybe she can trace Ms. Gloria Evans. Maybe if she's been hiding a kid from his father, there'll be a reward. Wouldn't that really be a surprise for Bernie?

With a satisfied smile, Penny went back to the car, the drawing securely held between her gloved fingers. She laid it on the passenger seat, looked down at it, and frowned. Something was sticking in her mind, it felt like a sore tooth that was starting to throb again.

Darned if I know what, she thought as she started the car and drove away.

# 70

On Saturday morning, the normally intense satisfaction he would have felt at seeing the pictures of Zan splattered all over the tabloids was missing. He had endured a miserable night of restless dreams involving him trying to outrun the hordes of people who were relentlessly chasing him.

Shooting the priest had unnerved him. He had tried to hold the gun against the old man's robe, but at the last minute the priest had pulled to one side. According to the news report, he was in critical condition.

Critical condition, but not dead.

What was he going to do now? He had told Gloria to meet him at LaGuardia tonight, but thinking about it, that was a lousy idea. She was worried about being caught. She was suspicious that he would not deliver on the money. I know her mind, he thought. I still wouldn't put it past her to try to get some of that reward money. I wouldn't be surprised if she was dumb enough to think she could make a deal with the cops and let them put a wire on her before we meet. If she gives them my name now, it's all over.

But if she thinks it through, and is greedy enough to hang on, waiting to get her hands on my money and not go to jail, she may opt for that, he thought.

I can't take a chance of someone spotting me in broad daylight around that farmhouse. But I've got to get up there before she leaves to meet me at LaGuardia. I'll take everything personal in the house that belonged to her and Matthew with me. Then when the real estate agent finds them dead, nothing will be around to suggest that Gloria was impersonating Zan.

He had planned to kill Zan and make it look like a suicide. In a way this was better. She would never get over losing Matthew for good.

When he thought about it, that was infinitely more satisfactory than putting a bullet through her heart. How much fun it had been all these years, even before Matthew was born, being able to observe almost every moment of Zan's life at home whenever he wanted to tune in. In these last two years, he had loved being able to watch her lying in bed, hear her sobbing in her sleep, then waking up in the morning, and, not knowing he was watching, reach over and touch Matthew's picture.

It was eleven o'clock. He dialed Gloria. But she did not answer her cell phone. Maybe she was already on the way into New York, and on her way to the cops?

The thought terrified him. What could he do? Where could he run?

Nowhere.

At 11:30 and then at 12:30, he called her again. By then his hands were shaking. But this time she answered. "Where are you?" he demanded.

"Where do you think I am? I'm stuck here in this damn farmhouse."

"Were you out?"

"I went to the store. Matty just isn't eating anything. I got some hot dogs for his lunch. What time do you want me to meet you?"

"Eleven o'clock tonight."

"Why that late?"

"Because there's no need to do it earlier. And by then, Matthew will be sound asleep, so you won't have to lock him up alone for too long. I'll have all the money. It might raise too many questions to wire it. You can take your chances on carrying it through airport security or sending it parcel post to your father, but this way you'll know you have it, Brittany . . ."

"Don't call me that! You shot that priest, didn't you?"

"Gloria, I need to remind you of something. If you still have any thoughts of going to the police and making a deal, it won't work. I'll tell them that it was you who begged me to kill that good old man because you were stupid enough to blab to him in confession. They'll believe me. You'll never go scott free. This way you still have a chance of doing what you want to do, to have a career. Even if you cut a deal, you won't get away with less than twenty years. Believe me, there isn't much of a market for either actresses or makeup artists in prison."

"You'd better have that money with you."

He could tell that if she had had any intention of going to the cops, she was wavering. "I'm looking at it right now."

"Six hundred thousand dollars?" she asked. "All of it."

"I'll wait tonight while you count it."

"What about Matthew saying I took him from the stroller?"

"I've been thinking about what you said. He was just three years old. There's nothing to worry about. They'll think he's mixed up about whether his mother or someone else, meaning you, took him that day. You know they arrested Zan last night? The cops don't believe a word that she's saying."

"I guess you're right. I just want this to be over."

You're making it easy for me, he thought. "Don't leave around any of the stuff you wore when you looked like Zan," he said.

"Stop worrying. Every bit of it is packed. Did you get my airline ticket?"

"Yes. I'm sending you by way of Atlanta. It's better if you don't have a direct flight. I'm just being careful. Use your own ID when you fly from Atlanta to Texas. You're booked on the 10:30 Continental tomorrow morning from LaGuardia to Atlanta. That way if you want to send the money to your father, parcel post, which I think is a good idea, you'll have time to do it. I'll meet you in the parking lot of the Holiday Inn on the Grand Central Parkway. I made a reservation for you there."

"I guess you're right. And like you say, if I meet you at eleven o'clock, I only have to put Matty in the closet at 9:30."

"Exactly." Then, making his voice sound tender, he added, "You know, Gloria, you are a superb actress. These times you've been out, you've not only looked like Zan but you moved like her, too. I could see that in the photos that tourist took. It's uncanny. I'm telling you, those cops are convinced it's Zan in them."

"Yeah. Thanks." She clicked off.

I wasted a night's sleep, he thought. She won't go to the cops. Once again he picked up a newspaper with Zan's face on it. "I can't wait to see your expression tomorrow when that real estate woman and her buyer find Brittany and Matthew, and you get the sad tidings," he said aloud.

And like that he figured out the solution that was at his fingertips. It would take money, but that kind of money he could willingly spare.

He just didn't have the heart to kill the child himself.

# 71

It was late morning when he got to his desk after seeing Brittany La Monte's roommates. Wally Johnson leaned back in his chair. Totally ignoring the phones and conversations going on in the big room, he studied Brittany's photo montage. There is a slight resemblance to the Moreland woman, he thought. Angela Anton had said that La Monte was a consummate makeup artist. He held the montage against the front page of the *Post* showing Alexandra Moreland coming out of the courthouse. The headline read: ZAN SCREAMS, "I AM NOT THE WOMAN IN THOSE PHOTOS."

Was there even the faintest chance that she was right?

Wally closed his eyes. On the other hand, was Brittany La Monte still alive, or had Bartley Longe managed to carry out his threat to her? She had not been seen in nearly two years, and the postcard could well have been a phony.

The tape of that phone call was enough to bring Longe in for questioning. But suppose . . . Wally Johnson did not finish the thought. Instead, he reached for his cell phone and called Billy Collins. "Wally Johnson, Billy, you at your desk?"

"On the way in. I had to stop at the dentist. Be there in twenty minutes," Billy answered.

"I'll take a run up. I want to show you something."

"Sure," Billy said, mildly curious.

*          *          *

The night before, Billy had gone directly from Zan Moreland's arraignment to a play at Fordham University on the Rose Hill Campus in the Bronx. His son, a senior, had one of the leading roles in it. Billy and Eileen had heard about the shooting of Fr. Aiden O'Brien in the car on their way home to Forest Hills.

"I'm sorry we won't get this case, but it happened in another precinct," he had told Eileen heatedly the night before. "To shoot a seventy-eight-year-old priest when he's in the process of offering you forgiveness has to be the worst form of lowlife. I just spoke to Fr. O'Brien earlier today, something about the Moreland case. The crazy thing is that Fr. O'Brien was warned about that guy. Alvirah Meehan, the friend of Zan Moreland I told you about, had seen someone watching that priest Monday evening. She even went to view the church security camera tape, but couldn't get a decent look at him."

All Friday night, Billy had kept waking up, feeling as if he had, in some way, personally failed Fr. O'Brien. But we *did* look at the tape, he thought. The glimpse we got of that guy with a lot of dark hair was useless. He could have been anybody.

The first thing he did in the morning was to phone the hospital, where a police guard had been placed outside the intensive care unit. "He's holding his own, Billy," was the reassuring answer to his inquiry.

At the precinct, Jennifer Dean was waiting at his desk with David Feldman, one of the detectives assigned to investigate the shooting of Fr. O'Brien.

Although Jennifer Dean was outwardly calm, Billy knew her well enough to sense that she was tense. "Wait till you hear what Dave has to tell us, Billy," she began. "It's pretty explosive."

Feldman didn't waste time on preliminaries. "Billy, as soon as the medics got the priest on the way to the hospital, we looked at the security cameras." The crinkles around David Feldman's eyes were proof that the detective was by nature a man who frequently smiled, but now his expression was grave. "We had a description from some of the people who were in the atrium after they heard three popping sounds. They saw a six- or six-foot-one man with a bushy head of black hair, trench coat, upturned collar, and dark glasses run out of the Reconciliation Room. It was easy to pick him out on the camera, entering and leaving the church. I think that mop of hair is a wig. No way that we could get a decent look at his face."

"Anyone see which way he headed?" Billy snapped.

"A woman came forward who saw a man running toward Eighth Avenue. He may or may not have been our guy."

"Okay." Billy knew David Feldman had more to say but would do it his way, meticulously covering the step-by-step of the investigation.

"This morning the church handyman, Neil Hunt, came back. He had been to an AA meeting last night and went straight home and to bed after it. He didn't hear about the shooting until this morning. But get this." Feldman pulled his chair closer to Billy's desk and leaned forward. "Hunt used to be a cop. He got thrown off the force after being sent to the farm twice to dry out. Drinking on duty. The third time he was told to turn in his shield."

"Billy, wait till you hear the rest of it," Jennifer said, a note of barely concealed astonishment in her voice. "Remember that Alvirah Meehan told us that she had been in church Monday evening, and didn't like the way that man sprang up from supposedly praying when Fr. O'Brien came out of the Reconciliation Room? It bothered her enough that she went back and looked at those security tapes."

Feldman darted an annoyed glance at Dean for interrupting him. "We took a look at those tapes from Monday night, Billy," he said. "It's the same guy who was on the cameras last night going into the atrium of the lower church and leaving it a few minutes later, the one who shot the priest. You couldn't miss him. Mop of black hair, big dark glasses, same trench coat. The priest had no idea who he was.

"But, Billy, get this. We believe that Zan Moreland was in the church Monday night, too. She came and left before Alvirah, but the man in the black hair may have followed her in. He didn't leave until he saw what Fr. Aiden looked like."

"Was Moreland dropping in to say a prayer, or do you think she's connected to the guy who shot the priest?" Billy snapped. "Or did she go to confession and maybe that guy got worried?"

"I think it's a possibility," Feldman answered. "Billy, there's something else going on. As I said, the handyman who showed us the security tapes, Neil Hunt, used to be a cop."

"He wasn't the one who showed us the security tape yesterday," Jennifer Dean interrupted again.

"He claims he has a photographic memory," Feldman continued. "He bragged that I should look up his record in the department on that. He swears that Monday night, right after the Moreland woman left the church, he was walking home and a block away, a woman who looked just like her stepped in front of him and got in a cab. He said he'd have thought it was the same person, except the one who got in the cab had slacks and a jacket on. The one in church was dressed up."

Billy Collins and Jennifer Dean looked at each other for a long minute, each thinking the same thing. Was it possible that Alexandra Moreland was telling the truth, that there really *was* someone who looked exactly like her out there? Or was this ex-cop trying to capture a moment of self-importance by making up a story that no one might be able to prove or disprove?

"I wonder if our former brother in New York's Finest has read the morning papers and figures this is a good way to get someone to pay him for an interview?" Billy suggested, even as his gut told him that wouldn't be the case. "Dave, let's get Neil Hunt in here and see if he sticks to his story."

Billy's cell phone began to ring. Deep in thought, he picked it up and barked his name. It was Alvirah Meehan. He did not miss the triumphant note in her voice. "I wonder if I can come right over and see you," she said. "I have something of great interest to tell you."

"I'll be right here, Mrs. Meehan, and I'll be glad to see you." He looked up.

Wally Johnson was making his way swiftly through the uneven rows of desks to come to him.

# 72

Kevin Wilson spent more than an hour in the exercise room of his apartment late Saturday morning. During that time he switched the remote from channel to channel, trying to see every possible news clip showing Zan leaving the courthouse. Her agonized protest, "I am not the woman in those photos," cut through him like a knife.

Frowning, he watched as a psychiatrist compared the photos of Zan in Central Park after Matthew disappeared and the ones of her taking Matthew from the stroller and carrying him away. "There is no way that woman is not the mother kidnapping her own child," the psychiatrist was saying. "Look at these photos. Who else would be able to find and change into the exact same dress in the space of a few hours?"

Kevin knew he had to see Zan today. She had told him she lived in Battery Park City, only fifteen minutes away. She had given him her cell phone number. Keeping his fingers crossed, he dialed it.

It rang five times, then her voice came on. "Hi, this is Zan Moreland. Please leave a number and I'll get back to you."

"Zan, this is Kevin. I hate to do this to you, but I'd really like to get together with you today. We're getting the workmen started Monday on the apartments and there are a few things I need to go over with you." Then he added, hastily, "No problems, just choices."

He showered, then dressed in his favorite kind of clothes: jeans, a sport shirt, and a sweater. He wasn't hungry, but he had some cereal and coffee. He sat at the small table that overlooked the Hudson while he read in the paper about the charges that had been placed against Zan. Kidnapping, interfering with parental custody, lying to the police.

She was ordered to surrender her passport and could not leave the country.

Kevin tried to imagine what it would be like to stand in front of a judge and have charges like that hurled at him. He had been a juror in a manslaughter trial once and had watched the frightened defendant, a twenty-year-old kid who'd been high on drugs when he rammed a car, killing two people, sentenced to twenty years in prison.

His story was that someone had slipped something into his soda. Kevin still wondered if that was possible, but the kid had a history of being arrested for pot.

*I am not the woman in those photos.* Why against all the odds do I believe her? Kevin asked himself. I know, I absolutely *know*, that she is telling the truth.

His cell phone rang. It was his mother. "Kev, did you see the newspaper about the Moreland arrest?"

You know I did, Mom, he thought.

"Kevin, are you going to hire that woman after all this?"

"Mom, I know it sounds crazy but I believe that Zan is a victim, not a kidnapper. Sometimes you just know something about someone else and that's the way I feel."

He waited, then Cate Wilson said, "Kevin, you've always had the biggest heart of anyone I know. But sometimes people aren't deserving of it. Just think about that. Good-bye, dear."

She had disconnected.

Kevin debated, then pushed Zan's number again. He hung up when her voice started to direct him to leave a message. *I'll get back to you.*

It was nearly 1:30. You're not going to get back to me, he thought.

He got up, put a few dishes in the dishwasher, and decided to go for a walk. A walk that will take me to Battery Park City, he thought. I'm going to Zan's apartment and knock on her door. If nothing else, I would guess that this job is more important to her than ever—her legal bills have to be piling up already.

He was reaching in the closet for his leather jacket when the phone rang again. It better not be Louise crowing about Zan's arrest, he thought. If she is, I'll fire her.

His "Hello" was close to a bark.

It was Zan. "Kevin, I'm sorry. I left my cell phone in my coat last night and the ringer was off. Do you want me to meet you at Carlton Place?"

"No, I've had enough of being on the job for a week. I'm just about to go out for a walk. You're fifteen minutes away. May I come to your apartment and we can talk there?"

There was a moment of hesitancy, then Zan said, "Yes, of course, if that works better for you. I'll be here."

# 73

Come on, Matty, eat your hot dog," Gloria coaxed. "I made a special trip to the store to get it for you today."

Matthew tried to take a bite, then put it down. "I can't, Glory." He thought she'd be mad, but she just looked sad and said, "It's a good thing this is the end, Matty. Neither one of us is going to last, the way we're living."

"Glory, why did you pack up my stuff? Are we moving to a new house?"

Her smile was bitter. "No, Matty, I told you, but you don't believe me. You're going home."

He shook his head in disbelief. "Where are *you* going?"

"Well, for a while I'm going home to visit my daddy. I haven't seen him in the whole time you haven't seen Mommy. After that, well, I guess I'll try to get my career on track. Okay, I'm not going to make you eat that hot dog. How about some ice cream?"

Matthew didn't want to tell Glory that nothing tasted good anymore. She had packed away almost all his toys and cars and coloring books and crayons. She had even taken the picture he was drawing of Mommy, the one he had put back in the box because he didn't want to finish it. He didn't want to throw it away, though. And she had packed the bar of soap that smelled like Mommy.

Every single day he kept trying to remember what it was like to be with Mommy. Her long hair that sometimes tickled his nose. Her robe and how it felt when she wrapped him inside with her. All the animals in the zoo. Sometimes he said their names over and over when he was in bed. Elephant. Gorilla. Lion. Monkey. Tiger. Zebra. Like A, B, C, D. Mommy had told him that it was fun to put letters and words together. E is for elephant. He knew he was forgetting some of them and he didn't want to. Glory sometimes gave him DVDs with animals in them, but it wasn't the same as seeing them with Mommy at the zoo.

After lunch, Glory said, "Matty, why don't you watch one of the movies on your DVD. I have to finish packing. Close the door of your room."

Matthew knew that Glory probably wanted to watch television. She did that every day, but never let him see it. His television only worked on the DVD setting, and he had a lot of movies. But he didn't want to watch one now.

Instead when he went up to his room, he laid down and pulled the blanket up over him. He forgot and his hand crept under the pillow for the soap that smelled like Mommy, but it wasn't there. Matthew was so sleepy, he closed his eyes and hardly noticed that he was crying.

Margaret/Glory/Brittany finished the hot dog that Matthew had barely touched and sat reflectively at the kitchen table. She looked around. "Crummy house, crummy kitchen, crummy life," she said aloud. Her anger at herself for having gotten into this situation in the first place had been mingled with a sense of sadness. It had come over her during the night and she knew it had to do with her father.

Something was wrong with Daddy. She knew it in her bones. Her hand reached for her cell phone, but then she pulled it back. I'll be with him by tomorrow night, she thought, I'll surprise him.

She said it aloud. "I'll surprise him."

The words sounded hollow and even foolish to her ears.

# 74

Alvirah was reveling in her story as she sat at Billy Collins's desk, and word for word she described her meeting with Tiffany Shields to him and his fellow detective Jennifer Dean. The shoebox with the sandals Tiffany had given her was on the desk. She had taken one of the sandals out. What she didn't know was that she had placed it on top of Brittany La Monte's photo, which Collins had hastily turned over, facedown.

"I don't blame Tiffany," she said. "She's had one hard time of it being lambasted by the media and all the do-gooders. When she thought Zan had kidnapped Matthew, you can understand why she'd feel furious and betrayed. But when I explained to her that Zan had never blamed her, and reminded her that she would be under oath in a trial, she soon changed her tune."

"Let me get this straight," Billy said. "Ms. Moreland bought two pairs of identical shoes and had a third pair that was very similar, except for the strap."

"You've got it," Alvirah said heartily. "We talked about it, and Tiffany remembered a little more. Zan told her that she had ordered them online and by mistake got two pairs in the same color. Then when she realized that the sandals looked so close to a pair she already owned, Tiffany said, Zan just gave her one of the new pairs."

"Tiffany's memory seems to move around a bit," Jennifer Dean suggested. "Why is she so positive that Zan Moreland was wearing the sandals with the thinner strap that day?"

"She remembered because Zan happened to be wearing the same ones that Tiffany was, the pair with the thin strap. She said she had noticed it that day, but she wasn't in the mood for joking and Zan was nervous and in a hurry."

Alvirah looked at the two detectives. "I came straight here after I talked to Tiffany. I didn't happen to have with me those pictures showing Zan wearing one pair of sandals when she supposedly kidnapped Matthew and a different pair when she came back to the park after he was gone. But *you* do. So go look at them. And tell your experts to study them. And then wonder why any woman about to kidnap her child would bother to go home and change her shoes."

Billy and Jennifer Dean looked at each other, once again knowing what the other was thinking. If what Alvirah Meehan was telling them was true, the case against Zan Moreland was unraveling. They had both been startled by the resemblance of Brittany La Monte to Zan Moreland, once Wally Johnson pointed it out, and by the fact that La Monte was a makeup artist who had disappeared in exactly the time frame when Matthew Carpenter had been kidnapped, and who had worked for Bartley Longe, the rival Zan Moreland insisted was responsible for Matthew's disappearance.

In this high-profile case it was necessary to move very carefully. Billy did not want to admit that he was shaken—more shaken than he had ever been in any investigation he had ever worked.

We spoke to Longe, Billy thought. We dismissed him as a suspect. But now? With all this going on? Was the ex-cop Neil Hunt on target when he said he saw someone who looked like Zan Moreland getting into a cab near that church? He even remembered the hack number so we could check cab records for Monday night at that time. That was next on Billy's list.

Was Tiffany Shields a reliable witness? Probably not. The kid had changed her version of the morning she began to babysit Matthew Carpenter to suit her imagination.

But what if she was right about the shoes?

Alvirah was getting up to go. "Mr. Collins, last night after her terrible experience of being arrested and placed in a holding cell, Zan Moreland, Matthew Carpenter's mother, begged me to start out with the premise that I believed in her innocence. The minute I decided to do that, I sought out Tiffany and reminded her that she'd be under oath in a trial and she told me what I believe is the truth."

Alvirah took a deep breath. "I think you're a decent man who wants to protect the innocent and punish the guilty. Why don't you do what Zan begged you to do, too? Assume that she is innocent. Really investigate the man she believes to be responsible for Matthew's disappearance, Bartley Longe, and start digging. You see, even though she's been arrested, she still got the big job instead of Longe—of decorating some fancy new apartments. If Longe did figure out how to kidnap Matthew, and if Matthew is still alive, this might be enough to make him try to get back at Zan again and with the only weapon he may have. Her son."

Billy Collins stood up and extended his hand to Alvirah. "Mrs. Meehan, you are quite right. Our job is to protect the innocent. That is all that I am free to tell you right now. I'm very grateful that you encouraged Tiffany Shields to tell you what is perhaps a more accurate account of what happened when she met Ms. Moreland at her apartment the day Matthew disappeared."

As he watched Alvirah make her way to the exit, his instinct was telling him that she was the one on the right track and that time was running out.

As soon as she was out of sight, he yanked open the drawer and pulled out the photos of Zan Moreland that had been in newspapers all over the world these past few days, the original ones of her at the park after the kidnapping and the ones that just surfaced from the

British tourist. He laid them on the desk and reached for a magnifying glass. He studied them and handed the glass to Jennifer.

"Billy, Alvirah's right. She's not wearing the same shoes," Jennifer whispered.

Billy turned over the photo montage of Brittany La Monte and aligned it with the other pictures. "What could a good makeup artist do to change a similarity to a look-alike?" he asked Dean.

It was a rhetorical question.

# 75

When Zan opened the door for Kevin at 1:45, he looked at her for a long minute, then, feeling as if it were the most natural thing in the world for him to do, he put his arms around her. For long seconds they stood still, her hands at her side, her eyes searching his.

Kevin said firmly, "Zan, I don't know how good your lawyer is, but what you need is a private detective agency to turn this situation around."

"Then you *do* believe that I'm not a wacko?" Zan's tone was tentative.

"Zan, this is me. I trust you. Trust me."

"I'm sorry, Kevin. My God, you're the first person to say you believe me. But it goes on. The Mad Hatter's tea party goes on. Look around you."

Kevin looked around the warm and tastefully decorated living room with its eggshell walls, roomy pale green sofa, striped chairs, and deep green and cream geometric carpet. Both the couch and the chairs had open boxes on them from Bergdorf's.

"These just arrived this morning," Zan said. "They're charged to my account. I didn't buy them, Kevin, I didn't buy them. I spoke to a salesclerk in Bergdorf's I know pretty well. She said she didn't handle the sale Monday afternoon, but she recognized me and was a little hurt that I hadn't asked for her. She said that I bought the same suit a few weeks ago. Why would I do that? The one I have is in the closet. Alvirah thought she saw me on the security camera in the church on Monday evening wearing a black suit with a fur collar. I didn't wear that suit Monday evening. I wore it the next day, when I met you." Zan threw up her hands in a gesture of despair. "Where does it end? How can I stop it? Why? Why?"

Kevin covered her hands with his. "Zan, hang on. Come on. Sit over here." He guided her to the couch. "Have you ever noticed anyone following you?"

"No, but Kevin, I feel as if I'm living in a fishbowl. I've been arrested. Someone is impersonating me. The media is hounding me. I feel as if someone is walking in my footsteps, shadowing me, imitating me. *That person has my child!*"

"Zan, let's go back. I saw the photos of the woman you swear is not you in the paper, taking your son out of the stroller."

"She was wearing the same dress that I have, the same everything."

"That's my point, Zan. When did you wear that dress on the street where you could be seen?"

"I went out on the street with Tiffany. Matthew was asleep in his stroller. I grabbed a cab to Sixty-ninth Street to go to the Aldrich town house."

"That means even if someone saw you, and wanted to look like you, in the space of an hour or so, she would have had to find a dress that was exactly like yours."

"Don't you see? One of the columnists brought that up in the newspaper. They said it would be impossible for anyone to do that."

"Unless someone saw you while you were getting dressed, and already had a dress identical to the one you chose to wear?"

"There was absolutely no one in the apartment except Matthew while I was getting dressed."

"And this identical clothing continues to this day." Kevin Wilson stood up. "Zan, do you mind if I look around the apartment?"

"No, take your time, but what for?"

"Just humor me."

Kevin Wilson walked into the bedroom. The bed was made and piled with pillows. A picture of a smiling child was on the night table. The room was orderly, with a single dresser, a small writing desk, a slipper chair. The valance of the large picture window matched the blue and white pattern on the bed.

But even though Kevin's subconscious was aware of the pretty bedroom, his eyes were darting around the room. He was thinking of the time three years ago when a client had bought a condo after a bitter divorce between the sellers. When the workmen started to pull out the wiring, they had discovered a spy camera in the bed-room.

Was it possible that Zan might have been under scrutiny when she chose the dress she was wearing the day Matthew disappeared? And was it possible that she was still under scrutiny from an un-known observer?

With that in mind, he went back to the living room. "Zan, have you got a stepladder?" he asked. "I need to take a look around this place."

"Yes, I have one."

Kevin followed her to the hall closet, then reached past her and took the ladder from her hands. She followed him into the bedroom as he stood on it and slowly, carefully, began to examine and run his finger over the crown molding on the bedroom walls.

Directly opposite her bed, and over the dresser, he found what he was looking for, the tiny eye of a camera.

# 76

The *Post* and the *Times* were delivered to the Aldrich town house every morning. Maria Garcia put them in the pocket on the side of the breakfast tray for Nina Aldrich, who enjoyed breakfast in bed. But before Maria brought up the tray, she looked at the headline with Zan Moreland's cry, "I AM NOT THE WOMAN IN THOSE PHOTOS," splattered across the front page.

Mrs. Aldrich lied to the police, Maria thought, and I know why. Mr. Aldrich was away and Bartley Longe dropped in on her. And *stayed*. And stayed a long time. She knew she was keeping that young woman waiting and she didn't care. And then she lied bald-faced to those detectives. It was easier than to try to make an excuse for keeping Ms. Moreland waiting so long.

She brought up the tray and Nina Aldrich, propped up on pillows, grabbed the *Post* and saw the front page. "Oh, they did arrest her?" she said. "Walter will be furious if I'm dragged in to testify. But I'll simply repeat what I told the detectives, and that will be that."

Maria Garcia left the bedroom without answering. But by noon, she could stand it no longer. She had the card Detective Collins had given her and, being careful to see that Mrs. Aldrich was not on her way down in the elevator, dialed his number.

In the precinct, Billy Collins was waiting for Bartley Longe who, in a rage, had accepted Detective David Feldman's invitation to come in to the Central Park Precinct. Billy picked up the phone. He heard a tremulous voice say, "Detective Collins, I'm Maria Garcia. I'm afraid to call you because I don't have my green card yet."

Maria Garcia, the Aldrich housekeeper, Billy thought. What now? His voice soothing and reassuring, he said, "Mrs. Garcia, I didn't hear you tell me that. Is there something else that you want to say?"

"Yes." Maria took a long breath, then nervously burst out, "Detective Collins, I swear on my mother's grave that Ms. Moreland was told by Mrs. Aldrich to meet her here at the town house that day almost two years ago. I heard her and I know why she's lying about it. Bartley Longe, the designer, had stopped in to see Mrs. Aldrich on Beekman Place. They were having an affair. She let poor Ms. Moreland do all the work to get the job and gave it to him instead when he started flattering her. But that day, she was leaving to meet Ms. Moreland here on Sixty-ninth Street when Mr. Longe arrived. She knew perfectly well that Ms. Moreland was waiting for her, and that she'd sit there waiting until Mrs. Aldrich decided to show up."

Billy was about to respond when Maria Garcia gasped, "Mrs. Aldrich is on the way down. I have to go."

There was a click in his ear, and Billy Collins was processing this new chink in the evidence in the case against Alexandra Moreland when, accompanied by his lawyer, a furious Bartley Longe arrived at the precinct.

# 77

At quarter of one on Saturday afternoon, Melissa phoned Ted. "Have you seen the papers?" she asked. "They're all talking about how generous I am to offer that wonderful reward for your son."

Ted had managed to beg off from seeing her again on Friday night on the basis of his ongoing flu-like symptoms. At Rita's loyal insistence, he had called Melissa after her announcement to the media and groveled his gratitude to her.

Now, clenching his teeth, his voice robotic, he said, "Beautiful lady, I predict that a year from now, you'll be the number one star on this planet, maybe in the universe."

"You're sweet." Melissa laughed. "I think so, too. Oh, good news. Jaime-boy had a fight with his publicist again. Isn't that a riot? The big all-is-forgiven scene lasted only twenty-four hours. He wants to meet you."

Ted was standing in the living room of his handsomely furnished duplex apartment in the Meatpacking district, the apartment where he had lived for eight years. It had been his crowning achievement when he had been established enough to buy and furnish it. Bartley Longe and Zan Moreland, his assistant, had done the interior decorating. That was how he had met Zan.

That was running through his head as he reminded himself that he could not afford to offend Melissa. "When does Jaime-boy want to meet me?" he asked.

"Monday, I guess."

"That would be *great*." Ted's reaction was genuinely enthusiastic. He was not up to meeting Jaime-boy today. And Melissa was flying to London to attend a celebrity birthday party. He knew that, concerned as she was with catching a flu bug, she still did not want to go unescorted to the party.

He felt an almost uncontrollable desire to laugh. Wouldn't it be perfect if someone did somehow find Matthew, and Melissa had to shell out five million dollars?

"Ted, if you start feeling better, hop a plane to London, or else I'll find someone else at the party. British guys are soooooooooooo attractive."

"Don't you dare." His slightly stern voice, his "Daddy knows best," was a good sign-off. Finally he was able to get off the phone. He opened the door of the terrace and went outside. The cold air snapped at him. He looked down.

Sometimes I wonder if it wouldn't be good to jump and be done with it, he thought.

# 78

When Willy got back from his daily walk in Central Park, he realized that he was hungry. The problem was that he and Alvirah often liked to have lunch out on Saturdays, then drop in on a museum or go to a movie.

He tried to call her cell phone, but she didn't answer. *I should think that whatever that Tiffany Shields kid has to say, it would be said by now,* he thought, *but maybe Alvirah stopped to do a little shopping.*

*I won't spoil my appetite,* he decided when she still hadn't returned. But fifteen minutes later, he was wavering. And then the phone rang.

"Willy, you just won't begin to guess what I'm going to tell you," Alvirah began. "I'm so excited, I can hardly stand it. But listen, I just left Detective Collins and Detective Dean at the Central Park Precinct. Let's meet at the Russian Tea Room for lunch."

"I'm on my way," Willy promised. He knew that if he began to ask Alvirah questions, she would spill the beans immediately about what was exciting her and he'd rather hear it over the lunch table.

"See you there," Alvirah confirmed.

Willy replaced the receiver and headed for the closet in the foyer. He pulled out his jacket and gloves. As he was opening the front door of their apartment, the phone rang. He waited in case it was

Alvirah calling back. Instead, when he did not pick up, he heard the beginning of a message. "Alvirah, this is Penny Hammel. I tried you on your cell phone but you're not answering. You won't believe what I'm going to tell you, Alvirah," she began. "I swear I think I'm right. This morning—"

Willy let the door close behind him on Penny's message. Later, Penny, he thought as he rang for the elevator.

The message he did not wait to hear was Penny telling Alvirah that she was willing to bet that Matthew Carpenter was the child Gloria Evans was hiding in the farmhouse.

"What should I do?" Penny asked the answering machine. "Call the cops now? But I guess it would be better to hear from you because I have absolutely no proof. Alvirah, *call me!*"

# 79

Kevin, what does this mean?" Zan asked. "You're telling me that my bedroom has had a camera recording every minute I'm here?"

"Yes." Kevin Wilson did not waste time thinking about the terrible sense of invasion that Zan would be feeling when the full awareness of all that this discovery involved sank in on her. "Zan, somebody installed this or had it installed. Somebody probably bugged your other apartment as well. That's why it was possible for your look-alike to dress in exactly the same clothes."

From staring into the camera, he turned to look at her. Zan's face was ghastly white. She was shaking her head in protest. "My God, my God. Ted sent that guy he knew from his hometown in Wisconsin, Larry Post," she cried. "He's Ted's driver, cook, and handyman. He does everything for him. He installed the lighting fixtures and set up the television here and in the other apartment and my computer system in my office. Maybe that is how my accounts were hacked into. And all this time I've been blaming Bartley Longe."

"Ted has done this to me!" she shrieked, her voice rising with every word. "It's Ted. But what has he done to my son?"

# 80

Shortly after two o'clock Larry Post reached Middletown. The job that Ted had laid out for him was not easy. I'm supposed to make it look like Brittany shot the boy and then killed herself. That's easier said than done.

Larry had not been surprised that Ted had changed his mind about driving up there and finishing them off himself. Ted was worried sick that Brittany would go to the police, and he now realized that the boy might be able to convince the cops that Zan had not taken him from the park. If that happened, Ted knew the police would eventually come to him.

Larry could understand why Ted couldn't bring himself to kill his own son, but why was it at this point even necessary? I'm no bleeding heart, but I can't say that I ever thought that working for Ted would ever end up like this, Larry thought. But he did point out to me that if the cops keep digging and find those cameras in Zan's apartment, she'll know that I was the one who installed all the lighting and set up her computer.

When Zan decided to leave Ted and take that apartment on East Eighty-sixth Street, and then again when she moved to Battery Park City after Matthew disappeared, big-hearted Ted was the one who had helped her get settled both times. He sent a plumber to check all the pipes and me to install new lighting fixtures. And the cameras. The day she moved from Eighty-sixth Street I got rid of the original cameras. I had already installed the second cameras in her new apartment.

For the first three years it was enough for Ted to just spy on her anytime he wanted. But then she was getting successful in her business and she and Matthew were such a team that he couldn't stand it. And that was just the time when he met Brittany at a party and hatched this whole crazy plan.

Ted is right. If we don't act now, the cops will be knocking on my door before too long. I'm not going back to prison. I'd rather be dead. And he's going to give me the money he's already put in Matthew's trust fund. Let's face it. Ted needs me and I need him.

Ted had said that Brittany had become too much of a loose cannon and was now a big threat to both of us. He said that she's nutty enough to think that she might be able to make a deal with the police and still get the five-million-bucks reward that witch Melissa has put up in her big publicity stunt.

Larry laughed out loud. If that kid ever got home safely, Melissa would have a coronary. But that's not going to happen. He and Ted had figured out how he would get this done.

Brittany will recognize the truck when I pull up the driveway, he thought. Hopefully she won't panic when she sees me because she knows that I've been in on everything all along. When I'm near the house I'll phone her and say that I've got two big boxes full of cash, six hundred thousand dollars. I'll say that Ted wanted me to show her that he wouldn't double-cross her about the money and give her time to send it to Texas. In case she gets suspicious and is scared to open the door, I'll be carrying one of the boxes and she can look through the window and see the hundred-dollar bills on the top layer of the box. She won't be able to tell that the rest of the box is stuffed with newspapers.

When she lets me in, I'll do what I have to do. If she doesn't let me in, I'll blow the lock off the door. If that happens, it won't look like a murder-suicide, but there's nothing I can do about it. The main thing is that neither one of them will ever be able to talk.

# 81

Billy Collins was unimpressed by Bartley Longe's show of bravado. "Mr. Longe," he said, "I'm glad you have your lawyer with you. Because before we exchange a meaningful word, I am telling you that you are a person of interest in the disappearance of the woman known as Brittany La Monte. Her roommates kept a tape of your threat to her."

Billy had no intention of telling Longe that he had just come under suspicion of hiring Brittany La Monte to impersonate Zan Moreland and to kidnap her child. *That* possibility he was hugging to his vest.

"I never saw Brittany La Monte after she left my home in early June almost two years ago," Longe snapped. "That so-called threat was made because she had vandalized my property."

Wally Johnson and Jennifer Dean were sitting with them. "Your wigs and toupees, Mr. Longe?" Johnson asked. "By any chance have you replaced them with a set that includes one with a thick mop of black hair?"

"Absolutely not," Longe snapped. "Let's get this straight. I never saw Brittany after that day. Give me a lie detector test. I'll pass it with my eyes closed." He turned to Wally Johnson. "Have you followed up on any of those names my secretary gave you?"

"Two are out of the country," Wally Johnson shot back. "Perhaps you knew they're not easily reachable."

"I don't keep track of my many friends who are successful producers." Longe turned to his lawyer. "I would like to insist on having a lie detector test immediately. I will not be hounded by these detectives any longer."

Jennifer Dean had not said anything. Sometimes they worked an interrogation that way. Billy asking the questions, she listening to the answers. Billy Collins felt that his partner was sometimes better than a lie detector test for spotting the liars.

But not always, he reminded himself. If Zan Moreland is right about being impersonated, we both sure missed it.

And if she was, it didn't answer the question, Where is Matthew Carpenter? Is he still alive?

His telephone rang. It was Kevin Wilson.

Billy picked up his phone and listened, his face impassive. "Thank you, Mr. Wilson. We'll get right on it."

He turned to Bartley Longe. "You can leave at any time, Mr. Longe," he said. "We will not press any charges against you for the threatening phone call. Good-bye."

Billy jumped from his chair and headed out of the room. Trying not to show their surprise, Jennifer Dean and Wally Johnson followed him. "We've got to get to Ted Carpenter's apartment," Billy told them tersely. "My guess is that if he happens to be looking into his computer, he'll know that it's all over."

# 82

She couldn't wait any longer. She had to hear her father's voice. She had to tell him that she was coming home. But first . . . Glory tiptoed upstairs to make sure that Matthew's door was closed.

She had expected that he'd be watching one of the movies, but he was asleep on the bed, under a blanket. He looks so pale, she thought, as she bent over him. He's been crying again. The realization of what she had done to him swept over her as, careful not to awaken him, she tiptoed out of the room, closing the door behind her.

Standing in the kitchen, she picked up the last of the unregistered cell phones that he had given her and dialed her father's home in Texas. The call was answered by a stranger.

"Uh, is Mr. Grissom there?" Panicked, Glory knew that she was going to hear bad news.

"Is this a family member?"

"It's his daughter." Glory's voice became high-pitched and breathless. "Is he sick?"

"I'm sorry. I'm with the EMT service. He called 911 and we got here immediately but it was too late to save him. He had a massive heart attack. Are you Glory?"

"Yes. Yes."

"Well, ma'am, I hope what I am going to say is some comfort to you. Your father's final words were, 'Tell my Glory that I love her.' "

She pushed the button to disconnect the call. I have to go home now, she thought wildly. I have to put my arms around him one last time. What was the reservation that had been made for her? Yes, 10:30 tomorrow morning at LaGuardia, Continental Airlines to Atlanta. I'll change the reservation. I'll go straight home. I have to see him. I have to tell Daddy, I'm sorry. I'm sorry.

She opened her laptop. Half out of her mind with grief and regret, her fingers moved automatically to the Continental Airlines Web site. For a few minutes her fingers raced over the keys. Then she stopped. I should have known, she thought. I should have known.

There was no reservation in the name of Gloria Evans to Atlanta at 10:30 A.M.

There was no Continental Airlines plane leaving at that time to Atlanta.

Margaret/Glory/Brittany closed the computer. He'll be here soon. He won't have the money. I'll never escape him. He'll hunt me down with the same hatred he has hunted Zan Moreland. Her sin was not to want him and mine is that I am a threat to him.

He would be here soon. She knew it. She was standing at the window facing the road. A white truck was slowly passing the house. She gasped. Larry Post had been waiting in a white truck when she left Central Park with Matthew. If he was coming here now, it was to make sure she never had the chance to give Ted up to the cops.

It was too late to get Matthew and go to the car. Her eyes wild, she knew what might work. Rushing upstairs, she picked up Matthew, who was still asleep on the bed. The same way he was when I took him out of the stroller, she thought. She carried him downstairs and put him on the inflated mat in the closet.

"Are you going now?" Matthew asked drowsily.

"Very soon, Matty." She knew she didn't have to warn him not to make a sound until she came back for him. I taught him well, poor kid, she thought.

The sound of the bell ringing resonated through the house.

She locked the door of the closet and dropped the key behind the server in the dining room on her way to the door.

A smiling Larry Post was looking in the kitchen window. "Brittany, I've got a present for you from Ted," he called out.

# 83

T hat was a good lunch," Willy said complacently as he sipped the last of his cappuccino.

"Yes, it was. And, oh, Willy, I just know that Detective Collins is looking at all this in a different way. I mean, it's going to be as plain as the nose on your face that no woman about to kidnap her own child would bother to change her shoes for an almost identical pair. But what scares me is that whoever is behind this might start to panic if he finds out that the detectives are starting to believe Zan."

"And the question is whether after all this, even if Zan can prove her innocence, there's a limit on how much longer she can keep herself going if Matthew isn't found."

Willy agreed, his expression now weighted with concern. Then, as he reached for his wallet, he said, "Honey, just as I was leaving the apartment to meet you, Penny Hammel called. I didn't pick up."

"Oh, Willy, I feel kind of mean. I had my cell phone turned off when I was meeting Detective Collins, but when I called you I saw there was a message from Penny and frankly I didn't want to be bothered listening to it. I was too excited thinking about the fact that maybe the tide was turning for Zan."

She looked around. "I know it's not polite to use your cell phone in the restaurant, but I won't be talking, just listening." Alvirah turned away from the table, trying to give the impression she was reaching down for her pocketbook. She opened her phone and pressed the number to receive her messages. Then as she listened her face went pale.

"Willy," she said, her voice shaking. "I think Penny may have found Matthew! Oh, sweet Lord, it makes sense. But the woman who looks like Zan is packing to leave, oh, Willy . . ."

Not waiting to complete the sentence, Alvirah sat up straight and dialed Billy Collins's cell phone number.

A number she now knew by heart.

# 84

Would it work? Ever since he had sent Larry to Middletown over an hour ago, Ted Carpenter had agonized over what he had set in motion. He knew he had no choice. If Brittany went to the cops, he'd spend the rest of his life in prison. Even that wouldn't be as bad as watching the joyful reunion of Zan and Matthew.

*My* son, he thought. She didn't want me. I gave her a child and she claims she didn't know she was expecting him when she dumped me.

Thank you very much for your kindness and good-bye, he said to himself, playing her role. You never expected to have a child, so you don't have to pay for him. That wouldn't be fair. But how nice of you to check out the apartment I moved into and then the one that I rented after Matthew disappeared. How kind to see that the plumbing and the heating and the light fixtures work.

Of course it wouldn't be fair, Ted raged, because you really didn't want to share him. He was *yours*. You told me to start a trust fund for him but that really wasn't expected of me. Well, lady, that trust fund is going to pay for speeding your little precious into eternity today.

I wonder if she's home now? I didn't bother to watch her last night. I was too tired and worried, but now Larry is on his way to Middletown. With any luck, things will work out.

Ted turned on his computer and entered the code that would get him into Zan's apartment. Then, horror-struck, he watched as, directly facing the camera, Zan shrieked his name.

# 85

Cold and stiff, Penny Hammel was waiting in the woods behind Sy's old farmhouse. After studying the childish drawing and being sure that she was right, that Gloria Evans resembled Zan Moreland, she had driven down the road and called Alvirah and left a message. Then she came back and saw that the Evans car was back, so she drove around the road again and took up her vigil.

She couldn't let Evans get in that car and drive away. If I'm right that she had Matthew Carpenter in Sy's house, I can't let her disappear again, Penny thought as she stamped her feet and flexed her fingers to keep them from freezing. If she tries to leave, I'll follow her to see where she goes.

She wondered if she should try calling Alvirah again. But she was sure that the minute she got the message Alvirah would call back. I called her at home and on her cell phone, Penny reasoned. But after a while she thought, Maybe I should try once more.

She took her phone out of her pocket and opened it. Her fingers were inside her mittens. Impatiently, she pulled off a mitten but before she could go to her list of numbers, her phone rang.

As she had hoped, it was Alvirah. "Penny, where are you?"

"I'm watching that farmhouse I told you about. I don't want that lady to get away and she was packing this morning. Alvirah, I'm sure she has a child in there. And she looks like Zan Moreland."

"Penny, be careful. I called the detectives who are on this case. They're calling the Middletown police. They'll be there in a few minutes. But you—"

"Alvirah," Penny interrupted. "There's a white truck stopping in front of the house. It's parking in the driveway. The driver is getting out. He's carrying a big box. Why would she want any big box if she's planning to leave? What would she want to put in it?"

# 86

Billy Collins, Jennifer Dean, and Wally Johnson were being driven in a squad car to Ted Carpenter's apartment. Billy had briefed the other two on Kevin Wilson's call. "We never looked at the father," he berated himself. "Carpenter never made a single false move. Never. Outraged at the babysitter falling asleep. Outraged at Moreland for hiring a young babysitter. Then publicly apologizing to Moreland. Then outraged after the pictures in the paper. He was playing us all along."

Billy's cell phone rang. It was Alvirah relaying Penny Hammel's message. Billy turned to Jennifer Dean. "Get the Middletown police to the Owens farmhouse on Linden Road pronto," he snapped. "Tell them to proceed with caution. We have a tip that Matthew Carpenter may be hidden there."

Ted Carpenter's apartment was downtown. "Turn on the siren," Billy directed the officer who was driving. "That guy has got to be feeling cornered."

But even as he said it, he had a feeling it would be too late.

When they arrived, the crowd milling around the building told him that what he had feared might have happened. Even before he got out of the squad car, he knew that the body that had just plummeted through the canopy and was lying on the sidewalk was that of Ted Carpenter.

# 87

Help me, Brittany prayed. I don't deserve it, but help me. With a smile she waved to Larry Post, as she walked over to the living room window. She still had her cell phone in her pocket. He was opening the cover of a large box. She could see rows of hundreds lined up in it, each packet with a printed tape around it.

I'll open the door, she thought. Maybe I can stall him. I don't have the security system on. If he tries to open or break a window, he could do it in a minute. He thinks I'd never call the police for help. I don't have a chance. But maybe . . .

"Hi, Larry," she called. "I know what you've got. I'll open the door for you."

As she turned her back to him, she took out the phone and dialed 911. When an operator answered, she whispered, "Home invasion. I know the man. He's dangerous." Knowing that the local police were familiar with the location of the farmhouse, she cried, "The Owens farmhouse. Hurry. Please hurry."

# 88

I'm going in there, Penny decided. If that guy gets Evans and the child into that truck, no telling what will happen. I'll bring in the drawing and say that I found it when I was walking and thought it had to belong here. The cops may be on the way, but those 911 calls can get mixed up.

She hurried from her observation post in the woods. She ran across the field and stumbled over a heavy rock. Some instinct made her bend down and hoist it up. Maybe I'll need this, was the thought that ran through her head. She rushed up to the house and looked in the kitchen window. The Evans woman was standing there. The man Penny had seen carrying the box from the truck was a few feet away from her, holding a gun.

"You're too late, Larry," Brittany was saying. "I dropped Matthew in a mall an hour ago. I'm surprised you haven't heard about it if you had your car radio on. It's a big story, but I guess it won't make Ted too happy."

"You're lying, Brittany."

"Why would I lie, Larry? Isn't that the plan? That Matthew would be in a place where he's surely found, and I go home with the money and we're all happy—happy that we're finished with it?

"I know Ted is worried about leaving me out there as a potential problem, but you can reassure him that I won't be one. I want a life again. If I turn him in, I'll go to prison, too. And now you've brought the money. All of it, I guess. All six hundred thousand dollars. The trouble is that I can't celebrate because my father just died."

"Brittany, where is Matthew? Give me the key to the closet where you hide him. Ted told me about it."

Brittany saw the look of desperation in Larry Post's eyes. He'd find the closet easily enough. It was right at the end of the hall and he would find a way to open it even without a key. How could she stop him before help came?

"I'm sorry, Brittany." Larry was pointing the gun at her heart. His eyes were devoid of emotion.

Penny had not been able to hear what was being said, but she could see that the man in the kitchen with Evans was about to shoot her. There was only one thing she could do. She pulled back her hand and with her ample strength sent the rock she was holding crashing through the window.

Startled at the slivers of glass that cascaded around him, Larry Post fired the gun but the shot sailed over Brittany's head.

Realizing her one chance, Brittany threw herself on Larry, causing him to lose his balance, stumble, and fall. He opened his hand to protect himself from smashing against the stove and dropped the gun.

Brittany swooped down and picked it up as police cars raced up on the lawn. Holding it on Larry Post, she said, "Don't move! I don't care if I use it on you and I know how to do it. My daddy and I used to go hunting together in Texas."

Without taking her eyes off him, she backed up and opened the kitchen door for Penny. "The blueberry lady," she said. "Welcome. Matthew Carpenter is in the closet down the hall," she said. "The key is behind the server in the dining room."

Larry Post scrambled to his feet and began to run. He threw open the front door and ran into a sea of blue uniforms. Other police-men pounded past them into the house. Margaret Grissom/Glory/Brittany La Monte had slumped into a chair at the kitchen table. The gun she was holding was dangling from her hand.

"Drop the gun! Drop the gun!" a cop shouted.

She laid it on the table. "I only wish I had the courage to use it on myself," Brittany said.

Penny found the key and rushed to the closet, then paused. Slowly she opened it. The little boy, who had obviously heard the shot, was huddled in the corner, his expression terrified. The light was on. She had seen enough of his pictures in the paper to be sure it was Matthew.

As a broad smile came over her face and tears filled her eyes, Penny bent down, picked him up, and held him close to her. "Matthew, it's time you went home. Mommy has been looking for you."

# 89

Detectives Billy Collins, Jennifer Dean, and Wally Johnson were standing in the lobby of the late Ted Carpenter's trendy apartment building. The detectives from the local precinct had cordoned off the area around Carpenter's body and were waiting for the arrival of the crime scene unit and the medical examiner's van.

Their expressions grim, they were desperate to hear the outcome of Billy's urgent call to the Middletown police to respond to the possibility that Matthew Carpenter was being held in the Owens farmhouse.

Was Alvirah Meehan's friend in Middletown correct? Was it possible that a woman who strongly resembled Zan Moreland was hiding Matthew Carpenter all this time? And following Kevin Wilson's phone call about the camera in Zan's apartment, where was Larry Post now? They had just run his name through the computer at headquarters, and discovered that he had served time for manslaughter. It's a sure bet that he's got some part in this whole scenario about Matthew and not just the bugging of Moreland's apartment, Billy thought.

Billy's cell phone rang. Holding their breath, Jennifer Dean and Wally Johnson watched as a broad smile came over Billy's face. "They've got the kid," he said, "and he's okay."

Jennifer Dean and Wally Johnson answered in unison. "Thank God," they said, "thank God."

Jennifer, her voice low, said, "Billy, we were *all* wrong about Zan Moreland. Don't beat yourself up. Everything pointed to her."

Billy nodded. "I know it did. And I'm very happy to be wrong. Now let's call Matthew's mother. The Middletown police are on their way to our precinct with him."

Fr. Aiden O'Brien heard the breaking news from the police officer who was guarding him at the hospital. His condition now upgraded to "critical but stable," he whispered a prayer of thanksgiving. The sacred seal of the confessional that had cloaked his sure and certain knowledge that Zan Moreland herself was a victim would no longer haunt him. Her innocence had been proven in another way. And her child was coming home.

# 90

Zan and Kevin raced to the Central Park Precinct to find Alvirah and Willy already there. Billy Collins, Jennifer Dean, and Wally Johnson were waiting for them. Billy had told Zan on the phone that the Middletown Police assured him that while Matthew was very pale and thin, he looked okay. He'd explained to her that while ordinarily the police would want to have Matthew checked out by a doctor right away, that could be done later today or tomorrow. Billy had told them to get him home.

"Zan," he cautioned her, "from what they know so far, Matthew has never forgotten you. Penny Hammel, the woman we can thank for finding him, showed the police a drawing that they think Matthew made. She found it in the backyard of that farmhouse. I hear it looks a lot like you and it has the word 'Mommy' printed on the bottom. But it would be a good idea if you brought a toy or a pillow or something that he loved. It might comfort him after what he's been through."

From the moment she entered the precinct, other than fiercely thanking and hugging Alvirah and Willy, Zan had not said another word. Kevin Wilson, his arm protectively around her, was carrying a large shopping bag. When they heard the sound of sirens approaching the entrance to the precinct, Zan reached into the bag and pulled out a blue bathrobe. "He'll remember this," she said. "He loved to cuddle with me inside of it."

Billy Collins's phone rang. He listened and smiled. "Come into this private room," he said gently to Zan. "They're bringing him in downstairs now. I'll go get him."

Less than a minute later, the door opened and little Matthew Carpenter stood bewildered and looked around. Zan, with the robe draped over her arm, ran to him and dropped to her knees. Trembling, she folded him into the robe.

Tentatively, Matthew reached for the lock of hair that was falling over her face and held it against his cheek. "Mommy," he whispered, "Mommy, I missed you."

# Epilogue

*One year later*

Zan, Alvirah, Willy, Penny, Bernie, Fr. Aiden, Josh, Kevin Wilson, and his mother, Cate, watched with hearts overflowing as six-year-old Matthew, now restored to being a fiery redhead, blew out the candles of his birthday cake.

"I got them all," he announced proudly. "With only one breath."

Zan ruffled his hair. "Good for you. Do you want to open your presents before I cut the cake?"

"Yes," the boy answered decisively.

He's made a remarkable recovery, Alvirah thought. Zan had brought him regularly to a child therapist and he had blossomed from the timid child whom Zan had wrapped in her bathrobe when Penny brought him home to an outgoing, happy little boy who would occasionally still cling to Zan saying, "Mommy, please don't leave me." Most of the time he was an enthusiastic first-grader who couldn't wait to go to school and be with his friends.

Zan knew that as Matthew got older and began to ask questions, she would have to deal with his inevitable anger and sadness about what his father had done and how he had died. It will be one step at a time, she and Kevin had agreed. And they would handle it together.

The party was being held in Zan's apartment in Battery Park City, but she and Matthew wouldn't be there much longer. She and Kevin had chosen their wedding day to be just four days from now, on the anniversary of Matthew's return home. Fr. Aiden would be presiding at the ceremony. After the wedding, they would be moving into Kevin's apartment. His mother, Cate, who had already become Matthew's trusted babysitter, relished her soon-to-be role as grandmother.

Alvirah thought of the tabloids she had read this morning over breakfast. On page three they were rehashing the story of Matthew's kidnapping, the impersonation of Zan, the suicide of Ted Carpenter and the sentencing of Larry Post and Margaret Grissom/Glory/Brittany La Monte. Post had received life in prison and La Monte got twenty years.

As Matthew began to open his packages, Alvirah turned to Penny. "If it weren't for you, this wouldn't be happening."

Penny smiled. "Thank my blueberry muffins and the truck I saw in the foyer that day and then the drawing that I found stuck in the bush behind Sy's farmhouse. As Bernie had to admit, sometimes being nosy can pay off. The most important thing, the only thing, is that Matthew is safe. The reward money from Melissa Knight is a bonus."

She means it, Alvirah thought indulgently. Penny really means it. Melissa Knight had used every trick in the book to weasel out of paying the reward, but in the end she had written the check.

Now Alvirah watched as Matthew, suddenly serious, finished opening his presents and put his arms around Zan. He brushed a lock of her hair against his cheek.

Then he said contentedly, "Mommy, I just had to make sure you're still here." Matthew smiled. "Now, Mommy, can we please cut the cake?"

# Read About the Inspiration Behind Other Classic Novels
## by Mary Higgins Clark


### Stillwatch

When I was about twelve years old, there was a murder in the rectory of our local parish. The priests were lingering over coffee. The housekeeper, a young woman of twenty-eight, lived in the basement with her husband and five-year-old daughter.

Suddenly shots were heard. The priests rushed downstairs. The housekeeper's husband had murdered her and killed himself. The next day the newspaper read, "Their five-year-old daughter, bathed in the blood of her mother, was screaming and screaming."

That was the basis for *Stillwatch*. I wondered how much the little girl remembered of the terrible scene after she grew up. I decided to set the book in Washington because it is obviously the center of the political world in America and I wanted to use that background as well.


### Weep No More My Lady

At the time I wrote that book I had just gone to a famous spa, Maine Chance in Arizona. It was the ultimate in luxury and something I could never have afforded if I hadn't by then become a successful writer. I asked myself, wouldn't it be interesting if in a place like this, where everyone is waited on and pampered, that a killer is stalking his victims and waiting in a wet suit at the bottom of the pool to drown them? The prospect gave me the shivers, and I was on my way. Incidentally, that was the first book that Alvirah Meehan appeared in, and she's been my good friend ever since.


### While My Pretty One Sleeps

When I was eighteen, I worked on Saturdays in a Fifth Avenue department store because I have always loved clothes. At that time, Dior had just changed the fashion landscape when he came out with his new look. I thought, suppose a talented young woman is murdered for the fashion look she has created and twenty years later her daughter uses fashion to find her mother's killer. Just for the record, when I wrote that book I was a widow. Many people have asked if my husband was the inspiration for it because of my description of the man who is the father of the main character. My answer was no. I dreamed up the man I wanted and twenty years later I found him.

### The Anastasia Syndrome

I took a course years ago in which the instructor hypnotized people and brought them back to previous lifetimes. I took it out of curiosity, not because I believe in reincarnation. When I heard startlingly vivid descriptions of former lifetimes from people under hypnosis, it didn't make me a believer, but it did make me realize that I was going to write a book on that subject. Since I'm a history buff, I loved setting the back story in the time of Charles the First and Charles the Second of England.

### Let Me Call You Sweetheart

I love jewelry and have a few pieces that once belonged to my mother-in-law. One pin especially is unique. I thought it would be interesting if that pin could get someone on a path to murder. As a secondary theme, the idea of a plastic surgeon giving a number of women the same face, I thought offered a meaty plot because why would any doctor do that? A third plot element was the idea of a young man in prison for a murder he didn't commit. I threw these together—the jewelry, the plastic surgeon, and the innocent prisoner. *Let Me Call You Sweetheart* was the result.

### Silent Night

A friend of mine was nineteen years old when he was in the Battle of the Bulge. A bullet hit the Saint Christopher Medal he was wearing, and the medal saved his life. I always knew that there was a story within that story, and when I was asked to write a Christmas novel, I knew the Saint Christopher Medal had to be part of it. The other plot element involved a young woman who had been in prison, sees a wallet, picks it up and may be accused of having stolen it. I thought that is the kind of predicament that people can sometimes get into. Afraid to tell and afraid not to tell is a desperate situation for a lone young woman with a dependent child. That situation tied to the Saint Christopher Medal produced *Silent Night*.

### Moonlight Becomes You

My mother-in-law had a recurring nightmare perhaps twice a year. It was that she was in a funeral home in a casket. She was alive, and all the other people in the other caskets were dead. It is easy to trace the origin of that dream. Her mother was a young girl in England when the flu epidemic killed thousands of people. People were buried immediately, and later it was found that some of them were still alive. The coffins had scratch marks as they frantically tried to lift the lid and escape. In those days the rich people would have a string around the supposedly dead person's finger and would have a bell on the ground at the end of the string. They paid watchers to sit by the grave for a week just in case the person was not yet dead and tried to signal them. I thought that is a darn good basis for a suspense novel.

### Pretend You Don't See Her

So often an article I have read triggers a book. For this one I read a long article about a family in the Federal Witness Protection Plan and the excruciating loneliness that they were experiencing living in a strange place, unable to discuss their backgrounds and only contacting the rest of the family through a Federal Marshal. I ask myself why a young woman would be forced into that position and what it would be like if an assassin breaks through the code of secrecy and learns where she is.

**All titles by Mary Higgins Clark are also available as ebooks.**